Mary
In Search of a Legend

A novel devised and written by
Gordon Douglas and Gary Mitchell.
Dedicated to the memory of Gordon Christie.

Edited by Susan Wilson.

Gordon Douglas

Contents

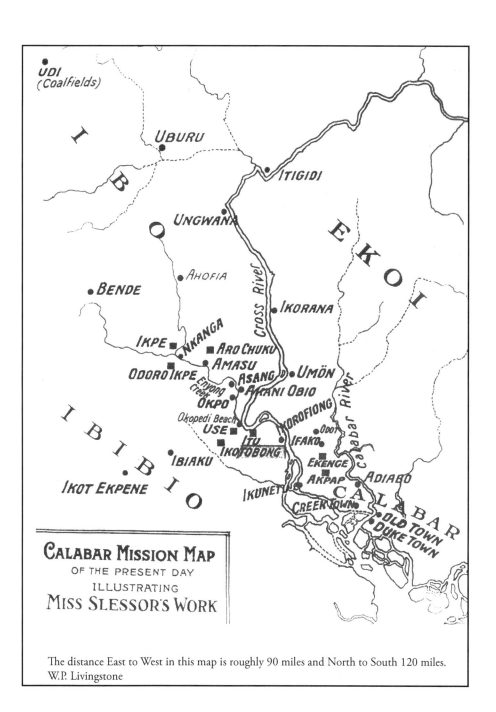

UDI
(Coalfields)

I B O

UBURU

ITIGIDI

UNGWANA

E K O I

Cross River

AHOFIA

BENDE

IKORANA

IKPE NKANGA

ARO CHUKU

ODORO IKPE

AMASU

Enyong Creek

ASANG

UMÖN

AKANI OBIO

OKPO

Calabar River

Okopedi Beach

KOROFIONG

USE

ODOT

I B I B I O

ITU

IFAKO

IKOTOBONG

IBIAKU

EKENGE

IKOT EKPENE

AKPAP

ADIABO

IKUNETU

C A L A B A R

CREEK TOWN

OLD TOWN

DUKE TOWN

CALABAR MISSION MAP
OF THE PRESENT DAY
ILLUSTRATING
MISS SLESSOR'S WORK

The distance East to West in this map is roughly 90 miles and North to South 120 miles.
W.P. Livingstone

Introduction

This book is dedicated to the work of Mary Slessor, to honour her life and her love for all people. We have chosen to write this book, not as has been done excellently before by a retelling of her works and adventures, but by extracting those highlights we felt most relevant to the story of a remarkable woman. This Mary is fiery, brave and outspoken, with a will of iron when necessary, attributes which were always prosecuted with genuine, caring human emotion. We have used some invention, and a certain amount of speculation, based on information gleaned from books, letters and the complex political history of the time, to give substance to and to illustrate her life; her letters, especially, give a great insight into her character and language, great sense of humour and political acumen. We have given people she met a voice, one that is based on reported events and meetings; we hope by this method these ghostly figures can speak and more fully play a part in her story.

What she brought with her from her Scottish upbringing was a deep knowledge and experience of the poor gathered from her work amongst the forgotten, helpless and hopeless of Aberdeen and Dundee. This gave her a unique understanding of poverty and its consequences, poverty which was both financial and educational. Her ability to learn and speak the local African dialects fluently, and therefore comprehend the complex native tribal questions and answers, gave her access to their intentions, strengths and weaknesses, dreams and fears; her determination to live as they did gave her a deeper understanding of their wants and needs. Mary's fighting spirit and the respect in which she was held by them and by many outside her normal sphere of activity, including government officials, gave her a power to negotiate on their behalf, which she fully exploited.

The fact that she was a missionary is not crucial to our telling of her story, as conversion to the Presbyterian faith was by no means her only driving force; in time, proselytising ceased to be her main function; in Mary's own words, when asked how many people she had converted, as always self-effacing, she said, *"just ain or twa"*. For example, Ma Eme Ete whom she called 'sister', for many years undoubtedly her closest friend and greatest ally, was never to be converted to Christianity. This omission cast a shadow over Mary's career within the missionary community but did not diminish the two women's friendship. For large periods of her life, in her search for social justice, it was Mary and her Lord against all the foes of Africa, whichever form they took.

As Mary always impressed upon others, one's legacy was not one's work on earth but the work that continued after death. In Mary's case, her many achievements were significant and enduring; she changed attitudes to local ritual, native trade and industry, women and children; and she left behind her a network of schools, trade routes, industrial training units, refuges for women and children, hospitals and churches.

These things and many more make Mary's story as magnificent and relevant today as when she walked among us.

Language

All conversations between native Africans and Mary, with the exception of those with King Eyo and certain of her adopted children, have been written in English. Although there were some who tried to improve Mary's conversational English, her drift in and out of her broad Scottish dialect happened as her mood dictated, the more enthusiastic and passionate she became, the more she relapsed into her native tongue.

Please note - there is a small dictionary at the end of the book to guide you through the Scots words used in this novel.

Acknowledgements

Apart from the back cover photograph (Dundee City Council Central Library) and illustration of Wishart Arch & Calabar (Missionary Record), images provided by: Dundee City Council: Dundee's Art Galleries and Museums. Our thanks go to both library and museum for their staff's enthusiastic and knowledgeable input into this book. Special thanks to Susan Wilson (editor) and Dave Mitchell (graphic designer) for their patient endeavours above and beyond the call of duty.

Disclaimer

As there is so little written documentation covering Mary's life and, the fact that she destroyed all of her incoming correspondence before she died, we have had to use a certain amount of licence to tell her story. Many people may have played a much greater or lesser part in her life than we have illustrated; this we apologise for in advance, but it was done with the best of intentions to tell her story to the greatest effect. Attitudes to her, inferred in the text, are based on research, but to make the point may have been exaggerated or lessened as the case may be. We have not set out to impugn any character and we hope that our honest endeavours will be accepted in good faith and be met with approval.

To contribute to Mary's living legacy, visit **www.maryslessor.org**.

Gordon Douglas & Gary Mitchell

Mary
In search of a legend

It is 1895 in Africa, the 'Dark Continent' made infamous by stories, legends and tales of barbarism, cruelty, savage ritual and wondrous beauty; also known as the White Man's Grave, a land where death is not always at the hands of man. Death by disease haunted the steps of all who were brave enough to venture there; if death remained a few steps behind that would be perfect, but most found it waiting for them a few steps ahead.

To be more precise, this is West Africa, on the river inland from Calabar and Duke Town. It was late afternoon as the small Government steam launch, known by the natives as a smoking canoe, slipped, slithered and meandered through the African mangrove swamp to its appointed destination. The journey had started well; it had begun closer to the coast at Duke Town where the air was fresh, but as the river twisted and turned through ever thicker bush, the air became thinner, and what little there was to breathe was filled with the pungent, choking, sweet odours of rotting vegetation. The dense tree canopy seemed to act as a lid to keep in the intense bush heat and smell, refusing to allow fresh air to percolate. Only when the river widened was there any glimpse of sky, not the blue skies of Scotland, but white, and as hot as an oven. The captain kept a close eye as the skies began to darken and the surrounding bush became eerily quiet.

"Mistress Mary, you'd better take shelter, there's a storm on its way."

The single woman passenger he addressed took his advice and moved aft to sit beneath the little canvas awning fitted for these occasions. She was a very striking thirty-three year old young lady, dressed in an elegant long black skirt with matching high necked jacket, with signs of a white blouse visible at the neck and cuffs, and highly polished boots; a fine hat at a jaunty angle, and a veil, completed her ensemble. She would have been well-dressed in Knightsbridge, but this was Africa not Knightsbridge. All was deathly still and, for now, the birds and wild animals had ceased their squawking and roaring. As the river widened they could see that the bright sky was now the colour of 'bruise', purple-black.

On the captain's instructions, the crew members had grabbed sheets to cover the lady's many cases, and now they sat and waited for the storm to break. It was not long before the earth seemed to growl with a low moan from beneath, as if from the bowels of Hell. Then, as the roar increased

1

and the vibration intensified, the sky and the bush around them seemed to explode, the thunder screamed and sheet lightning lit the dark sky. Almost immediately, the rain descended in continuous veils of bullet-like rain, which battered the river and tossed the small boat like a piece of driftwood. The water surrounding them boiled and became wild and furious, the boat's steam engine struggled to move them forward, steam flew everywhere, as cold raindrops condensed instantly when they hit the machine's hot outer shell. The captain tried to allay the fears of the young woman; he shouted over the cacophony of the storm - *"Hold on, it'll soon pass"* - his words were more in hope than expectation.

He was well aware that his passenger was of great importance, as he had been informed that her arrival in Calabar was much celebrated. She had been met from the boat as if she were visiting royalty by no lesser persons than the Governor General, Sir Claude Macdonald, and his lady wife. The young woman's name was Mary Kingsley, the headstrong niece of Charles Kingsley, the author of 'The Water Babies', who now, in her own right, was being hailed as the most influential explorer and travel writer of her time. She had arranged an appointment, as ladies do, to meet one of the most important voices in Africa. The legend of the woman she sought had travelled far; but was this just another 'tall-tale from Africa'? Would it prove to be all bluster and no substance? She needed to find out for herself.

The captain knew the river well, and after the storm had lost its rage, it ended as quickly as it had begun. The boat safely reached the shore, which was to be their landing stage before continuing the journey on foot to the area known as the Okoyong. Miss Kingsley's cases were decamped on to the sandy beach and she dutifully followed; she was famously unafraid but, for good measure, she always kept a loaded pistol hidden in the leg of her boot. The captain, attempting to keep up her spirits and hoping she might write a line about him in future chronicles, asked, *"Will you be writing of your adventures in Africa?"*

Well aware of the nature of his loaded question, she replied, *"I write of all the things that fascinate me, the special, the unique, and the original, Captain."*

They stood on the beach, gathering their equipment and their thoughts, unsure of what to expect; however it is unlikely that what happened next had been considered. The sound of birds screeching and animals calling could now be heard over the dripping of the rain drops. The captain, aware of the importance of his charge, heard movement in the bush immediately ahead; quickly he reached for his gun and shouted towards the direction of the sound, *"Halt, who goes there?"* Miss Kingsley smiled at the words and actions of the captain, and whispered to him, *"Not very original, Captain."* The captain chuckled and replied, *"Sorry miss, it's all I could think of!"*

A figure broke through the semi-circle of bush that surrounded the beach. At first it was difficult to make out quite what, or who, it was. It appeared to be a small woman toiling under the weight of a large gin crate, which she carried in the cradle of her outstretched arms; her smock dress had seen better days and was stained with what looked, at first glance, to be blood. The woman's face was tanned and lined, yet as she spoke her blue eyes lit up, as if at the flick of a switch. The stranger looked at the captain's gun, and said brightly in a broad Scots accent, *"You'll no' need that, I chased the leopards aff earlier!"*

She turned to the young woman, *"I'm Mary Slessor and you'll be Miss Kingsley, I've been expecting you. Well, I see you brought the rain wi' you."*

Miss Kingsley, after three months cosseted as the guest of Sir Claude and Lady Macdonald in colonial Calabar, was somewhat taken aback by the bedraggled figure standing before her, but thought as she looked at the lined face of this woman that she might have found what she was looking for. Once over the shock of the vision of this frail woman, Miss Kingsley approached and held out a helping hand, *"Can I help you with that box?"*

Mary smiled and replied, *"Thank you dear, but it's no' a burden. Follow my lead Captain, we've had a new path cut, I'll show you the way."*

Miss Kingsley asked, *"Is it far?"*

Mary replied with a touch of sarcasm, *"Well it's no' as far as the moon and it's further than just ower there. We'll get there when we get there."*

Distance in the bush is hard to measure; few measure it in miles, most measure it in time, as fallen trees, small streams swollen instantly into rivers by the frequent rains, and the constant danger of wild animals, can add miles, hours or days to a single journey; a straight line is very seldom followed, and 'we'll get there when we get there' is about as accurate as Africa would allow.

Miss Kingsley, although used to foreign travel and rough terrain, was still trying to adapt to the African bush. Due to the dense canopy of trees blocking the sun, and thick undergrowth blocking all else, there seemed to be no way to distinguish north from south, east from west; whichever way you looked, the thick bush was the same. As this was a newly-cut path, the ground was still fresh and dangerous to walk on; the machetes had cut the bush but had left sharp piercing spikes for unwary travellers. Miss Kingsley marvelled at Mary's pace in such brutal conditions, and that in bare feet.

In time they reached a clearing, not a natural one, but one that had been created by the hard work of natives, who had been making space for their homes and settlements by this method for centuries. Most houses were very basic mud walls with palm frond matting for a roof, the more important the person, the bigger the house. By native standards, Mary's house was a mansion, built on two floors with a verandah on the upper level. It was in the interests of the natives to be seen to welcome missionaries and help build them a fine house, which would act as church, school and hospital.

Miss Kingsley had heard much of Mary's work with young black children, and within seconds of their arrival, screams of joy of *"Ma! Ma!"* rose from the clearing. This preceded the arrival of a clutch of smiling, clapping infant native children, who gathered round her and hung on to her dirty smock. The boys and girls were all dressed in tiny pants made from striped and colourful material, typical of those Miss Kingsley had seen in mission boxes sent out from enthusiastic sewing circle ladies in Britain. She noted with great hilarity that one boy was so excited and animated that his pants slipped off his tiny body and were left abandoned on the ground; no one batted an eyelid until the hilarity had finished, when the young boy was reunited with his Sunday best.

Mary called to the children in Efik, the local language, and all but one vanished, *"Come awa' in. We'll get a cup o' tea."* She shouted to the remaining young girl, *"Jeanie, put on the kettle!"*

Miss Kingsley took a seat on Mary's verandah and removed her hat. The crew deposited the luggage and began their journey back for the rest of her cases. Mary instructed her children to help and show them the way. As soon as the children had gone, Mary's tone changed, she said, *"While we wait fir the kettle to boil, there is something I must take care o'."*

Miss Kingsley, keen to be of assistance asked, *"Can I help you with the box?"*

Mary looked at her doubtingly, *"Have you a strong stomach?"*

Miss Kingsley looked confident, as she always did, *"Yes, I've seen many shocking things on my travels."*

"If yer sure?" Mary replied.

Mary put the gin case down gently on the verandah and knelt beside it. As she slowly opened the lid, Miss Kingsley leant over in her chair to get a better view. The look on Miss Kingsley's face turned from one of curiosity to one of

4

horror; she turned her head away in disgust and covered her mouth in a vain attempt to stifle an anguished cry. No matter how hard she tried, she couldn't stop exclaiming, *"Oh my God, babies! Dead babies?"*

Mary said ruefully, *"It's twins,"* and offered a quick prayer.

Miss Kingsley took a deep breath and, once she had sufficiently recovered her composure, admitted, *"I'm sorry for my reaction, Miss Slessor. When you think you understand Africa and have the stomach for its ways, it finds another method of confounding the imagination."*

Mary, almost oblivious to Miss Kingsley's admission, continued to stare into the box, *"The death of twins seems savage to civilised people, but in many societies twins are a bad omen. They believe that one of the children is the father's, and the other is the devil's, but which one? So both must die and the mother banished."*

Miss Kingsley, with tears in her eyes, examined the babies, *"Poor baby, its skull crushed, but look, the other one still breathes!"*

Mary picked up this infant, wiped the blood off his naked body with her smock, and cradled him in her arms. *"God is looking after him."* Miss Kingsley gave Mary a questioning look but omitted to ask a question.

Mary shouted towards the house, *"Adiaha! One of your children is still alive!"* A distressed young native woman dashed out of the house, dressed in a bloodied and tattered smock, but was too frightened to come any closer. Mary, as if addressing a naughty child, shouted angrily, *"Come here! It's safe, I have blessed him, and he needs fed. Be grateful that Abassi has saved your good child!"* Out of respect for the woman they called 'Ma', she did as she was told.

Mary continued her explanation, *"That poor lass gave birth last night and has walked for hours for sanctuary here, not on the road or paths, but through the thickest bush; if she'd used these paths, they would have been cursed for ever for her tribe. Once the twins are born, they cannot be touched, so they are thrown into boxes or stuffed into pots and left in the forest to die of hunger and thirst, or to be eaten by ants or wild animals. Rituals like these often start as legends, but we wouldn't do it in the civilised world would we?"* Mary huffed aloud, *"Well, don't ask those accused of being Scottish witches, who were tortured and burnt tae ashes, usually for nothin' more than livin' alone, or ownin' a black cat, yes, **we** were civilised."*

The sound of happy children returning filled the air and removed much of the gloom. Mary's attitude changed almost immediately, as if an enormous weight had been lifted from her small shoulders, the glow on her face mirrored the cheerfulness of her children. *"Here are my happy accidents, my bairns, all abandoned and left to die. We'll have a cup of tea and then feed these cheery wee faces."*

Once the children had been fed and washed, they were all put to bed on pallets on the house floor. Miss Kingsley watched in admiration as Mary sat with each child in turn, and spoke as a natural mother might do, and listened to their prayers. Miss Kingsley was not a religious woman and had a great mistrust of the motives of those who were, but here she could see that, for one family, it did much to bind and comfort them. She was almost envious of the peace it seemed to afford them, but was still far from convinced it had any place in **her** life.

When the children were settled, Mary wrapped the dead child in a white cloth and the two women walked into the yard where, at a secluded spot, Mary dug a hole and placed in it the gin box containing the baby. Mary turned to Miss Kingsley, *"I have heard you are not religious Miss Kingsley, so if you will give me a minute."* Mary knelt beside the grave and with a silent tear prayed for the child's soul. Miss Kingsley was moved by Mary's kindness and humility, her love for a child she had never known, or had any relationship to. It seemed that all the stories she had read or been told might be true, but she would need to find out much more.

When they returned to the house, Mary and Miss Kingsley sat out on the verandah to enjoy the cool of the evening. Jeanie, Mary's eldest child, before going to bed provided them with a couple of lamps and more of her mother's favourite tipple, yet another cup of tea. As Jeanie left for bed and Mary sat stroking a large yellow cat on her lap, she confessed, *"I know you're not supposed to have favourite children but I am ashamed to say that Jeanie is mine."* Mary giggled like a mischievous schoolgirl, *"Yer no' supposed tae but it's true. She's been with me fir thirteen years, the poor wee lamb's mother died when she was born, and she was thrown out into the bush and left to die. She had been abandoned to her fate and survived for over a week without water or food. A woman had heard a babe whimperin' in the bush, and while no one would dare go and look for her, she came to me and told me all she knew o' the tragedy. Straightaway I ran off to look for her, and found the child in the most wretched condition, covered head to toe with flies and ants, just alive. It was a miracle that she had survived, and only God knows how she did, and I thank Him every day for his kindness, and the blessing of such fine lassie."*

The tea ceremony continued, and they settled down to a well-deserved rest.

There were many questions in Mary Slessor's mind so she began by asking the young woman, *"Whit brings a lass like you to Africa? I dinnae think it was God. And that's no' a criticism."*

Miss Kingsley, used to being interviewed wherever she went, began with her stock answer, *"To learn more of fowl and fetish,"* but added, *"I believe you are an expert on both, and may I say that it is not a talent I would normally associate with a missionary."*

Mary thought for a moment, *"I think many missionaries find religion first, and come here expecting to find God in their 'good works'. But God is no' here,"* she waved her arm around, *"or in Scotland or England, He is here,"* she touched her heart, *"in yer heart, and no amount of 'good works' will make Him appear. No amount of travel will bring you closer to Him, He is in the hovels and back streets of Dundee and in the big houses in Edinburgh. No amount o' money will make Him visit you, or bless you, though the rich are not excluded from His care and guidance; mind you, many of them are mair in need o' it than the poor."*

Miss Kingsley had read a little in the Missionary Record of Mary's past, and knew that she was not from the traditional missionary class, *"I must say, you are not what I expected, do you not miss your family and your home?"*

Mary smiled, and avoided the question as if it was painful to discuss, but she answered, *"These wonderful bairns are my family, **this** is my home."*

Miss Kingsley, seeking an answer, attempted to rephrase the question, *"What on earth brought you here?"* She raised the palms of both her hands upwards and looked around and added, *"What brought a woman like....!"*

Mary, aware that Miss Kingsley was struggling to finish her question, finished it for her, *"Like me? Doing here? A mill lassie from a family that was poor in money, wha never had twa farthin's tae rub thegither, but we were rich in a'thing else."* Mary's eyes glinted in the lamp light and she smiled a cheeky smile, *"Are ye up fir the tale?"*

Miss Kingsley agreed excitedly, *"Of course, that's why I came here, to find the real Mary Slessor."*

Mary took a deep breath, and looked to the heavens, *"Well, tae the best of my recollection it was 1848 that I was born, although it could have been 1849. It was a long time ago and I was only wee,"* she chuckled, *"I ken it wis Aiberdeen."*

The first cry of many

To avoid Mary's blushes, I shall take over the narration of her life, for, as she said, *"it was a long time ago,"* and she was only wee.

It was on the 2nd of December 1848 that her life began. It began by her being held up unceremoniously by the ankles and spanked into life. It seemed a tough start, but the life which was to follow would be even tougher. The town of her birth was Aberdeen, on the North East coast of Scotland, a town famous for farming and fishing; but the expanding industrialisation of Great Britain saw more and more families depend solely on the topsy-turvy, boom and bust, of mill and factory employment. A molten, almost nomadic, existence was created for families who, for centuries, had been masters of farm and fishing work, at one with nature. Once sure in the knowledge that hard work would put food on the table, they depended on that hard work, and the kindness of the seasons, not the vagaries of 'free trade'. In this new world, seasons came and went, almost unnoticed within the dingy confines of soulless factory walls. Aberdeen, like most industrial towns and cities, was now a place that operated all the hours that were available, smoke belched from countless chimneys and, for those in employment, a hard crust was earned.

The small house in which she was to take her first breath was on the outskirts of the town, in a district with the inauspicious name of Mutton Brae; in fact the house was not the family home but that of Mary's grandmother. This reflected the matriarchal powerbase of many Scottish families, women wielding authority over their husbands, and if not them, then their daughters' husbands. Mary's grandmother had never been happy with any man her daughter had been courted by, and when she fell in love and married Robert Slessor, she felt that she had married well beneath herself. The couple had lost two babies in the past, one at childbirth and another, named Robert, died in infancy, so this time the grandmother decided to take complete control of the circumstances of the birth. Her interference did little to improve relationships between Mary's mother and father; the previous deaths had been unavoidable, but they had no argument to use against her involvement in this birth.

Robert and Mary were very much in love, but times were hard, work was slow, and Robert's own trade as shoemaker was suffering, which led to a spiral of petty squabbles and self-doubt. Time spent idle never improved their situation and for Robert alcohol increasingly began to fill the gap between waking and sleeping; it seemed to take the sting out of his loss of self-respect, replacing it with a drunken bravado. The drink in itself was comparatively cheap, but it robbed the family of more than the pennies it cost to buy. Robert was elated at the promise of a new child and felt that its birth would mark the turning point in all their lives.

As he waited outside the house on the cold steps in the winter's drizzling sleet, he heard the cry of the new-born baby and became increasingly impatient that he be allowed to enter. In her own time, his mother-in-law opened the door and granted him entry to the room, dimly lit by three small candles. She stood between him and those he had come to see, and said with pride, and not a little triumph in her voice, *"You have a healthy wee girl,"* then stepped out of his way.

Robert walked beyond her and knelt down at the bedside, tenderly taking his wife's hand in his and kissing it. In her arms she cradled the beautiful little bundle. He looked at the baby and said to his wife, *"She's beautiful, just like you. Can we call her Mary?"* The proud mother wiped away a tear, *"Yes that's what we'll call her, Mary,"* and added, with great affection, *"Would you like to hold her?"* Robert stood up in readiness and said, *"Of course,"* but his mother-in-law stepped between them and insisted, *"Don't be silly, he's soaken wet."* Realising she sounded too severe, she smiled, a big smile, and added in a more caring tone, *"This is no place for a man. I've been saving this for such an occasion,"* and from her apron she produced a shilling and handed it to him, *"Go and do what men do best on these occasions, go wet the bairn's head."* Robert looked at his wife for some guidance, she in turn looked at her own mother then at Robert, and said, *"You are soaken wet, you might give the child a chill,"* but added, reluctantly, *"Go on, enjoy yourself, you'll have a lifetime with the bairn."*

He was shepherded out, he stepped into the dark street and was cloaked in a fine drizzle. His emotions were a confusion of anger and a great love for wife and family. Should he go and drink? As he looked longingly back to the house, he saw his mother-in-law wave to him from inside, with his babe clutched in her hands. Should he go for a drink? Why not? He turned up the collar on his jacket and walked slowly towards the nearest alehouse.

On nights like these, when winter arrived before it snowed, it was a dreich landscape. Everything turned grey, the short duration of winter sun failed to provide any warmth, freezing the fingers and the soul. The only colour that could be seen emanated from the window of the local hostelry, like a lighthouse in a wild sea. Robert Slessor was drawn towards its warm yellow light, like a moth to flame. He opened the big wooden door, which creaked noisily as he entered the bar. A fiddle player sat in the corner and played a sad low air, the locals looked round, and only when they had recognised the newcomer, did they smile, shout a welcome and continue their conversation. The room was lit with a few candles, but the main light came from the big welcoming open fire. The landlord, a rotund, jolly-looking man, welcomed Robert, *"Well, fits new, Bob? Hivnae seen you fir a twelvemonth."* Robert, happy at least that someone was glad to see him, said, *"A gin, Jack,"* and handed over the shilling coin.

The landlord took the coin, looked closely at it, then bit it, *"Hivnae seen ane o' they fir a while. Taken up heghway robbery, Bob?"* The locals all laughed. Tam, a local, sitting at the bar, turned around and spoke to anyone who would listen, *"And the way things are going, it'll be the last any o' us'll see, we'll a' soon hae empty pooches. The wages at the mill are being reduced again. Whit they dinnae see is that when the wages fa', abodie loses."*

Robert glad to have his mind taken up with others' problems, asked, *"How's that Tam?"*

He replied, *"Well, when the mills are daein' fine, abodie prospers. Eh ca' it the moose's share."* He used his hands to illustrate his argument. *"Ye see at the tap are the Laird and the Mill owners, wha hae a' the money and the land, next we hiv the La' and the Kirk, tae keep us a' in oor place, then there's the workers and their families, and just alow us, we hiv the animals. You see, when us workers buy food tae feed the bairns, we a' get fat including the moose in the corner. Ye'd maybe see the moose as a pal, and feed him a wee touch. Cause when you're rich, the crusts fa' easy fae yer plate."* His attitude hardened, a crazy look came into his eyes, *"But if I see a moose noo, when I'm wretched poor, a' he'll get fae me is the heel o' my shoe!"* He slammed his drink down violently on the table, *"It's what makes thieves o' good fowk and beggars o' us a'......... And whit's yer joab, Bob?"*

Robert replied, *"I'm a souter."*

Tam nodded in appreciation, then continued, *"A shoemaker, a fine trade, but you'll soon be as poor as the moose!"* They all laughed.

"How do you work that out, Tam?" asked Robert.

Tam smiled and continued, *"Well, like the moose, yer at the end o' the queue. We a' need shoein' but wi' the drap in wages, wha cares how comfy yer feet are, if yer belly's empty? Ye'll maybe get some boot repairs, but naebodie'll need new shoes till oor pooches are fu'.'* Tam stared into his drink. *"Aye, it's a gey drearie sermon, sometimes drink's the only way tae mak sense o' this mad world."* All went quiet until Tam said, *"Another glass o' sanity, landlord!"*

A sound was heard from the street, there was a loud knock on the alehouse door, the landlord walked to the small window to see who was there, *"Oh it's fine, it's no' the bobbies, it's Crimea Bill."* The landlord lifted the latch and held the door open to allow a legless man on a wheeled trolley to enter. The young soldier, draped in a sodden and stained military jacket from the Crimean campaign, said to the landlord, *"Do you mind Jack? It's just fir a heat."*

The landlord welcomed him, *"Come in by."* The soldier began to pull himself towards the open fire, the roughly-made wooden sledge roared and screamed as the soldier dragged it across the bare floorboards.

Tam whispered to Robert, *"A hero o' the Crimea, that's how we treat war heroes, left tae fend fir himself, lives on what little scraps the poor can afford tae gi' him. As fir the rich? They dinnae gi' a damn. As fine a sodger as you could hiv, we sent him aff fae here, a' wavin' an' cheerin'. So proud tae be wi' his pals, he gave a'thing fir his country, and his country gave him a medal fir his bravery, and a sledge fir his legs."*

Robert whispered back to Tam, *"Whit would he say if I bought him a drink?"*

Tam replied with a word of caution, *"He might snap yer nose aff fir yer pity. He lost mair than his legs in the Crimea."* He paused, and then added, *"He'll hae a gin."*

Robert paid the landlord for the drink and took it over to Crimea Bill. The soldier looked up with hatred in his eyes for Robert's pity, but reality prevailed, and he raised a filthy, wet, shaking hand and accepted the drink. The soldier, avoiding eye contact, replied in a hushed voice, *"I thank ye Sir."* The bedraggled man gripped the cup in both hands and, while he continued to gaze intently into the flames, very slowly and gently, sipped the comforting drink. Robert took his seat back at the bar and counted the money he had left in his pocket. He pondered whether or not to have another. There was no contest, he turned to the landlord and said, *"One mair fir the road."*

Nine years on

We have moved on nine years to see how young Mary has progressed; the house, their family home, if that is not too grand a title, is a single room with an outside ash pit. The family has increased in number since we last visited them - there were now three children, Mary aged nine, William aged seven, and Susan aged three. William had been christened as such, but in honour and affection for the infant who had died, he was always addressed as Robert.

As had become their usual practise, the children would spend the evening playing their favourite game, a game inspired by their mother's ambition that her son Robert, when of age, should apply to be a missionary in Africa and follow in the footsteps of the hero of the day, David Livingstone. The children's game starred Robert as the gallant missionary, Susan played the part of a native child, keen to learn the scriptures from 'the great white man', and Mary played an especially wild savage, if you will. It would seem that the children were well suited to their roles; Robert was studious, obedient and pious, and Susan his devout follower, but Mary was fast turning into an unruly child, her red hair a signal to others to beware her quick wit and matching temper. During the last few years, life had not been easy for the Slessor family, no matter how hard they tried. The grandmother had stepped in to help with the growing brood, Mary's mother had found work, but the hours she was given made a happy, contented family life impossible. Mary's father, over the years, had become increasingly unreliable; he left each morning to find work but always returned empty handed, compounding his misery and penury by visiting the alehouse on his way home to drown his sorrows.

Mary's grandmother called for the children to stop their game and prepare for bed; as with most children they were slow to obey. She was used to being obeyed, and their prevarication caused an increase in volume and urgency as her request became a command, *"Bed, now!"* she screamed. Mary pleaded with her, *"Can we not stay up till mither comes in? We never see her."* The grandmother was losing her temper and wanted to be gone before Mary's father returned. *"Mary, do what you're told, please."* Mary could hear a rare softness in her voice and reluctantly complied.

With the children in bed, the grandmother sat quietly by the fire, and spoke while staring into the embers, *"If yer faither would settle to a job, she'd have a bit mair time fir you. Yer dad is worthless, I told yer mother he was beneath her, but she wouldn't listen to me, headstrong that's what she is! Where she gets it from, I don't know. If your father would spend more time looking for work, and less time in the public house, we'd all be much better off. Yer mother's working her fingers to the bone, while your father drinks his life away."*

As she finished her soliloquy, she heard Mary's mother's footsteps on the wooden stairs; she could now identify the sound of those tired steps as they wearily reached the stairway landing. There, Mary's mother met her neighbour, a white-haired, seventy year old lady called Mrs Hepburn, who asked, *"You're early Mary, did you see Annie on yer travels? You look awfie weary, lass."*

As always, Mary's mother tried to be polite through her fatigue and frustration, *"I'm fine, but the mill's been put on short time. Annie'll be along presently, we were sent home early as there's no work fir the rest o' the week."*

Mrs Hepburn shook her head and then said pointedly, *"How will ye manage? It's bad enough wi' a full wage, never mind what you'll get noo."*

Mary's mother was in no mood to put up with snide insinuations, but tried not to lose her temper, *"I don't know whit you're referring to. If you'll forgive me, Mrs Hepburn, I've bairns tae mind."*

Mrs Hepburn, well aware that she was out of order, feigned offence, *"Oh! Forgive me fir askin'!"*

The grandmother had listened at the door and announced to the children as brightly as she could, *"Well, here's yer mother now, she's early."*

As the door opened, Mary jumped out of bed and rushed to greet her mother. At the attentions of wee Mary, the tired lines on her face seemed to vanish and her exhaustion to lessen. The lass took the small loaf of bread from her mother's hand, and young Robert helped her with her shawl. Mary led her to the fireside, sat at her feet, and removed her boots. Mary saw that both shoes had holes in their soles, which she playfully stuck her fingers through. Naively, the young lass asked, *"Why doesn't father mend your shoes, mither?"*

Mary's mother quickly grabbed the boots from her daughter, hoping that it could be kept a secret, but it was too late. The grandmother grabbed one boot and looked at its awful state, *"My God Mary, when will you see sense, and see that man for the waster he is!"*

Mary's mother had had enough, *"Mother!"* She looked towards her children, who were just visible in their bed in the alcove, their noses and bright eyes peeking above the covers, *"I'll speak to him the night!"*

As the grandmother hurried to put on her shawl, she warned her daughter one last time, *"Mak sure you do, there's tongues waggin' at the kirk that…"*

Mary's mother, now exhausted and exasperated, tried to end the conversation, *"Enough mother! I'll see you the morn. Quick, Robert could be back anytime."*

As the grandmother got to the bottom of the dark stairs, she came face to face with her son-in-law. He stopped her dead in her tracks, a petrified look on her face. Robert, the worse for drink, seemed manic and approached her with his hands raised aggressively. He grabbed her by the shoulders, his vile breath made her recoil. *"Boo!"* he bellowed. The old woman screamed, freed herself from his clutches, and rushed off into the night. Robert laughed loudly and shouted after her, *"I don't want your greetin-face to darken my door again! Run, run ye auld harpy! Good riddance tae bad rubbish."*

Mary's mother had heard the shout from the street and warned the children, *"Oh Lord, it's yer faither, get under the covers bairns, please. Pretend tae be asleep."*

The sound of heavy stumbling steps on the stairs drew closer and culminated in the door being burst open. The drunken man came half-way into the room, then turned and yelled outwards, *"And you, Mrs Hepburn, can tak a lang wak aff a short pier! You nosey interfering auld witch."* Robert staggered into the room and sat down heavily in a chair in front of the fire. There was an ominous silence, then he began, *"I saw that monster o' a mother o' yours in the street. I told her this is my house. I don't want that woman here ever again!"*

Mary's mother had swung the soup pot over the fire and knowing from sad experience that there was no good time to break bad news, said *"Robert, we've been put on short time at the mill."*

Her father closed his eyes and scratched his brow; he exhaled heavily and asked, with venom in his voice, *"Well, what do you expect **me** to dae about it? I cannae get work!"* He softened his tone, *"I've tried Mary love, believe me, this is no' my idea o' a life."*

Mary's mother moved towards him and placed a nervous, but comforting, hand on his shoulder, *"We'll just hae to tighten our belts."*

Robert, taking this as a personal criticism, stood up aggressively and, face to face with his wife, he yelled, *"What dae ye mean! Whit are ye sayin'?"*

Mary's mother tried to defuse the situation, *"Never mind Robert, hae yer tea."*

She handed him a bowl of soup with bread. Robert, full of guilt and self pity, staggered and lurched threateningly towards his wife. He waved his arms wildly and knocked the plate and bread out of her hand on to the floor. He lunged at her and pinned her to the door. Wee Mary had seen enough. She whispered to Robert, *"Look efter Susan,"* then leapt out of bed and set out to separate her fighting parents. From the corner of her eye, Mary's mother had seen her wee lass rise from her bed, and called to stop her, *"No Mary, please! Go back to yer bed. Please!"* But young Mary was not for stopping, she grabbed her father's arm. Without thinking, he swung his arm to free himself from her grasp and as he did so, he gave Mary an almighty smack in the eye with his elbow, sending her tumbling across the room and knocking her unconscious. Unaware of the damage he had done, he released his wife and shouted, *"I'll go somewhere where e'm wanted!"*

He slammed the door shut, shaking the entire building and causing the little wall mirror to fall and crash, breaking into pieces on the bare floor. The drunkard staggered down the stairs and into the anonymity of the black night. Mary's mother lifted up her daughter and carried her gently to the fireside chair where she held her close and wept. In the dark corner of the room, a mouse nibbled on the discarded bread.

The lesson at Church

It was Sunday morning and the Slessor family were preparing for church. The three children, all dressed in their Sunday best, stood obediently while the finishing touches were being made. The two women inspected Robert, and then Susan, and agreed they were looking fine, but when they looked at Mary they both shook their heads. Mary's mother said, *"There seems no way to make it look any better."* She tipped wee Mary's hat down to one side but the grandmother shook her head and replied, *"No, that just looks ridiculous!"* and tilted the hat the other way. Mary turned around to see her reflection in a broken piece of mirror, her face was expressionless, the silly jaunty-angled hat could not hide her enormous black eye. Mary giggled at the sight. Mary's mother was resigned, *"Well, it's the best we can do."*

She took wee Mary aside for a quiet word, *"You know your father never meant you any harm."* Mary looked gravely at her mother, then smiled and, with a touch of steel in her voice, said, *"I know mither, but he'll never do it again!"*

The grandmother offered a compromise, *"You could always miss the Kirk fir a week?"*

Mary's mother was shocked at the suggestion, *"We need all God's blessings we can get, He never takes a week off from His care and love for us. He will not look unkindly on Mary's keaker."*

The grandmother was not so sure and added wryly, *"But others will."*

When the Slessor family, minus the father of course, reached the street, they came upon Mrs Hepburn who was gossiping with a crowd of women; she appeared to be acting out a fight. As they approached they heard part of Mrs Hepburn's conversation, *"..... and the wee lass has this enormous black eye.....* "Taken by surprise, the neighbour greeted them sheepishly, *"Hello Mrs Mitchell, Mrs Slessor, how's the family?"*

The grandmother tried to put her in her place, *"Oh fine, fine, just mindin' our own business!"*

Mrs Hepburn sniffed at this obvious rebuke and turned away. The Slessor family, their heads held high, walked proudly to the Kirk and though the church-goers all nodded politely, many whispered as they passed. Mary was far from being a Christian at this time, the church did little for her, but Robert junior was entranced. During the long sermon, a well-dressed boy, bigger than Mary, sat across the aisle from her and attracted her attention; he pointed to his eye, pulled down the bottom lid and pretended to cry. Mary ended this awkward social interaction by sticking her tongue out at him. As she averted her gaze, unfortunately she found her grandmother scowling back at her.

When the service ended, the adults chattered to one another outside the church, the children standing obediently by their families - though of course, not all children. While Robert sat and read to some younger children the latest issue of the Missionary Record, his mother and grandmother talked alone, well out of earshot. Mary's mother had some unwelcome news, *"I think it is time we should move on."*

Her mother was shocked and asked, *"What do you mean, Mary?"*

She replied, with a choke in her voice, *"There's little enough work here fir me, I think that if we move to Dundee it may change our fortunes. There's supposed to be lots of mill work there, and the waggin' tongues are making life hard fir us a'. We need a new start."*

Her mother was much more sceptical, *"You know as well as I do that that will no' happen."*

Her daughter, by way of justification, said, *"Robert has managed to get a lift in a van to Dundee on Wednesday. We won't take up much space, we have little but ourselves tae flit."*

Her mother looked at her, paused then said, *"A van? In your condition?"*

Mary was taken by surprise, *"Oh, you know?"* She rubbed her stomach, and looked down towards a very small bump.

Her mother sniggered, *"I may be auld but I'm no' blind. Is Robert up for the move?"*

She replied, with added conviction, *"He seems to be keen tae leave, a new town, a new house, mak a new start."*

The grandmother, suddenly aware that she had not seen wee Mary since the end of the service, asked, *"Where's Mary? Poor wee lamb, he's knocked the child out o' that bairn. Get rid of that worthless husband and things will get better."*

Behind the church in the tree-lined graveyard, wee Mary was busily climbing a tree. The boy who had bothered her in church appeared, obviously intent on her further humiliation; he stood at the bottom of the tree. *"Well, well, what are you up tae monkey girl?"* he shouted, *"abodie kens that your drunkard of a faither gave you that black eye."*

Mary, never one to back away from a bully, warned him, *"You'd better run afore something happens to you."*

The boy laughed mockingly and walked round and round the tree, continuing his cruel taunt, *"Is yer drunk faither going to come and do the same to me? E'm no faird, I'll get the bobbies on him, he should be in the jail anyway, that's what my dad says, he says it's only a matter o' time. He says the jails are full o' drunks like him......"* The young lad, so intent on making his speech to Mary, had stopped looking up at her. Suddenly he felt a tap on his shoulder and with some surprise he turned round, just in time to see Mary's fist smack him in the eye and knock him to the ground. The boy squealed, *"I'll get the bobbies on you!"*

Mary stood above him and said, *"And tell them what? That a wee monkey girl gave a big bruiser like you a black eye? I dinnae think so! Just say ye were climbing this tree and you fell. That, they wid believe!"*

At that moment, Mary heard her mother shouting her name and turned to the boy as if nothing had passed between them, *"Well, I'll see you later,"* then danced a skip in the direction of her mother's call. Her mother took her hand and asked, *"I hope you've been behavin'?"* Mary replied dutifully, but with a cheeky smile on her face, *"Yes mither, you can be proud o' me."* It was with a nagging doubt in her head that her mother led the family homewards.

1857
Moving on

It was very late on Wednesday night, a time when the children would normally have been tucked up in bed, but tonight it was all hands on deck for the flitting. Each family member carried something to be packed into the horse-drawn van; not in suitcases, all items were wrapped up in oft-mended blankets. In a quiet moment, wee Mary looked into the food basket, which had been prepared for the journey, broke off a piece of bread, and placed it in the corner of the room.

The family left as quietly as they could, the creaking of the wooden stairs the only clue to their vanishing into the night. They all climbed into the back of the horse-drawn covered wagon filled with someone else's belongings, for their long journey from Aberdeen to Dundee. The three children, like so many mice, found little spaces between the furniture, made themselves as comfortable as they could, and hoped that wherever they rested their heads, they would soon find sleep. The driver of the van was Tam Scott, from the alehouse; he was as polite and philosophical as ever, *"Hello Bob, good evening Mrs Slessor, a braw nicht fir a new start."*

Mary's mother sat behind the two men, resting on a bundle of clothes, *"This is awfie kind o' you, Mr Scott."*

Tam sat with the reins in hand, drew on a clay pipe, and replied, *"Not at all, Mrs Slessor, after a' we're a' God's creatures, this load is fir Dundee, and as lang as naebodie kens, naebodie'll mind."*

As the journey began, back in the old house, a mouse scurried to the corner of the room and contentedly nibbled on the crust that Mary had left.

At long last, their journey nearly completed, Tam drove his van to the crest of the hill overlooking Dundee. The town sprawled beneath, like a dark stain on the snowy landscape, under a veil of smoke that day and night spewed from countless smokestacks. Tam pulled up the horse and allowed it to have a well-earned rest. He took the opportunity to re-fill his pipe and look at the view. He couldn't resist a word of warning to Robert, *"Some say this place is their saviour, for many others it is just a means to an end. Whar nicht never ends, and daylight never starts. There is nae mother nature, only ill-nature, and hard work."*

Mrs Slessor's voice was heard from behind, *"There is God, Mr Scott, and wherever there is God there is goodness, kindness, forgiveness and love."* She added humorously, to relieve the air of doom, *"Ye auld cynic! And if you are quite finished your sermon, the quicker we can get there then the quicker we can find work."*

Tam touched the brim of his hat in mock obedience and recommenced their journey, *"Hup lass!"* At his order, the horse reluctantly moved off and the cart creaked slowly down the steep hill towards the outskirts of the town.

A new beginning in Dundee?

We rejoin the Slessor family two years later, blessed by another child named John. The low murmur, that had been their soundtrack in Aberdeen, had been replaced by the incessant industry and clatter of machinery that came from the mills and factories which lined the Dundee streets. Dundee was nicknamed 'she town', due to the number of women who were employed. The mills, where the women and children worked long hours, were built to operate at full production; anything less meant a drop in profits for their owners. The children, small and agile, with seemingly tireless energy, ran constantly between, and under, massive moving metal monsters for their meagre wage. Working amongst such savage machinery, many fingers, hands and limbs were lost, mere slaves as they were to this pitiless industrial master. The small, cramped and overcrowded houses and streets were full of these workers; there was little or no fresh water and that was only available from natural wells and was often little better than purified sewage. The ashpits, which held all the waste from this mass of people, were emptied manually by scavengers in seaboots at four in the morning and deposited on the packed earth streets for collection. This foul-smelling effluent would soak into the earth and no amount of chloride of lime could hide the stench or remove the germs. Diseases, such as scarlet fever and typhus, ran rampant in the dirty, dark streets, lanes and closes, through which men, women and children trudged to work each day.

Mary had seen from early days that the poor were at the mercy of the rich and at no time were they in charge of their own destiny; it was simply a means of keeping the wolf from the door. At Lochee on the outskirts of town, the Camperdown Works was the largest factory in Europe employing 14,000 workers, mainly women and children for whom work was readily available. Men, and older boys once they had reached the age to be paid a full wage, were thrown on to the scrap-heap. These men were given the title of 'kettle bilers', as they were expected to stay at home and take charge of domestic duties. Mary's father had apparently traded the misery of one town for another, though the only positive aspect for him was that in Dundee there were more alehouses in which to lose himself. There were only so many hours that Mary's mother and brother Robert could work, so as soon as was practicable, at the age of eleven, Mary started work at the mill, rising at five and working from six in the morning till six in the evening, with an hour for breakfast and an hour for dinner. The day was long, tiring and arduous, but Mary, now a keen reader, always took a book to read in her free time, or prop up on her machine, in an attempt to improve her education. Yet, irrespective of the hardships, she took great pride in working for her family; even at such a young age, Mary had realised that if there was no work, there was no pay and they would go hungry. She was aware that the poor had no power, and no voice, and the mill owners knew just how little to pay in order to keep the workers at their machines. There were no complaints, except in hushed tones amongst themselves, and as there were a hundred redundant workers only too happy to take their place, there were few arguments. Mary's mother was a good and conscientious worker, not that she had any choice, but as she walked to her work in the early morning rain, she felt twice the age of her thirty eight years.

As she reached the large doors of the factory, the noise increased in volume. Inside, there was a violent contrast to the still dark morning, a scene of apparent bedlam and total animation, the huge machines remaining in full production while the night shift turned seamlessly into the day shift. The cogs crunched, fingers worked quickly, people conveyed messages by sign language over the furious sounds of the clattering machines. As daylight began to shine down from the high windows through clouds of dust and stour, young women and children coughed and spat. Children ran through the factory with arms full of bobbins, and hurried from machine to the bin and back again. Angry overseers bellowed and stared, looking for a machine, or machinist, in need of their 'help and encouragement'.

Mary's mother was hard at work at her machine when she spotted a young, heavily pregnant girl, who was struggling at hers. She managed to attract the attention of an old woman nearby and signed to her her concerns. As the overseer scanned for slackers, the old woman signalled back, by simply touching her eye and pointing to the loom, *'keep your eye on your own work'* she reminded her. A few minutes later the girl collapsed, and before Mary could help, the old woman grabbed her arm and instructed her to keep working. The young girl was lifted out of the factory by the overseer and was immediately replaced. The 'bummer', a loud, high-pitched alarm sounded for lunch time. Hordes of workers left the dusty atmosphere and simply stood outside the factory doors, and smoked, or talked loudly - the constant racket blighted the hearing of all the workers. Mrs Slessor spotted the old woman, but when she attempted to speak to her, *"what happened to the young lass?"* she seemed to be ignored; the old woman smoked her clay pipe and did not respond.

One of the other women spoke, *"No point in speaking to Auld Bessie, she's as deaf as a post, been here a' her days. What did you want?"*

"What happened to the young lass?"

The woman pointed to the ashen and frail young girl returning. Mrs Slessor was taken aback; the woman explained, *"Oh her, she's aff to finish her shift!"*

Mrs Slessor, almost dumbstruck, asked, *"Finish? But she wis pregnant!"*

The woman shook her head and said simply, *"That's right, but if you give up your machine, you lose yer job! She's had her bairn, now she's back to mak up her time. I've seen lassies gi' birth standin' at their machines, rather than lose their pay."*

Mrs Slessor shook her head, *"God save us!"*

Her workmate scoffed and replied, *"There's little time fir God in the mill. When you work here you've made up yer mind 'atween God and mammon! Best leave God at the door, you can see Him efter yer work."*

Mrs Slessor looked down at her hands and said, *"God is with us even in here, if you will pray with me, just quietly, we will ask for God's blessing."*

When she received no reply, she looked up and saw that she was alone; all the workers had shuffled back to work. Quickly she prayed, gathered herself together and followed.

To pawn or not to pawn

Later that night, young Mary was helping her mother get the other children ready for bed. While young Robert, now eight, led them in prayer, Mary remained pottering about. Her mother looked disapprovingly at her; Mary tutted, then reluctantly knelt with the others. The children, Susan, aged four, and John aged two, once in bed, were soon asleep, and Mary and her mother prepared the tea for her father. A noise on the stairs startled them and apprehensively they listened and waited. To their great relief, the sound of the footsteps continued on up the stair, past their door and collectively they breathed again.

The room they lived in was dark and lit by one candle and the remains of a small fire. The shape of the room was oblong, the door about a third of the way along one of the long sides, the open fire about a foot from the door on the same wall. The length of the room was shortened by curtains at either end; behind one was the bed for the children, and the other, a bed for the parents. This was as much privacy as their small wage could afford them. The furniture was rudely built, and included two chairs, a bench, stool and table. There was a sense of tension that pervaded the sad scene at this time of day and each bang, squeak, and footstep threatened grief.

Mary's mother broke the anxious silence, *"Mary, would you take that bundle to the pawn shop till pay day. Tell Mr Grieg that you'll be back for them afore Sunday. Go now afore your dad gets back, quick lass, aff wi' yea."*

Barefooted, Mary, glad to escape from the house, grabbed the large bundle of assorted clothing and rushed down the stairs, as if the devil were after her. She stopped at the entrance to the close and, before running quickly down the dark wet wynd, looked over the top of the bundle to check that the road ahead was clear. The closes and wynds, lit by the weak gas light, were seldom empty; people were often to be found sleeping in these dark places, where homeless and forgotten children wandered at all times of the day and night, sometimes taking refuge on warm bakehouse roofs. Mary, ever watchful, spotted a group of older boys up ahead and hid to avoid being seen. The boys were playing noisily and were being chastised for their rowdy behaviour by people in the tenements; thankfully she knew a way around them and took it. The shop sign ahead, 'Grieg's Pawn Shop', creaked loudly in the wind. Mary dashed to the door, knocked, and ran in. It was late, and the proprietor was in the process of shutting up shop; he called out gruffly, *"I'm shut!"* The old man turned to see who was bothering him so late, yet saw no one, until he leant over the counter and there was young Mary. His brusque manner changed, *"Ooh it's you Mary. Well I daresay I can stay open for such a regular customer as you. Same as usual?"*

As Mary put the bundle on the counter, Mr Grieg went to his money box, took out a few coppers and handed them to her. Mary looked at the small remuneration in her hand, shook her head, and said with tongue in cheek, *"I'm no' sure that this is enough, Mr Grieg, these are awfie good quality items, our Sunday best,"* she took a deep breath, *"we might have tae tak' our business elsewhere."*

Mr Grieg, used to Mary's manner by now, played his part, *"Dinnae dae that Miss Mary. Let me ken in advance, I depend so much on your custom, I'd go out o' business!"*

Mary tried to hide a smile and decided to let him keep his livelihood, *"Oh a'right then."*

Mr Grieg laughed, and as he locked up for the night, he shouted, *"See you Seterday Mary!"*

She took the coins and placed them carefully into the hem of her shabby, though clean, skirt. She skipped playfully out of the shop and into the rainy night. Suddenly she saw the boys head in her direction. In a flash, she had climbed a tree in the backyard of a house and there, from the safety of the high branches, she watched them go past. The biggest of the boys had a rope with a lead weight on the end, which he swung in the air; much to the enjoyment of all the others, he inadvertently hit one of the gang on the back of the head. Once they had gone, Mary climbed down and hurried home. She walked slowly up the stair, paused and sat down on the top step to catch her breath and listen to what was happening inside. Her heart sank as she heard her father drunkenly abusing her mother. There was a bang, and then a crash, at which Mary rose immediately and burst into the house. The sight she was confronted with sent her into a fury – the table and chair were overturned and the dinner plate and its contents were now sizzling, spitting and smoking in the fire; the children, hiding in their alcove, protected by Robert, huddled terrified and afraid to move. The father screamed at the top of his voice, *"This food isn't fit fir pigs, I should go and leave you, then see whit happens to you."*

Mary's mother pleaded with him, *"No' so loud Robert, the neighbours."*

Her father, out of his mind with drink, continued to rant, *"Damn the neighbours! Damn you!"*

Mary's mother saw young Mary in the doorway gathering her anger, and to block her advance she stepped in front of her. In his rage, he grabbed his wife and threw her out of the way, sending her crashing to the ground. Mary ran between them, stopping her father in his tracks. He was standing in front of the fire and as he moved towards her, his shadow grew larger and engulfed the little girl. He sneered and spat out at Mary, *"And you!"* She stood like a wild dog in a dog-fight, teeth bared, her hands like claws, her back arched; she said bitterly, *"Go on, hit me! Why don't you go? I hate you, we all hate you, hate you! hate you! Naebodie would miss you if you left!"*

Her father made a drunken lunge for Mary, and her mother, aware of the likely consequences, jumped in-between and took the blow herself. She managed to hold on desperately to her husband and screamed to Mary, *"Get out lass, for God's sake, run!"*

As Mary tumbled down the stairs, the row continued to rage above and the family's shame echoed through the narrow lanes. She fell into the street and ran and wept. Little thinking of anything else, she turned a corner and bumped straight into the crowd of bullies. The head of the gang smiled a cruel smile and said, *"Well, if it's no' Carrots, it's wee Mary o' the pawnshop, we've got you now, hand it over."* He held out his hand. Mary slowly backed away, shook her head, and said defiantly, *"No!"*

The gang had blocked her escape and now Mary had her back to a high wall. The head bully, standing a distance away, began to swing the heavy lead weight above his head and inch towards her. In Mary's mind, she saw flashing images of the violence of the fight between her father and mother; what was happening now seemed as nothing compared to what she had just been through. As the bully got closer, Mary stared straight into his eyes, and didn't bat an eyelid. She said without flinching, *"Do yer worst!"* The bully saw no fear in this little girl, he had no stomach for actual, physical harm, his sport was in making people afraid and watching them run. He could now see that this one was not going to run, her steely blue eyes convinced him of that. He could see that she was unafraid, unshaken and unbowed. He stopped his advance and began to lower the swinging lead weight, hitting the same gang member once again in the back of the head. He turned and walked away and the others followed in confusion.

The bully with the sore head rubbed the two large bumps and asked, *"What about the money?"* The head bully, embarrassed by the experience, was in no mood to explain, *"Shut it!"*

Mary, not quite sure what had happened, watched them leave. Had she been so afraid of her father that any further threat had no effect? Mary sought sanctuary so climbed her favourite tree and sat there and sobbed. In time, her mother arrived at the bottom of the tree and whispered softly, *"Mary?"*

Mary was surprised to see her, it was obvious that her mother was nursing the beginnings of a black eye, *"Wait, I'll come down."*

Her mother looked around and, not knowing where her husband was, said *"No, I'll come up."*

Mary was astonished to see her climb the tree. The night was lit by a half moon just visible between the high tenements and together the two sat for a time in complete silence. Her mother said, quite calmly, *"I can see why this tree is your favourite place. It's good for the young and fit, but as you grow older you'll find you need something mair practicable. I worry fir you, lass."*

Mary smiled and placed her hand on her mother's, *"E'm fine."*

Her mother laughed, *"I ken ye are, but, I know you're young but..... do you know what love is?"*

Young Mary had never been asked such a question, *"I know I love you and Robert, John and Susan."*

Her mother tried to explain, *"What you said to your faither, it wasn't right. When you go to Sunday school and read about the black sheep, your faither is ours. The choice is yours Mary, your faither loves you the best, and you get the worst o' his temper, but if you want us to leave him we will."*

Mary looked shocked and confused, *"But you cannae forgive him fir the way he treats you..... can you?"*

Her mother continued, *"Do you remember the bracelet your Gran gave you, the one you caught on a branch and broke, we all spent hours trying to find the loose beads in the grass?"*

Mary remembered it fondly, *"I still have two beads left."* She searched in the hem of her skirt and pulled them out. *"I loved it."*

Her mother asked, *"Why do you keep them?"*

"To remind me of the thing I loved so much."

Her mother pressed on, *"You love them as much now as you did when the bracelet was complete, don't you? It's more than the memory of it. As long as you have part of it, in your heart it is still complete, still perfect. With God's help, I still see the man I married, a loving caring man, who loved me and adored his bairns. Your faither is living through a fever, God knows it's a lang fever, and it may kill him, but I pray that we may see him return to be the man we know he is. Men are so often weak and childlike; when they lose self-respect they become bitter and mad wi' the world. He is as much a prisoner o' his drink as we are. In his eyes I see my man trapped, begging fir help, begging fir forgiveness."*

Up to a point Mary understood, but asked, *"Look at your eye mither, it surely cannae go on?"*

Mary's mother took her daughter's hand between hers, and squeezed it, *"Love is no' a choice, it is unconditional, the Lord teaches us to believe in Him and we need fear nothing, fear no one; if death itself holds nae fear, then fear loses its power."*

Mary tried to understand, *"Do you not..... hate him?"*

Her mother smiled warmly, *"Hate is a word that those without God use, you can live wi' fear, but hate will poison your soul, you cannae live wi' that."*

Mary, with a young lassie's logic, pointed out, *"That's no' fair."*

Her mother laughed, *"You'll find that life will often seem unfair, the poor* get poorer and the rich get richer, but poverty is no' a sin, neither is money, don't despise either, whit is sinful is that money is often wasted on the wealthy, the undeserving and indolent. But we're rich, we have health and food, and best of all I have you Mary." She hugged Mary tightly. "There is so much goodness, and a little too much fire in you, Mary. When I am weak you give me such strength. Like this tree, you wrap its branches around you and it protects you fae the storm. I believe you have God within you lass, all you have to do is to ask Him and He will answer. He will say, trust in Me, and I will lift your heart and lighten your darkest shadow, there's nothing you can ask Him that He will not listen to, and give His advice and solace." Her mother paused, thought, and then said, "If we are the focus of yer faither's ire, can you live with that?"

Mary nodded in agreement, and her mother added, "The day you say move on Mary, we will, but if you take God into your heart He will see you through all things." Her mother rubbed her eye, "Though I may ask Him tae improve my footwork."

Once they considered it safe to return, the two climbed down the tree and, hand in hand, headed home.

In a period of relative calm which followed at their home, Mrs Slessor, true to her convictions, gave birth to a beautiful baby girl named Jane Ann Slessor.

Land sharks

1870 was a traumatic year for the Slessor family; there were two deaths, the first was Mary's father. In time, Mary had learned how to deal with her father's drunkenness and avoid his fists and ill-temper, yet since his death, her relief had been tinged with a great sadness and anger that the demon drink had robbed her of a good father. Her younger brother Robert, studious, warm hearted and responsible, who, from an early age had had a career as a missionary mapped out for him, had died of tuberculosis at the age of twenty; this was a much harder death to accept; Mary could tell through the tears that in the last few months the injustice of his death had tested even her mother's faith.

By now Mary was twenty two and a bright attractive young woman, but no less wild; she still hitched up her skirts and climbed trees at any opportunity. But Mary's world was now very different, her role had changed; could she fill the gap left by her 'responsible' brother? She doubted she was good enough, but for the family's sake she would have to try. Susan, aged fifteen, John aged twelve, and Janie aged eight, were all now actively employed, and Mary's mother, due to ill health, had left her work at the mill and now ran a small shop in which they all helped. Mary had risen to the challenge and was also lending a hand at the Wishart Church Sunday School, reading to the young children excerpts from the Bible and tales of missionaries from many lands that were regularly featured in the Missionary Record. One of the Church elders, a marine insurance agent called James Logie, had watched her with the children and was impressed by her kindness and patience; he asked if she would like to join him in his evening missionary at Queen Street Mission to work with the poor, sick and elderly in Dundee. Mary at that time felt unworthy of such a responsible position and believed that currently her life was hard enough and busy enough without taking on any more, so she politely thanked him and declined the invitation.

The Wishart Church, an imposing, three storey building, was situated at the eastern corner of Cowgate where it intersected with St Roque's Lane. The top two floors had been converted into one large space to accommodate the impressive church; the bottom storey was cut through by a vennel. The left-hand side of the ground floor was occupied by the Sunday school and access to the church above was by a wooden stairway. The premises on the right was for a very different activity - a large public house called the John O' Groats which, to her shame, was one of the many places in which her father had tried to drown his sorrows. This corner had been given the nickname 'Heaven and Hell'. It may have been thought by some an unsuitable site to encourage religious devotion, but the more enlightened in Dundee believed that the poor were as deserving of salvation as those who lived in the more affluent precincts. Even on Sunday when such drinking dens were officially closed, this corner, situated as it was so close to the large harbour, was habitually populated by the flotsam and jetsam of society. The harbour was the heart of the town's commercial power, the owners of the nearby mills would have men sit in the tall minaret-type towers attached to each factory and, by telescope, watch day and night for their eagerly awaited ships to appear on the horizon. By employing this early warning method not a minute was wasted; by the time the ships were ready to discharge their goods, a fleet of horse-drawn wagons was ready and waiting to convey the cargo to its destination. This area of Dundee was a noisy, bustling, constant hive of activity. The influx of traders and sailors into Dundee's busy port led to the harbour district being filled with an eclectic mixture of accents, cultures and ethnic backgrounds due to the extensive trade with the Far East, India, the Black Sea ports and Europe, not to mention the divergent nature of the large fishing and whaling fleets. Consequently, the narrow streets, lanes and countless public houses overflowed with a fluid, thirsty and often lawless, transient population.

It is Sunday, and Mary is on her way to church with her mother and family. With the exception of Mary, the others entered the building and climbed the stairs to the church. While she waited at the bottom of the stairs to welcome in the worshippers, Mary met Mr and Mrs Logie, who asked her again if she had thought any more about helping with the Dundee Mission work; still feeling undeserving, she shook her head and once again declined. Out of the corner of her eye, Mary had noticed a young Negro man with a sailor's bag standing outside the church, looking agitated. She approached him and asked, *"Can I help ye, sir?"*

The tall, handsome man replied, *"Oh Miss, I'm just off the boat, I wonder if there is somewhere I can stow my bag?"*

Mary was only too happy to help, *"I'll pit it in the Sunday school room until the service is ower."*

He seemed greatly relieved, *"I thank you so much, that is very kind of you."*

He climbed the narrow wooden stair to the church and took his place in an unreserved pew towards the back of the congregation. All during the service he sang lustily and with great conviction, catching the attention of an elderly, respectable, well-dressed couple, who looked down on his enthusiasm disapprovingly, as if he were an interloper in 'their Church'. At the end of the service, Mary waited for him to return; with work still to do, she told her family to go home without her. Not wishing to hurry the sailor, she waited patiently for him, but when the last of the congregation had left and he still had not appeared, she lifted his bag and climbed the stairs to the church.

She opened the door and saw him sitting alone, praying. The door creaked and with some alarm he turned to see who was there. He immediately recognised Mary and sprang to his feet. Full of apologies, he took his bag, *"Let me take that from you, I am so sorry, to repay your kindness with such thoughtlessness!"*

Concerned, Mary asked, *"You seem troubled? Are you very far fae hame?"*

The sailor smiled a wide smile then said, for Mary's benefit in broad Dundonian, *"No, no, I'm fae Dundee."* Mary was understandably surprised. *"Ah yes, I am black, but my mother was brought here as a maid with a wealthy family. They had returned to Dundee after a good life in Africa, and here she met my father, who was also a sailor like me, and they married,"* he paused, and then smiled even more broadly, *"the consequence was me, Gift!"*

Unsure of his meaning, she asked, *"Gift?"*

The young man pointed to himself and told her proudly, *"It is my name, Gift."*

Mary smiled back and asked, *"Have you faimlie here?"*

"My mother and father have gone to a better place. But I have a beautiful wife and daughter." He rifled through his pockets and pulled out a locket which he opened and showed her the picture inside. He continued with great pride, *"She is named Patience, her skin is like ivory, and her hair like rays of sunlight."*

Mary was almost speechless at the image she beheld, *"She is such a bonnie lass, so very beautiful."*

His enthusiasm grew, *"And our child is called Victoria, she is the blessing of my life,"* he paused, *"yet I do not love her as I should, and for that, I ask God's forgiveness."*

"Your bairn?" asked Mary.

Gift shook his head, *"No, dear Patience, my wife. Her parents did not approve of our friendship, and that was all it was, a childhood friendship. But as we grew to be adults, Patience believed she loved me as a man, and that drove a wedge between her and her mother and father, and while I was at sea they threw her*

Wishart Arch

29

onto the streets such was their shame. Hearing of her situation when I returned, no matter where I looked, I could not find her, but I was looking in the wrong places. The streets can be cruel to beauty, and often drags it down to its own wretched image; she had taken to drink, and had to earn money the only way she could. Drink, evil men and illness, all aged her, and robbed her of her mind and her beauty. But I love her as the girl I knew, and have worked hard to save her. Each blow she took brought her down further and further. God has given me the sublime mission to save her soul." He paused, then asked, *"Would you come with me and meet her?"*

Mary enthusiastically replied, *"Aye. I would love to."*

She led him down the stairs at the bottom of which he hesitated.

"What is wrong?" Mary asked.

Gift scanned the street from the Wishart Arch towards the 'Heaven and Hell' corner, then quickly stepped back, *"Land sharks!"* he said dramatically.

Confused by the term, she asked him, *"Land sharks, whit are they?"*

With fear in his eyes, he spoke quietly, *"Thieves who infest the harbour. They know the movements of all the ships and who has been paid-off. I'm sure they can smell the money and they have the scent of mine."*

Mary spotted the four rough men lurking nearby, but she knew the area and suggested, *"I know another way, come quickly."*

The two left by the back door of the church, climbed a wall, and were soon in the comparative safety of the labyrinth of lanes.

Gift smiled at Mary, *"God has been good to send such a friend as you."*

She introduced herself, *"My name is Mary, Mary Slessor."*

Once he got his bearings, he led her to a dark lane and up three flights of even darker steps to the attic room. As they reached the top they heard a noise inside, followed by wild shouting; the door burst open and a well-dressed, but slightly dishevelled, young man rushed out, pushing them aside. As they entered the room, lit only by the dim firelight, all that Mary could make out was the shape of a creature sitting hunched on the floor. Gift, uncertain of what might happen, said softly, *"Patience?"*

In a flood of tears, the woman sprang to her feet and then fell to the floor, screaming; she grabbed his legs, *"Oh my dearest Gift, Gift, Gift, Gift!"* she cried.

Mary could hardly believe that this sad, pathetic being was the same beauty she had seen in the miniature; only a few of her front teeth remained, her blonde hair was filthy and had the texture of rats' tails. The tragic woman flashed an evil look at Mary, staggered to her feet and kissed Gift with public passion, rubbing herself against him as if she were a feral cat marking out her territory. Suddenly her attitude changed as she pawed at the sea bag he was holding. In a juvenile voice, she asked, *"Have you brought a present for Patience and your beloved Victoria?"* Mary presumed that the baby was asleep, wrapped in the bundle of rags in the corner of this dirty, stinking room. Gift looked into his bag and his eyes lit up with pride, *"I carved a toy for Victoria from whale bone and I brought you a fine seal skin."* Patience became angry and grabbed the bag and with a great flourish, as if she were a magician's assistant pulling a rabbit from a hat, produced a bottle of gin.

Patience held the bottle closely, *"Oh thank you Gift, I am so thirsty."*

To Mary, this seemed unlikely, as countless empty gin and whisky bottles littered the floor. Patience slowly turned her head and stared coldly at Mary; she sneered, took a step towards her, and spat out, *"And you're not getting any of **this**, this is for working girls!"* The woman removed the cork and took a long swig out of the bottle; apologetically Gift looked towards Mary. While Patience sat cross legged on the floor and drank greedily, he took Mary aside and asked, *"Will you look in on us tomorrow? She may be better then."*

Mary realised Gift was sorely in need of a friend, *"Of course e'll come back, if you want."*

The sailor opened the door and for the time being said goodbye, *"Thank you so much, may God be with you Mary, you shall see Victoria and I play such games."*

Purely by touch, Mary made her way down the dark stairs, always keeping to one wall until safely at the bottom. As she reached the dark wynd, she thought she heard voices whispering close by. Though she took the time to look, she saw no one but, for safety's sake, took to her heels and ran all the way home.

True to her word, after work Mary retraced her steps to Gift's house. The stairs were in total darkness but luckily she had remembered to bring a candle and match to light her way. She approached the attic room and, with some trepidation, knocked on the door which swung open. The room was pitch black. She carefully stepped over the threshold and called out, but there was no reply. The sight which confronted her was terrifying; she could see signs of a violent struggle, the few items of furniture they possessed lay in pieces, strewn across the wet floor. Gift's precious carving was crushed into tiny fragments, and there, in front of the grate, lay Patience; she had evidently been beaten and her throat had been cut. When Mary realised that the liquid which now seeped into the floor was blood, she turned away in horror and slipped, falling to the ground and spilling the candle as she did so. The wick sizzled and extinguished as it hit the floor. Frantically, her hands searched for the candle, her sense of panic and alarm grew the longer she remained sightless in this hellish darkness. When at last she recovered and re-lit it, she saw that she lay face-to-face with another body; by the flickering light she could see that it was Gift. A quick glance told her that he had also been beaten and though still alive, was surely close to death.

He opened his eyes, *"Mary, is that you?"*

Mary took his hand in hers, and asked urgently, *"Where is Victoria?"*

He whispered, *"Yesterday, not long after you left, I found that she was already dead, how long she had been so I do not know, my poor, poor child."*

Mary lifted his hand and held it to her cheek, *"Oh meh God!"*

Gift squeezed Mary's hand and said, *"But Mary, she is safe now. She is safe in the arms of the Lord and I will be with them both soon, and we shall all be happy."*

Mary tenderly stroked his hand, *"Oh Gift, how did such a thing happen?"*

Gift's throat gurgled, and his voiced weakened, *"The land sharks did for us."* He squeezed her hand again and said, *"Don't mourn for me."* There was a sense of triumph in his voice. *"I'm with God, Patience and Victoria. I'm free and we are as one at last, Mary."* Gift's grip tightened then loosened and he was gone from this mortal world.

Mary sat and wept uncontrollably and mourned at their passing. After an hour or more, she stumbled out of the house and into the lane, her clothes, hands and face covered with blood. In shock, she wandered through the deserted Dundee streets and struggled against the gathering storm, her warm tears merged with the freezing driving sleet which ran down her face. In a daze, she came eventually to the doorstep of Mr and Mrs Logie's home at 13 William Street, Forebank. She knocked politely at their door, as if it were a pleasant afternoon in spring; she was aware of hearing footsteps from inside the house. The door was opened gingerly and only very slightly by Mrs Logie, and through the narrow opening, her left eye was all that was visible.

Mrs Logie spoke very loudly, *"Who is it? I have a very fierce, vicious dog here, he will eat you, yes he will. Down brute!"*

It meant nothing to her in her state, she simply asked, *"Is Mr Logie here? I'd like to enrol in his mission."*

Mrs Logie, only too aware of the lateness of the hour, complained, *"Well goodness gracious, whoever you are, this is neither the time nor the place for such foolishness....."* Suddenly she thought she recognised the late night visitor and stopped her charade, *"Is that you? Is that you Mary?"*

The driving winter rain was washing the blood from Mary's face and skirts, making thin red streams between the cobbles like the veins of a city, and although Mary began to shiver violently, she felt nothing. Mrs Logie called to her husband, *"Mr Logie, it's Mary. I'll get a towel."*

Absent-mindedly Mrs Logie closed the door and left the young woman standing outside in the rain. Mr Logie could only imagine that all was not well and left the comfort of his fireside chair to open the door; as he did so, Mary collapsed into his arms. Without delay he carried her into the drawing room and as her body quivered in his arms, laid her gently onto the carpet in front of the fire. He shouted to his wife, *"Mrs Logie, would you remove Miss Slessor's wet things and avail her of some warm, dry clothing?"*

"Certainly, Mr Logie," she replied, as if the thought had crossed her own mind, which of course it hadn't.

"And after that, would you be so kind as to fetch some hot tea for the poor child? I will wait in the hallway."

After an appropriate time, Mr Logie returned to the room and saw Mary dressed and wrapped in a blanket, sipping a cup of tea by the fire. Mary said apologetically, *"I'm so sorry, I cannae think what got into me, I just didnae know whit to do, whar to go. We must send for the bobbies, it's murder Mr Logie!"*

Mr Logie, a man of some authority and experience, thought it best to hear the cause of her distress before taking any further action, so sat down beside her and said quietly, *"Before we do that, Mary, tell me all."*

"It may be too shocking fir Mrs Logie."

Mr Logie agreed, *"Mrs Logie, may we have another pot of your fine tea?"*

His wife concurred, *"An excellent suggestion, Mr Logie."*

Mrs Logie was a small delicate woman but with great inner strength, a loyal supporter and staunch ally of her husband in all his endeavours, despite appearing eccentrically 'dizzy' - though that may have been more by design than by lack of mental acuity. When she had completed her task, with tea tray in hand she knocked at the drawing room door and dutifully waited for her husband's instruction to enter. The room was silent, Mr Logie, his hand gripping the mantelpiece, stood staring intensely at the fire while Mary sobbed into her blanket. Mrs Logie sensed the sadness and said nothing, but continued with the 'tea ceremony', patiently awaiting her cue to re-enter the conversation.

Mr Logie checked the time on his pocket-watch, and asked, *"Mrs Logie, will you keep an eye out for the beat police officer? He should be on the corner in three or four minutes."*

"Of course, Mr Logie," she dutifully replied and withdrew.

Mary said, *"It may not be the right time, Mr Logie, but could I help you at the Dundee Mission?"*

Mr Logie, unsure if she was capable of making this commitment in her current state, asked, *"You wish to, even after this?"*

Mary sadly replied, *"No, 'cause of this!"*

Still doubtful, he asked, *"Are you sure you have the strength for it?"*

Mary shook her head, yet replied, *"No, of course not..... but to see the belief that Gift had, in such a miserable situation - there was nae anger or revenge in his heart, even after the deaths of Patience and Victoria. Nothing could diminish his love and his faith. Such devotion gave him such strength when a' purpose and hope wis lost. Death was no' an end but his beginning, his faith shone like a beacon tae me; with the power of that faith, surely nothin's impossible."*

At that moment, Mrs Logie returned with the constable; Mr Logie greeted him and walked into the hallway to have a word in private and, soon after, Mary and the officer departed in a cab into the night.

Once she had gone, Mr and Mrs Logie talked in only general terms about the late night visitor; Mrs Logie asked no questions and Mr Logie told her only what he wanted her to know. As they prepared for bed, to avoid his wife having nightmares Mr Logie changed the subject, *"Did I hear you speak earlier of, and to, a dog, Mrs Logie?"*

Her reply was prompt, *"A burglar's invention sir, a mere burglar's invention."*

Mr Logie smiled and asked, *"And do you find this ruse successful, Mrs Logie?"*

"To your knowledge, have we ever been burgled?"

He laughed and continued to pursue the playful deceit, *"And where, may I ask, does this 'wild beast that would eat a man' abide when I am at home?"*

Knowing that the game amused him, Mrs Logie thought carefully before replying, *"I keep it safe in a kennel in my mind."*

Mr Logie was happy to end the evening on a more cheerful note, *"Good, we wouldn't want a vicious beast like that to go roaming about the house, would we, Mrs Logie?"*

Mrs Logie ended victoriously, *"No, Mr Logie, we would not."*

Death and the three-legged stool

Over the past few years, the health of Mary's brother John had taken a turn for the worst, and in the hope of aiding a full recovery he had emigrated to New Zealand to begin a new life. Sadly that was not to be; within months of his arrival in that country the Slessor family received the sad news that, due to his weak constitution, he had died. Mary's mother's dream to have him take Robert's place as a missionary was now only that, a dream.

Mary soon became a committed mission worker in the streets and hovels of Dundee and a great aide to Mr Logie; he could see that her endless patience, and good humour, set her apart from many others who did their work out of a sense of Christian obedience, self satisfaction or moral crusade. To Mary, all were equally deserving and no situation taxed her bravery, morality or honour. Due to the ill treatment of missionaries in the town, it was the mission's policy that they should always work in pairs; but soon she went unaccompanied into any home, bringing with her, her new found God, a God who gave her the strength to face any situation no matter how perilous. She asked no payment, or thanks, or Christian devotion for her work, but the confidence she exuded encouraged many unfortunates to believe that her belief was one to wonder at and admire. She entered houses cursed by plague or fever, sexual depravity and abuse, death or desertion, and treated all in want of aid as friends in need. She talked fondly of her God, as if he were a friend and not a master; her actions were that of a human being who sincerely cared about their specific condition and circumstance, speaking to them, not preaching at them. Mr Logie believed that she was indeed a rare flower.

Mary had been sent to visit an old woman, Mrs Riley, who was close to death and who lived alone in a single room which held her few belongings; she had no friends and no family had survived her. As Mary entered the woman tried to raise her spirits, but could only lift a hand in welcome; Mary sat on the bed beside her and tried to make her comfortable. The only light was from the dying embers of the fire. The old woman croaked an apology that there was no candle, and explained that as she knew that she was not long for this world, the purchase of a new one would have been an extravagance; Mary agreed and sat with her until her time.

The old woman, cheered at the young lassie's care, said, *"Mary, should you get cauld, brak', the leg aff the three-legged stool, as I'll no' be needin' it in heaven."*

The two began to talk of the old woman's long life; she remembered all of her eleven children's names, dates of birth and exactly where they were born and where they died, recalling, with only a little sadness, how the 'parish' had put two of them in the poorhouse to die, commenting that, *"the parish has a public soul, but no hert."* She told Mary how, to put a roof over their heads, she had taken a job sewing sacks and she remembered that *"sewing wis nae sae bad, it wis carryin' a' the sacks back and fore, to and fae the mill, that took it oot o' me."* She talked of her husband, only a little more fondly, *"Oh, he was a lang streak o' misery, a real skinnymalink, but he was braw wi' the bairns."* She giggled, *"I mind he had awfie cauld feet. Funny what you remember at the end o' yer days, is it no' Mary?"*

She recalled which was each bairn's favourite corner, where and what game they played, and how she'd seen all her children die of disease and illness, and wondered, without bitterness, why she had been saved for so long to grieve over their passing.

The old woman apologised to Mary, *"Sorry, I can leave you nothin' dear Mary, no' even the end o' a candle tae see yer way hame."*

Mary, touched by the generosity of the poverty-stricken old woman, said, *"You have given me mair than I deserve. If I'd never met you, I'd never have kent such strength of spirit, never met such kindness wi' no thocht o' reward."* She lifted the old woman's wrinkled hand and kissed it. As the old lady's eyes closed, Mary continued to sit and wait; her silhouette against the dying fire embers betrayed the tears that fell from her eyes.

In the faint light of dawn, Mary was awoken by a loud scream. The old woman cursed, *"Ooooooooooh!..... Damn it! I'm no deid, I'll hae tae buy anither candle!"* The two women laughed at the happy catastrophe.

Mary made her a hot drink and took her leave, sure that she'd see her after her shift at the mill.

On her return later that day, as she approached the stairs to the old woman's house, she felt instinctively that there was something wrong. She climbed the last few steps and saw through the open door Mr Logie standing over the motionless old woman; Mary stood in the doorway and sobbed gently at the sight. Mr Logie turned to speak to her, *"Ah Mary, I was here at the end, she's not long gone. She asked me to go out and buy her a new candle, but strangely she never lit it, she said it was for you, she said to give you these."* He picked up the candle and the three-legged stool, which now sported only two, *"I don't know what happened to the other leg."*

Mary turned to look at the fire, and smiled as she spotted the remnants of the third leg smouldering in the grate. Mary clutched what remained of the stool and replied, *"It's fine, I do."*

Mr Logie looked around the room and said, *"Sadly, they'll be no stone to mark her passing. This place holds little to show for eighty years of hard work. It's a shame."*

Mary sprang to the old woman's defence, *"This is no' a sad place, this room is packed full of memories and life, no' the trophies of life, those that you cannae tak wi' you. But her heart was full o' riches, those will never fade, they are gems beyond price. She was a princess, nah, a queen of life; she needs no monument to death, and widnae thank you for it. She did not see death as an end, but only as another rung on the ladder to her just reward. A pauper's grave has a glory that no mausoleum can overshadow, what matters is how you live your life, no' the size of the monument you leave on your death. We have grand cemeteries built wi' the wages of the poor, wi' tall gravestones, as if the closer they reach to heaven, the better the lives they led. If only that were true."*

Tea and acrimony

Mr Logie's belief in Mary's devotion and dedication had suggested a course of action, which did not please all those associated with the church. In their comfortable home, he and his wife had taken it upon themselves to coach Mary in etiquette and help her improve her education. This would be essential for her personal growth, and would greatly improve her prospects for the job of missionary. They were sure that she had the goodness, intelligence and stamina, but her attitude to those in authority was another matter altogether. The question was, could that be controlled? Only time would tell.

Firstly they invested in a smart suit of clothes for the young woman for the social evenings that the Logies had planned. The weight and the constricted movement of these garments made Mary feel a prisoner to propriety, a feeling she would never overcome, but as it was for a noble cause Mary bore it well, or at least as well as she could.

After one of these events, a dinner at which Mary could mix with the gentry, the three discussed how the evening had gone. Mary knew their report would be less than glowing, as one of the wealthy visitors had promised to *'give a little something to charity'*, and Mary had been critical of his meagre gesture. Mr Logie stood with his back to the open fire and after much thought and deliberation started to speak, *"In polite society, Mary, we should never criticise* or reproach our betters. *The rich and highly-advanced among us often seem, let us say, artistically eccentric, other-worldly. You have so much to learn of morality."*

Mary nodded, wide-eyed in sarcastic agreement. Mr Logie pretended not to see Mary's reaction, so continued, *"We must know our place Mary, to be respectful of those who wield the power in our society, as they do so by their expertise and wisdom and we may gaze and admire them,"* at this point he changed the tone of his voice, *"and not sneer at them from below!"*

Mary, squeezed by the constriction of her corset and high-buttoned jacket, was exasperated by the criticism, replied, *"The rich hae nae priority in His eyes, they are no more learned nor wise, there's nae first-class passage to heaven."*

Mr Logie was shaken by her disrespect, *"But the mill owner gave you work, a chance to earn a living, without that you would have starved. There is plenty work for those not too lazy to find it."*

Mary tried to undo her tight collar, *"Is that how you see it? Well, let me tell you, that if yer lucky..... by the time yer fourteen they let us lassies work the full fifty-eight hours. Lassies can find regular work, but the poor lads, and men, are treated like auld workhorses. When a laddie grows to be a man and would get a man's wage, he is no longer onie use, and put on the street. The women, on the other hand, on half his wages, and the bairns on a quarter, fill the owners' pockets, build their grand houses, pave their fine Dundee streets. Aye, the mill owner's expertise and wisdom? Well ye hae tae hand it to them, they are wise enough to expertly fiddle ye out o' yer wages! Then be seen as benefactor - wi' yer ain money? I can no longer haud my tongue! These so-called friends have no more right to my respect than the news seller or the doxy on the street!"*

Mr and Mrs Logie stood close together, with arms around one another, shocked by her outburst. To avoid hearing any further castigation of the establishment, Mrs Logie went to the dinner table and carried away some of the dishes to the kitchen, *"If you'll excuse me!"*

Mary, still disgruntled, continued, *"At least we know how and why a lady of the streets earns her pennies, she gets paid for providing a service that some **man** wishes. She hisnae thousands who do her work and then are kept as close to penury as the masters can get awa' wi', workin' all hours tae mak massive profits fir them. You talk of morality, what about the morality o' the sweatshop? Of course they'll gi' tae guid causes, because of the sweat o' my mither and many others! They hae it to give - halls, parks, streets named efter them, but the lassie that works hard for a livin', puts what she can intae the mission or the collection plate on Sunday. THAT is giving, THAT is sacrifice. Although she is a step away from* starvation, she does it no' fir a brass sign in Dundee. There's no' a separate heaven fir fowk wi' money. That's only in this world!"

Mr Logie, when faced with the unanswerable, hid behind the scriptures, "He that hath pity upon the poor lendeth unto the Lord; and that which he hath given will he pay him again, Proverbs chapter 19 verse 17."

Mary looked down at the table, thought for a moment then, with a smile, said, "Bread of deceit is sweet to a man: but afterwards his mouth is full of gravel, chapter 21 verse 17."

Mr Logie was taken aback at being out-quoted, so changed tack, "So would you turn down the rich person's £10?"

In frustration she replied, "No, giving is kindness, but the mill owner will gie only a tiny wee pert o' the profit he maks, and gets the honour fir it, but the mill girl gives her all, and trusts only to God fir her reward."

Mr Logie, again felt that he had been bested, "You have a streak of wilfulness in you that I do not admire, you seem to think that God will supply all." He returned to his quotations, "The rich ruleth over the poor, and the borrower is servant to the lender."

As quick as lightning she replied, "He that oppresseth the poor to increase his riches, and he that giveth to the rich, shall surely come to want."

There was an uncomfortable silence; Mary raised her eyebrows in mock victory, "I know that your respect and position dictates your sense Mr Logie, I ken these are not your own words, it's no' your heart that says these things."

Mr Logie was losing patience, "Mary, the sharp edge of your tongue may cut the strings of our friendship and, though I sincerely hope not, your pride may see us go down very different paths. That is something you may wish to dwell upon."

Mary knew then that she had said too much and had offended the kindness of her hosts, but replied, "I'm proud that my God has chosen to share His love wi' me, I cannae see truth in things I find false, I cannae see kindness in guilty pity, I cannae see love where it disnae exist."

Mr Logie could not agree, but knew that in her world she spoke the truth; to do other would have been a betrayal of her heritage. "You may find that choices are not always so easy to make," he said. "I hope your beliefs never get in the way of the correct decision; you may discover that it is not always so easy to put the spiritual need so far ahead of the earthly; it is a long road to Africa, and prayer alone will only take you so far."

Their falling out was over for another night; they would do so again. He knew that her fiery spirit would get her into trouble, but he was sure that her faith, both in herself and in her God, was more than a match for most adversaries. He continued to sponsor her application to be a missionary, and in 1876, they received the news that she had been accepted to train for the role in Edinburgh.

A new Mary?

Mary's weeks in Edinburgh were intended to turn her into a 'good missionary', to hone her English language skills, improve her Bible knowledge and establish her suitability for the role. As the time passed, cosily wrapped in this cosseted life, her character began to change now that she was free of the pressures she had experienced hitherto. Edinburgh had brought her into a new social circle, a different class of young person; many of her fellow students had never worked a day in their lives, yet she admired their ambition to give up security and comfort for such a dangerous and uncertain future. On many occasions, Mary stayed at Darling's Regent Hotel, a temperance hotel in Edinburgh's Waterloo Place where, thankfully, their family and friends kept her firmly anchored and, though in a different social sphere to Mary, judged her solely by her goodness and by no other criteria.

She had become a familiar face as she walked daily to and from the school; unlike Dundee, the streets were tidy and uncluttered and she enjoyed the promenade in the fresh air and bright sunlight. Early one evening, while returning to her lodgings, carrying her Bible, she mulled over the lessons of the day and how well she was doing, how well suited she was to her new life. Dundee seemed as far away as Africa. As she admired the style and dresses of the fine ladies who passed by, she suddenly became aware of a shadow behind her; it seemed to be keeping pace, and for the first time in the metropolis, she became uncomfortable. In an attempt to lose her pursuer, she decided to look into the window of one of the many small shops which lined the street. She stopped, took a deep breath and turned to face the owner of the shadow; to her relief, there was no one there. Happy to have avoided a confrontation, she turned to continue her walk home and found the shadow's owner blocking her way; before her stood an old man, grinning. He was over sixty years of age, as far as she could tell, and was wearing a suit, or at least the shredded remnants of one. He held out a spindly arm, at the end of which he cupped his bony hand, and asked, *"A farthing for a beggar, Miss?"* For a moment she was too surprised to speak. The beggar was determined to engage her in conversation, *"Is that a Bible you have there?"*

As a good Christian she knew she had to reply to the question, but before she could answer, he asked, *"Are you going to Africa to do missionary work?"*

Surprised and annoyed by the intimacy of his question she replied, *"Yes, that is my intention."*

He pressed on, *"Why do you want to go?"*

Mary became more annoyed, but attempted to remain civil, *"Not that it should concern you, but to save the heathen and teach them God's word and Christian ways."*

The beggar chuckled, *"Eloquently put, but it sounds as if you were reading that from a card. Were you?"* He grabbed her gloved hand, and opened it to look; Mary shrugged him away, and rubbed her new glove clean. It did not stop him. *"What if that were impossible to do?"* he enquired.

Mary, flustered by his insistence and impertinence, replied, *"Well, I wouldn't give up!"* then said haughtily, *"and take to begging on the streets like you."*

Without taking a breath, the beggar replied, *"Oh, so you don't think that God cares about the entire human race? Is the beggar in Edinburgh any less one of God's children than the King, the meenester, the mill owner, the African, or Chinaman?"* There was a long silent pause; he began to pace then he continued, *"If you believe in God, then you must believe in the Community of Man. God does not choose between rich and poor, black or white, Scot or Turk, Protestant or Mussulman, that is man's choice. To close your mind to these things is to close your heart to God."*

Before Mary realised what was happening, he had reached out and grabbed her Bible, opened it and began to go through its pages. As if not wanting to touch them; he held it open on the flat of his hand and blew the thin paper pages over. He read, and nodded at the passages he recognised, speaking quietly and very quickly, *"The Lord's my Shepherd dum de dum...... The Bible,"* he laughed, *"may be God's word but its interpretation is man's; you should take your strength from **His** deeds, understand **His** meaning, not man's."*

Mary felt that, metaphorically, she had her back to the wall; all she could think of to say was, *"Who gives you the right to question me?"*

The beggar laughed again, *"I was once a missionary."* He paused and said gleefully, *"and I live to tell the tale! I went with great enthusiasm, empty pockets and a head full of psalms and good intentions. Like yourself, I went to teach the heathen, though I ended up unable to tell who were the heathens and who were the teachers."* He cackled. *"The missionary soon becomes driven by the politics of* the Church and proscribed text, and other politics beside; all fine in the streets of this grand town, producing conversations only fit for drawing rooms and pulpits, but of little solace in the heat of the jungle or during perpetual fits of malaria." He stopped and hit his head with the palm of his hand, as if trying to shake something loose. Once that was seemingly accomplished, he smiled broadly again and continued, "You will need to use your mind and your heart. There you will find God, and you will need every ounce of strength He can give you. The scriptures are for those who lack your belief, young lass."

Mary, confused by his advice replied, "An old man like you should mark his words, you should remember that missionaries do God's work."

The beggar took a huge breath and then sighed, "If only that were true..... my dear lass, I am 40 years old, my life abroad, the worry and malaria has aged me beyond recognition......" He lost the thread of the conversation for a moment, then returned to it, "what the native needs is not high-minded, well-intentioned Christian conversion, but they do need saving," again he giggled, "sadly it's mostly from our exploitation, the Empire builders, Britain, Germany, France, Belgium dum de dum....."

He returned Mary's Bible, clasped his hands behind his back, put his head down, started to pace backwards and forwards, and continued his lecture. "The missionary preaches that his God has come to save the savage; but once we have their trust, we stride further into their territory. In our shadow, in our very footprints, stalk the merchant and the gin dealer, there to steal their crops, land, pride and birthright. I became the anointed, the appointed standard bearer for greed and speculation; a fine parade we made, a parade of charlatans, each one giving less and taking more as we trampled our way into new territories. Any good work I could achieve, which was often very little, was soon destroyed by those real savages who would profit by it. In my Holy quest, doing God's work, I stopped looking over my shoulder." He smirked, "Proverbs chapter 13 verse 20 'He that walketh with wise men shall be wise: but a companion of fools shall be destroyed.' Yet it was we who destroyed their beliefs, culture and dignity, and left them with empty rhetoric. Converted them not to God, as in return for their trust and their crops and land we gave them slavery, but slavery by another name; we made them dependant on the scraps we would throw them from the wealth that was once their own. If we do not understand who and what they are, we are the losers; if you open your eyes there is much they will teach you - love, kindness, loyalty. Yet they have grown up with such idolatry and savagery, inflicted upon them, then adopted by them, their faults are obvious and easy to deplore, but ours *are much, much more devious and poisonous. If you can earn their trust, use that to help them build a future, and on no account betray it!"*

Mary stood, completely stunned by his words; to escape his presence, she opened her purse and offered him a small coin. The beggar recoiled at the sight of the money and screamed, *"No, no Miss!"* His right hand rose and shook as it reached for the coin, his left hand grabbed his right and pulled it away, *"No, I fear that you will need all that you have, and much, much more, if you are to match the same age as mine."* He began to walk away but stopped, looked back and said, *"I wouldn't have told you these things if I didn't think you had God in your heart, Mary. You walk in God's footsteps not man's. God bless you."*

Mary looked down at the pavement and tried to gather her thoughts; when she lifted her head to speak to him, she realised that he had vanished. She never saw the beggar again, and as time passed, she put the incident to the back of her mind as if it were a strange dream.

Before she had finished her stay in the capital city, Mary had made many friends; one woman in particular, Mrs McCrindle from Joppa, on the outskirts of Edinburgh, took a special interest in Mary's progress and they would remain great friends throughout their lives.

On her return to Dundee, Mary and her family eagerly awaited news of Mary's mission report. When it arrived, apart from a criticism that her knowledge of the scriptures was not up to standard, she was accepted as a probationer in Calabar, West Africa. They could not have been happier, or more proud, though Mary's mother's joy was clouded by a sense of sadness; she knew it was a noble path that her daughter had embarked upon, but the loss of her lass was a high price to pay. Their farewell at the entrance to their close at 17 Harriet Street was heartfelt, but the tears for the family were kept until the doors were closed and the train to Liverpool docks was well on its way. Mary was accompanied on the journey by the Logies; in the carriage there was little conversation, but much private thought and prayer.

1876
The Liverpool farewell

Mary stood on the dock and waited to depart on the six-week journey to Calabar on the S.S. Ethiopia; she was dressed in her new finery, a long black dress and high-necked jacket, sturdy boots and gloves; she carried the compulsory pith helmet, which would protect her head and long red hair from the worst effects of the sun. The Logies stood silently beside her, leaving her time for reflection until invited to speak. Mary stared at the large metal ship, and admitted, *"I'm not very fond o' water."*

Mr Logie now felt free to speak, *"You're looking every inch the missionary, Mary, how do you feel?"*

Mary confirmed, *"I'm excited..... and sad to be leaving all those who mean so much to me. I can only hope that they won't miss me as much as I'll miss them; my heart is full and empty at the same time."*

Mr Logie looked intently at her then out to the water, *"I have a feeling that this will be an adventure like no other, lass."* He turned to face her, *"You are such a singular soul, Mary; Calabar does not know what is coming."*

Mrs Logie fussed at Mary's dress collar, *"You must remember to keep covered at all times, high buttons and....."* she paused and then whispered, *"always keep some wool next to the skin."*

A commotion behind them made the three move aside as a fellow traveller went on board, immediately followed by two porters carrying a newly-made coffin. Mrs Logie attempted to cover Mary's eyes, *"Oh Mary, don't look."* Mary looked quizzically at the long box, Mr Logie explained, *"Sadly it is something often taken out as part of their luggage..... for safety's sake. It's not called the white man's grave just to frighten the children."*

Mrs Logie continued her fussing with her list of do's and don'ts, *"Don't eat any native food and never, never drink any water that hasn't been boiled."*

Mary, touched by her concern, replied, *"Yes, yes of course."*

Mrs Logie, efficient to the last, enquired, *"Now, do you have everything?"* She flitted around the porters locating and counting Mary's bags.

Mary looked at her luggage and resorted to her Dundee tongue, *"Ev mair claes than the raggie man."*

Mr Logie looked at her disapprovingly. She corrected her English, *"Sorry, I have more raiment than a draper's."*

Mr Logie smiled with mild frustration, *"Slightly better, but the tone needs adjustment, and remember....."*

Mary quoted his words, *"Yes I know, 'speak clearly and properly',"* adding triumphantly, *"but I shall be as loud and clear as a bell for the Lord."*

With a hint of reproach in his voice he told her, *"Remain modest in all things, and obey, not only Him; give your masters no reason for complaint."*

Mary raised an eyebrow towards Mr Logie, as he did to her, and replied with mock obedience, *"Of course."*

As the porters lifted Mary's luggage on to the ship, there was a shout from a steward, *"Last call for boarders!"*

Mrs Logie gave Mary a hug, kissed her goodbye, then ran off weeping profusely; Mr Logie looked at Mary and took her hand, *"You are indeed a contrary lass, but I have never met anyone quite like you, one who has such belief. Many may talk of servitude to God, but in reality they believe themselves to be the masters, not the servant..... but with you Mary?..... I could not have wished for a better pupil; you have taught me so much."*

Mary blushed and said without thinking, *"Awa!..... Oh sorry, go away with you!"*

Mr Logie had a last request, *"Will you come back one day and tell us how you fared amongst our heathen brethren?"*

"Of course."

The steward called, *"All aboard!"* Mr Logie looked at Mary, and after an awkward pause, they formally shook hands. Mary turned and took the first step on her own up the gangway, the first step towards a new life. Once safely on board, Mr Logie, with a comforting arm around his weeping wife, said in a loud whisper, *"Mary go, go take on the world!"*

Into the African fire

Once on board, Mary sobbed. As the ship left the dock, she waved farewell to Mr Logie whom she could see supporting his wife, who continued to weep uncontrollably. The six-week journey would be good for Mary, time to acclimatise to her new situation, including the rapidly rising temperatures. Though she was now on this magnificent adventure, she remained at odds with her new role; she found it difficult to make conversation as the 'new Mary', but answered politely and made small-talk whilst sweltering in her new clothes and silly, preposterous hat. She felt stifled in this persona, but did not want to let the Mission, or the Logies, down. She watched the children run and play and envied them having fun in the minimum of clothing, and though she was tempted to join them, she knew she could not. After a week of keeping her own company, on one bright, sunny, but almost gale-force afternoon, she battled up the narrow metal stairs onto the windswept deck. As there were no others out in such conditions, she had her pick of deck chairs; she settled in the most secluded spot she could find. Hidden from view, she felt liberated enough to remove her thick stockings, boots and hat, and for the first time she relaxed. She stood with difficulty in the strong gale and struggled to move forward to reach the handrail and let down her long hair to blow free in the wind. At last she was able to take in all the wonders around - the countless sea birds that followed in the ship's wake, the magnificent dolphins which acted as vanguards to the rusting hulk. She marvelled at everything that swam or flew, their colours and shapes, all the sights and sounds that she had never seen or heard before. In a wave of emotion, she fell to her knees and gave thanks to God for all that she had been given and this chance to serve in His name.

As the weeks passed, her ability to converse with her fellow passengers improved. She made up her mind to seek out one passenger in particular, Mr Thomson, an architect from Glasgow, whom she had overheard talking and wanted to hear more. As they talked she learned that after a stay in Africa he had decided to close up his business in Scotland and buy himself a plot of land high in the mountains of Cameroon. His notion was based on his experience of life in the tropics; he knew that missionaries, throughout the district, regularly became exhausted and unwell while working in the intense heat and in locations associated with disease; this enemy to health he described as 'areas of bad air'. They became so unwell that their only option was to take a break, or 'furlough', which entailed a costly and time-consuming return trip to Britain. These furloughs were often delayed until cover could be found to fill their posts. As they waited their condition often worsened; this naturally extended their rehabilitation time, which could last for one, two, or even three years, a long time away from their missionary duties. Mr Thomson had had the idea to build a retreat high in the mountains, where the air was fresh and as far away from the 'bad air' as possible. Mary, yet to experience the extremes of the African bush, listened intently without knowing the significance and sense of his scheme. He also told her of day-to-day life in Africa and its many hardships; he described its creeks, streams, and rivers filled with all manner of animal life; he related journeys to other parts of Africa and encounters with elephants, tigers, leopards, snakes and every kind of creeping, crawling insect. She sat enthralled as he described torrential rainfall, enormous storms of thunder and lightning, ferocious hurricanes which ripped up trees and destroyed houses. As Mary lay in her berth that night, she played over each event in her mind as if they were stories from an adventure book, but as Mary would soon find out, these were not fanciful tall tales. Sadly, within months of his arrival in Africa, Mr Thomson would die, his dream of a retreat never to be realised.

Mary's arrival in Calabar

As the journey came to its end and the boat skirted the African coast, Mary stood aboard transfixed and amazed by the vibrant colours; her senses reeled with the perfumed scents carried on the gentle breeze. For a lass from Scotland, who had lived all of her life a virtual prisoner of the narrow streets and wynds and rank-smelling alleyways, where the light was often only glimpsed between high, dark, grey-brown buildings, this was another world. The lush green landscape ahead, above her a sky that appeared to go on forever, cries of hidden animals, and strange birds that flew up from the jungle, each one more fantastic than the last, took her breath away. As the ship pulled into the harbour at Calabar she felt that her heart might burst. The ship's eagerly awaited arrival created much excitement; the whole port viewed almost in miniature from her vantage point was alive with frantic activity. The vista from the harbour up to the imposing buildings, which sat imperiously overlooking the wide bay, seemed so perfect, so idyllic; surely this couldn't be the dark, dangerous Africa of Livingstone's stories? First impressions of course can be misleading, and Mary was easily impressed, as a child might be, unaware of the challenges that lay before her - unlike those longer in the tooth or with more to lose. For Mary it was different as she was not forsaking a well-to-do upbringing, or suffering the consequences of a loss of position or status; the mill lassie was starting a new adventure and all she could forfeit was her life, which, some time ago, she had placed securely into the hands of God. She stood spellbound and watched as the harbour quickly filled with small boats; other, larger boats of buyers and sellers of exotic goods, as yet 'strange cargo' to Mary, sailed this way and that. Her impatience to stand on this new land was overwhelming and she grabbed her bags in a most unladylike manner, ran along the deck high-stepping over luggage and cargo in her way, showing a lot more ankle than one would imagine appropriate for a young woman in her position. As she reached the bottom of the ship's gangway, looking impatiently left and right, she heard someone call her name. In her enthusiasm she misidentified the caller and believed it to be a man in a small boat filled with large bales of material. He saw her wave to him and motioned her to come aboard; his gesture and broad welcoming smile were all that the impatient young woman needed, so it was with great gusto that she threw her bags into his open arms. The boat was more than a 'genteel' step away; Mary took a step backwards, ran, jumped and landed bottom first on the soft bale. The boat's crew applauded her athletic effort, laughed and shouted loudly; aboard the ship, Mr Thomson and his friends joined in the applause. Mary, oblivious that she had had an audience, turned and looked at them with embarrassment, smiled coyly, and waved them farewell.

As it happened, a boat has been sent for her from the Mission; quite how she missed seeing it was difficult to fathom, as it was, by comparison, an impressively large vessel with a white awning, manned by six local boatmen called Krumen dressed in undershirts, red caps and dark loincloths; aboard, a young, well-dressed white man shouted and waved to attract her attention. He was the Mission administrator, Alexander Ross, a pernickety and fastidious young missionary.

"Goodness gracious another weak spindly woman, it's strong men we need for this work," he spoke loudly to himself, *"she's hardly more than a child, give me strength."* He smiled fawningly towards her and shouted, *"Miss Slessor, I have been sent by the Mission to gather you!"* With the aid and assistance of the crew, she was safely decanted into the boat. The young man took a seat beside her, *"I trust your journey went well, Miss Slessor?"*

Mary flushed and out of breath replied, *"Indeed, it was a wonder."*

As if speaking to a child, he asked condescendingly, *"I believe you had quite a storm; were you not afraid?"*

Mary reacted to the tone in his voice and inadvertently slipped back into her best Dundonian, *"I cannae believe that God wid send me a' this way just to drown in a ship."*

Ross smiled awkwardly then introduced himself, *"My name is Alexander Ross. You shall be met officially at the Mission jetty by Mrs Sutherland. You will find Mrs Sutherland a fine and upright person with a great deal of experience to take guidance from; she has long been a servant of God and the Mission."*

Mary said diplomatically, *"I will be guided by her, thank you, Sir."*

Mr Ross picked up Mary's helmet and handed it to her; obediently, though reluctantly, she put it on. Enjoying every second of her new life, and still in somewhat of a dream, she allowed her hand to drop and drift into the warm water of the harbour, a world away from the cold, muddy, tidal-brown water of her beloved River Tay.

The boat reached the jetty at Duke Town and the sight awaiting Mary was beyond her understanding. In front of her was an elderly woman with white hair, dressed, not as she would have imagined, but in a plain smock; she was closely attended by a group of beaming young native children, in brightly coloured clothes, acting as a guard of honour. Mary's words came from her heart, *"Oh my goodness, whit a welcome!"*

This 'honour' was beyond Mary's wildest expectation or experience; at no time in her life had she been treated with such respect. She could say nothing, but stood in stunned humility that God had seen fit to allow her to witness this wonder; tears burst like a dam and streamed down her face. Mrs Sutherland, moved by Mary's genuine and touching emotion, approached her and placed her arm around Mary's shoulder and introduced herself, *"Miss Slessor, I am Mrs Sutherland, or as I am called by my young friends here, Akamba Ma."*

Unsure of what to say in reply, all that Mary could manage was to gaze in joy and wonder at the children. Mrs Sutherland said, *"If you have all your luggage, we should climb to the Mission house to meet the rest of our happy band."*

They all proceeded in a snaking line from the harbour up through the town to the Mission house set high above. The ascent was difficult as the roads and paths which weaved their way through the many small houses were dangerous and hard to negotiate. The roads, if such a term could be used, which radiated downwards, were basically dry river beds constantly rutted, deepened and eroded by regular flash flooding during the rainy season. The heat was stifling and Mary struggled to keep pace with the others, laden down as she was in her heavy regulation missionary outfit; each step seemed to take more of her energy and to slow down their progress. Mary had never known heat like this - she had read of a 'wall of heat' in books, but to actually experience it was a completely different matter; not a cloud in the sky, not the trace of a breeze, no matter how hard she tried it felt as if there was no air to breathe. Although she was young and fit, nothing had prepared her for such all-consuming, intense heat, from which there was no shelter, no relief, no escape: it was a beauteous, cruel heat. She knew that she must push on; this was her first test and she could not afford to fail. As they meandered towards the top, Mrs Sutherland, seeing her distress, linked arms with Mary to aid her stumbling steps, and though Mary had been determined to do all things by herself when she arrived in Africa, she had to admit reluctantly that accepting help was not always a weakness. With the old woman's kind assistance her first test was almost accomplished.

Mission impossible

At the Mission house, most of the town's European ladies had been invited to greet the latest member of the mission from Scotland. The Scottish contingent at Calabar consisted of four ordained missionaries and their wives, and eight teachers, with an additional eighteen African agents and one ordained African. As the missionaries waited outside, inside two of the merchant wives, Mrs Crabbe and Mrs Smylie quietly gossiped and discussed the new arrival.

Mrs Crabbe was the first to snipe, *"I hear that she is a mill girl..... from Dundee! I was hoping she would be from Edinburgh so I could get some news of home, who is marrying whom, the latest fashion..... I doubt she knows where Edinburgh is."* They both sniggered, then Mrs Smylie said, *"She may know the latest fashion in clogs!"* They tittered; Mrs Crabbe picked up her small round glasses and peered through the window, *"My goodness, they will accept anyone nowadays, not like the old days, no, no, they were only taken from the best of families! She won't live to see the year out, you mark my words, death by disease or disappointment! Probably both!"* she added and she and her companion laughed cruelly.

As Mary and the odd parade neared the Mission house, Mrs Sutherland gave her some unwelcome news, *"We have organised a small get-together of prominent citizens to welcome you; it can be tedious but they feel that any news from Britain makes them feel less homesick."*

"Oh hivins!" blurted Mary, then, *"sorry."*

Hearing the alarm in Mary's voice the old woman asked, *"I hope you don't mind?"*

Mary stuttered and attempted to hide her terror of public events, *"Oh, of course not, I would be delighted,"* she lied. Each step Mary took only increased her anxiety, she hoped that she would remember all the lessons that Mr Logie and Mrs Logie had so kindly taught her, but she doubted her ability to use them in the heat of drawing room battle. Once they reached the Mission house, the sight of a line of well-wishers eagerly awaiting Mary made her feel faint. The attentive Mrs Sutherland saw her obvious discomfort and said to the guests, *"I'm sure you all know how trying the climate is to our new recruits, plus the arduous nature of the climb. We should give Miss Slessor a few minutes to catch her breath before we hear of her news from home."* The kind old woman led Mary through the main room to a back bedroom which was, thankfully, darker and cooler. Mrs Sutherland took Mary's hat and said, *"I'm sorry, but the job does come with certain social responsibilities, especially with Reverend and Mrs Anderson away on furlough at the moment. I will do my best to lead you gently through the wagging tongues. Some of the merchant and military wives live only for gossip and speculation. They mean no ill but they do it all the same."*

Mary, glad to have a friend, asked, *"Would you think it ill of me to have a few moments?"*

Mrs Sutherland smiled, *"Of course not,"* and left the room closing the door behind her. The second Mary was alone she flopped down onto the bed, loosened her collar and dress, removed her boots and stockings, picked up a fan and cooled her sweating brow. *"I'm sweatin' like a brewers dray, surely no one has faced such awfie trials!"* she moaned.

She heard a noise behind her and turned towards the window where she spied two young black children, who smiled at her, giggled and ran away. This was the spur that Mary needed, to remind her of the importance of her new role, and that her selfishness was an affront to God. She knelt down and prayed and asked His forgiveness. After a few minutes, Mrs Sutherland knocked at the door and opened it. Mary stood before her dressed, composed and ready for the fray. *"Miss Slessor, are you up for the task?"* she asked.

"Please, call me Mary. Yes, into the lion's den."

Before they entered the main room, Mrs Sutherland asked her, *"I believe you are from Dundee, Mary?"*

"Yes," Mary replied.

"Good that'll cut down the idle chatter," she took Mary's hand and said reassuringly, *"trust me."*

The room was full of the 'polite' society of Calabar. Mrs Sutherland took control, *"As I introduce Miss Slessor to you, the latest addition to our Mission, I'm sure she will speak to you of what she knows, and will tell you of her home in Dundee. I have to say, I know little of the town, so as I know you have more knowledge than I, I will be fascinated to hear your questions. So who has a question about Dundee?"*

As she had expected, the room fell silent. *"Well, never mind. I'm sure Mary will have lots to tell you as she circulates. But firstly I would like to take this opportunity to thank God for the safe delivery of Miss Slessor."*

Mary placed her hand on Mrs Sutherland's and asked, *"May I?"* At a nod from the old woman, Mary fell to her knees, the house children doing the same and, with some reluctance, the military and merchant contingent followed suit. Mrs Sutherland smiled at Mary's bravado. *"Dear God on high, I thank you for our blessings and for my safe delivery to this wondrous place, where with God's grace we may help bring light by Thy radiance, wisdom by Your word and peace by Your example. God I beseech you to give me strength and that the trials of the past are not used as reproaches for the future, that jealousy, ambition, fear and envy are banished from every heart that carries Your word. That love, compassion and understanding be our weapons in the battles ahead, not intolerance and violence against our brothers and sisters."* The merchant ladies raised an eyebrow. *"Grant us leave to act in Your name, Amen."*

Once back on their feet, Mary was surrounded by the mission staff who fussed excitedly around her. The two merchant ladies stood and tutted, *"Where would we be without the might of the military with these savages? The girl knows nothing, six months I give her,"* said Mrs Crabbe. No longer the centre of attention and, with noses well out of joint the two ladies took their leave of the building. Mrs Sutherland noticed their departure and smiled.

Later that evening, Mary saw for the first time a gloriously breathtaking sunset turn, in what seemed like seconds, to a moonlit night filled with more bright twinkling stars than she could ever have imagined. She and Mrs Sutherland sat on the verandah and blethered, *"Well Mary, are you up for the challenge?"* she asked.

Mary, amazed at God's wonders, answered, *"I'm no' sure if my enthusiasm is enough to sustain me, but He will give me strength..... if it is His purpose for me to stay....."* adding forcefully, and with determination in her voice, *"then in His name I shall."*

Mrs Sutherland placed her hand upon Mary's and reassured her, *"I believe you have the heart for it, but climate and disease are great levellers; sometimes the greatest heart cannot survive. Tomorrow I'll introduce you to my aide, Ma Fuller. There is much work to be done."*

When Mrs Sutherland had finished talking, she turned to Mary only to find that, tired and exhausted, she was fast asleep. She took two blankets and covered Mary knowing that the warm evening would turn into a bitter chill overnight. As the day dawned, the household awoke, the mission staff and house children went about their business quietly so as not to waken Mary. Those passing the sleeping lass began to point to her and whisper. Mary awoke forgetting where she was and opening her eyes she saw a bulbous pair of eyes looking back at her. She screamed and pulled the blankets over her head. The big green lizard took fright, ran off into the bushes, and all the mission workers and children laughed. Mrs Sutherland explained, *"It's only a lizard, Mary, they're harmless, but you'd better get used to them."*

The Andersons return

After three months Mary was almost feeling at home, but Mrs Sutherland had warned her that things would change with the return of the senior missionaries, the Andersons. Mr Anderson was a good man and a renowned preacher, but Mrs Anderson had a fearsome reputation as a stickler for punctuality and discipline. The household was in an excited uproar at their imminent arrival, with everyone polishing, washing and pressing; the house children were also washed and polished and paraded for inspection. Mrs Sutherland took Mary aside and gave her some last minute advice, *"Well Mary, up until now I've left you free to learn about the challenges that lie ahead, but now you must deal with more exacting aspects. The return of Mrs Anderson may cramp your style and rein in that wayward streak, but facing reality is not always a bad thing."*

Unlike Mary's trek up from the harbour, the procession she watched approaching was almost military in its speed and precision. The large-hatted woman who led the 'charge' was quick and determined; Mary wondered who it might be, but was fairly sure she knew. Similar to Mary's arrival, all the great and the good were gathered at the Mission house to act as a welcoming committee. As soon as Mrs Anderson reached the mission grounds she was surrounded by the European contingent, who flittered around her like moths around a flame. Mrs Anderson, while being polite to all those who chattered, did find time to catch the eye of Mary, and, as soon as there was a lull in the proceedings, she headed for the new recruit. Mrs Sutherland, forever watchful, acted as an intermediary, *"Mrs Anderson, may I introduce the latest addition to our group, Miss Slessor."*

Mary curtsied awkwardly and Mrs Anderson bowed her head, *"I hope you are finding life here to your liking, Miss Slessor."*

Mary replied, giving little away, *"It is all I expected and more."*

Mrs Anderson was not sure what to make of her reply, so asked, *"So you have high expectations, Miss Slessor?"* As Mary prepared an answer, Mrs Anderson said, patronisingly, *"You must tell me later,"* and walked away.

"A bit of a cold-fish," Mary whispered to Mrs Sutherland.

Mrs Anderson's entrance into the house had been greeted with the excited noises and squealing of the house children, but they had remained in their place. She now called out imperiously, *"Mrs Sutherland? the children?"*

At her word, the children were released and they ran to Mrs Anderson and hugged her. Mary was surprised by the children's spontaneous enthusiasm and was now even less sure of what to make of the stern Mrs Anderson. Mrs Sutherland turned to Mary and whispered, *"Cold fish?"*

Mr Anderson appeared in front of Mary, he was watching his wife and the children with great admiration. He turned to her and remarked, *"Isn't she amazing?"*

Mary, who could not take her eyes off the children and their expressions of genuine affection, replied without moving her gaze, *"Amazing, quite, quite amazing."*

Mr Anderson asked, *"And how are you settling, Miss Slessor? Have you had time to visit up river, to the wild country?"*

Mary, caught off guard, hastily replied, *"At times I find Duke Town as wild and as untamed as my experience can accommodate."*

"I have no doubt, but what happens in Duke Town is far from the misery or depravity of the Okoyong."

Mary replied without thinking, *"I have more faith in winning the fight with the heathen than against those who should know better."*

Mr Anderson looked startled, *"I hope in time we will have a chance to see how well you succeed against both."*

Mary realised she had sounded immodest, *"Of course..... I didn't mean....."* But at that moment, Mr Anderson was called for and he excused himself. She turned to Mrs Sutherland and confided, *"Well, that couldn't have gone much worse."*

Mrs Sutherland replied, with tongue in cheek, *"With my limited knowledge of you..... I'm not so sure."*

The return of the Andersons had brought the obsequious out in force. Their influence far outstripped that of Mrs Sutherland and Ma Fuller, and the many bees that swarmed around the honey pot meant that the house was abuzz. Mary was aghast at the opulence, intolerance and downright discrimination that she had witnessed since her arrival, and worse, here it was openly displayed and seemingly tolerated by the Mission. After a preliminary and suitable amount of small talk, Mrs Smylie turned to Mrs Anderson, *"I mean no disrespect,"* which Mrs Anderson knew was almost always a precursor to exactly that, *"but since you have been away the scandalous number of darkies wearing little or no apparel in the town - men, women and children - I have to say is disturbing; we are after all a Christian community, are we not?"*

Mrs Anderson gave a withering look towards Mrs Sutherland whose responsibility it was, in her absence, to keep everyone happy.

Mr Anderson smiled and assured her, *"I shall attend to that, Mrs Smylie."*

Mrs Crabbe lowered her voice as if passing on a confidence, *"Indeed the other day I saw one of the Negroes wearing nothing but a black stove-pipe hat with a red scarf tied round it!"*

The synchronised raising of eyebrows in disgust was almost an art form amongst these ladies. Mrs Smylie coughed, loosened her collar and continued, *"It was most disconcerting, I was attending to my roses at the time!"* The rest of the ladies shook their heads and said, *"Ohh,"* almost in unison.

Mary had had enough of this foolish and idle chatter and attempted to slip out for some 'fresh air'. The ever-eagle-eyed Mrs Anderson spotted her and cried out, *"Miss Slessor, won't you join us?"*

Mary stopped in her tracks and through clenched teeth replied, *"Of course, delighted, that would be so nice."* She entered the women's circle with as much relish as if walking into a snake pit.

Mrs Anderson pointed to a small gap between the two fairly stout merchant wives recumbent on the sofa who reluctantly moved to let Mary squeeze in between. These ladies, while courting the company and influence of Mrs Anderson, were less than happy to share their throne with the 'help'. Mrs Crabbe turned and asked, *"Miss Slessor, you must find life so different here compared to the mills of Dundee?"*

Mary was beginning to lose her temper, *"Yes, the struggle and toil of the constant poor, the atrocious working practises, the rich getting richer, the wealthy oblivious to how the poor survive,"* she paused and smiled, *"obviously I see nothing of that here."* At the end of her statement there was total silence.

Mrs Anderson almost spat out her tea but managed to regain her composure. *"You may go now Miss Slessor. I forgot that you are on house wake-up duty for the next **month**. Mrs Sutherland will give you your orders. Thank you, Miss Slessor."*

As Mary retired from the room, the two merchant wives smiled smugly at her put-down and, within her hearing, Mrs Smylie commented, *"You just can't get the help these days"*, their bustles retaking the region of sofa previously conceded to the young upstart.

Once all the visitors had left, and in her free time, Mary went out, still 'dressed to the nines'. As soon as she was out of sight of the prying windows, she ran to her favourite secluded place to remove the offending articles. Off came the boots, the underskirts, the stockings and the hated hat; once the high-buttoned dress was loosened for breath she hitched up her skirt and was all set for tree climbing. In the tree, her thoughts flew by, as did the time in this neutral territory and before she realised it the sun had set. *"The sun has set?!"* she screamed, *"Eh'll be late!"* Mary in her haste and blind panic tried to dress and hurry at the same time, which, as we all know is not possible. Had she dressed as if in a bedroom, it would have been more expedient and she would have avoided careering on to her face more times than was good for a body. By the time she reached the Mission, everyone was at the dining table, and grace was being said by Mr Anderson. Mary crept in on squeaking boots that all who were gathered at the table could hear and, more in hope than expectation, she took her seat.

Mr Anderson finished saying grace, *"Amen!"*

All eyes turned immediately towards Mary, then to the end of the table, the 'domain' of Mrs Anderson. Mrs Anderson smiled; anyone who knew her knew that that was not a good sign. She spoke very quietly, *"Good evening, Miss Slessor, we are glad you have found the time to join us. You must give us your engagement diary so we know when to expect you. I don't know what you must think of us, starting without you. I hope you don't mind if **we** continue?"*

Starving with hunger, Mary replied, *"Oh..... of course not."*

Mrs Anderson continued to smile, *"You're so very kind."*

Mary prepared to rise from the table, but was stopped by Mrs Anderson, *"Please Miss Slessor, you must stay and give us your company, your ideas, indeed your wisdom."*

This was no polite request but an order to *'stay exactly where you are and watch us eat'* - a severe punishment for the starving lass. Mary's mouth watered as she looked at the table laden with food, but she could not weaken; not only did she have to watch the company eat, she was also excluded from all conversation during the meal; but when Mary's eye caught Mr Anderson's, he smiled kindly.

Once the tortuous meal was over and the evening chores were done, Mrs Sutherland located Mary, who sat sulking in a corner, and they talked. *"Well, Mary, you have much to learn, you make enemies like bees make honey. You may know God and the scriptures well enough, but now you must learn patience and diplomacy. You are like a bull at a gate. You cannot take on all of the devils of Africa by yourself; you will need God **and** strong allies. After six months you seem* *to have lost none of your fire, but it's not a fire that warms, but one that burns and destroys. Use that fire to light torches to show the way, use it to burn away disease, set fire to idolatry and ignorance, let it be the beacon for hope, understanding and learning, or it will destroy you; indeed your impatience may yet be your undoing, lass."*

Mary had no excuse but reasoned, *"But I canna live wi' such hypocrisy, such arrogance, such intolerance."*

Mrs Sutherland explained further, *"Intolerance? It does indeed swing both ways. But fortunately we are not sent here as judges - a judge must see all sides. Thankfully that arduous task is for others wiser than us. Remember we are here as His servants."*

Mary sat quietly and reflected on her wise words.

After a few moments, Mrs Sutherland continued, *"Anyway, you have been given the job of rousing the house for morning prayers at 5.30. Do it well and you will be forgiven. Now it's time for bed and in the morning you must be alert. Goodnight Mary, God bless."*

After her private prayers Mary went to bed. She lay holding her stomach, as if that would allay her hunger pangs. Under her pillow she felt something solid. Hoping it was not a lizard, with some trepidation she carefully lifted her pillow to find, to her delight, three bananas. Where they had come from she had no idea but before devouring them she thanked the Lord, *"I know that I'm not worthy of this bounty but, thank you, oh thank you Lord!"*

Mary knew that her failings were many but she believed that time-keeping was not one of them, even though this was different from rising for work at the mill in Dundee. She would normally wake up automatically for work as her senses told her the time to rise, whether on dark winter mornings or slightly less dark summer ones; she had never let her family sleep in. Here the sun rose and fell with the speed of a blink of the eye and the silence of a whisper. There was no chapper-up here, no dawn chorus of birds coughing chimney smoke to awaken her. But it seemed a much greater felony to let down someone who disliked you than someone who loved you. As she pondered the answer to this she fell asleep.

She awoke with a guilty, panic-ridden start and sat bolt upright, her eyes fully open. She realised that the room was full of light casting ominous shadows; it was morning and she had overslept! Mary jumped from her bed and raced to find the bell; she looked for its long handle, picked it up and began to ring it with all her might. There was no sound; no matter how hard she shook the candlestick, it would make no noise. Realising her mistake she threw it down, found the bell and, praying that she wasn't too late, walked through the house ringing it with the urgency and cacophony of a fire alarm. When she reached the verandah and gazed out to the bay, she thought to herself, *'what a beautiful moonlit night it is.'* Immediately she dropped the bell with a final clang; apart from the shuffling of bare feet behind her the silence was deafening. She turned to face the dark look and the inevitable smile of Mrs Anderson. *"Miss Slessor, you may take my watch and count down the hours, minutes and seconds to 5.30 until you need to ring the bell again. We shall speak in the morning. Now, with the exception of Miss Slessor, all of you, back to bed!"*

Hard at work in Duke Town

The next two years at the Mission were hard for Mary as illness was never far away; the stifling heat and malaria took a much worse toll on better and braver souls, but she was determined to stay. Mary worked hard trying to learn Efik, the language used by most of the natives who lived in and around Duke Town; she believed this ability, if mastered, would give her access to hearts and minds. Mrs Sutherland and Ma Fuller, a former West Indian slave, were keen to help her in any way they could and encouraged her to be independent of them, so that when ready she could be left to her own devices. Until then, Mary was only too happy to help where and when she could; they regularly visited nearby townships to minister and, with the most basic of equipment, could treat all kinds of ailments. As the two senior women had lived there so long, they understood the people and their local remedies; using a mixture of these and traditional medicines, they treated conditions such as hydrophobia, malaria, diarrhoea, and fever, as well as vomiting, insect, snake and rat bites; with faith and good practise, their remedies assured them of a welcome in even the most distant native yards.

One memorable visit was to a troubled native woman who was in difficult circumstances. She was the youngest and most beautiful of the local chief's many wives and lived in a separate house. As Mary and Mrs Sutherland approached her doorway, there was suddenly a loud, angry scream and the sound of a great commotion inside. Ma Sutherland was forced to duck to avoid being hit by a human skull. Instinctively, before she knew what it was, Mary had caught the missile. When she realised what she held, she dropped it immediately. The slaves inside the house, in fear for their lives, scattered every which way, raising clouds of dust as they escaped. Mary and Mrs Sutherland also retreated to a position of safety. *"Ah, this is the house of Etuk, who recently lost her baby. I was rather hoping this might have resolved itself. We must be careful,"* Mrs Sutherland cautioned.

As the slaves peeked out from their hiding places, the screaming inside restarted, causing them to take flight and disappear into the bush. Ma Sutherland shouted in the direction of the doorway, *"Etuk, it's Akamba Ma."* There was no reply, so cautiously they entered the dark hut. After the bright sunshine, it took some time for their eyes to adjust. Inside there were two thin vertical windows which gave two narrow beams of light illuminating the form of a young black girl, naked to the waist, holding in her hand a bottle of gin. The air was fetid; the only sweetness was from the evil liquor, a smell only too familiar to Mary. The room was full of native charms; all the belongings the young girl possessed were scattered across the hard mud floor.

Mrs Sutherland whispered to the girl, *"Etuk?"*

Etuk turned slowly and menacingly in the direction of the two women, her head bowed. She raised her head slowly and stared with hatred in her eyes; they seemed to burn as she spat out the words, *"Old women, you no use here, go!!!"*

Mrs Sutherland attempted to defuse the situation, *"I know your pain is like fire and it still burns inside."*

Etuk stood angrily before them, ready to pounce. *"Get out, gin will put out the fire,"* she screamed.

Mary shook her head and with her improving, yet limited knowledge of the local language replied, *"Gin may dampen the fire tonight, but will burn twice as fiercely tomorrow."*

Etuk, further angered by Mary's words, raised her arm and pointed in her direction, *"You withered mission men, you know nothing of a mother's pain,"* she hissed, *"It is a young woman's pain!"* She spun her hand in a circle in the air as if invoking a spell then stepped slowly forward, her long fingernail touching the tip of Mary's nose. *"This for young women, not old crones,"* she said with contempt.

Mrs Sutherland could see this was not going well; using only her eyes and eyebrows, she attempted to convey to Mary the need to avoid involvement, but to no avail. Mary lifted her arm and slowly took hold of Etuk's finger and gently moved it aside. Mrs Sutherland's sign language to Mary was now in overdrive, her head shaking from side to side, faster and faster signifying 'no,' but it was too late. No one had ever stood up to Etuk before. One slit of light had now fallen across Mary's face and Etuk seemed paralysed, hypnotised by her piercing blue eyes and flaming red hair. The young woman dropped the gin bottle and fell to her knees, covering her eyes to escape Mary's stare. There was no sound but for the rhythmical glug, glug, glug of the bottle spilling its contents on to the mud floor.

Slowly Etuk, with head still bowed, uncovered her eyes and said to Mary, *"You see my pain!"*

Mary sat down beside the young girl on the floor of the hut and tried to comfort her, *"I do, as I saw my own mother's pain."*

Etuk asked, *"Did she drink much gin?"*

Mary hid a smile, *"No, her God put out the fire. She lost three children."*

Etuk put her hands to her face in horror, *"All at once?"*

Mary smiled, *"No, she put the spirits of her children in the hands of the Lord and He took away her pain and thirst, and blessed her with another child."*

Etuk's eyes lit up, *"Was that babe you?"*

Though not correct, Mary agreed, *"Yes, it was me."*

Etuk stroked Mary's hair and lightly brushed her pale cheek, *"Will God give me another child?"* she asked, and added enthusiastically, *"one like you?"*

Mary smiled and replied, *"God in his wisdom will make your child as beautiful as you."*

Etuk's anger had gone and tears and sadness took its place. She rested her head on Mary's shoulder and together they sat in the middle of the floor amidst the settling dust. Mrs Sutherland, bewildered by the turn of events, shrugged her shoulders and left them alone to make their peace.

Later, when Mary caught up with Mrs Sutherland, the old woman in admiration admitted, *"I am impressed, Miss Slessor,"* she paused and to clear her confusion asked, *"What? Why? ..... How did you do that?"*

Mary's thoughts seemed to be elsewhere but she replied, *"Isn't it strange? Isn't it strange how tears show that the mother-heart is the same all the world over?"*

Mrs Sutherland, still bewildered by Mary's singular talents, asked, *"Did you try to convert her?"*

Mary looked surprised by the question, *"No. Why do you ask?"*

Mrs Sutherland continued, *"Is that not why we are here? Or so says Mr Ross."*

Mary shrugged, *"I don't think so. I am here to help the Lord do His work, to listen, to give solace, to understand."*

"*I wouldn't say that too loudly,*" advised the older woman. "*Can I ask you Mary, who are you here to serve, the Mission or the Lord?*"

"*Surely there is no difference?*" she replied.

Mrs Sutherland chuckled, "*You have much to learn, Mary. Oh, so much to learn.*"

As the two women walked through the bustling streets of central Duke Town, their attention was drawn to a fracas outside one of the European stores. They stopped to see its cause. They recognised Mrs Smylie, who was beating a young black man over the head and body with a broom. The man was cowering on his knees and she was hitting him mercilessly, though fortunately for him, the blows were more constant than effective. Mrs Smylie was as smartly dressed as ever, yet her actions were less than ladylike. She continued her tirade of abuse, "*you lazy, good-for-nothing useless black.....*" Suddenly Mrs Smylie glimpsed the two mission ladies observing her. Immediately she froze mid-wallop and miraculously the broom appeared to stop half way between the vertical and horizontal; with feigned innocent surprise she turned to face them, as if they had interrupted her beating a carpet. Mrs Smylie smiled and said, "*Ah, Mrs Sutherland, what a fine day, ah and Miss?.....*"

Mary nodded politely, "*Slessor..... Don't tell me you're having problems with the help, Mrs Smylie?*"

Mrs Smylie caught off guard began to panic, "*Oh no, no, no, this boy and I were just cleaning out the back-store.....*" - she tried to pull him to his feet, though as she did so he cowered away from her, expecting more blows - "*when a small lizard crawled into his hair and got tangled.....*" she paused and Mary finished the fairytale for her, "*and you were helping him to get it out?*"

"*Exactly,*" said Mrs Smylie and grinned sheepishly. She stared at her young worker; obediently he smiled at the two mission ladies while a trickle of blood dripped from his scalp. Mrs Smylie grimaced at the sight, "*Oh it must have bitten him, oh poor boy, let's go in and I'll tend to that immediately. Good day, ladies.*"

Quickly she ushered him into the store and as soon as the door had closed they heard a smack and a male voice exclaim, "*Ow!*"

The two women began the climb towards the Mission house stopping to rest half-way up the steep hill, finding some shade from the intense heat of the sun. Mary looked exhausted and unwell and exclaimed, "*I must get awa' fae here.*"

Mrs Sutherland looked concerned, "*You've been here for two and a half years* and you work too hard; you don't take enough care of yourself. Are you sick again?"

Mary said with a lack of conviction, "No, only homesick. I long for the cold streets of Dundee, the snow, the rain, the wind. I never thought I'd see the day! And oh, to see my mither and dear Janie and Susan."

"Don't they write?"

Mary was keen to explain, "They do, often, but the words make me more desperate to see them again and I fear that, unless I can escape from Duke Town, I see no future for me here. This is not why I came to Africa. I want to make a difference, not sit and play games with those who have the power, who use it to make their own lives more comfortable while the poor around us become more wretched by the day. I've begged them to allow me to move upriver, but they refuse to listen. I cannae stay here, I cannae do it, I winnae!"

Mary's emotions took over, "Dinnae let Mrs Anderson see me like this, they'll send me awa' and no' let me back!" As she finished her last words, she fell back into a faint. Mrs Sutherland shouted for help and quickly two young boys carried Mary up to the house.

A week later in the main room of the Mission, Mr Anderson was pacing nervously when Mrs Anderson appeared, having been visiting the invalid. He asked her, "And how is Mary?"

Mrs Anderson said sadly, "The doctor says her malaria has returned, worse than before, she's exhausted."

Mr Anderson put his hand on his wife's shoulder, "It's only a week into the fever. We have seen many who were much worse and who still survived."

She stroked his hand, "The doctor thinks we should send her home, if....." she corrected herself, "when, she is fit enough to travel. Though I have my doubts that should she get home, she will ever return."

Mr Anderson confided in her, "She has a rare fire for the work."

His wife seemed frustrated, "But does she have the strength? We have seen many come here with spirit, but the Lord has seen fit to release them early from their mortal duties. We can only pray that she will be spared."

Her husband confessed, "She has been continually pleading to be sent upriver, but we never thought she was ready."

Mrs Anderson replied, "I often wonder whether upriver is ready for Mary Slessor!"

They could hear the sound of moaning. He asked his wife, "Who have you assigned to look after her?"

She appeared slightly embarrassed and looked down at her shoes, then admitted, *"I..... I thought that I would do it."*

In surprise, her husband raised his eyebrows but avoided eye contact with her. As she left the room he added, *"Let me know if I can help."*

As Mrs Anderson entered Mary's room, she was greeted with shouts of *"Mither, mither!"* Mary was standing by the window, her eyes ringed with dark circles, her long hair hung over her shoulders, wild and unkempt. She stared, unblinking, towards Mrs Anderson, then with a smile and a change in her manner, said, *"Ah, it's you mither, thank goodness, I wis havin' the strangest dream, that I was in Africa; imagine a wee slip o' a lass like me in Africa. And there was this wifie that didn't like me at all,"* Mary giggled, *"Mrs Anderson, who is the age o' Methuselah and as cauld as a December frost, wi' wee glasses, wi' teeny wee eyes in them, like....."* Mary made a sign for 'small' with her thumb and first finger, *"like wee cauld river pebbles!"* Mary covered one eye to focus better on the face before her, but failed and shook her head.

Mrs Anderson told her gently, *"Come back to bed Mary, you're not well."*

With a big smile on her face, Mary skipped back to bed like an obedient child; Mrs Anderson tucked her in and sat down on a chair beside her. Mary complained and patted the bed covers, *"No, no, sit here."*

Though not used to being given orders in her own house she did as she was told; Mary laid her head on Mrs Anderson's lap and her hand on the back of the older woman's. Mrs Anderson was quite taken aback, never having had to deal with such informality, but she was deeply touched by its sincerity.

Mary pleaded, *"Read from the Bible, mither, just like before."*

"Of course."

Mary was soon asleep. Mrs Anderson sat with her own thoughts and waited for the morning sun.

1879
Back in Dundee, sick and homesick

It was a difficult journey home, but Mary was too ill to tell the difference between malarial nightmares and real ones. As it was, she was glad of the gale which blew away the Calabar cobwebs. She had learnt in her two and half years that no one is ever ready for Africa; she had experienced so much and still knew little or nothing. What she had come to realise was that a woman's lot was the same the world over - so much responsibility but with no power. She was determined to discover how that could be changed. She couldn't imagine how the Foreign Mission Board would look upon her first report; in Duke Town, Alexander Ross was writing that report, '... *Mary Slessor was teaching at Duke Town...*' he paused then huffed audibly '*when not indisposed.*'

As Mary recuperated on the boat back to Scotland, though still weak, her head began to clear. She recalled the best and worst of her time in Africa, its people, its places, her successes and her failures. She was glad that she had done nothing to be ashamed of, although she had a nagging memory about someone having '*eyes like wee cauld river pebbles*', but as she couldn't recall who had said it or its context, she put it to the back of her mind; undoubtedly in time it would come back to her.

After weeks of sea travel, the train journey was a pleasant distraction and as it skirted the Fife coast, Mary began to relax knowing that she was close to the end of her journey, but she was in for a surprise: she was to travel over the newly-completed Tay Railway Bridge. If she had not been so terrified of falling into the River Tay, she might have marvelled at this unbelievable sight. But one glance at the track, supported on what seemed exceedingly thin and fragile legs, caused her to hold her breath and close her eyes as the train crossed the river, and to grip tightly to the arm rests until the train came to a halt, and not until she heard the guard announce, '*Dundee station!*' did she open them again.

Though she managed to regain her composure, it was all she could do not to break down at the sight of her mother, who looked pale and frail and so much older, but Mary was perfectly aware she was no oil painting herself. She knew that she had to be strong so they wouldn't worry about her when out of sight. She was greeted with warmth, grace and pride by her mother and two sisters but no more than that; she knew they worked as hard as she did and for a pittance.

Her mother suggested, "*We'll get a cab Mary, it's rainin'.*"

Mary, though weak, was in need of fresh air, "*No!..... No, please can we walk?*"

Janie tried to reason with her, "*It's cauld; are you well enough?*"

Mary smiled, "*It's never cauld in Africa, and the rain will wash away my weariness.*"

They walked out into the damp Dundee streets; Mary raised her face to the sky, closed her eyes and drank in the raindrops. She vaguely remembered how ill she was and that her constant fear in Duke Town had been that she would never see her beloved Dundee or family again.

She offered a simple prayer, *"Thank you Lord for the strength to endure."*

Her mother, Susan and Janie noticed that Mary was unsteady on her feet, and they gestured to each other to help her. The four linked-in, Mary oblivious of the family support; she was just delighted to be close to them and back in the bosom of the family. They took a leisurely half hour to near their house. As they climbed the steep incline of Albert Street, which led to the city's Stobswell district, Mary was re-introduced to the darker side of Dundee life. The streets were full of drunken carousing men, women and children. A public house door swung open and a man was thrown out bodily into the street where he lay in a drunken stupor in the muddy puddles, singing. The drunkard spotted the women; he lifted his wet bonnet and slurred out politely, *"Ladiesh!"* then his head dropped back into the mire.

Though Mary paused to help him, her family quickly ushered her down one of the many dark pends. In the almost pitch darkness, Mary's mother reached into her apron and found, by touch only, a candle and match. The four then climbed the wooden stair, and entered the small room; the fire had been set and once lit the hearth was alive with heat and light for their comfort.

Mary, so glad to be home, observed, *"The room is much wee'er than I remember."*

Her mother smiled, *"Yet you are no' much bigger, lassie."* She began to cough, a hard hacking cough and Janie, Susan and Mary looked at one another with some alarm but said nothing. Mary studied her ailing mother and chastised herself, *'how could I have been so selfish, what was I thinking, making mither walk from the station?'* She thought sadly, *'when we do well, we have no concept of those who do not, and when **we** are unwell, we imagine there is no pain other than our own.'*

Mary's mother, aware of the silence, explained, *"It's no' the cauld that maks ye cough, it's a' the stour."*

Susan removed her shawl and shook it in front of the fire; a cloud of dust and small fibres floated upwards then descended, some into the fire, igniting and sparking into ash, the rest falling to the floor. Janie swung the soup pot round on an iron bracket to settle above the flames.

Mary's heart warmed at the thought. *"Mither's own soup, how often I dreamt of this,"* she said, *"I cudnae be happier if I wis wi' the Lord. The food o' the Angel's."* Her mother scowled at her. *"Sorry Mither."*

Soon they were all seated on odds and ends of chairs and stools around the wooden table, ready to tuck into a meal of bread and soup.

"Will you say grace, Mary?" asked Janie.

They bowed their heads, closed their eyes and clasped their hands. *"Dear Lord, you have seen fit to keep me and mine safe and well, to bask in Your glory, to do Your service on earth, and pass on the wonder of Your goodness."* Her mother began to cough again. Mary peeked at her mother. *"We pray for those who are unwell,"* her mother looked back disapprovingly, *"and for all the women and children of the world, that You will save them from the injustice that poverty inflicts, and from the wretchedness and evil which we all carry within us, but that with Your guidance and love we can banish from our lives forever. Amen."*

Without further conversation they began to eat.

During her furlough it was not all rest and recuperation. On the advice of the doctor and with money she had saved from her mission work, Mary managed to move her sisters and mother to a better house in the healthier air of Downfield, at Mains of Strathmartine on the outskirts of Dundee. And when at home, the role of agents and missionaries was not simply to repair body and mind; it was also an opportunity to raise awareness of missionary work and collect donations for its successful continuation. Giving talks was something Mary would always fear, but as fund-raising was an essential part of their work she knew that one day, sooner or later, she would have to face up to it. As it happened, a month or so later while on a visit to the Mission Board in Edinburgh, she was unexpectedly called into action. It was a Sunday and Mary was attending the children's church when she was approached by the Superintendent, *"Miss Slessor, I've told the children who you are, and they would all love to hear something of your travels and work in Africa."* He smiled and indicated that she should mount the platform. Caught completely off guard she panicked, *"Oh no, I cudnae dae that."*

The Superintendent was unfamiliar with missionary reticence and asked, *"Are you unwell, would you like a glass of water?"*

Mary was stuck for words, *"Oh no, it's not that, it's just..... I can't, I've never....."*

The Superintendent looked surprised and disappointed. To give Mary some time and in the hope that she might change her mind, he chose a hymn for the children to sing. As their voices filled the air and Mary heard the sweet sound and looked at the eager faces of these young children she knew at that moment, for His sake, she must overcome her shyness; it was His work that she was doing, she would not be speaking with her voice but His. Yet, as the hymn ended, she still wasn't prepared. Mary took a deep breath and asked, *"Gie me a moment, please?"*

Again the Superintendent prevaricated, *"Let us pray."* Mary began to gather her thoughts. The Superintendent 'sneaked a peek' at her; she shook her head *'not yet! not yet!'* so he continued to pray. The next time he looked she was as calm as she was going to be and, much to his relief, she nodded to let him know that she was ready. To the obvious delight of her juvenile audience, she stepped on to the platform and talked with great enthusiasm for over a quarter of an hour. Mary would never be comfortable speaking to an audience and it remained as hard a trial as the Lord ever set for her; where the words came from she did not know, but she had a good idea.

Before Mary left Scotland, she was in the vicinity of one of the Nation's greatest disasters, the fall of the Tay Railway Bridge. The news, when it first reached the newspapers, reported that almost three hundred passengers had died in the disaster, and though that proved to be incorrect, it was no less a catastrophe. It had occurred on the last Sunday of 1879 and as usual blame was attributed to both the guilty and the innocent. The fact that it happened on a Sunday allowed the Sabbatarians to have a field day, blaming the disaster on those who had chosen to break the Sabbath. Mary was sad that such a tragedy should be manipulated for religious ends; however she was glad to see the Dundee Advertiser report the reactions of other local religious figures to this accusation and to the event itself:

Reverend Father McGinnes, St Mary's Roman Catholic Church... *I have this week heard and read, "They had no business to travel on Sunday." What are we, Jews? Must we pass the lord of the Sabbath and go back to Moses for rules of Sabbath conduct? No the modern Pharisees who speak thus themselves bear the burden they would place, without warrant, on other's shoulders? For God's sake let us have none of this. The occasion is too solemn for cant and hypocrisy...*

Reverend David Macrae in the Kinnaird Hall said... *But we need to beware of judging others, and especially of coming to the conclusion that a terrible calamity has befallen them, or sudden destruction upon them, must be greater sinners than we are, and have the mark of divine displeasure... We have to remember that God attached penalty to the violation of his physical as well as of his moral laws... Gout is God's on luxurious living, fever and pestilence are God's judgment on dirt and bad drainage. And the Tay Bridge Disaster is God's judgment on defective engineering.*

Mary felt deeply the tragic loss of the friends and families of those who lay dead in the wreckage of the train and of those who had so far been found. She read of the makeshift mortuary set up in the train station ticket office:

Tay Bridge Disaster Mortuary

... along the wall to the right are displayed caps, umbrellas, and many other little articles of personal attire, all labelled and waiting identification; while stretched in front along the floor lies another ghastly row of newly recovered corpses not yet consigned to coffins, and covered with glazed cloths that show the outlines of the bodies below stretched in the repose of death.

Behind a folding-screen in the bottom of the room some stout-hearted women are busily engaged in the kind offices for the dead – stripping the bodies of their sanded, soaking garments, and clothing them in garments of the grave.

There lay the stoker, a poor lad, his face scorched, his teeth firmly set, and his white blanched hands stiffly clenched. He was only 23, and his world was no doubt bright and radiant with the hope and buoyancy of youth. But he died at his duty, as these brown marks upon his features tell, and those lips, now sealed forever, will disclose no hint to wondering humanity of how he was overtaken by an enemy swifter and more powerful far than most locomotives the poor lad will ever ride.

Mary wept and prayed for their souls as she read the touching account and thought to herself, *'This was what the disaster was about, it was not about the Church or religion, the bridge or the train, it was about the people'.*

1880
Back to Africa

It was not long before Mary became restless to return to Africa, and when news reached her that the Goldies were to travel back on the next boat, Mary decided that, though it was not yet the end of her furlough, it would be the perfect time to leave. Mr and Mrs Goldie were the elder statesmen of the Calabar Mission, who had moved there from the West Indies to set up a Mission House, bringing loyal workers, including Mrs Sutherland and Ma Fuller and many years of patience and experience with them. Mr Goldie, a small man, now grey haired and bearded, was a larger than life figure who had worked tirelessly for the natives of the region; his tenacity and fighting spirit on behalf of the Efik-speaking people was legendary. It was not only this which Mary wished to understand; he had also written the first dictionary of the Efik language and it was said that what he didn't know about the language and people of West Africa wasn't worth knowing. It was patently obvious to Mary that an ability to speak to and understand the people was crucial.

The journey was an invaluable learning experience for her and as such seemed to last for days rather than weeks. Mary's efforts to understand Efik had so far been sketchy and taken in very small stages, but on the long trip she found Mr Goldie to be a priceless fount of knowledge, who delighted to talk the language to her and challenge her understanding of it; they played language games in which Efik words, turned upside-down and inside-out, began to come alive. Now she no longer looked for the English word but saw the light shine from within the Efik.

Although a junior in mission circles, Mary was surprised to learn that Mr Goldie had heard of some of her exploits. He confided in her, *"I have to tell you, that Mr Ross did say you were one to watch. Praise indeed?"*

"Praise? Methinks no' fae Mr Ross."

Mrs Goldie and Mary smiled knowingly at each other. The Goldies were a perfect couple who never interrupted one another, when one spoke the other listened attentively and unless asked for an opinion held their own counsel. Mary supposed that due to spending so many years together in Africa, and being devoted to their work and each other, they had found such harmony. She felt they spoke with one voice, so when she confided anything of a personal nature to Mr Goldie, it was a confession shared.

While relating her experiences in Africa so far she admitted, *"Often these wild, Godless, cruel men do indeed seem like savages."*

Mr Goldie was surprised and disappointed by her choice of language, *"Savages, Miss Slessor? In relation to whom? The civilized Europeans? Huh! Is it the way they dress? the way they talk? their rites? Thank the Lord they are not Europeans; the French hate the Germans, who hate the Portuguese, who hate the Belgians, and they all hate the British. Is that civilisation? Missionaries often refer to the natives as children. What is wrong with children - are they not the purest of our race? - children who have not yet learned malice, or greed, or envy, or deceit. We talk fondly of the innocence of youth, and yet, at every turn, we try to turn them into miniature versions of ourselves. We want them to crave what adults crave, think what adults think, so we can manipulate them more easily. We are full of righteous indignation when we think of the African dealing in slaves, but not so long ago the wealth of our country was built on that very trade.*

We paid them well to keep the supply of men, woman and children flowing so we could work them on our plantations for no wages, or sell them to someone who also wanted free labour. Slavery had been a way of life that we encouraged for centuries. Then one day, we told them to stop, or we would punish them. We removed their lucrative source of income, and their power, and turned them from allies to enemies in one Act. Can something be morally right one day and wrong the next?"

Mary had no argument and Mr Goldie had not finished, *"For example, do you think that the military are here to protect the natives? It may appear to be the case, but they are here primarily to take the land so that no one else can have it. The hunger for land of the European statesman is all consuming; conquest and colonisation is all. The cost of that colonisation is great, the race for Africa's wealth, known and unknown, leaves little time for compassion or pity. Over the years I have found that the politician, merchant and the military use the missionary as a divining rod, a signpost for safe passage into uncharted territory. Who is there to save the African? We, you and I, must on their behalf give them a safe, secure future, free from the reliance of government hand-outs. Help mould them into traders, not tinkers. As the native is often inconsequential in the scheme of things, we know that they have the ability; we must give them respect, responsibility, purpose and the platform to succeed, and pray to God they will accept it and prosper."*

Mary, unsure of her ground, asked, *"But surely converting heathens to follow the word of the Lord cannot be wrong? It can do no harm."*

He pointed out, *"But they have a God, they call him Abassi."*

Mary disputed this, *"But, but, but..."*

"But what?" he enquired further, *"It is not **your** God?"*

Once again, Mary struggled to answer.

He smiled, *"Because we don't understand their belief system, we in ignorance, call them heathens, an opprobrious term used to slight that which is beyond **our** understanding."* He thought for a moment, *"Maybe it is their strange rites and religions that are un-civilised? They worship strange gods and perform strange rituals, and of course, the Europeans practise in no such manner, do they? The magnificent harvest festival we love to celebrate at home - are these not offerings which are brought to church and set in front of the altar? Wheat, barley, flowers, fruit and vegetables - are they not given in thanks for continued success in the fields and orchards?"* He looked sympathetically at her, *"Do you see no resemblance?"* He smiled impishly, with a glint in his eye, *"Miss Slessor, the leopard is not the* lamb and the lamb is not the leopard, nothing will turn one into the other."

Mary tried to counter his argument and, when unable to do so, asked naively and in desperation, *"Have you no faith in the Lord, Mr Goldie?"* Mrs Goldie became almost animated at Mary's question, but said nothing.

Mr Goldie put his hand on top of Mary's, *"I was like you when I arrived, more years ago than I care to remember, believing that there was only one truth; but in time you will find that truth, like some people, has more than one face. To answer your question, of course I believe in God, but not one who is cruel, dogmatic and without wisdom or understanding. God is patient and caring and believes that the African has his own place on His earth. My work on the Efik dictionary helped me to understand their belief..... and mine."*

It had become clearer to Mary, *"I think I understand, but it makes me more afraid than ever, I feel a homeless soul even more. And with very few exceptions it seems I am no more at home with the natives than with the Mission. As you may gather, Mr Ross, especially, would be glad to see me turn round and run off home."*

Hearing the frustration in her voice he asked, *"Does he diminish what you do?"*

She dismissed his suggestion, *"Of course not!"*

"Have you faith in a God that you can trust?"

Enthusiastically she replied, *"I do, I do."*

Mr Goldie squeezed her hand, *"Trust in Him, He is not **a religion**, He is faith; if you stand with Him, He will never abandon you; with Him, you can move mountains. Most missionaries arrive here with all the answers, to present the Church's vision of the perfect world to the natives. Mary, you seem to be attempting to find answers and ask questions of the world all at the same time. It's not an easy path and has many pitfalls, demons, and enemies, and no certainty; you may lose everything if you continue, but if can stay strong, with God in your heart, you may do miraculous things."*

Mrs Goldie, who had sat in silence beside them, nodded to Mary in agreement. The rest of the journey continued in this vein, Mary happy to have her beliefs, motives, and misconceptions challenged in such a constructive manner.

On their arrival, the welcoming committee was there to meet them and in the most awkward circumstance. There was much cheering on the dock as the launch approached and, befitting their rank, Mary sat towards the front of the boat with the Goldies at the rear. With the exception of a wave hello from Mrs Sutherland and Ma Fuller, it was as if she had ceased to exist.

Alexander Ross was busily orchestrating the event, gesticulating and ordering the Krumen to do his bidding. The Goldies were the nearest thing to royalty the Mission had and they were out in force to greet them. Mrs Goldie, tall and bespectacled, was a severe-looking woman and had seen and done it all before and, aware of Mary's lack of social standing in the community, sensed that she could have fun with the situation. The launch came to a halt and as Mary was about to step on to the pier she heard the voice of Mrs Goldie, *"Miss Slessor..... Mary, would you mind helping an old woman?"*

Mary knew that Mrs Goldie was more than capable of disembarking by herself, but spotted the mischievous look in her eye and returned to assist her in her game. Mrs Goldie acted the old woman and Mary the faithful retainer as if they'd spent a month in rehearsal. *'This is braw'*, Mary thought. On the pier, it was as if Mary was newly-born as no one could speak to Mrs Goldie without acknowledging her. Through the crowd Mary saw the disapproving gaze of Mr Ross, who had been usurped in his role as Mrs Goldie's right arm for the walk to the Mission house. Once in the confines of the house, Mrs Goldie relieved Mary of her duties in ringing tones, *"Thank you so much Miss Slessor, you've made an old woman very happy. Now I'm sure you have much to attend to."* Mr Goldie waved a very public wave which Mary returned in like manner. Once this pantomime was over, and out of the public's gaze, she was glad to be back, but in her solitude she had time to consider what tomorrow would bring. What was to be her future?

Early the next morning Mr Ross sent for her; in doubtful expectation she knocked on his door. *"Come in Miss Slessor,"* he shouted. He sat behind his desk, dressed as usual in Presbyterian black jacket with white shirt and tie, the official garb which he wore whether on official business or not. He looked over his small reading glasses which perched on the end of his long nose, *"Please sit!"* he barked.

Mary remained standing, waiting for Mr Ross to change his tone.

After a moment he said, a little more kindly, *"Should you wish to, Miss Slessor?"*

Mary smiled and sat down. Mr Ross looked down at his papers, smirked aloud and said, *"Well, it would seem that you have been hard at work,"* he paused and added sarcastically, *"working behind my back!"*

Not sure to what he was referring, she asked, *"Sorry? I've nae idea what you mean."*

His tone was accusatory, *"You have asked the Mission Board to allow you to* go upriver, where, as we all know, women can do no good," adding dismissively, "you know my opinion of female missionaries."

Mary knew it only too well, "Oh yes, we should a' be men, and built like prizefighters. Do you not think that a weak wee woman can spread the word o' God?"

Not used to being challenged, Mr Ross asserted, "These people need to understand....."

Mary interrupted, "Whit? That God is a bully? That God only recognises the strong?" She got to her feet and leant over the desk; taken aback, he rocked unsteadily in his chair. "Let me tell you Mr Ross," she continued, "that if you think any prizefighter can defeat me and meh God, you are so wrong. You mistake compassion fir weakness. Show me a man wi' compassion, and I'll find you a stone wi a hert!"

Mr Ross overbalanced, the chair tipped and he landed in a heap on the floor. Standing above him Mary carried on, "Yer a fool if you mistake power for strength, and you are as daft as you look if you think that women are below men! Most men are like you, full o' pride and ire, you aye know the answer......... but you never listen to the question!!!"

With some difficulty Mr Ross got to his feet, brushed the dust off his clothes and sat down, trying to regain his composure; he located his glasses and again picked up the letter. In a much more conciliatory tone he resumed, "What I was about to say, was that your request has been granted," and added with emphasis, "you are to go **on your own**, to Old Town, **with immediate effect**."

Mary hid her delight and said in a matter-of-fact manner, "Oh, I thank you, Mr Ross." Again she leant over the desk and he moved backwards not knowing her intentions. She picked up his hand, shook it, and left his office.

Outside, it was as if a massive weight had been lifted from her shoulders; she danced and sang all the way back to her room and when inside fell to her knees, wept, and thanked the Lord. This was the last time that Mary and Alexander Ross would officially cross swords. In 1881, as Mary's Presbyterian Church was in discussion to unify with other churches, the outspoken Mr Ross, while in dispute with the Synod, was ordered home but he refused to leave; he set up his own independent mission at Henshaw Town. This caused great confusion later amongst the native tribes causing awkward questions to be asked of Mary, did Christians worship two Gods? Unfortunately, Alexander Ross died three years later, leaving much of his work unfinished.

Off to Old Town

The following day she dressed formally, gathered her belongings, and with two native bearers set off on her journey to Old Town. As she walked through Duke Town, she was observed by the two haughty European merchant women who sat comfortably outside their store while native boys struggled behind them carrying large bales and heavy boxes.

Mrs Crabbe observed, *"Well, off she goes, the mill girl goes to Old Town."*

Mrs Smylie commented, *"You know why she's going there - to save money. It's so much cheaper to live there; she can send her money back to Dundee. At Old Town she can live on leaves and bugs."*

Mrs Crabbe laughed, *"Almost like home."* They both sniggered. *"She won't last long, you mark my words."*

Mrs Smylie added, *"No, no, she'll be back..... carried slowly in a box."* They both laughed heartily.

The natives of Old Town had no love for missionaries, merchants, or soldiers. Twenty five years previously they had fallen foul of the Europeans when they had broken new laws and, in retaliation, the warship Antelope was ordered to open fire and destroy the town, almost razing it to the ground. For years the bush reclaimed what it had given, until the British allowed the town to be rebuilt; until two years before her arrival the mission house had been occupied; since then it had been abandoned and had fallen into disrepair. If Mary had wanted a stiff challenge she could hardly have chosen one more difficult.

The three mile journey took until the sun set and it was now as dark as the *inside o' an undertaker's hat*; the bush became a much more fearful place, the sound of wild animals echoed. The native Duke Town carriers were brave in the daylight but were now petrified of every noise and shadow; it took all her time and patience to keep the unhappy band together; a few well-chosen newly-learnt Efik phrases kept the carriers moving in the right direction. Eventually she decided that a rousing hymn would not only help to raise their spirits but also block out the animal screams and roars from the bush. They marched on to Old Town to the strains of 'the Lord's My Shepherd'; their caterwauling would have scared the *De'il himsel'*.

Though the natives had been told of the arrival of a new missionary, her entry was hardly noticed; there was no welcoming committee, in fact there was little sign of any life apart from the frantic scurrying of rats, snakes and huge, many-legged beasties which slithered and ran from every corner of the dilapidated ruin of the old mission building. Somewhat despondently Mary sat on the cases which contained all her worldly goods, her clothing, Bible, books and medicines. She was wondering how it could be any worse when a thunder clap almost deafened her and instantaneously lightning lit the entire world around her and rain descended with ferocity through the tree canopy above. Inside the old mission house, the rain fell only slightly less torrentially but she was thankful for that. She felt like Noah in his ark as many of the beasties that had fled when she arrived returned to shelter from the downpour in the mission doorway and on the verandah. Though terrified of the creepy crawlies she realised, *"We're all God's creatures"*, and said to them, *"well, if you behave you can bide, but only until the mornin'."*

When she awoke, as far as she could establish, the sun had risen. The cover of high trees and thick bush blocked the sun for most of the day, but the intense heat indicated that above the canopy the air was bakingly hot. The house animals had gone, or at least they had found a hidey-hole out of Mary's sight. The yard with its broken fence and the single room wattle-and-daub mission building with its collapsed roof were in a much worse state than she had thought the previous night. She woke the two bearers, made them some food and a cup of her precious tea and gave them their orders for the morning. Native workers often seemed lazy to the Europeans but she had observed that they worked as ruled by the heat of the day and not by some overseer's pocket-watch; they rested when the day was at its hottest and made up time when it was cooler. This infuriated their European masters who ordered *"the work done now!"* while they themselves sat in the shade and looked on. Mary realised that if they were to respect her and work for her, she must work with them, as hard if not harder. She remembered the words of her hero David Livingstone, *'My views of what is missionary duty are not so contracted as those whose ideal is a dumpy sort of man with a Bible under his arm. I have laboured in bricks and mortar, at the forge and at the carpenter's bench, as well as in preaching and in medical practise. I am serving Christ when shooting buffalo for my men, or taking an astronomical observation, or writing to one of His children.'*

Singing songs together seemed to make the time pass more quickly and help make the tasks seem less arduous. Within hours she could at last see the parts of the building that were worth preserving and the locals had become more curious. Some had never before seen a white woman and by the middle of the afternoon she had collected quite an audience. Many of the natives were brought by their children to see the crazy white woman with the fiery hair. An audience doesn't mean that they sat in rows at the front of the yard, but they were observing her from behind bushes and trees. Mary hoped that they may have also been attracted by the singing, as during some of the hymns the choir's volume appeared to be amplified by singing bushes; at least it was a start. Mary believed that music and goodness was in their souls and that, at last, her journey had begun.

As night fell she decided to write a long letter to the Missionary Board to complain, sorry, to make them aware, of the situation in Old Town and ask them for some further assistance in repairing the mission house. She had sent the bearers back to Duke Town for building supplies and to deliver news of her situation and, by the morning of the third day, she was beginning to grow weary and feel desperately alone. At night especially, Mary felt the greatest sense of isolation, when her work was over and there was no one to confide in, no one to help her as she struggled to move forward. Fully aware that this was what she had pleaded for, would anyone have any sympathy for her? Or was she now getting what she deserved? In the morning she rose from her bed, washed, cleaned her teeth with a chewing stick and put on the water for her cup of tea. Suddenly she thought she heard the boards on the verandah creaking. She picked up the stout stick which she always had by her bed and hid behind the doorpost prepared for the worst. She looked out and saw that the verandah was laden with plantains, bananas and yams. She searched to see if there was anyone she could thank for such a wonderful gift, but as usual there was no one in sight. Mary felt like weeping, but knew that that would not improve her situation; she approached the food, went down on her knees and thanked the Lord. Hidden from view behind a tree, a young native woman spoke to another, *"She thinks Abassi brought her food, it was me!"* They both laughed and continued to watch. The following morning there was a further delivery from Mary's phantom good neighbour, yet still no contact; an idea began to form in her head, but that could wait until tomorrow.

The boys returned with the building supplies so at last they could begin to make the house watertight. They hammered and sang, sang and hammered and with new oil lamps were able to work long into the night. After eating their evening meal, Mary felt that the three of them should have a service of thanksgiving. The two boys were Christian mission workers and took part with passion and humility; it was good for their souls and for those of the invisible audience. By nightfall she knew that sleep would come easily. She was aware that she must waken very early to put her plan into operation, so decided to sleep outside, behind the fence.

Next morning, at the slight sound of the verandah creaking, Mary awoke. At first it was difficult to see, but soon she could make out the figure of a native woman slowly creeping away. Quickly Mary ran across and blocked her path; the native woman still giggling and looking backwards over her shoulder didn't see Mary till the very last second. When almost face-to-face the young girl stopped, screamed, turned around and ran. Undoubtedly it was not the girl's intention, but she ran straight into the mission house from which there was only one way in and one way out. Mary was sure that as soon as she realised her mistake she would speedily exit, but when she didn't reappear Mary decided to follow her into the house. As Mary reached the verandah, she called out a greeting in Efik. There was no reply, but as she listened she could hear the faintest whimper coming from inside. She said quietly, *"Don't be afraid, it's only a kind spirit come to thank you."* This only increased the wailing. When she stepped inside the room the intruder was still nowhere to be seen. *"Don't be frightened, I just want to thank you."* Mary stood stock-still and listened. She traced the origin of the whimper to beneath her bedcovers and, pulling them back, saw a half-naked woman cowering and shaking uncontrollably. Mary sat down beside her and very gently placed her hand on the girl's head. The girl closed her eyes, screwed up her face, as if Mary was going to strike, and screamed. When no blows came, the shaking seemed to subside and the girl opened one eye. That eye stared and darted left and right, up and down, examining all around her; the other eye soon opened and, though she seemed to relax, she grabbed the bedcover and pulled it up to just beneath her nose, the trembling began again.

Mary tried to reassure her, *"I am Miss Slessor. What is your name?"*

The girl mumbled through chattering teeth, *"Efiaaaaaaaaaaaaa, Efiaaaaaaaaaa,"* and when at last she became calm, *"Efia."*

Mary repeated her name, *"Efia?"* She stood up, crossed the room and looked into her bags of clothing. There she found a fine cotton smock and presented it to the girl. At first the young girl, although still frightened, stared at its bright colours and perfect weave, as if it was in some way made by the gods, or by bad ju-ju, but as its touch caused her no harm, she ran her long elegant fingers over the fine material. Mary turned away to make them both some tea and when she turned back the girl was wearing the striped garment

77

and stroking it lovingly.

The moment was quickly over for they both heard a mumbling sound emanating from the direction of the courtyard. Mary looked out and saw that over fifty natives had gathered outside the compound, standing as if they were held behind an invisible rope tied across the courtyard perimeter, not one foot or toe strayed over the line. Mary looked back to Efia, who rose from the bed and, as if wearing a magnificent ball gown, promenaded into the yard as proud as a princess. She nodded to Mary in thanks and joined the throng to no doubt tell of her experience at the hands of the woman with the fiery hair.

This was more than she could have hoped for and was the beginning of her acceptance as an outsider. She had learned enough from life not to ask for too much, but to be thankful for small mercies.

A barrier to progress, the wall of skulls

Within a few weeks, Mary had set up Bible classes and a school, where she also administered to the sick from throughout the district; her life was now extremely busy, her loneliness gone. Sundays especially began early and finished late. The Missionary Board was interested to see how well she was doing, though there were those who may have been more interested in how badly. Her first visit was by two grand gentlemen Mission Board members, in pursuit of answers. She had been told in advance of their arrival and was concerned that all would not go well; but as there was little she could do to influence the outcome, as always, she put her faith in Him.

Her first service of the day was to be held at the nearby village of Qua. The church building in Qua was unlike any seen back home where walls of human and animal skulls never feature. She had gradually gained the trust of some of the natives by working around problems, not charging through them; she had found during her comparatively short time in Africa, that change happened slowly, and acting like a bull at a gate served no purpose. At a meeting with the local chiefs, Mary raised the matter of the forthcoming visit of the Missionary Board and the wall of skulls; it had not gone well. The chiefs sincerely believed that they had done more than enough to welcome the white woman into their village; the removal of the wall of skulls was a step they were not prepared to take. The skulls were the tribes' trophies of war and, though most had been fought for long ago, they were still potent signs of their power and bravery. After the meeting Mary met with Efia and Isan, her infant son, and told of her frustrations; she explained that while she could accept the importance of these skulls to the tribe she could not guarantee that repercussions would not follow the Mission Board's visit. There seemed only one solution to them both, to hide the skulls.

Late on Saturday night, the two women walked to the village and, behind the makeshift pulpit and platform, pinned up a white sheet at the far end of the room to conceal the offending items. Efia had warned the natives of the importance of the men's visit and on Sunday morning they turned up in numbers to see and be seen; so far so good. At Qua the entrance to the compound was decorated with feathers, animal bones and other native charms. Mary introduced herself to Mr Marshall and Mr Williamson, the two men from the Mission Board, both of whom were suitably dressed for a slightly cool day in Scotland; how they survived in the stifling heat of Nigeria Mary could not imagine. Mary had by now adapted her clothing to suit the conditions and while her appearance was acceptable, certain items had been discarded to cope with the scorching heat. Before she led them into the church she thought it wise, in case something was to happen, to mention that *"the decorations inside were not of my choosing and in time all will be removed."*

Mr Williamson asked, *"Should the temple not be cleansed, Miss Slessor?"*

Mr Marshall, the bespectacled and older of the two by some margin, seemed to be more understanding, *"I'm sure that Miss Slessor will, but Rome wasn't built in a day, Mr Williamson."* Mr Williamson remained unconvinced.

The service began with an address by Mary in Efik, which she followed by leading the congregation in a recitation of the Ten Commandments. The two gentlemen, seated on a bench on the platform nodded their approval, totally unaware that hidden underneath the sheet behind them was a wall of skulls. What they would have made of that fact she wasn't sure but she believed that out of sight out of mind was the best policy. Before they rose to give their address Mary introduced the two men to the congregation. Mr Marshall's sermon, which she translated as best she could into Efik went well, but Mr Williamson preached his own brand of fire and brimstone at great length, during which some of the congregation, especially the children, lost concentration. Mary saw Efia wave to her; Mary, content that things were proceeding well, simply smiled at her in return; Efia then began to point with great urgency in the direction of Mr Williamson. What Mary hadn't seen was that Isan had toddled past the platform and was now playing behind the two speakers. Mary looked behind her and saw the child pulling at the sheet hiding the skulls. As the toddler fell backwards he brought the cloth down with him and the congregation, aware of the situation, gasped collectively as quietly as they could. As part of the Efik translation of Mr Williamson's address Mary added quickly, *'that the congregation should not draw attention to the skulls, as it would be impolite.'* As luck, or lack of it would have it, one of the skulls slipped, but at first did not fall; it slipped again, but still remained. Mary held her breath and prayed that it would not drop, but not all prayers are answered and it tumbled from the wall. Making almost no sound, it rolled along the ground and stopped between the feet of Mr Marshall who, thankfully, was exceedingly short sighted. As the skull hit his heel, he reached beneath the bench and picked it up. Seeing only the round domed top he whispered quietly to Mary, *"I think you should take this Miss Slessor, the child has dropped his ball."*

At the end of the service Mary and Efia orchestrated the entire congregation to come forward and surround the two men in celebration. This was a stroke of genius as it had the dual purpose of giving the impression of great devotion as well as hiding from view the now exposed wall of skulls. The two gentlemen accompanied Mary to all the services she carried out for the rest of that day, and at their departure, though exhausted, they seemed genuinely pleased by what they had seen; as Mr Marshall later noted, *"especially our exceedingly enthusiastic reception at Qua."*

Trade and twins

The trade path to Duke Town ran through Old Town and its use was jealously guarded by the men of the village, not because its use by others would do them any harm, but because someone else would benefit by it; in that respect they were very European. More and more incidents had occurred involving inland tribesmen, laden with palm oil, trying desperately to find their way past the possessive and greedy locals, but in the most recent dispute, when blood was spilt, Mary felt enough was enough. Her influence was now becoming a power for good in the area and, mindful of the bloody history of the place, she made a point during her meetings, or 'palavers', of inferring that she had great powers at her beck-and-call without saying what they actually were. Indeed had they known that the only power she had at her disposal was the conviction of a wee Scots woman, they might have dealt differently with

80

her. While they did not wish to incur her wrath, they still did not want to allow safe passage to the traders. But what if she were to use the mission yard as a doorway, a safe gateway to Duke Town? The local chiefs rarely visited the compound as they could only enter by her invitation, so she thought that if she were to allow the inland traders safe passage through the mission grounds, it would be a form of sanctuary and they would not be harmed. When the chiefs arrived by invitation to palaver, there was at first much grumbling and banging of tables, but after some debate they grudgingly allowed it to happen, not because they were in favour, but because they had no argument against it. Her busy days now meant equally busy nights; with her knowledge of the area she led the traders safely through the mission grounds, past the guards at Old Town, and through Duke Town to deliver their goods.

In 1878 there had been a treaty to stop the murder of newly-born twins and treating their mothers as outcasts, but things changed slowly; live twins were still stuffed into clay pots and cast upon anthills to be devoured. The sight of such barbarity made even Mary doubt her faith in these people, but given their ancient customs it was almost understandable while remaining totally unforgivable. The treaty was observed as well as any could be, but telling people not to do something was only that, to not believe in a law but to simply obey is an almost impossible task. In effect the bush had no law, only nature's law, man's law was something else; even the threat of fierce retribution as they had suffered in the past, was not one they recognised.

Mary had stood resolutely against this evil practise but realised you can't break a spear with a feather; fortunately, the feather which was capable of beginning that process arrived unexpectedly one evening. Mary was sitting on the verandah, enjoying the cool of the evening and playing with Efia and Isan, when they heard the crying of an infant some distance away. As they continued to listen the sound intensified; Mary stirred and eventually, through the darkness, she saw a figure approaching the compound entrance carrying the wailing bundle. She recognised him as the trader Mr Owen; this time his trade was very much alive and kicking. He was carrying a baby wrapped in his jacket. Mr Owen was like many men with weeping bairns, glad to get them off their hands. With great care he gave the baby to Mary and reclaimed his jacket. She could see that this wee lass was no more than half a day old and was screaming like a banshee.

Mr Owen said appreciatively, and with great relief, *"Oh thank you."*

Mary cuddled her closely and whispered, *"My, my, what a beautiful bairn,"* and turning to Mr Owen asked, *"where did she come from?"*

"I found her in the bush." His manner changed ominously. *"She was one of two,"* he continued, *"her poor twin brother was not so fortunate; he was half-eaten by ants. She would have been next. I wasn't sure what to do with her; it's not the first time I've seen abandoned twins, but for some reason I could not walk past this one."*

"It was the Lord that made you stop. Efia! Could you get a blanket and some powdered milk?"

Efia looked at the wee one, *"Let's pray the Lord will let her live."* The child screamed loudly, her arms and legs flailing. Mary smiled. *"This one will not give up life cheaply, she's a real fighter. She's like a' the Slessors. I'll call her Jeanie after my sister."*

When the others had left, Mary fed Jeanie and gave her a bath in warm water. It was a brand new start. The two lay together in bed and, while the infant slept, Mary watched her breathe in and out until she too succumbed. News spread quickly in the district, undoubtedly aided by the tale told by Efia that Mary had taken in a twin. No doubt many would question her wisdom and they would give the mission a wide berth for a time, but as the little one began to grow without horns or a tail, she was accepted. Here was living proof for all to see of the kindness of God's word versus a cruel ritual. Over the months that passed, Mary's household grew in number with other abandoned children. Her happy band now numbered six and she began to be known as *"the Ma who loves babies"*.

News had reached Mary that the Egbo tribe were in a major palaver with the British Council and the Missionaries; she heard little of its context but feared the worst. The Egbo was a secretive sect, the finest, the most feared and ferocious of warriors in this part of Africa. Should the Egbo runners, or messengers, come through your village all must hide - man, woman or child - or else; a severe beating was the least they could expect. During the palaver there had been many runners through Old Town; their increased frequency indicated that the talks might be coming to a conclusion, whatever that might be. Was it to be war? A war that would send all missionaries home, forfeiting all they had worked for? Would gunships again try to bring peace by blasting the Africans into submission? Perhaps there would be good news. She doubted it, but it was what she prayed for.

The sound of drumming preceded the arrival of the Egbo runners, a warning to all to clear the paths and disappear out of sight. As the drums grew louder and louder and louder, she quickly gathered the children and took them into the house; by the volume of sound this was no small band of runners. She did a quick head count and realised that one of the children was missing. No matter how many times she counted, or how hard she searched, she could not find her beloved Jeanie. Mary, aware of the tragic consequences, realised to her horror that she was not in the house. With dread in her heart she looked outside and saw the most amazing sight. In the middle of the yard was Jeanie, barely able to walk, standing facing over fifty Egbo runners who, armed with spears, whips and machetes and wearing hideous, brightly-coloured masks, were standing at the entrance to the compound. The drums were now playing slowly, rhythmically, and the men were gently swaying side to side and chanting. Jeanie was copying their every movement. Mary was transfixed. Was this a dream? Was this a miracle? Mary walked out very slowly towards Jeanie and stood behind her. The two were joined by the rest of the children and soon all were chanting together as one. The bush rang out with the joyous sound. Mary was sure that the chanting could be heard all the way to Duke Town. She prayed that they could hear it in Dundee.

What had transpired was no less of a miracle. The palaver had produced a law, after its own fashion, to outlaw the murder of twins; to Mary this would appear to have been an act of diplomatic genius. The law, previously imposed on the natives, had been just that - imposed - but Mary believed that this version had more than a chance of success. She was convinced that one could not change things by simply imposing one's will, it must be done with the consent of those involved; though not always easy, it was a lesson she would follow from now on. The Egbo runners had come to announce to everyone that the law **had** now changed and, if broken, they would be offending the Egbo, which carried a greater threat of retribution than if one disobeyed the Colonial Government.

It was what they had all been praying for and they had every hope that from now on the law would be upheld. The good news travelled quickly and Mary and the bairns were soon joined in the yard by the mothers of twins who gathered to celebrate their freedom from exile. They wept and crowded around screaming *"Sosono! Sosono!" Thank you! Thank you!* As the Egbo runners continued to chant, the women and children danced in celebration and hugged and wept together. This was as joyful a night as Mary could remember.

A few days later at a great ceremony, the treaty was signed and the new king, Eyo VII, was crowned. It was a scene Mary could never have dreamt of even a week before; on the platform in front of thousands of Africans, and amongst other dignitaries, sat the mothers of twins. The assembled women wore crimson silks and satins and were decorated with earrings and brooches and all kinds of finery, each one dressed as extravagantly as she could afford. The men wore uniforms created in the image of European generals, admirals and captains, trimmed with gold and silver, and wearing magnificent jewelled hats and caps. Many, usually naked, bodies were covered with beadwork, silks, and damask - Mary even recognised the imaginative use of red and green tablecloths edged with lace; no doubt the traders' fabric stores had been emptied. Many of the hats were immense, flamboyant affairs, with sparkling brooches and huge feathers of all colours; native legs were circled with brass beadwork and unseen bells that tinkled constantly and added to the general chaotic noise. In fact the noise was so loud that the Consul asked the new King to call for quiet during the reading of the treaty. The King replied that there was little he could do about it as it was the fault of the women. He turned to Mary and asked, in his best broken English, *"Ma, how do I stop these women mouth? How can I do? They be women – best put them away."* His English, though very far from perfect, was better than most Europeans' knowledge of Efik. As there seemed no other way for the ceremony to continue, some of the louder women were made to leave but allowed to return after the formalities were over. It was a wondrous occasion and the celebrations went on long into the night and into the next day. However, as the new King was a good Christian, many of the excesses usually associated with such an event were forbidden by him. Over the next few months the murder of twins was driven underground; what had once been practised openly was now carried out only in secret, but in Mary's mind at least it was a beginning.

Mary's feet were never still, her adventurous spirit carried her further and further from the now comparative safety and security of Old Town. The new King had kindly taken Mary under his protection and when he heard of her intention to visit the district of Ibaka to see an exiled chief named Okon he strongly objected. Mary had once met this chief and though he now lived thirty miles upriver in an area they said was haunted by elephants, she was determined to visit him. Eyo knew only too well that once her mind was set nothing would stop her and yet he continued to try to dissuade her. As she was preparing for the journey on which she was to take the house children, Eyo sent her a gift and what a gift it was. The first she knew of it was when

Efia came into the mission house, breathlessly excited, and screamed, *"It's such a sight, Ma. Ma, they have come for you!"*

Mary was confused, *"Who have come where? To do what?"*

"The King has sent a boat for you, come, come!"

Efia grabbed Mary's arm and hurried her down to the shore. Mary was aghast; the boat he had sent for her was his magnificent state canoe! The brightly painted canoe, over 40 feet long with a small canopied 'cabin' in the centre, was manned by a crew of thirty-three. As if that were not enough the King had come personally to see her off; he had learned not to argue with her, and without sending an armed guard to protect her, had done the next best thing.

Mary was genuinely touched by his kindness, *"This is so good of you, King Eyo."*

The King replied, *"Ma must not go as a nameless stranger to a strange people, but as a lady and our Mother."*

"I am so honoured, God be with you," Mary said humbly. The King reciprocated, *"God be with **you**."*

The long journey in the torch-lit canoe was a joy, and as the crew paddled throughout the night, led by a drummer, they sang softly, *"Ma, our beautiful beloved mother is on board!"*

Mary and the children slept soundly. Only when she had a legitimate reason to stop and rest did she realise how exhausted she had become. But in the morning she felt refreshed, ready to face the challenges ahead.

Ibaka was a different world from the one she had left in Old Town. The natives here were poor, naked and dirty, and as much as she wanted to attend to their spiritual lives, their medical needs came first. Most had never seen a white woman before and it took time for some of them to let her touch them. Their medical requirements far outstripped her supplies and, at times, her expertise; she soon had to send for more medicine and as the patients she had treated became well, more and more came to her. She began to realise that there must be many thousands of people like these all over Africa who needed ministrations to both their bodies and their spirits. They soon began to trust her honesty and her word, which was just as well; Mary was finding out that the further she travelled from the seat of power in Duke Town, the more difficult became her work and, in her isolation, she became impatient to make the natives see the wisdom of her ways.

Chief Okon, whom she had met in Duke Town, had seemed a reasonable man, but that was in her territory, now she was in his. One morning she was shocked to learn that Chief Okon was to punish two of his wives by giving them each one hundred lashes. Immediately Mary set off to intervene, if she could; she had to hope that her word would hold some sway with him. When she arrived, a group of men stood behind the Chief, all baying at two young women who were standing cowering, heads bowed; they were just slips o' lassies, no more than sixteen years old.

Mary asked, with respect and a growing sense of anxiety, *"May I enter, Chief Okon?"* He gestured to her to join him.

Mary tried to establish the facts, *"Chief Okon, may I ask..... what is their offence?"*

"They went into a yard that was not their own."

Incredulously she asked, *"And for that, they get a hundred lashes?"*

The Chief tried to stop Mary from losing her temper, *"We will rub the wounds with salt, they will soon heal; it is the law, they must learn, it is the only way to make women obey."*

Mary, trying not to appear to insist, asked, *"Would you bring the people for a palaver?"* She turned to the girls, *"You have done wrong and according to your law you must be punished."*

A crowd gathered, and when she saw the men behind the Chief grin at the thought that they would get their way, it was too much for her. She faced the men and, with hands on hips, gave them a piece of her mind, *"A hundred lashes is too cruel. Shame on you! These lassies are little more than children, they should not be wives. Childhood is a time to play and learn. The lesson you will teach them is one of cruelty so unimaginable, so barbaric, it is unworthy of you!"*

An elder native shouted angrily at Mary, *"Who are you to come and question our laws? Little woman! you are here under our protection. You say too much of that you do not understand!"*

The Chief whispered to his aide who listened and, with a look of surprise, removed the girls so that the punishment could be carried out. Mary stayed with the Chief and knelt and prayed while she heard the lashes and counted as each one scored the young girls' flesh. When the lashes stopped at ten the laughter ceased and the sound of grumbling took its place; it seemed that the punishment was over. Mary was well aware that she had not won and felt no joy but some little satisfaction that she had challenged their authority and made a small difference to the outcome. The Chief on his way out to the yard, stopped by her and said quietly, *"We have much to learn from each other Miss*

Slessor, but one step at a time."

She attended to the girls' wounds and prayed that she could change things more quickly; she knew there was much she would alter in European society if she could, but she also knew that to change things in Africa would be a long, long journey, possibly without end.

It was the now the season of storms and it never disappointed. On her return to Old Town with the bairns and accompanied by Okon and one of his wives, they were caught in a tornado. Okon's canoe flooded and when the crew lost control and their wits, they were forced to find shelter in the mangrove. On reflection, sitting in the waterlogged canoe until the storm passed was not the smartest idea, but they were already soaked through and there seemed no practical alternative. Needless to say, by the time they neared Old Town Mary was trembling with fever. Okon and his wife, seeing her distress, held her close between them to keep her warm. Once at home, Mary could not rest until she had made the bairns a hot meal and put them to bed; until then she would have to drip dry. Unsurprisingly, by morning, she was deep in the grip of the worst of fevers. It had become so severe that those around her decided that to save her life they had no alternative but to send for a doctor, who advised that they should send Mary on furlough at the earliest opportunity. Whilst marking time to leave Old Town, another tornado lifted the roof from her house and, while safeguarding the children, she was drenched once again. The state of her health was now a matter of the greatest urgency. She was carried on to the steamer at Duke Town; through the haze of fever, all she could remember was insisting that Jeanie accompany her to Scotland.

1883
Jeanie's Scottish baptism

With the collapse of the Tay Bridge in 1879 and the rebuilding only partially complete, Mary's train pulled into the station on the Fife side of the river at Ferry-Port-on-Craig and the passengers took the ferry across the Tay. Accompanied by her beloved Jeanie, Mary was almost her old self again. The wee girl was mesmerised by all the sights and sounds, indeed everything that passed her by. Such simple pleasures refreshed Mary's jaded senses and reminded her of the miraculous gifts that the world had to offer. Children investigate and explore all that we take for granted, and have the ability to

Ma Eme, Mary & Edem, Ekenge (1889).

play 'boo!' over and over, and over again. *'Thank God for bairns'*, thought Mary, even if growing up is not all that it should be. What her mother and sisters would make of Jeanie she did not know, but she was sure they would make her feel as if she were one of the family.

Due to illness at home there was no reception at Dundee and, as night fell, Jeanie and Mary made their way to Downfield. Despite the latest news she had received of her sister Janie's illness, Mary approached the house with hope and expectation but felt that a brave face would also be needed. She put Jeanie down behind her, knocked at the door, opened it and entered the house. Her mother and sisters looked at her and smiled broadly, yet there was an air of disappointment in their greeting, until, from the back of her skirt and the tangle of Mary's legs, Jeanie peeked out and, as bright as a button with a grin that would have made even Alexander Ross smile, said *"Boo!"* There was an explosion of laughter. Mary's mother came over as fast as she could and scooped up Jeanie in her arms; joy filled the room. The child could not have been more welcome and Mary told her family that while in Dundee she would have her baptised Jean Annan Slessor.

The day of the baptism at Wishart Church was beautiful with bright sunshine and a cool clear air. All Mary's attempts to rein in wee Jeanie's enthusiasm were fruitless; she was in no doubt that she wanted to run free, or should we say, toddle free. Mary called her back and scolded her gently, saying, *"Jeanie, come back, will you do what you're told, behave!"* Mary's mother glanced at her, raised an eyebrow and said, *"Oh Mary, the things that children teach us."*

Mary knew that her mother carried fond memories of another little girl who wouldn't do what she was told, but felt that being reminded of it at this time was hardly fair; instinctively she stuck her tongue out at her.

Her mother chastised her with mock indignation, *"Mary! Behave!"*

They all laughed and continued through the streets to the church where Jeanie was baptised in front of a captivated audience at the Wishart Memorial Sunday School.

So far Mary's time in Scotland had been a great success, due perhaps to the spotlight being transferred to her daughter and not on her unworthy self. Her talks seemed relaxed with the wee one beside her and the public gave so much money for the Mission that she began to question whether she was using the 'poor wee soul', but she could go nowhere without her. Jeanie would sit on the stage and enchant the audiences who thrilled at the sight of the beautiful child. Mary told stories of her life in Africa and, with Jeanie's presence, her experiences truly came alive. While Mary talked, the wee one would sit patiently and eat biscuits, which she consumed with great gusto and freely shared with all those on the platform, much to the delight of the audience who applauded each time she did so.

When Mary and Jeanie returned to Dundee after their latest sojourn, the winter clouds were gathering. Mary knew well what it signified, and hoped that this particular event would soon happen. The winter sun had long vanished, yet much of the chill had also gone. 'All good signs' thought Mary. Instead of heading directly home, she carried Jeanie to a nearby stretch of grass and put her down to play, just as the first snow flake fell. Years of Scottish winters blunted most adults to the joys of snow; it only meant slippery streets, wet slush and general inconvenience. Yet Mary, with the facade of a grown-up woman, given the opportunity was still as much a child as she had always been. In this quiet suburb, she watched Jeanie stand transfixed as she waited for these strange flakes to land on her hands and face. The little girl knew rain well enough, rain that would make everyone run for shelter, but here she stood beside a watchman's fire with palms upturned and let the snow fall and vanish before her eyes, her face turned upwards towards the swarm of flakes. She screamed and giggled in excitement. Mary could hold back no longer and joined her; the old watchman smiled and marvelled at their actions so similar in exultation of this miraculous event. Mary wanted no reason or explanation for snowflakes; it was a gift her Lord had given to children and to those adults who were still children at heart.

When they returned to the house, later than expected, wet and rosy-cheeked, Mary's mother looked at her daughter and was about to speak when Mary pre-empted her, *"I know mither, behave."* Her mother smiled and said, *"No Mary, I was going to say, I hope you never have to grow up."*

As Mary's furlough was coming to its end, she felt the need to announce her plans to leave Dundee, but this was delayed as worryingly Janie's health had deteriorated. The doctor was called and after he had examined her he asked to speak in private to Mary and her mother. He led the two out into the street; his mood darkened and he had trouble finding the words. Seeing his awkwardness, Mary interjected. *"We know she is very ill. Is there anything more we can do?"*

The doctor knew how much Mary had already done to help her family. *"You have done as much as you can by moving them out here, but I fear it will not be enough."*

Mary asked, *"Do you mean there is something else that can be done?"*

He laughed gently, *"Could you improve the climate?"*

Mary thought for a moment, *"I suppose I could ask the Mission Board if I could take her with me to Africa."*

The doctor shook his head, *"While that would help greatly, that might be too much of a change"*

Mary considered the proposal but admitted, *"Where else could we move her? Broughty Ferry?"* There was no reply. She asked again, *"Perth??"* Still no reply. *"Edinburgh???"*

The doctor shook his head, *"I would recommend the South coast of England."*

Mary and her mother looked at each other with blank expressions; it seemed as likely to move her there as to a but-and-ben on the moon. She took a deep breath and said, *"Well, if that is what she needs then, with God's help, that's what we will do."*

Thanks to good friends of the Mission, and others, in February 1885 she was able to arrange to move Janie to a lovely small house at 48 The Strand in Topsham, Devon; her mother remained in Dundee to see that her sister Susan was settled before joining them. The Mission Board was good enough to extend her furlough until both were settled in their new home; however in April of that year they were to receive shocking news. They were informed by letter that Susan, on a trip to Edinburgh to visit friends, had dropped dead on arrival. While her mother and sister remained with Jeanie, Mary made the sad trip up to Scotland to attend to the funeral and close up the Dundee house.

On her return to Devon, Mary, unable to stay idle for long, and being the only able-bodied, surviving, breadwinner, knew that there was a pressing need to keep the wolf from the door; she found work at Exeter hospital. This was not only a financial boon but it also had the added bonus of greatly increasing her medical knowledge, which had now become an increasingly important part of her missionary work. With both 'the invalids' in the bright fresh air improving daily, her need to return to her duty in Africa pressed upon her; she knew she would need to tell them soon. As they relaxed on the back lawn of their new home which stretched down to the river Exe, with wee Jeanie playing amongst them, a pause in the conversation gave Mary an opportunity to raise the topic of her leaving, but before she could her sister broke the silence, *"Mary, we've been talking, mither and me, we think that it's time for you to go."*

Mary, feigning offence, replied, *"You want rid of me?"*

Her mother rose to her humour, *"Behave! You have work to do and it's time to get on wi' it, get back to helping others, we're fine now, get away with you."* Her tone softened, *"You are my child given to me by God, and I have given you back to Him."*

Mary protested, *"But, but....."*

Her sister added, *"We've made your mind up fir you, you know it's what you must do. You'll aye be with us, whatever you do, and wherever you go, and we'll aye be with you."*

Her mother had the last word on the subject, *"Love is no' measured or diminished by distance. We have a' witnessed love too weak to radiate atween twa people sitting next to ane another, but atween **us** there's no place you can go that you are not with me, whether you are in Africa or India or China, you will always be right here."*

There was a long pause while they collected their thoughts. She knew they were right, they both knew what was in Mary's mind and in her heart. Mary put up no argument and thought only of the goodbyes yet to be said. When the day came their farewells were not sad, though they couldn't hide the grief in their eyes. They all knew that they would meet again, but did not know exactly where or when.

This time the journey back to Africa seemed to last an age, and Mary was glad to have the bairn with her to stave off the veil of sadness that can descend when sorrow is your only companion. The long trip did give her time to catch up with the news from Africa that she had missed since she had been away; the ship was abuzz with the outcome of the recent Berlin Conference. From reports she read, all the European powers with vested interests in Africa had assembled to divide and rule the nation. Mary thought to herself *'magnanimous of them, was it no'?'* It would appear that they had decided that the spread of population, controlled by small pockets of tribal power, seemed the best way to keep the peace, while answering to courts run by Europeans and set up throughout the regions to arbitrate along European lines. To that effect, a British Consul had now taken up a post in Duke Town as part of the Oil Rivers Protectorate. In her opinion, as long as the competing European bodies did not fall out amongst themselves, this appeared, on the surface, to be a reasonable resolution, but only time would tell. As the ship neared the home port, her spirits lifted and though happy to think of her mother and sister in the sun, it was sad to think of all those left in Dundee. She often dreamt that if she was ever to be left a fortune she would move all the poor from Dundee to come and live with her in Africa.

1885
Move to Creek Town

On her arrival, she learned that she was not to return to Old Town. This saddened her but she was convinced that as this region was now comparatively settled, her talents could be put to better use further inland at Creek Town; so once again they were on the move. Though Creek Town was a notoriously difficult place with many problems, she was pleased to be reunited with Mr Goldie and King Eyo, two of a handful of men she knew she could trust. The King was keen to learn and they would sit and talk for hours. Owing to his conversion to Christianity, and his controversial choice to have only one wife, he had lost the support of some of his followers, hence there remained much overt disobedience by those outwith his control. Since they had last met, the King had been learning some geography. He wanted to show off his new-found knowledge and asked, *"Ma, you are from England?"*

Mary, proud of her heritage, replied, *"Awa! No, no, no, Scotland!"*

The King was confused, *"Is that not England?"*

Mary tried to hold her tongue but couldn't, *"Goodness no!"* She used her extended arms in an attempt to describe the distance between the two. She pointed to her left hand, *"this is Africa,"* she fully extended her arms, *"and my right hand is China,"* he nodded and she repeated the demonstration, *"left hand England, right hand Scotland, see?"*

The King seemed satisfied, *"Ah, now I understand. How can I learn about Scotland?"*

Mary replied, *"You should speak to my mother, she'd tell you all about it."*

The King nodded and continued, *"Mary, can I ask you a question? It has been troubling me for some time, and it may offend."*

"Of course."

"Many of my people who are not Christians ask me this. We know that many of our laws seem strange, I have heard them called barbarit, that is not good, yet we only punish those who have done wrong according to our laws and tradition."

Mary corrected his pronunciation, *"I think you mean barbaric."*

"Thank you, but you allowed the barbaric....." - he nodded to her to make

sure he had said the word correctly, she nodded back and smiled, he continued
- *"punishment of God's only son, you allowed him to be nailed up through the hands and feet on a cross and left to die. Are **you** not the cruel people? My people see that their punishments are very small in the face of this."*

Mary, taken aback by the question, had to think quickly of a suitable reply, *"It was the law at the time, and it was wrong."*

The King said, *"But laws cannot be made and changed to suit the speed of the river or the height of a mountain. Surely if a law is made it must be correct, and obeyed? Did these men, who did this to Jesus, die on the cross to make amends?"*

"No, they were forgiven." Mary replied.

The King still perplexed, smiled, *"I will write to your mother and see if she can explain, and she can tell me of Scotland."*

Sometime later Mary was delighted to hear that the King had written to her mother and to ask her about Scotland; tragically she was never to read his letter; three days before its arrival, on Hogmanay, 31st December 1885, her mother died. Then in March 1886, while still grieving and feeling such great remorse, the news of her sister Janie's death of tuberculosis reached her. How alone she felt, wracked with guilt and shame; it was as if her entire world had collapsed and her heart would break. In one year she had lost all her points of reference; her sounding board was no more and she felt that the child in her had gone. Mary experienced the loneliness of an orphan, and had it not been for the strength He gave her, and the love of her bairns, she could not have carried on. With no close friends or relatives to confide in, she felt that Heaven was nearer than Britain and she knew that she could not share her misery with Jeanie. Her nights were now full of the ghosts of the family that she had lost, of precious moments that they had shared, but most of all she knew that she must honour them by carrying on the work they were so proud of.

With no family left to worry about her, she made plans to make her most difficult and ambitious move yet, to the wild untamed region of the Okoyong. She wrote immediately to the Mission Board and requested that they let her go.

An uncertain future

Back in Duke Town, Mr Anderson sat at his desk in the Mission House, looking at the letter from Mary. He shook his head then said, *"Well Mr*

Chairlie Ovens, Mary & John Bishop

Goldie, Miss Slessor seems determined to go up to the Okoyong. That is surely ridiculous, she is too frail, and even without her recent loss this is something we should not even contemplate."

Mr Goldie seemed less concerned, *"She understands."*

Mr Anderson said angrily, *"We all know that is not enough! We would be remiss in our duty to even consider such a preposterous move. The area is beyond her guardian angel King Eyo and full of fierce tribesmen who would turn her sad short life into a tragedy."*

Goldie agreed, up to a point, *"There is no doubt that the task is great, but sending an army of missionaries, armed with Bibles and maxim guns, would be useless, but Mary is something else entirely. She carries an armoury of goodness, kindness and purpose. She is much more than a one-woman army, she has no fear, all she fears is letting down her God."*

Mr Anderson was becoming flustered, *"But surely it would be like sending ....."* Goldie interrupted, *"like sending Daniel into the lion's den?"*

Mr Anderson tutted but Goldie continued, *"In the past she has done the difficult well, it will be interesting to see how she copes with the almost impossible."*

Mr Anderson threw the letter on to the table, stood up, turned his back on Goldie and said in desperation, *"In all conscience, I cannot sanction sending Mary to her death."*

Mr Goldie picked up the letter and while reading it smiled and said, *"She seems very determined to go. If you are to turn her down you'd better think long and hard about it."*

Mr Anderson remained gazing into the distance and in frustration said, *"She lacks....."* he paused, having to think of a reason, *"she lacks the Bible knowledge to convince the natives....."*

Goldie interrupted, *"But she has the love of the natives at heart, and understands them, and to be perfectly honest I have the feeling that if we don't agree to her request she will go on her own; now **that** would be something to have on your conscience!"*

Mr Anderson returned to his chair, put his head in his hands and seemingly resigned to his fate, exclaimed, *"God save you Mary!"*

Mary knew that life so far from the control of the Mission, the military, and King Eyo would take all her skill and patience, so over the next months she paid three short visits to the Okoyong, mostly to administer to their medical needs and take in the lay of the land, while introducing them to her ways. She found these people very different from those she had previously encountered, tall, handsome, brave, fearless in fact, with strong features and piercing eyes. They seemed self-assured and insular and their reputation had been long established; retribution to any incursion into their territory or challenge to their authority was swift and savage. Her accommodation on such visits was less than salubrious; she described her sleeping arrangements to a friend, *'I am not very particular about my bed nowadays but as I lay on a few dirty sticks laid across and covered with a litter of dirty cornshells, with plenty of rats and insects, three women and an infant three days old alongside, and over a dozen goats and sheep and cows and countless dogs outside, you won't wonder that I slept little!'*

On her last visit to the Okoyong she went alone for she knew it was her last chance to make the move work. As she passed the armed native guards, they were taken aback by the sight of a single white woman, walking amongst them, showing no fear. The benefits that they might gain from 'book' - education - were great and, should at least some of the tribe accept religion, they would be more readily acknowledged by the Europeans; but it was undoubtedly their intention that only women and children be allowed to be touched by the white God.

Chief Edem, who was head of the Ekenge branch of the Egbo and whose word was law, had summoned a palaver. When Mary entered his hut, unarmed and alone, his normal aggressive manner lost its purpose. Though he treated his own women like chattels, he seemed to see in Mary an annoyance that

Mary's first home at Akpap with Chairlie Ovens.

97

would not go away, no matter how badly he treated her. It may have been that Edem believed his acceptance of her to be a mere gesture, to promote himself as a friend of the Europeans without risking too much. To allow one small woman into his district, what could she achieve? What did he have to lose? The palaver ended, and it was reluctantly agreed that Mary be allocated a piece of ground that no one would be allowed to enter without the Chief's permission. She was then introduced to his sister, Ma Eme. At first the woman seemed cold and distant, hostile even to Mary's presence, a challenge to her own laws and religion, yet as they talked and sparred, Mary found her strong convictions and bright mind refreshing; she was beginning to understand that progress, if it were to be achieved, often made some very strange bedfellows. While they agreed on very little, they shared a passion that was deep and sincere, a love for the people. Eme's reasons for seeking her out became clearer as she spoke, *"I have heard you are a good man, but I want nothing of your God!"*

Mary tried to explain, *"But if you take God into your heart....."*

Eme put her hands over her ears and sang loudly to drown out Mary's words. When she could see that Mary had stopped speaking, she began to talk again, *"But I am sick of the fighting, and bloodshed, and cruel death by sacrifice. The tribes will not be content until all are dead. This we must stop!"*

Mary surprised by her inclusion questioned, *"We?"*

Eme proposed a pact, *"Yes, if you make no more God noise at me, I will help you."*

Mary laughed, *"Yes, no more God noise. I thank you for your help."*

Eme told something of her life, *"I lost my man a time ago, and me and his other wives were blamed for using bad ju-ju to make him die. At the trial, they took a white bird and cut its head off, and if it ran this way I was guilty and if the other I was not. The bird ran well, and I escaped being buried alive, but I was kept away from others, and would have starved to death had my brother not relented, and allowed me back to the village. Women are but slaves in this race of men, who make war and children for **their** pleasure. We live or die by their word, and we fear their anger, and the demons in the gin bottle. You must walk quietly amongst us, until you can walk past without shaking the ground. Then they will let you live, then you must do great magic, and save us all!"*

Eme clapped and laughed with all the innocence of a child at the thought of a better future. Mary was well aware that making friends with Eme would not be viewed well and could create further animosity between herself and those missionaries who believed their sole purpose was to convert all they came upon to be good Presbyterian Christians. But Mary knew well enough that her God did not take sides; He recognised a good soul, regardless of creed, colour or religion.

1888
Alone in the Okoyong

Before Mary's departure from Creek Town, King Eyo called for her and told her, *"Mary, I ask you to reconsider this foolishness. It would seem that you are as headstrong as ever, and I am wasting my words, but I still ask you to think again. These people are not good like the Efik, they are not to be trusted, they are savages, my name and reputation will do you no good with them, we defeated them in battle a time ago, they are not Christians, they do not forgive. You will find that they still obey all the old laws, and make me ashamed; you must walk with light feet and a hard heart as they will not be kind as we are. You must prepare for the worst, and hope that it does not come to pass. You shall be in my heart, and in my prayers, and God will have to be very wide awake to keep you safe. May the Lord lead your steps and guide our Mother safely back to us."*

At the dock at Creek Town, the crew's reluctance to make the long and dangerous journey north meant waiting hours in the pouring rain. The wailing of the women, who had come to mourn Mary's leaving, darkened the already sombre mood; it took the arrival of King Eyo to focus the crew's minds to get on with the job in hand. Mary was beginning to 'lose her rag', and in a rare moment of weakness and desperation, she asked for help, this time not only from the Lord, but for a volunteer to come with her on her journey. At first there were no takers, and she began to think that this was a mission too far; but help came and from the most unlikely of quarters - the Mission printer John Bishop, a fellow Scot, stepped up and volunteered his services. In the confusion of her leaving, she had failed to recognise the volunteer whom she had met at the Darling's Hotel while studying in Edinburgh; it seemed a life-time ago. She was surprised and almost turned down his offer of help; why, she did not know, possibly because he was not the kind of person she was expecting to enlist, but quickly, and fortunately, she accepted and soon they were belatedly on their way.

At the height of the rainy season, the trip to the Okoyong in Eyo's state canoe with Mr Bishop and her current brood of five bairns was far less joyous than the previous one. The crew who were petrified at the thought of passing through such dangerous territory, unarmed and filled with the fear that their heads would end up on spikes, made any progress torturously slow. For the bairns' sake, Mary tried to make the journey as much fun as she could, and they managed to pass many hours singing silly songs and rousing hymns. Mary had her paraffin stove with her and she heated up a tin of beef stew for the bairns. When they had finished eating she decided to make a cup of tea for herself and Mr Bishop; in the cramped conditions, and in the pouring rain, she could only find one cup and two saucers. Although not a disaster, in the scheme of things it felt a bitter blow that she was to be denied one of her few real pleasures. She took a deep breath and handed the cup and saucer to Mr Bishop; she would make do with the empty steak tin. Unfortunately as she washed it out over the side of the boat, it slipped from her fingers and disappeared into the murky waters. Mary grasped the side of the boat in frustration and as she turned saw Mr Bishop trying to hide a smile; this helped her put the accident into perspective and she settled down to drink her tea from the saucer. She said to Mr Bishop, *"If you use what you have, you will never want!"* He nodded in agreement and they both had a pleasant, if unorthodox, afternoon tea together.

To be fair to the Egbo rowers, it was a dangerous time for them, as they could be all killed at a whim. As warriors they were a larger and more legitimate target than a missionary woman, her bairns, and a Mission printer; there would be little honour in killing a wee Scots lass, but death was death, however it came. They were landed as near to Ekenge as they thought safe, and once Mary and the bairns were safely decanted, Mr Bishop was left with the rest of the carriers to catch up as soon as they could. The first party set off to walk the last four miles of the journey with the bairns and what they could carry. Night descended. They made very slow progress through the dense bush; the brave wee bairns, now beyond exhaustion and 'out on their feet', wept openly and in all honesty, despite her efforts to cheer them, it was all Mary could do not to join them. Her feet hurt so badly that if she were to continue, her shoes would have to be removed; her feet were so swollen that the rough ground was preferable to being tightly shod. When they eventually reached Ekenge, the word was quickly passed around and shouts of, *"Ma has come! Ma has come!"* rang out into the night air. A young native boy stopped her and in admiration, said, *"You are so brave to come here alone."* Had she not been so exhausted she would have been delighted, but as she was 'ready to drop' she couldn't raise much more than a smile. The children, scared and tired, huddled round her wet skirt and continued to weep, and the joy of the moment was lost. They were shown into a ramshackle of a building in which to sleep, and once left on their own she began to make hot food for them. While the bairns scoffed their tea, she cleared a space and laid out sacks for them to sleep on. Once fed, and prayers said, one by one they fell asleep.

There was no sleep for Mary as she waited for the carriers to arrive with the rest of their belongings. She waited and waited until, eventually, she glimpsed the bedraggled figure of Mr Bishop enter the yard; laden with as much as he could carry, unfortunately he was on his own. Breathlessly he managed to say, *"Miss Slessor, I'm sorry, I couldn't get the carriers to come with me, no matter what I said. They said that until they had word of safe passage, they wouldn't leave the canoe."*

Barefooted, Mary stormed out in a fury, *"Will you stay with the bairns, Mr Bishop?"* She brushed past him and shouted at the top of her voice, *"I'll gie them safe passage!"*

The boy who had welcomed her, caught up with Mary as she crashed through the dense undergrowth and into the night and offered to light her way. When she reached the boat's mooring place on the opposite bank, there was silence; the crew were fast asleep in the canoe. Incandescent with rage, she plunged into the river and stormed across. On reaching the boat, the water now almost up to her chin, she banged with all her might on the side of the vessel and put the fear of the Okoyong into the sleeping rowers. Unaware of which kind of water devil was awakening them they panicked, for Mary's temper rivalled that of the hippo's, in or out of the water. When riled, Mary would almost always revert to her Scots tongue, which had the effect of scaring and confusing her victims at the same time. *"Ye lazy scunners, get aff yer backsides and dae some work, ev' left the bairns and walked miles tae get ye out o' yer beds! Get this stuff moved **now**!!!"*

Her angry words echoed throughout the forest and made the ground shake; birds took flight, and the scariest beast awoke with a shudder and left that area of the bush. Her anger was so great, that not one of the crew dared question whether they had been given safe passage or not. Soon Mary was driving the human chain back to Ekenge and heaven save the hindmost.

In the morning with her goods around her, including her newly-acquired portable reed organ sent by friends in Scotland, she thanked Mr Bishop for all that he had done, and waved goodbye to him and the bearers. As the day progressed, she was joined by Ma Eme, who informed her that most of the tribe had gone to Ifako to celebrate a funeral, and that they would be away, and drunk, for days. While this seemed an opportunity to get things done, the following day was Sunday and Mary could not begin work. Though she had found an ally in Ma Eme, there was nothing she could do to bring the women to her church service. As Mary began to preach, there was only her own small family band in attendance. If she had doubted it before, it was now confirmed that this would be a hard place in which to minister.

The tribe's arrival back in Ekenge was a sick parade of humanity; hangovers, as she knew only too well, brought misery, self-pity and grief. Mary remained out of their way for as long as she could, but when Ma Eme told her that the boy who had guided her on the night of her arrival was to be punished for absenting himself from the funeral, she marched out to do battle with them on his behalf. Sadly, she was too late to defend the Good Samaritan; his cries were all she was witness to. For his sins they had poured boiling oil on his hands; she could only comfort him and tend his wounds. Although King Edem wished his people to have knowledge of the Bible and to be educated, he was less than enthusiastic about Mary's presence and with this obstacle, she could not see how any success was to be achieved. She prayed to the Lord for patience and guidance, knowing that He would have the answers; right now she had none.

The weeks passed and Mary kept a low profile, only doing what she was asked; her skill as a healer brought her closer to many reluctant natives and, largely by this means, the Sunday congregation slowly began to grow. The sanctuary of her yard, safely away from the gaze and reach of the ill-tempered men, encouraged women and children to gather. It would be easy to construe that their enthusiasm to sing hymns with joy had something to do with their apparent conversion; in reality it was because they had music in their hearts and they loved to sing; the sound was wonderful. Mary looked out at the choir and thought how different this was from services at home; the process was similar, yet the performances were worlds apart. The psalms and hymns were transformed by the natives' movement and rhythmic clapping, even the youngest child moved as if born to it. This was a heartfelt celebration and she prayed that one day they would also do this with God in their hearts; but for now she sang and clapped and shared in their joy. Mary watched with interest Ma Eme, who stood outside in the yard and sang and danced with the rest, and she laughed as Eme covered her ears when she made God noises.

Undoubtedly, Edem kept a watchful eye on Mary, but he did it from a safe distance. His tribesmen continued to fight, drink and abuse their slaves and womenfolk and Mary realised that without his acceptance, her mission would end in failure. The amount of drinking and debauchery filled her with great sadness, but as ever, God was looking out for her. An order had come for Mary to visit Edem's hut as he wished to palaver, but she was in no mood to be ordered by him and took her time packing her bag with Bible, medicines, glasses and tea. The messenger became so nervous at the length of time she was taking that he left without her. Mary strolled leisurely through Ekenge, but as she approached Edem's hut she saw him screaming at the messenger. When she came into the yard, the shouting ceased, the messenger stole away and Edem's manner immediately became conciliatory, *"Miss Slessor, I am glad that time is not pressing upon you."* He smiled. *"It would seem a devil has bitten my favourite wife on the arm and the wound has become angry."*

Mary had been alerted in advance by Eme that it was Edem who had bitten his wife during a night of drunken lechery and, to his great annoyance, the witch doctor had not been able to cure her. The decision to ask for Mary's help was a course of action Edem had not taken lightly.

"What hideous devil would have done this to such a lovely wife?" Mary asked. *"Surely no man, unless possessed by demons, would be so cruel?"*

The Chief became nervous; he did not know what Mary knew of the circumstances, but he was suspicious. Mary was having fun at Edem's expense, but to go any further would serve no purpose. On further examination of Edem's wife she saw that the wound was badly infected; once she had washed and treated her injury, there was little more she could do but pray.

Thankfully over the next few days the Chief's wife recovered fully and, as the consultation had happened in the full glare of the tribe, Mary's success was transmitted throughout the district and beyond. Proof of that came a week later, when a messenger arrived from a district many hours distance. He had, with some difficulty, crossed the swollen Cross River with a gift of brass rods accompanied by a request for help and a bottle of gin as payment. The messenger explained in desperate terms that their Chief Otu was dying. In normal times, this would have had her reaching immediately for her medical bag, but she was becoming ill and 'running out of steam'. With a touch of weariness, she asked, *"What will happen should he die?"*

"By our custom, all his wives and slaves will be put to death."

The weariness left her heart, if not her body, and she told him, *"I will come with you."*

The arrival of the messenger had created a stir in Ekenge. Although Chief Edem had not accepted Mary as a missionary, she was there under his protection. *"Ma you must not go!"* he warned, *"What happens should he die?"* *"Many will also die."*

Edem said sternly, *"And you will be among them."* He continued in a vein reminiscent of King Eyo, *"They are a cruel people and you will not be safe. The river is big with rains. You will not be able to cross."*

Mary would not be dissuaded, *"I thank you, but the Lord will protect me. If I can save the Chief, much bloodshed will be avoided."*

Edem was equally adamant, *"But Ma, you risk all to save what there are plenty of - children, slaves, women - but there is only one Ma."*

On any other day Mary might have argued with him though she did appreciate his concern, *"But to God, each one is one to be saved."*

He kept trying, *"But God he is Chief, like Edem."*

She explained, *"In God's tribe, all are equal, His power is used to protect each one. They love him for His kindness, not His anger. He will protect me if I carry Him in my heart."*

Edem, unable to sway her, said, *"Ma, will you take me in your heart also, and we will both protect you."*

Touched by his kindness, Mary replied, *"Of course, it'll be an honour, Chief."*

It was now time for her to leave, but though she had the determination, she was unsure her stamina would be up to the task. She thought to herself *'God will hae to gie me a hand this time'.*

The journey on foot through the bush in the pouring rain, with only an umbrella for protection, took over eight hours. During the arduous trek, her clothes were torn and then shredded, but there was no alternative but to carry on. As she passed through small villages on her way, she couldn't imagine how she looked, barefooted and bareheaded, bedraggled and drenched to the skin. What would they think if they could see her in Duke Town? Without doubt many tales of the wet, crazy, white woman are still told to this day to frighten the bairns, but when there is work to be done, there is work to be done.

When she arrived at the village there was no opportunity to rest. First of all, she was given a pile of odd, exotic-looking, native garments to choose from, while the remains of her own clothes dried in front of the fire. As she readied herself, she could hear the murmur of raised voices and the crashing of spears upon shields; had she arrived too late? Was the Chief dead? The Chief's warriors were 'in a right lather' and ready to carry out their threats of murder. Fortunately, God was watching. When she was shown into Chief Otu's house, though she found him weak, thankfully he was still alive. His men gathered around menacingly, but Mary was in no mood to put up with such foolish intimidation and shooed them away, bellowing at the top of her voice, *"Get out, stay out, aff we ye, scoot!"* Whether it was her manic appearance or her fiery temper that made them flee, it didn't much matter, as long as she was allowed to do her work. She was aware that failure to save the Chief would result in ritual slaughter; despite her rising fever, she knew her hands must be steady and sure. For three days and nights she watched and waited, nursing him through crisis after crisis until, at last, on the fourth day, he began to rally. As Otu continued to improve, Mary permitted the senior members of the tribe to file past the door and pay him tribute. It would seem that her time in Exeter Hospital was proving as valuable as that spent at the Edinburgh Missionary School.

She stayed on until he had fully recovered and was surprised and delighted that the natives were keen to be taught 'book'. During her stay she came into contact with many new chiefs; one in particular drew her attention. He was physically different from the others, statuesque, tall and lighter-skinned, who always remained in the background, but his piercing eyes keenly observed Mary's every action. Through enquiry she learned the history of this man; he was King Eze Kanu Okoro whose home was further north at Arochuku. He was the king of one of the most powerful, infamous and feared tribes in West Africa, the Aro. Late one night, in a quiet moment, she observed King Okoro and another warrior, both with beaded breast-plates and tall wooden staffs in their hands, standing stock-still outside her yard. Intrigued and a little perturbed, Mary left the safety of her house and stepped out into the oppressive night air. Still they did not flinch. She sat on the ground, determined to engage them in conversation, yet they remained silent. To goad them into a dialogue, she proffered, *"I know little of the Aro. Are they as bad as they say?"* Okoro's eyes moved, he took one step closer but no further; his lieutenant stood sentinel. Mary looked up and asked him directly, *"Sit by me?"* The tall man thought for a few seconds, approached her, bowed his head, put down his staff and sat cross-legged facing her.

She began, *"I hear you have great power, King Okoro."*

The Chief bowed his head in supplication and repaid the compliment, *"I can see that* **you** *have!"*

Brushing aside his reply, she tried to differentiate, *"I believe mine to be another kind of power."*

"You make those around you do as you wish, do you not?"

As she could not deny it, Mary laughed, *"Well..... they believe in my word,* **I** *do not do it by fear....."*

He interrupted, *"You do it by belief.* **We** *believe in our Oracle! By our belief, for centuries we have lived in the most beautiful place on earth. If we do not continue to keep him happy, it will be taken away from my people."* He leant towards Mary, *"Would you not fight?"*

Mary agreed, *"Of course....."*

He interrupted her once more, *"I heard you were to be here and walked many miles to seek you out, to watch your power. Do you bewitch?"*

"Goodness sake, no!"

Okoro looked satisfied with her answer and confided, *"I think they may soon drive us away, and turn our land into dust. Is* **that** *right?"*

Mary could only answer as a Christian, *"Of course not, much palaver must come before arms are raised."*

Again he seemed happy, *"Should it come to pass, before they lift their arms, will you say these words?"*

With determination she agreed, *"Of course I will!..... And mair besides!"*

He stood, picked up his staff, bowed his head and said, *"Ma, you are a good man, and I believe you are to be trusted. You have African eyes that see the good, and can understand the bad. We may meet again."*

He turned and walked away, the two men quickly fading into the night. While Mary could not assimilate much of what he had said without further knowledge, from now on she would keep one eye on the comings and goings of the Aro.

By the time she left the village, she had made many new friends who were sad to see her go; but they were content, as she had vowed to send them a teacher and agreed to their request that *'she would always be their mother'.*

The scalding

Her long trek back to Ekenge took most of the strength Mary held in reserve; she was sorely in need of rest, yet again it was not to be. As she approached the outskirts of the village, she recognised the unwelcome sound of the Egbo

106

drums and the noise of men shouting. When the drums of the Egbo called *'all to attend'*, all attended. The sound led her to Edem's yard where there was a great furore. At the edge of the yard Mary met Eme who, beside herself with grief and through a flood of tears, explained that a male slave had done some work for a woman's husband but had not been paid. The slave had badgered the woman, who had then paid him with half a yam. When this became known, the woman was accused of breaking the tribe's code because her actions were interpreted as a prelude to adultery. Her punishment was to be the burning of her body with boiling oil. Mary tried to push her way through the crowd and the sight that greeted her filled her with dread and disgust. In the middle of the baying crowd lay a naked young woman, staked out on the ground; the more the girl struggled, wept and wailed, the louder the crowd screamed for the punishment to be carried out. As Mary broke through the warriors' inner circle, her eyes met with Edem's; Mary stood and glowered at him. A warrior had just dipped a ladle into boiling oil and was approaching the hysterical girl. Mary hesitated for a moment, hoping that her appearance would encourage Edem to demonstrate leniency, but not a word did he utter. Without a further thought, Mary stepped between the man with the ladle and the girl. The drums stopped and the baying crowd fell silent, even the girl stopped screaming and looked up in astonishment. Mary's heart was pounding as she stared straight into the eyes of the tall, fiercely-painted, ladle man; he grinned a broken-toothed grin and began to swing the ladle slowly towards her face. The drums began again as he drew closer, his grin became wider as the boiling oil dripped from the swinging ladle. Mary had learnt that bullies often deal in fear rather than actual physical harm and she prayed that this was one of those times. The ladle was now only inches away and some of the boiling liquid splashed out on to the ground just missing her bare feet. Every sound stopped as the oil fell; there was a sharp intake of breath by all who watched. If they had expected her to 'lift her sark and run', they were mistaken. Mary did not move, other than to look down at the bubbling liquid on the ground and on raising her head to look at her antagonist; she saw that his grin had gone. The steel had vanished from his stare, he looked towards Edem for some instruction on how to proceed, but Edem gave none. The chiefs who had surrounded Mary, now surrounded Edem and, after much shouting and remonstrating, Edem took Mary alone into his house. He sat down and asked her to join him. *"Ma, we are glad you return safe to us."* He continued with greater emphasis, *"Your God is good to*

107

*you..... We have a troublesome woman who needs to be looked after. Will you take her under your roof and **away** from mine?"* Mary agreed.

Edem, with a more than a touch of exasperation in his voice, said, *"Thank you Ma."* He turned away from her and yelled an order, *"Release the girl to Ma!"*

When Mary left Edem's house the Egbo had unchained the girl and, without another word, and hardly a sound, the two women left the yard. Whether the Chief had tried to complete the punishment before her return or not, she would never know; she was only happy that it had coincided with Edem's change of mind.

That night, Mary's yard was filled with excited, chattering women and children, who gathered together to celebrate the great work that Abassi had done that day. Mary began to ponder whether her proselytising was counterproductive to what she now believed her real mission to be. Many of these natives had the same trust in their God as she had in hers, and just as she could not give up her God they would not give up theirs. She began to think that their God, who they called Abassi, might be hers by another name and that it would be a similarly thankless task to try and convince those already converted and who worshipped as Baptists, Catholics, Methodists, or Muslims, to worship as Presbyterian, to have arguments over words and not what those words meant. She considered the notion, *'If believers in goodness and fairness could unite, would that not make a better world for all?'*

The caravan and trading places

The men of the Okoyong, like most men who have evolved their power through countless generations of unchallenged dominance, ruled by fear and divine right, and had scant regard for those who were weaker or poorer. It was a sad fact, the world over, that many of those in power gave nothing and took all they could and used outdated convention, ritual, and law to inflict cruel punishment. If Mary had been born a man, she would have boxed their ears and made them see sense, but as she wasn't, she would have to 'ca cannie'.

As word of her healing hands and fearless reputation spread, her congregation grew and, with the help of Abassi, they all prayed together. However, Edem's promises of a new house had not materialised and her patience was quickly running out. The present mission house, situated next to Edem's harem, was not a place conducive to quiet contemplation, so she went in search of a more suitable site. She spotted an ideal place on the edge of the village, away from the noise and bad habits. Early one morning, she and the bairns began to clear the site, Mary turning the chore into a game, and they spent many happy hours planning and building their new house. The news of her building work was not long in reaching the ears of Edem and it left him with no choice but to send men to give her a helping hand. They drove strong stakes into the ground, between which they wove beaten branches to make walls; these were daubed with red clay and left to dry. Soon, two large rooms began to take shape. The men pounded a flat clay floor with their feet, singing as they worked; it was good to see them working, happy and content, at least for the time being, as their idleness was a constant concern to Mary. The two rooms were fashioned into a bedroom and a kitchen and, with the addition of the palm-frond roofing mats, the building was made watertight. For Mary, the women, and the bairns, the making of the furniture was great fun. Together they moulded a sideboard out of clay, with shelves to hold plates, cups, pots and pans, and a fireplace with a mantel; she could have any piece of furniture she wanted, as many chairs, a fine table. To finish off the building a spare room was built on each end, to be used for storage or for house guests, creating a U-shaped structure with a verandah at the front. It was a dream come true, though she felt a great sadness that her mother and sister would never be there to enjoy it with her. For the first time in the Okoyong she felt at home, a home to keep safe her new family and possessions, a home in which to keep her sewing machine, books and precious reed organ, which she could now play to her heart's content without 'annoying the neibours'.

One of the first letters she would write in her new house was to the Missionary Record, to ask for the services of a carpenter to help her finish the building. Charles Ovens, a carpenter from Edinburgh, read her letter and her prayers were answered. In a comparatively short time - that is, African time - he arrived to put in the finishing touch of windows and doors. At last this was her house, constructed by the community, and freely given from the natural bounty of the bush. It reminded her of the tinkers' homes on wheels she'd seen in Scotland so, in honour of them, she called it the caravan. The many women who came to visit were enthralled by the house, the furniture especially; they lovingly stroked the chairs, tables and sideboard as if they were in some grand mansion in Dundee's well-off district of Broughty Ferry. These simple items were easily within the grasp of everyone, but there was no appetite for work which seemed to have no practical benefit.

For the men of the tribe, their acts of drunkenness and debauchery were generally their only activities. She decided it was time to talk to Edem about trade and to use as an example her experiences in Old Town.

"Could you not put your men to work; do some trade with other tribes, or with the Europeans?"

"We do trade!" Edem said proudly. *"We trade with many tribes. We trade in heads!"*

Mary gulped hard, and took a breath, *"No, I mean, if you would harvest palm oil and yams. There is much to be gained by it."*

Edem shrugged his shoulders at the suggestion, *"They will kill us and take our goods all the same. No, we give them heads, and they pay, or else!"*

Old battle scars ran deep between King Eyo and Chief Edem, so Mary decided to send a message to Eyo and the Duke Town traders to ask for a guarantee of safe passage for the men from the Okoyong. Initially it was not well-received, but she was determined to press on and give these natives another purpose in life, other than conflict. Many, many palavers later, once she had received a promise of safe passage, Edem reluctantly agreed to give it a try. An exploratory trip to Duke Town was organised; as usual, the tribe's enthusiasm far outstripped their experience, as the first overloaded canoe sank at the harbour; a second attempt, which Mary oversaw, was more successful.

She had hoped to keep her part in the venture to a minimum so that the tribe would feel that any success was by their hard work and endeavour, and she could concentrate on her missionary work. But for the moment, the Lord had other plans for her. As she stood back and observed the second loading of the canoe, she noticed something metallic sticking out from beneath a pile of yams. She lifted up some of the cargo and her worst fears were realised; she found guns, swords and knives underneath. In a fit of rage, she began to throw the weapons on to the landing stage. She picked up a rifle and threw it behind her; out of the corner of her eye, she saw one of the warriors bend to pick it up. She stopped her frantic activity, turned and stared at him. Under Mary's hostile glare, he stepped back and fell over a load of yams and, though hilarious, no one dared to laugh. She continued to throw knives and swords across the baked-clay landing, the loaders leaping and hopping out of the way of the sharp spinning blades. Once sure that the canoe was empty of weapons, she turned to face the natives. Many of them had now vanished into the bush and those who remained stood cowering in a huddle behind their women. Mary yelled at them, *"You ca' yersels men? Huh! Move it!"*

Their cargo, without weapons, consisted of yams and plantains to be given as gifts to the people of Duke Town, plus bags of palm nuts and a barrel of oil for trade. At Duke Town, King Eyo was as good as his word and when Mary and the five chiefs arrived, he showed great kindness and humility towards his guests. Before the palaver began, he proudly took them on a tour of his large house. For the first time they could witness for themselves what successful trading could achieve as opposed to endless, bloody and pointless battles, which only served to perpetuate animosity. They had never seen such opulence and never before had they had any reason to believe that such could be possessed by a native African. This was the sea change she had prayed for, and such a demonstration of wealth had saved her years of endless palavers. Mary had opened their eyes to the benefits and potential that honest work could achieve. The talks went well, and many old squabbles were settled peacefully. A whole world of opportunity now opened up in front of the men from the Okoyong; for the first time there was a promise of life beyond drinking and fighting. Mary prayed that that would remain the case, but if she had believed that from now on life would run smoothly, she was in for a rude awakening. The tribe's new found status led to a plethora of new buildings in the Okoyong; Chief Edem's son, Etim, was one of those who wished to have a fine new home.

Mary at Okoyong. Jeanie sitting on Mary's left (1890).

111

Death and retribution

Mr Ovens and Mary had become great friends in the short time he had been with her, kindred spirits in fact. Devotedly Scottish in both head and heart, their strong accents and great sense of humour were both a delight and a confusion to everyone who came within earshot. The tall, bearded Ovens, with a relaxed care-free demeanour, was a fine complement to Mary's more serious, over-worked and often short-tempered manner. The sound of their voices could sometimes be heard at a distance, long into the night, as they continued to work:

"O ye'll tak' the high road, and Ah'll tak the low road,
And Ah'll be in Scotlan' afore ye,
Fir me an' my true love will ne'er meet again,
On the bonnie, bonnie banks o' Loch Lomon'."

During one of their sing-songs, an extremely distraught Eme came rushing into the yard, *"Ma, Ma, you must come quick, much death to come!"*

Eme pulled at her arm to hasten her departure, but Mary wanted to know the reason for her panic. *"Quickly tell me."* Eme pulled. Mary insisted, *"Eme! Please."*

Reluctantly Eme let go, *"It is my brother Etim, a tree has struck him down, Death is in the room and waiting for him and they are preparing him for the journey."*

Mary, now only too aware of the urgency of the situation and its possible consequences, said, *"Oh goodness me! You should have pulled me harder!"*

Quickly she grabbed her medicine bag and they set off. Eme continued her story, telling her that Etim had been working close to a nearby village when a branch of a tree that he was cutting fell and struck him on the back of the neck. He was carried back to Ekenge and the news that the Chief's son had been struck down by the witchcraft of that village spread like wildfire. Eme told her there was vengeance in the air and, if he died, it would yet again end in the bloodshed of the innocent. When they arrived at the Chief's yard, the warriors were buzzing about like angry wasps, a frenzy of delirium, revenge and grief. As Mary approached Etim she feared the worst, and on examining him, found that no amount of medicine or prayer would save his earthly life; but until she could think of an alternative she would treat him as if there was still hope. After she had spent some time with the dying man, she told Edem,

"I have done what I can, I shall return in a few hours." The tribe's witchdoctor stood at Edem's shoulder and grinned.

Once back in her yard, she spoke with Mr Ovens, Tom his African worker, and Eme, and apprised them of the situation so that they could flee before Etim's death was announced. Eme wept, as much for the many who would soon die as for her brother; Tom and Mr Ovens seemed more concerned for Mary than themselves, *'bless them'*. Cries for vengeance would soon fill the air and the village where the accident happened would become the focus for the warriors' anger. How could it be stopped? Mary had no idea, but knew that sitting worrying about it would not help.

When she returned to Edem's yard, the witchdoctor was hard at work; these men were a crucial part of the natives' beliefs and a constant source of grief to her; there was no love lost between them and their distrust for her was returned in full. They reinforced every bad vice of the tribe they served and for any loss of a life within that tribe they attributed blame and exacted a terrible revenge. Their power was great and their influence unassailable. The painted man, adorned in animal skins, beads and paint, hovered over the lifeless body of Etim; his attempts to bring back life were based not on medicine but ritual. The room was filled with all the ju-ju of the witchdoctor, skulls, dead birds of every type and hue, charms containing human fingers, a palette of nightmares. He was holding a lighted palm leaf and blowing the evil-smelling smoke into Etim's nostrils; if that were not enough he was also rubbing pepper into his lifeless eyes and yelling chants and incantations loudly into his ears. It was a hideous scene. In the knowledge that she had done her best, all Mary could do was stand and watch. When he noticed Mary, the witchdoctor redoubled his efforts and blew, shouted and gesticulated more wildly as he circled the prostrate body. Mary had seen enough so left the room. She would have loved to have given the witchdoctor a great slap on the back of the head and tell him *'to behave'*, but for now she needed time to think, to make some kind of plan, and pray to God to help her stop the slaughter which was bound to follow.

The heavily-armed warriors were soon on their way to the offending village to do their worst; thankfully, Eme had sent word that Etim had died and many had already fled. As usual, almost every man had left the village; those who remained were helpless women and children. The warriors in no mood to leave empty handed, returned with this sad chain of prisoners to await execution. On hearing the news, Mary rushed to the compound to plead

113

with Edem for mercy. In the depths of his sorrow, the Chief was in no mood for leniency, *"Well Ma, your Lord has abandoned you. You save devil twin babies, yet you will not save my son. He is a cruel Lord."*

Mary tried to console him, *"He is now a son to the Lord, and he will be at peace."*

Edem was losing his patience, *"No more God noise! My eyes show me weak."* His tears betrayed his pain. He regained his composure and said with venom, *"But I am strong, and they will all die for my son!"*

Mary tried to continue, but Edem raised his hand abruptly to stop her speaking. Aware that she was wasting her breath, she said simply, *"I will honour your son, if you will let me."*

"It must be a great honour," Edem insisted.

Mary assured him, *"Oh, it will be!"*

She had nothing in her head but panic, but as she left an idea began to form. She ran back to the caravan to the accompaniment of the wailing of the terrified women and children prisoners, chained to posts like cattle awaiting their fate, and suggested to Mr Ovens, *"I'm going to go and sit by the prisoners, day and night, to keep the warriors at bay."*

Mr Ovens, normally a most genial man, said, *"No, that widnae work!"*

Mary was in no mood to be defied, *"I'm sorry Mr Ovens, but my mind is made up, and nothing you can do will stop me, so there!"*

He tried to explain, *"I only meant, you tak the day shift, and I'll tak the night shift."*

Mary, while on occasions endangering her own life, never asked others to do likewise, *"It's far too dangerous, I am a missionary, it is my work, you are a carpenter."*

He smiled and reminded her, *"Is there no other carpenter that comes to mind, that rose above his station?"*

Mary smiled at her foolishness and Ovens mimicked her earlier statement, *"my mind is made up, and nothing you can do will stop me, so there!"*

She scolded him, *"Mr Ovens, would you behave!"*

As soon as she had collected some clothes and props, she knelt down to pray and ask the Lord's forgiveness for what she was about to do. What she proposed was a moral dilemma for Mary; for this temporary 'sacrifice' she would put her Christian faith aside for native ritual, but innocent lives were at stake. She seriously doubted that others would see this act in the same light; she was sure that should it become known to her critics they would make much of it, yet she felt that her Lord would understand, and forgive, and that was all that mattered to her.

Before leaving for Edem's yard, she had raided the mission box of all the coloured silks, shirts, vests and brightly-patterned linens that had been sent from Scotland. She had witnessed many strange rites and rituals since her arrival in Africa, and noted that colour, ostentation and splendour were the features most admired and, on that premise, she set about her task. Firstly she dressed Etim in the finest suit she had, with a patterned waistcoat, and placed him in a magnificent chair; then she shaved his head and painted it yellow. Around his head she wound a bright silk turban and upon that, she placed a magnificent top hat draped in red silk with colourful feathers standing tall; over his shoulders she placed a fine linen tablecloth. To one of his hands she tied a carved walking stick and to the other his finest whip; to complete the bizarre display, a large, bright, striped umbrella was placed over him to shade him from the sun. On a table beside him were placed the skulls of his enemies, his weapons and some of his prized possessions and, for her own sake, she added a few candles, a little flicker of light in a grimly dark scenario. As a final act she placed a large mirror in front of Etim, so that, according to tribal lore, his spirit could see what had been done and be happy.

When the people came to see him, without exception, they yelled with delight and began jumping and dancing with joy; as she had hoped, all immediate thoughts of slaughter vanished from their minds. The scene was complete and, though not in any sense 'traditional,' was as fine a sight as any could remember. To begin the celebrations, they called for barrels of rum. Barrel after barrel was brought, opened, and consumed, guns were fired into the air, swords were brandished, and they sang and danced raising clouds of dust, all to the accompaniment of the pounding drums; it was mayhem. While it was far from the ceremony Mary would have wished for Etim, she had given them something to celebrate and, for the time being at least, it kept their minds off the executions.

Mary slipped away and left them to their celebration and, more resolute than ever, she and Chairlie Ovens took their positions as guards over the poor, chained, souls. The prisoners had waited hourly for their deaths to come, and as the burial of Etim could not take place without sacrifice, they all now held their breath and waited. Mary quickly wrote a note to Duke Town with a request and sent Tom to deliver it post haste. As the noise of the celebration began to subside, they were only too aware that time was running out. Edem had seemed content with the work Mary had done for Etim, but now, awash with rum, he was as ready as the rest of the tribe for the prisoners to follow his son. During the afternoon the drums had fallen silent and the drunken warriors began to congregate. The witchdoctor led Edem in the parade and buzzed in front of the Chief, weaving and waving, chanting and wailing, so much so that he tripped over his own feet. Impatiently, Edem shook his head, stepped on the prone witchdoctor and carried on.

A chair was brought for the Chief and placed in the middle of the yard; he took his seat, leant forward and glowered at the prisoners and their protectors. Mary stood up, preparing herself for what might happen next. The witchdoctor had picked himself up and continued his sorcery, his arms flailing and brandishing his fetish-adorned stick; suddenly he stopped and took from a pouch what Mary recognised to be Esre beans. This was bad news - the Esre bean, ground up and put into water, was poisonous and would be given to the accused to drink. It was believed that if guilty they would die and if innocent they would live. It reminded her of witch trials in Scotland, where the charge alone was a death sentence. The trial consisted of being ducked into water, and if the accused drowned they were innocent, and if they survived, they were found guilty and burned at the stake. Like this, it was a sham and she couldn't let that happen here. As the witchdoctor pounded the beans, she respectfully approached Edem and bravely asserted, *"They will not take the Esre bean!"*

Edem, full of rum and indignation, shouted, *"Ma, you have done enough, you must go!"*

The other chiefs and warriors became agitated by the delay, the drums and chanting began again, louder and faster. The witchdoctor ordered the guards to unchain one woman and she was led away. Unsure of what to do, and well aware that the woman would surely die if she didn't follow, Mary decided to go off in pursuit. By the time she caught up with them, the woman was raising the cup of poison to her lips; Mary ran towards her and shouted out, *"Don't, don't drink it!"*

The young girl threw the cup to the ground. The guards and witchdoctor turned their anger towards Mary. She took a few steps away from the girl and the warriors began to follow. She took another few steps and she let out an almighty shout to the captive, *"Run lass, run, go to my house!"*

By the time the drunken guards knew what had happened their prisoner had gone, it was all over in seconds. The witchdoctor ran off, undoubtedly to report to Edem, and the guards followed Mary back to the compound. She could see the witchdoctor tell Edem of her role in the escape, and the Chief's head fell, more in frustration than anger. He lifted his head and bellowed, *"Ma, you must do no more!"*

She replied, *"I must do what my God tells me."*

Edem reminded her, *"You are here under our protection. You must obey our laws."*

She had an answer, *"So be it. I ask that the prisoners take the Mbiam oath."*

This oath entailed the application of a foul-smelling liquid by means of a stick on to the tongue, head and foot of the accused, who, in a terrified state, believed that if they lied it would kill them, and though not pleasant, was much better than the Esre bean. She was now playing Edem's game, and if he was to be fair, he should allow it. The other chiefs consulted him and reluctantly they agreed.

Edem ordered, *"Let it be!"*

The trade-off worked and all but one woman and her infant were released. When Mary demanded that they should also be set free, Edem had had enough, *"Ma, if you will not stop now, my men will burn your house down and drive you out!"*

She could see that he had run out of patience; he had felt the loss of his son more deeply than she had thought, and this little white woman, challenging his authority in front of other chiefs, was pushing him to his limit. She felt for his plight, but in all conscience she could not let these two die.

Edem began to plead with her, *"We have done more for you than we have ever done. You will die and we will have our way."*

This was as honest a statement as she had heard in all her life; it was also the sad realisation that only her death would silence her. She now felt that any further obstruction by her would serve no useful purpose, but the Lord had another idea. The remaining captives were a young woman and her babe-in-arms but Edem's heart was hard. Suddenly Eme approached her brother, *"I ask you great Chief, to show mercy to this woman and child. There is much strength and wisdom in mercy. Your name will be carried far and wide by the mother's words, as she grows old, and by the son's, as he grows into a man."*

Eme wept and prostrated herself on the ground before Edem and continued to plead, *"Their skulls will add no honour to your house."*

Edem and the other chiefs looked shocked at Eme's passionate plea. He rose from his chair, stood before Eme and offered his hand; as she stood up he announced, *"In Etim's name, release the girl!"*

For the first time there would be no human sacrifices; the burial of Etim was accompanied only by the striped umbrella, the mirror and one slaughtered cow.

The next few days were difficult and dangerous; for safety's sake most of the captives had stayed with Mary until they could flee unseen into the bush. Tom returned with two missionaries and the equipment Mary had asked for; it was in the nick of time. The two workers, who arrived with the paraphernalia were extremely nervous, which under the circumstances she could fully understand. There was an oppressive air about the place and you could almost cut the tension with a machete. It was new territory for these men and, given the events of the last few weeks, it had taken an act of great faith to answer her desperate call. As the sun fell, the crowds began to gather. Word had spread so quickly that soon the area around the house was teeming with excited natives; they had come to see a magic lantern show. The people of Ekenge, those brave enough to face the unknown, came into the room and sat down; as usual it was mostly women and children, the men stood in the doorway ready to make a quick escape should devils appear. The projection of a picture on to a white sheet from a smoking light source was indeed like the devil's work. The first time Mary had witnessed lantern slides was in Dundee as a wee lass; it was as if by magic to see deep into the jungles of Africa or be amongst tigers in India. What would the tribe make of it?

The smoking projector spat sparks of fire as the liquid burned away, the audience watched every action and movement of the projectionist and, as the sparks flew, ducked down and 'oohed' and 'aahed' together. The projectionist's hand shook as he attempted to load the first slide; Mary placed her hand upon his to give him strength, smiled, and said, *"God is with you."* The young man looked at her and nodded, and with her guiding hand inserted the first slide. It was an image of Jesus' entry into Jerusalem, which was met with a chorus of delight, a sea of wide eyes and huge grins. She explained to her flock the image before them and they applauded. Edem, who was standing by the door, called to one of his men to check behind the house to see if Jesus was actually there. The man returned and shook his head; Edem stroked his chin and remained confused. A stunned silence greeted the slide of Christ's crucifixion; it seemed to deeply touch everyone who saw it. Tears were shed by some, mostly by those who had come to accept the Lord in to their hearts, but even the most hardened amongst them seemed to be genuinely moved.

For all the natives' rites of sacrifice, practised for generations, this kind of cruelty against a king they could not comprehend.

The mood lifted as they watched scenes of Scotland's cities, high tenements with broad streets, parks, carnivals, buses, horses, cows, sheep, ladies in fine dresses, men in smart suits, wonders they never knew existed. Towards the end of the show were slides of the military, not by her choosing, for Mary didn't agree with their general use, though at times the showing of these slides had saved many a life. The first was of a regiment of the British army, heavily armed with rifle and cannon, ready to fight. The next was of a warship, bristling with guns and bigger than anyone could imagine - the mission steam launch, 'smoking canoe', was the largest sailing craft most of them had ever seen. Mary turned to see Edem staring at the image, never seeming to blink, never taking his eyes off it. When the slide was replaced, Edem looked at her with a questioning stare, a look to suggest she had somehow betrayed him. The final slides were to entertain, moving from one slide to another gave the impression of movement. The subject was the stealing of a goose, the thief's eyes moved from side to side as he tried to escape with his loot, only to be apprehended by a stout policeman. That was followed by a juggler in action, which brought the proceedings to a successful end. Hopefully there had been enough in this show to occupy even the most idle of minds.

After the performance, when all was quiet, Edem came to Mary for a private talk. As they sat away from prying eyes, he began to open up his heart to her.

He sounded disappointed. *"Did you show these things to make us afraid of your powers?"*

The thought had never crossed Mary's mind, *"Were you afraid?"*

"You have said that peace would come from respect, not fear."

Mary agreed, *"You are correct Chief, but others do not have your wisdom."*

He was still unimpressed, *"Pah!..... You give great honour to my son, and give no honour to me."*

She apologised, *"That was not my intention, I honour you both."*

"But you don't! We have our customs, as you do, and you do not respect them."

"But you don't respect mine."

He countered, *"But it is **my** country!"*

She answered as best she could, *"Yes it is, but when bad customs mean death for innocent people, it is time for those customs to be questioned, and if found wrong, then to be changed."*

Edem, still confused, asked, *"If I went to your country, would you let me do the same? Are the only laws British laws?"* Mary had no answer and he carried on, *"Are you not sad at the death of the Lord's son? The death of my son makes me see the sadness of death."*

Suddenly, Edem fell to his knees at her feet and Mary stood up in shock and surprise.

"Ma, sit please, we have not been at ease, and you have battled as strong as any warrior for what you believe. But I grow weary of death and vengeance. I wish peace, so we can sit like you at the caravan, and not seek out another battle to fight, and lose more sons."

Mary, touched by his frankness, reminded him, *"There are always battles to fight, but not all battles kill. You must fight as hard for peace as war, fight to keep your mothers and children safe from hunger and disease. These are battles worthy of winning for a great Chief."*

It would be wrong to say that things became normal from then on, as there was no normal, no usual, no status quo. It would be more correct to say that the number of dramatic events lessened. The chiefs began to do regular trade with Duke Town and Creek Town; they had found a new outlet for their excess energies other than making war. Mary was now accepted as a friend who had the tribe's best interests at heart and she was regularly consulted to give judgement and officiate in inter-tribal disputes.

She now felt that the Okoyong was much safer, not because they had all accepted God, far from it, but they had found a balance to their lives, free from constant conflict; but that was not the same throughout the region. As her health once again began to fail, there was a call for her to settle a dispute between two warring tribes some distance away. The messenger reported to her that a battle was soon to begin and that many people would die. Equally concerning was the probability that it would spill over into the Okoyong and all her good work would be undone; so, despite her ill-health, she was determined to go. Edem was unhappy with her decision and could see that she was unwell; though he knew it was pointless to argue, he did, *"Ma, if you are to do this foolish thing, I will send my warriors with you."*

Mary knew that an armed bodyguard would only inflame the situation, *"I thank you Chief, but warriors would only make things worse; I must go alone."*

Despite her stubbornness, he continued to try and reason with her, *"But Ma, you are a woman alone, it is not your place, your place is in the Okoyong. You must take warriors, we will protect you, you are now an agent of the Egbo."*

Mary thanked him but declined, *"Give me two bearers and an Egbo drummer to keep me safe. Let the drummer clear my path to the edge of the Okoyong, from then on the Lord will protect me."*

Edem was happy to at least do this for her, *"As you will Ma, but they will not see you as we do."*

As early as she could, Mary dismissed her two guards and, led only by the drummer, stumbled long into the night. The Egbo drummer announced her arrival to the warring chiefs who had waited anxiously. Undoubtedly, had she arrived with armed warriors, blood would have been spilt immediately, but a woman alone was an entirely different proposition. As her fever began to take hold, her patience and negotiating skills sank to a very low ebb. The chiefs, seeing her weakness, began to surround her, shouting and waving their spears, and she feared the worst. The last she remembered was the sound of shouting, then a loud buzzing noise echoed in her head just before she collapsed in an untidy heap on the ground. When Mary awoke, she found that she had been taken to a quiet room; expecting to be a prisoner, she was happy to find that she was unbound and in bed. The first face she saw she recognised - it was Chief Otu whom she had previously treated and cured. Cheerily he asked, *"Ma, you come to see me?"* and then announced to the other chiefs, *"Stand back, this is the Great Ma!"*

Delighted to see a friendly face, she said, *"Otu, how are you keepin'?"*

Though happy to see her, he was very concerned, *"I am well Ma, but you are not, you must rest."*

Aware of the consequences of any delay, with some impatience she insisted, *"No, we must palaver."*

She sat up in bed and rose unsteadily to her feet. She knew her illness would only get worse and while she could, she must get on with the job at hand. Through her fever, she listened patiently to the arguments of both sides and, after some consideration, gave her judgement. Following further discussion, and some objections, this was accepted. Otu was grateful for her wise counsel, *"Ma, I hope you will take this as payment for your work."*

She was delighted that the war would not happen, but the payment for her work, two boxes of gin, was not appreciated. The chiefs had expected the gift to be opened immediately and shared by those attending, but Mary knew that that would be a mistake; and the more she refused to open the gin, as their thirst grew, the more threatening the mood became. Otu was having problems controlling the other chiefs as temptation turned to desperation.

121

Out of the fog of fever an idea came - they knew that as an Egbo agent they could not lay hands on her or her belongings, so Mary took off her shawl and threw it over the boxes. Howls of protest filled the air and, no matter how much they badgered her, she would not relent. Eventually, exhausted and in desperate need of sleep, she made a concession. She took one bottle out of each box, pretending that they should check that the bottles were not poisoned and, as they began to drink, she quietly instructed the bearers to set off for home with her bags and the remainder of the gin. While they drank and caroused, Mary slept. No matter how raucous they became, they could not interrupt her fevered sleep. In the morning, before the others awoke, Mary slipped out and made her way home.

Not long after her return, she finally succumbed to the fever's grip. Chairlie, with the help of the bairns, tried to administer what medical assistance they could, but when he discovered Mary in the deepest terrors of the fever, with scissors in hand cutting off her long hair, he decided he could do no more, and immediately had her taken to the hospital in Duke Town.

1890
The accidental visitor

After two weeks in the white-walled hospital, set high above the town, Mary sat up in bed and, although still weak, was beginning to improve. The nurse had done her best to make Mary comfortable; and she had trimmed Mary's chopped hair to make it at least presentable, though no amount of styling could hide the patently obvious fact that her hair was now very, very short. In this Victorian age, long hair was not only viewed upon as fashionable, it was seen as an essential requisite for all young women. Short hair was seldom seen and, if displayed, was regarded as a mark of subservience if not downright shame. This would be another black mark against her. Had she cut it to show her indifference to convention and wagging tongues? Or was it, that in the depths of illness, she simply wanted to cool her fevered brow?

While she grudgingly admired the work the nurses and doctors did on other's behalf, she always felt that she knew best, especially whether she was well or she was not. Mary was a reluctant patient and desperate to return to work, but being forced to take another week of bed rest set her at odds with those around her. In fact, she had so improved that she was becoming bored and impish. An elegant young man entered the room; he was tall, slim, with dark eyes, hair and moustache, dressed as all the young men of the Mission, in dark jacket, white shirt, tie and light flannel trousers. He had come to visit a patient who, he was informed, had been discharged earlier in the day. Mary watched him as she began to sup from a soup bowl. With no reason to stay, the young man walked towards the door. Mary, in a fit of pique, threw her spoon to the floor. The young man either didn't hear the clatter or, in his haste, chose to ignore it, so Mary called to him, *"Hey, laddie, would you mind.....? The spoon."* He stopped, returned to pick it up and hand it to her.

"Thank you, the soup's difficult tae eat wi' yer fingers," she said, with a deal of sarcasm.

He stuttered, *"I..... I..... hear you are the famous Miss Slessor."*

She shrugged as if offended, *"So do I..... though what it means in the scheme of things, only He can tell. And you?"*

The young man stumbled over his words, *"Oh, oh I'm fine, and, and, and not at all famous."*

She smiled and said, *"It's much better that way, they build you up, put you on a pedestal, just so you're easier tae knock aff it. I meant, what is your name? You have mine; now, in polite society, we should both know each other's. I can hardly go on calling you laddie, can I?"*

Apologetically he said, *"Of course, it's Charles."*

Mary waited to hear his second name, *"Your parents must have thought you an ugly bairn to no' have given you another name. Here was me thinking what a bonnie young man you were."*

Embarrassed both by the omission and the compliment, he blurted out, *"Charles, Charles Morrison. I'm sorry, you seem to have caught me off guard, I am not usually this tongue-tied. Do you have this effect on all men?"*

She gave him a cold stare and ignored the comment. Changing the subject, she asked, *"What brings you to Duke Town? And if you intend to say a boat, you can leave now."*

He was relieved that she had a sense of humour. A little more at ease, he continued, *"I am a teacher."*

She picked up her Bible from the bedside, held it up and asked, *"Book or....."* she pointed to the book he was holding, *"book?"*

Charles looked confused. She continued, *"Are you a religious missionary teacher?"* she asked, lifting the Bible again.

The difference now clarified, he was happy to reply, *"Oh, book? No just the normal kind, no, no, the Bible is for those such as you to teach, and the word is that you surpass all others in that respect."*

She gave the credit where it was due, *"The Bible is my textbook, I have little to do with it."*

He looked down at the book he was holding and asked, *"So have you no time for other books?"*

She was taken aback, *"Goodness lad,* **I** *also live to read, to learn, to be educated, amused, confused and bemused. But I daresay you have a talent to teach."*

Modestly he shrugged his shoulders, *"And your talent?"*

Mary, always uncomfortable talking about herself said reluctantly, *"My talent, if it could be called such, is probably patience; to listen, and with God's help, to understand whit others say; too often people only hear their own voice in any palaver. Mind you, there is often great goodness in silence, understanding in silence, honesty in silence, peace in silence; ye ken that wars never begin with silence. A hollow victory at such a great price, victory for power not sense, the battle won but the war lost."*

Enthusiastically he added, *"To read is to learn. If you don't, all you have is your own experience, one-sided, often shallow and self-serving. Reading brings contrary experience, laughter, tears and tragedy, and how others have been able to cope, how they put their woes behind them, put them in their rightful place."*

She lifted her Bible, *"A bit like my book?..... Eh?"*

The young man thrown off balance, nodded an agreement, then asked, *"Have romance and passion a place in your world?"*

She said, with an amount of embarrassment, *"The love o' God is my life."*

Aware he may have asked an inappropriate question, he apologised, *"Sorry, I didn't mean to be personal."*

She put him at his ease, *"No, it's fine, the subject seldom arises."*

There was an awkward pause as Mary seemed to tire. Thinking he may have outstayed his welcome, he asked kindly, *"Could I lend you this book? You may have time to enjoy it; it is 'Sketches by Boz' by Charles Dickens."*

Mary shook her head, *"Thank you, but I'm afraid my eyes are weary after so long in the bush, they strain easily in these bright Duke Town skies, though oddly, sleep is still a stranger to me. I fear it would take me a twelvemonth to finish a chapter."*

Enthusiastically he asked, *"Could I offer my services as your eyes for a time? I could read to you."*

"I'm no' a bairn!" she shouted then, softly, *"though I daresay a few pages would be a blessing. Thank you."*

He pulled up a chair and sat down beside her and, putting the book on the bed, he began to read. She made herself comfortable and closed her eyes. He began, *'Chapter one, Our Parish, The Beadle, The Parish Engine, The Schoolmaster, How much is conveyed in those two short words – The Parish!'*

Mary opened her eyes and took a sharp intake of breath at those two short words, the parish. He continued, *'And with how many tales of distress and misery, of broken fortune and ruined hopes, too often of unrelieved wretchedness and successful knavery are they associated.'*

Mary's memories and fear of the 'care' of the Parish in Dundee were still fresh in her mind; she nodded her head in agreement, and added, *"Aye, right enough!"*

As he began to read chapter two, he said, *"Oh I believe you'll like this Miss Slessor."*..... *'The Curate, We commenced our last chapter with the beadle of our parish, because we are deeply sensible of the importance and dignity of his office. We will begin the present with the clergyman.'*

Mary smiled in anticipation and giggled like an excited child, *"Ooh, this should be good."*

'Our curate is a young gentleman of such prepossessing appearance, and fascinating manners, that within one month after his first appearance in the parish, half the young-lady inhabitants were melancholy with religion, and the other half desponding with love.'

Mary rolled her eyes in mock swoon, Charles raced on, *'Never were so many young ladies seen in our parish-church on Sunday before; and never had the little round angels' faces on Mr Tomkin's monument in the side aisle, beheld such devotion on earth as they all exhibited.'*

"Aye, we've seen them, paper angels!" Mary laughed loudly under the bedcovers, hiding her face as if to conceal her enjoyment that she, Dickens, and Mr Morrison were mocking the clergy; he smiled at her joy. *'He was about five-and-twenty when he first came to astonish the parishioners. He parted his hair on the centre of his forehead in the form of a Norman arch, wore a brilliant (a diamond) of the first water on the fourth finger of his left hand (which he always applied to his left cheek when he read prayers), and had a deep sepulchral voice of unusual solemnity.'* As he continued to read, the soothing sound of his voice appeared to send her to sleep. He remained by her bed reading and as he did so Mary's hand moved, her fingertips touched the back of his right hand and rested there. When he turned a page, he moved his left hand and very gently stroked her small, sun-tanned, calloused hand. The shadows began to

lengthen and a nurse arrived with a lamp to allow him to continue reading.

After some time he whispered very softly, *"Well, that's the end of chapter four, shall we begin chapter five?"* At that moment the nurse returned and motioned him to leave. He took Mary's hand, gently placed it under the bedcovers and whispered, *"Goodnight."*

The next day, Charles rushed through the streets of Duke Town heading towards the hospital; Mary spotted him through the window and jumped back into bed; she quickly ran a comb through her hair and then hid it under her pillow. When he entered, he attempted to make it look like a chance meeting; he dusted himself down, straightened his tie and casually approached her bed.

He enquired nervously, *"Oh Miss Slessor, you are still with us? How are you? You are looking well."*

Mary still treated small talk with contempt, *"I thank you for yer kindness, but I know exactly how I look!"* she replied sternly. He was uncomfortable and shuffled his feet. *"Sit, sit."* she told him. And he sat.

To fill the awkward silence, he asked, *"Do you miss home, Miss Slessor?"*

*"Which 'home' do you mean? the place of my birth, or Ekenge? My heart is with God, and wherever he leads me, **that** is my home."*

He became reflective and confessed, *"Ah, home."* He breathed out heavily, *"As you may know, I am not long settled here from Scotland, and often find myself confused and, dare I say, alone and sometimes.......... a little afraid."*

She smiled, *"If you carry the Lord in your heart, you need not be afraid. We are weak, but with His strength we can do anything, fight all demons, love without fear or ridicule or reward. God and one is an army..... Laddie, if you are afraid you are at least still sane, there is little not to be afraid of here, the jungle, the wild animals, the drunken native, the drunken European, the disease, the military, evil and, especially, the curse of the self-righteous; each a danger of equal magnitude."*

He laughed and said, *"You seem to have scant regard for the pillars of our community?"*

As if sharing a secret, she leant over towards him and whispered, *"When I see how they treat those we are here to serve, I think - are not pillars to hold things up, not to hold things down?"*

She leant back in bed and closed her eyes. Not knowing how to respond, he changed the subject, *"Well, are you for more of our book?"* He clarified his question, *"Mine, not yours."*

She smiled and replied, *"Aye..... that would be grand."*

"I can't remember where we got to the last time." He began to flick through the pages.

With her eyes closed, she said, *"You had just got to the end of chapter four, and you were to begin the next."*

Charles looked shocked and glanced quickly down at the book, uncomfortable that evidently she had been awake during the hand-stroking episode; he tried to loosen his shirt collar and, before beginning, he wiped his brow with the handkerchief from his breast pocket. While thus occupied, he didn't notice Mary open one eye to view his discomfort, smile a warm smile, and once again close her eye.

Her final week in hospital passed and Mary was discharged. Chairlie Ovens came to escort her home, and as they walked through the streets of Duke Town, Mary kept looking over her shoulder but saw no sign of Mr Morrison. Unseen by Mary, Charles stood at his schoolroom window and watched her walk through the town, wishing that he had been brave enough to stop her and tell her what was on his mind and in his heart.

The letters begin

The journey back to Ekenge was strange; Mary was filled with new emotions and although no words had been spoken to that effect, she was suffering from a great attachment to Mr Morrison. It may have been simply a romantic conceit to believe a young handsome man, he twenty-four and she forty-two, could form any kind of attachment to *'an auld biddy like me'.* She returned to the Okoyong with a sense of loss, and though otherwise full of vim and vigour, her heart was back in Duke Town. Of course, that was until she was once again re-united with her bairns and with Eme and Edem. Her time in Duke Town may have been a flight of fancy, but now she had to put all that behind her and get on with her work. Once she had fed, washed, caught up with their tales, and prayed with the bairns, and when the last one was settled, she had time to reflect by herself. This did not last for long, as Eme soon arrived to welcome her back and have 'a blether'.

Eme asked, *"Ma, how are you? The last time I saw you, you were fighting fever devils and I feared I would not see you again."*

Mary explained, *"I was in the Lord's hands."*

Eme motioned to put her fingers in her ears, then tilted her head towards

Mary and observed, *"You have a strange shine from inside, the way a branch glows when filled with fire, and this time I do not think it is anger."*

Mary became uncomfortable at the direction the conversation was heading, *"You see river spirits, silly woman."*

Eme shook her head and said as a matter of fact, *"No."*

Mary stared sternly at Eme; Eme was enjoying her sister's discomfort. *"I shall go and let you sleep."*

"Yes, I think you should!"

Eme rose to leave but when she neared the door, she turned and said, *"Oh, I have a letter for you, it is in a foreign hand,"* Eme examined the envelope, she motioned with her hand and body, *"the lines sweep up and down like the waves on the river. The letter it glows like a....."*

Mary grew more impatient, *"Yes, I know!"* Quickly she rose from her chair and snatched the letter from Eme's hand. *"Out, out, this is not for **your** peepers!"*

Infuriatingly, Eme chuckled as she left. Mary gazed at the letter and her heart raced; as Eme had said, the handwriting did sweep like the waves of the river; she was sure it was from Charles. As if the missive were red hot, she dropped it to the floor, stood with her back to it, and tried to take control of herself. She blushed at her schoolgirl show of emotion and scolded herself, *"The letter can wait till the morning!"*

Mary checked the bairns and put the kettle on the fire for a cup of tea, and thought to herself, *'I may do some correspondence before going to sleep.'*

She was fooling no one, least of all herself. Once the tea was prepared, she sat and picked up a book. She read a paragraph but did not take in one word of what she had read. Out of the corner of her eye she could see the letter glow in the reflected light of the fire. She fell to the floor, picked it up and held it closely, afraid that it might vanish. Mary looked at the envelope, examining every character closely, over and over again. *"To Miss Mary M. Slessor, Ekenge."* She thought, *'if the letter was to tell me that Charles disliked all I had ever said to him,'* at least she would retain the envelope as a keepsake. Unopened, she put the letter down again and poured out a cup of tea. With mounting anticipation she once again picked it up and opened the letter very carefully to avoid tearing the perfectly-written envelope. Even if it were *'a demand for the return of the books he lent me'* she thought to herself, she would understand. Inside there was one full page, *'well, this is quite a long letter just to ask for his books to be returned'.* She began to read:

Dear Miss Slessor, ('*so far so good,*' she thought,)

May I take this opportunity to wish you well, and hope that you will continue to make a full recovery. My teaching goes well and hopefully my endeavours, and those of my pupils, will not be in vain. I hope that your good self, so very far away at Ekenge, will also soon be back to your outstanding best. I'm sorry if that last sentence gave the impression that you have to be at your 'outstanding best' to achieve success, (my pen sometimes says things before my head has time to consider them), but if I may make so bold, from our meetings at Duke Town, I think that you do 'outstanding' as standard. I hope that my frankness does not cause you embarrassment, if so please except my sincere apologies, but it is what everyone says of you, who talk of such things, and since having had the honour of meeting you, I humbly concur. Only to add that I am sure the great man Dickens, and his favourite characters, would be as proud of your acquaintance as I.

It has been preoccupying my conscience since our last meeting, so I must make a shameful and selfish admission to you. While visiting you in hospital, and wanting so much to see you well, I also had a wish that the doctors would not do their work quite so efficiently, and that you had been kept under their care for fully another two weeks, which would have given us time to finish what we had begun. I pray you shall forgive me, and hope that you will keep the books we were reading as a gift, a small token of my deep admiration for the wonderful work you do. I would like to think that you might find a few minutes, in the coming weeks, to write a reply. As I would like to be assured that you remain in good health, and that under your good guidance the 'bairns' continue to flourish.

I know that God will continue to share his blessings with you, as I can think of no soul who deserves them more.

Respectfully Yours,

Charles Morrison

The letter made her head reel.

For the next few months her writing became prolific - to friends, the Missionary Record and to Charles. At last she had found a soul mate. Over the months, their words became less guarded and they began to openly share their deepest fears and greatest expectations. Her visits back to Duke Town, a place she once had no fondness for, became, on the most flimsy of excuses, more frequent. On one of those visits, the two found time to sit alone and talk. It was a particularly fine afternoon. Happy to be together, they sat on the hillside overlooking Duke Town.

"*It is a wonderful country, is it not?*" said Mary.

He agreed but added, *"There is only one better."*

She knew the answer yet asked, *"Scotland?"* Charles nodded reflectively.

Mary confessed, *"I miss my family, but for me there are now only echoes of who I was in Scotland. My life is here now, and though I will go back, I have found a home here, the love of a family, and a love for a people and a country."*

He was glad that she could share this with him. *"That is good, but do you never feel alone? Do you never wish to share little things with someone, someone you can reach out to and touch? Someone who will tell you to have a seat and a rest, and will take your burden and carry it for a while? I know you have the Lord, and I wish that I had your belief, your strength, your conviction, your assuredness. I am weak, but when I am with you, you make me strong."*

She tried to reassure him, *"But loneliness comes from living without the Lord in your heart. Without His love you can be as alone in the vast deserts of Egypt as in the busy streets of Edinburgh. He is what makes us complete; He gives us love, protection, strength, power to do good works, and fight the darkest demons that hide in all of us."*

Charles wanted the certainty of life that Mary had, *"Will you teach me?"*

She smiled and said fondly, *"There is little I can teach you that you do not already know. He is inside you now, 'seek and ye shall find'."* Mary put her hand on his, *"But I will help you find Him,"* and added jokingly, *"I ken whar' to look."*

Charles smiled and held her hand and they sat quietly in the afternoon sun.

After a time Mary felt the need to ask, *"Is there no one in your life you depend upon?"*

He replied, *"I have my beloved mother, far away in Kirkintilloch, and a brother in America..... but the only one I want to spend the rest of my life with is..... you Mary."*

Mary said nothing, but continued to gaze into the distance; she smiled, nodded in agreement and squeezed his hand.

During the previous few months she had hoped that this moment would arrive; she knew that she was in love with Charles, and now that he had declared his love, she was concerned by what the world would make of it. Mary had thought long and hard of the potential repercussions of such a declaration and although her prayers had been answered, she felt that they would now have to be stronger than ever to weather the storm. They agreed to say nothing officially for the time being, and when he presented her with an engagement ring, she kept it with the rest of her treasured possessions until they had notified the Foreign Mission Board of their intention to marry.

Word of their liaison was soon known in Ekenge; as she knew, there was no secret which could be hidden indefinitely in this close-knit community. She became aware that the news had reached this far when Chief Edem asked to see her. Edem sat in his hut and welcomed in his old friend, *"Ma, it has been too long, come, come. You do well? I hear you take a young husband."*

Edem was never one to beat about the bush, but this must have been a record for getting to the point. As she could not deny it, she replied, *"Well, yes."*

"But you an old woman!"

For a few seconds Mary was speechless but once she had caught her breath, she defended her actions, *"What does that matter, if we love each other?"*

The old chief asked her to sit beside him, *"But marriage are for babies, you far too old. He is a young man, he will not stay with you if you do not give him children. It is in the nature of man to make many children! I know, I marry many times, and have many, many children, no old women!"*

Mary knew that he was trying to be kind; she tried to explain, *"That's as may be, but....."*

Edem had more to say, *"Ma, we wish you to be happy, you should marry an old man like you, he will not ask of you what you cannot give. We think if you are unhappy you will leave the Okoyong, and never return. All our bad old ways would come back, you have made us good. Though only some of us believe in your God, we **all** believe in you."*

Mary had no argument that would convince Edem, so told him, *"I thank you Chief. I will always do what I believe to be right. If I go, I will get a good woman to take my place. Until then you and I will work together, the Lord will tell me what is right, I must trust in Him."*

A few days later Mary was summoned again, this time to the office of the new administrator at the Mission, Mr Stibbles, who, armed with Mr Ross' notes and reports, was taking a similarly high-handed approach where Mary was concerned. Like an errant schoolchild called to the headmaster's door, she awaited his summons. *"Come!"*

Mary turned the door handle and entered his office. Mr Stibbles was sitting behind his desk and smiling, *"Please sit Miss Slessor, how are you progressing after your most recent illness?"*

Her answer had the same sincerity as the question, *"I am well thank you, and yourself?"*

He continued, *"I am in the rudest of health, I seem to thrive in this climate, better than most. I am seldom ill; actually, I find the air quite invigorating."*

Mary, impatient with his prevarication, asked, *"How can I assist you, Mr Stibbles?"*

He smiled a broad smile and said, *"That's what I admire about you, Miss Slessor, your spirit to confront things no matter how sord..... no matter how difficult."* He cleared his throat, *"I believe that you have formed a..... an..... an alliance."*

She knew exactly what Mr Stibbles was talking about, but she had no intention of making his task any easier, *"You have heard? Oh, I'm so glad. I was worried that you might not approve, he is a wonderful man but he is afraid I will leave him."*

Even if he could have found any words to say, Mr Stibbles was too shocked to interrupt.

"We have agreed that if I leave him, I'll get him another good woman to take my place."

While Mary continued, Mr Stibbles sat with his mouth wide open. *"He thinks I'm too old to have children, and that his bad habits will return. I'm not so sure, I think he has changed since I first met him."*

Mr Stibbles stumbled over his words, *"Wha..... Wh....."*

She decided to let him off the hook, *"Yes, Chief Edem is such a good man."*

Stibbles exhaled heavily and relaxed, *"I believe we are at cross purposes, Miss Slessor. I meant a more personal alliance? I don't want to be indelicate....."*

Stibbles hoped that Mary would volunteer the information, but she enjoyed watching him squirm, so asked, *"I'm afraid you will have to be, otherwise we'll be here a' day."*

At last he managed to say, *"It's to do..... with..... your marriage plans."*

She slapped her thigh, pretending to be surprised and delighted, *"You wish to congratulate Charles and me on our engagement?"*

"No, not exactly," he stuttered.

"You want an invite to the wedding? No sooner said than done."

His expression became more severe, *"I am sorry to say that such an action will never be sanctioned!"*

The delight vanished from her face. While narrowing her eyes, she said very slowly and deliberately, *"By you?"*

Stibbles looked sheepish and then returned to his pompous best, *"I must advise the Mission Board of the situation, as I see it. Mr Morrison is a fine, young,* and much valued teacher in Duke Town; his work is known to many, and he is highly respected; we would not countenance losing him."

It was obvious that his evaluation didn't appear to include her contribution to the Mission, yet she had to agree, "I believe Charles has been sent to do important work, I could not agree more."

He became suspicious of her apparent acceptance of his decision; there was now a hint of panic in his voice, "Does that mean..... that you wish to join him here?"

She couldn't lie, "If that is what the Lord ordains for me, of course I would."

He was not happy that she might return to compromise his position in Duke Town, "But, but, but..... what of your own work in the Okoyong?"

She pointed out, "As you don't mention it, I take it you think it of no consequence, so I would no' be missed."

Stibbles moved uncomfortably in his chair, "Obviously I wouldn't say that!" and added flippantly, "but as they say, 'a woman's work is never done'."

His patronising attitude released Mary's fiery temper, "You can't have it both ways Mr Stibbles! You are no different from the very worst of European, or African, men here; men have a' the power and the women do a' the work! I will leave it to God to decide my future, not a tin-pot, pen pusher like you. Good day Mr Stibbles!"

The sound of the door slamming echoed across Duke Town. As she walked away, she felt that 'losing her rag' might not have been the best course of action, *but it felt braw, oh, it felt awfie braw.*

1891
Engaged and home again

With her furlough overdue, she began to make plans for her absence. A palaver with Eme and Edem produced a guarantee that they would insist on good behaviour while she was away; whether it was a pledge they meant to keep, or simply a ruse to get rid of her for a while, only time would tell. With these assurances, Mary asked for a volunteer to take her place. When no one stepped forward, she resolved to stay despite her frailty. However, a comparatively new recruit by the name of Margaret Dunlop offered to serve. Due to her youth and lack of experience, Mary doubted her suitability and shared her reservations with Chairlie Ovens. "Miss Dunlop has agreed to come and serve while I'm away. I'm not sure that she can do the work."

Chairlie laughed, *"Why? Because she's a young woman? Because she's on her own? Because? Because? Because?"*

She knew she was being silly, but never liked to hear it, *"Dinnae be daft, you fair get my goat..... Yes, just because."*

Chairlie laughed loudly as Mary stormed away. Though she hated to admit it, of course he was right; it was arrogant of her to think that no one else could do the job that she was doing, no one is irreplaceable.

Her journey back to Plymouth made her profoundly sad; even Jeanie's smiling face did little to help. Mary was to spend time away from Charles and was now heading towards Devon to visit the last resting place of her mother and sister. As soon as she sighted the English coast, she decided to wear her engagement ring to give her strength. As it happened, when she reached Topsham, she would need all the strength she could muster. There she was greeted by the friends her mother and sister had made in their short time in the sun. Their words of kindness were of great solace to Mary, but they also filled her with shame and regret that she hadn't been there to share these treasured moments with them. The visit to the graves was a trial for her soul and, while she and Jeanie knelt in the graveyard and she said her final farewell to their earthly presence, she remembered their lives together and shed a quiet tear.

She prayed, *"I thank you Lord for my birth, and that I have shared this earth with these souls now departed, they, who taught me all I know - patience, understanding, forgiveness and, most importantly, love. There have been times recently, when I have questioned my conviction to continue with my work. I hope You can give me the strength to carry on in their absence; and for their sake, I know I must. I know I am a poor worthless orphan who doesn't deserve a second glance, but I pray that, whatever happens, with Your blessing, I can carry on. Please keep Charles and the bairns under your protection, even if ye hiv tae tak' an eye aff me. You ken what I'm like. I'll be fine. Amen"*

The loud noise and hectic speed of the modern world in Britain were now beyond her comprehension; had she spent too long in the bush? Or had the world changed out of all recognition? Mary began to have panic attacks in crowded streets; the mass of humanity was like a shoal of fish and trying to go in the opposite direction seemed impossible. She and Jeanie would find a quiet lane or alleyway to hide in until it was safe to move on. As usual there were the obligatory rounds of talks to be made. At one meeting, her fear of public speaking became so acute that, when she saw a man in the audience, she took up a position on the platform where she couldn't see him. Unfortunately she spotted another man looking at her and to her shame she delivered the lecture with her back to the audience. She would like to think that this had to do with the poor relationship she had had with her father but, since that time, she had stood up to far more belligerent men, and boxed their ears. She had never accepted the rules of a man's world, where women, after childbirth, became drudges, to cook, clean, fetch and carry, while the men sat around and decided on the shape of the world and their place upon it.

Jeanie and Mary spent some time at Edinburgh with Mrs McCrindle where, thanks to her kindness, Mary recharged her energies and the wee girl was spoiled. She gave talks in Bearsden and Morningside and found that the crowds were already aware of who she was, knew of her career and adventures. Her regular correspondence was now published in the Missionary Record and her letters were keenly read by the many who followed her story from the comfort of their own homes, church or school. Her next talk was to be in the YMCA Hall in Dundee, which she hoped would be a positive visit, despite her feeling that she was a very different woman to the one she once was. Walking the cold streets of Dundee towards the hall, she was struck by the lack of colour amongst a forest of chimneys, grim grey factories and tenements, and by the absence of the signs of the hand of God. There were many churches built by man, but so few trees.

She was met at the door by the Reverend Walton. Mary looked out at the audience, which, apart from the Minister, were all women, mostly from well-to-do families. It reminded her of the Okoyong and Edem and the chiefs paying lip-service to Christianity by encouraging their women to attend, while having little or nothing to do with it themselves. Had she come full circle? They opened the proceedings with a hymn, sung with grace and respect, but the words drifted listlessly to the floor, hardly echoing through the large and half-empty hall. These voices would not raise the roof, on this, or any other night. She decided that her talk would not only be about Africa, but also about the congregation itself, its belief, and about how little of the wealth she saw around her was given to foreign missions.

The local newspaper covered the event and reported her frustration: *'From my younger days in Dundee I could see that the church was becoming less fashionable among the upper classes, as well as the lower classes. Many seem to think that two services on Sunday was far more than anybody ought to expect to engage in. I recalled the joy at the services at the Okoyong. All such people who were blind to the beauty of their service at home should go to Calabar for two to three months, and they would come back and love the Sabbath. The country is large, out there the church has done little, what has been done was nothing as compared with what it was their duty to do.'*

At the end of her talk, the Reverend Walton looked a little surprised by the narrative, but gave her a vote of thanks. The newspaper report ended with the sentence: *'At her meeting last night she was accompanied by a little dark stranger from the land where she has been so worthily engaged.'* As usual, wee Jeanie stole the show.

Speaking of newspapers, one of the positive things about being back in Britain was that she could keep up with current affairs. In Africa, she was as up-to-date as the old newspapers sent from home would allow her to be, but she was an avid reader and constantly needed to feed her hunger for knowledge. The news from Africa was unsettling; after years of bickering, the British were to officially take over the running of West Africa. In the recent past there had been many stories concerning Sir George Goldie (not to be confused with Hugh Goldie) and his enforcer Frederick Lugard who, for financial gain, had ruled much of the country with imperialist zeal and a rod of iron. It would appear that the Government had lost patience with Sir George Goldie's style of conflict administration; but would the new regime, the Niger Coast Protectorate, with Sir Claude Macdonald as Consul-General, be any better? Only time would tell. Mary hoped and prayed that they would learn from the horrendous abuses of the past.

The scramble for Africa had seen many nations race for a piece of the land; consequently, most proceeded to terrorise and misrule the native population for economic ends. Mary had followed newspaper accounts, as best as she could, of the flawed campaign of General Gordon in Egypt, which tragically led to his death, and that of many others, before and after the siege of Khartoum. But her main concern was the fine balance in West Africa. Thankfully no 'El Dorado' had yet been discovered so, thus far, they had been comparatively free from military intervention and control. The great nations had bickered over thousands of square miles of new territory in the hope that there was easy money to be made. It was conquer and rule, just in case. The rattling of sabres and the loading of the hated Maxim gun were sounds she did not want to hear when she returned.

Another item that caught her eye concerned a subject very close to her heart;

it was a letter in the Missionary Record by a colleague of hers in Calabar, James Luke, which really 'got her dander up'. In his correspondence, he contended that the region was not yet ready for industrial training, a subject on which she had very strong views. Mary decided to write in reply; she described her own experience and the success that had been achieved by negotiating with all parties involved and co-ordinating organisation. She explained that the native skills she had witnessed were as advanced as their primitive tools would allow, yet with these basic implements, they fashioned useful and valuable items. She argued that, were the Mission and Government bodies to take the time and invest in teachers to develop these skills, the workforce could be harnessed to create a class of local artisan to rival any other.

She sent the letter to the Foreign Mission Board for their edification, but as she had had no reply to any of her requests, she did not expect a swift response. To her surprise and delight, this letter was acknowledged and, unlike her other suggestions, they hinted that it might be acted upon. Not long before her return to Africa, she was to receive a less positive response to her other letter. The Board's reply was cold and impersonal and did not actually deal with her request to be allowed to marry Charles; similar to Mr Stibbles' opinion, they simply explained that, in their view, Mr Morrison's talents were too valuable to be wasted in the Okoyong. Yet again, her people, and her work, were ignored in their summation of the future of the region. As they correctly supposed, she would not move from her important work upriver and, sure in this knowledge, it saved them from confronting her directly on the issue of her proposed marriage.

Although it was what she expected, it was still devastating news. She was beside herself with grief and, with Mrs McCrindle's good graces, she left Jeanie in her care and took a walk alone to reflect and mourn. Mary had never known love like this; the love of family, friends or God, though wondrous, she could fathom, but this kind of love seemed raw, it had filled her up and made her complete; now that it was not to be she felt completely empty. It seemed cruel that this powerful emotion could heal then hurt with such intensity. What had this kind of love to do with eternal joy? This passion had more pain than pleasure and while she would love him till she died, she would have to accept that they could not marry. She sat alone on the Scottish beach, facing into a howling gale and wept for every broken heart. She felt ashamed to be so vulnerable, for at this moment, even the Lord could not save her. He could only watch and wait until she found Him again. Mary knew that she had lost a part of her being and a part of her soul but, with the Lord's help, there would still be enough to keep her hard at work; as the rage and sadness subsided, she realised that no matter her feelings, she must go on. On returning to Mrs McCrindle's house, with the tears hardly dry on her face, to compound her grief a telegram was waiting for her. It was from Chairlie Ovens; in it he told her that Charles had been taken seriously ill with fever and that, due to his frailty, he was to be sent home. He suggested that, if she could return to Africa soon, she might see him before he sailed.

Mary made plans immediately for the journey and prayed that they would not pass each other unaware on a starless night on the ocean.

A sad farewell

On her arrival, she could see that Charles was there to meet her at the harbour. She was helped from the Mission boat by Chairlie who, aware of the delicate situation, took care of Jeanie. Mary saw Charles wave, her heart beat faster with every step, but she could see, even from a distance, by his pale complexion and ill-fitting clothes, that he was far from well; all thoughts of an affectionate embrace vanished from her mind. As they drew closer, the welcome kiss, which would have been their first, propriety would not allow and, given the situation, other than self gratification it would have served no purpose. The emotions they both felt had to be tempered by their roles, the time and the place, and hidden as their shared, private grief. As she approached Charles, she could see how desperately ill he was, and knew that should she weaken and weep, she might never stop. Tears would not help the gentle man she loved; she prayed for the strength to be the woman he needed her to be, not the woman he so passionately wanted; to be not only in love, but in control. He was probably no more fragile than she had often been herself, but with neither conceit, nor looking-glass, she was never a witness to her own illnesses. All she knew was that the sight of her love, in such wretchedness, was breaking her heart. Their greeting was very formal; the only informality being that they shook hands. Mary felt his hand in hers, the fever making him, simultaneously, hot, damp and cold. She desperately wished that they were alone on the verandah, speaking of Scotland, she cradling his head on her shoulder, or holding him, with supreme affection, not lust but real, enduring love. This handshake was the deepest love experience they had both experienced, a joyous welcome and tragic farewell at the same time.

The silence, although it lasted only for an instant, encompassed a lifetime of what-could-have-beens and if-onlys; the spell was finally broken by the approach of a fellow passenger. She introduced him, *"Oh, Mr Morrison, this is Reverend Ebenezer Deas."* The two men shook hands and together they set off for the Mission house.

Charles would soon leave for Scotland and, as Mary had returned to Ekenge, there was no time for precious words or private goodbyes. She hoped and prayed that when they next met, they would both be well enough to sit in the sun and make peace with life lived apart, but sadly that was not to be.

The death of a child

Mary once again buried herself in her work. Her house had become a nursery for all the local waifs and strays; unlike other mission houses, these children were not cared for by older mission children, but by Mary herself as part of her family. The children that she took in were, for the time they were with her, her children; they became *'ain o' the bairns'*. Naturally she had her favourites - bonnie Jeanie and Susie were two of them - but at night they were all fed, all washed, and made a fuss-over equally; bedtime was joyous, if chaotic, in her loving household.

Mary's bed was situated in the middle of the room and, for nights like these, she had constructed hammocks around her to hold all the wee ones, so they didn't have to share the floor with the beasties. To each hammock, she had attached a string, so that during the night, should a bairn cry, a simple tug on the string would cause the hammock to rock backwards and forwards and soon, with luck, they would fall back to sleep. She didn't know if it was her mill girl experience, years of controlling many machines at one time, that gave her this ability, as at night she would often have three or four 'rockers' going at the same time. Mary loved and admired these children, who had been the victims of such cruelty from their first breath in this world, who taught her so much, and whose smiles could lighten the darkest room.

One morning at breakfast, although Mary had warned the bairns often enough to stay away from the fire, in a hurried moment, wee Susie had come behind her back and squeezed passed unnoticed to give her a hand. It was only when Mary checked that everyone was seated that she noticed that Susie was absent. Then she heard a terrible scream. Mary spun round and saw that Susie had turned a pot of hot water all over herself. She lifted her up carefully and cradled her shaking body; she reached for her medical bag and, while fearing the worst, did what she could. After many hours of tender care and when she realised she could do no more, she wrapped Susie in a blanket and set off in haste for the nearest doctor.

It was a frantic dash through the bush in the darkness. Susie, badly scalded and in shock, wept when conscious, which only added to Mary's sense of despair. She raced on with no regard for herself; all she had in her mind was to save her darling Susie. On reaching the doctor's house, she was so exhausted that she simply fell to her knees and shouted for help. The doctor, dressed in his nightgown, opened the door. Mary was a dreadful sight; filthy and unkempt, her clothes in tatters, and her face, hands and feet bleeding, ripped and torn by thorns.

The doctor, unable to recognise Mary in this condition, asked, *"Who is it?"*

"Doctor, it's me, Mary."

He helped her to her feet and ushered them into his house, and quickly yet carefully he examined the child and did all he could to make her comfortable. Mary didn't need to ask him if she would survive; she could see by the look on his face that there was no hope. As she sat beside Susie, trying to hold back the tears, this tiny child, blistered and in pain, still found it in her heart to raise her hand so that her Ma could kiss it. Susie smiled at her one more time before the Lord took her.

It was the cruellest of all outcomes and the doctor allowed Mary to sit by her until the morning came. In the cold light of day, when the doctor had treated Mary's cuts and scratches, they wrapped Susie in a fresh blanket and Mary slowly carried her back to Ekenge. Many were waiting anxiously for her return, but the pathetic sight of Mary trudging towards them with the child in her arms told them all they needed to know; no words were spoken. Eme found her inconsolable, so immediately took care of the bairns. In her distress, Mary had to leave the details of the funeral to others. Susie would be laid to rest in the little graveyard behind Mary's house, where the remains of other children who were brought to her, ill and dying, were buried. Mary was so distraught that she could not attend the burial, the sight of Susie in her wee coffin, dressed in a white dress, wearing her favourite string of beads and clasping in her hands a white flower, was more than any mother's heart could take. In her sorrow, through the tears, she said these words from deep within her heart, *"Oh the empty place and the silence and the vain longing for the sweet and the softest caress and the funny ways. Oh, Susie! Susie!"*

When Mary returned to her senses, she sought out Iye, Susie's natural mother, who wept as she was told of the death of her surviving twin. From a distance, Iye had been a loyal mother and, in tribute, Mary paid ten pounds to Iye's owner to buy her out of slavery. Given her freedom, the young woman chose to come and work with Mary, where she remained a good and faithful mission worker.

Since the government changes and with the arrival of the new British Consul-General, Sir Claude Macdonald, Duke Town had become a very different place. It was now garrison to three hundred soldiers, turning it into a thriving and busy town. On the positive side, as the soldiers were billeted at Duke Town and providing the natives in other parts of the Oil River states behaved, the residents should have noticed little difference; but ominously, the river was now patrolled by gun-boats to create and protect a safe trade route with regions further up Cross River.

Mary came to believe that hard work was her only recourse to regain her faith and to let the world change around her. She had been concerned for some time that the Church had not seen fit to send one of their ordained ministers to preach to any of her congregations. It was bad enough that they hardly acknowledged her despite her resolve to continue to work on their behalf. Had they been forgotten? Perhaps the Mission was just too busy? Her success as an arbitrator in inter-tribal disputes had spread far and wide and when she heard the news that the new Consul-General was soon to begin appointing Vice-Consuls to act as judges, she decided to act.

Knowing how disruptive and dangerous the wrong appointment could be, she wrote to strongly voice her concerns. Not for the first time, her pen was to land her in trouble. Within a few weeks, the Consul-General sent a messenger and boat to transport her to Duke Town for a palaver. The town itself was much changed, with new roads and improved sanitary conditions and drainage. Sir Claude Macdonald's house was as grand as one would imagine for a British Consul-General. Mary was met at the jetty by two soldiers, who escorted her to his magnificent wooden house. She was led into his drawing room and invited to sit on a beautiful sofa, where she took the time to gather her thoughts.

Mary was concerned that she might not make a good impression and be taken for a mad, opinionated, bush woman, who talked too much. She mistrusted the military and the merchants, almost as much as she did politicians, be they of the Church, or Imperial kind. But she made a mental note to be polite, courteous and, most of all, to behave. An African manservant arrived with a tea tray and a dish of sweets, which he laid on the table before her; he poured two cups of tea, bowed his head, and left the room. Her eyes danced around the dish of glorious sweets; they were her favourites - toffees. She picked one out of the dish and looked at it adoringly, but when she heard the door handle turn, she panicked and stuffed the large sweetie in her mouth. Sir Claude entered the room, dressed in a light suit, shirt, and tie; she observed that he was studying her letter. He extended his arm, shook her hand, and sat down beside her. *"I apologise for keeping you waiting, Miss Slessor. I was just re-reading your lengthy letter, it is very illuminating. I hear you always have a lot to say."*

Mary realised that if she tried to speak, the toffee in her mouth might make her sound incoherent, so she simply nodded and smiled.

Sir Claude, surprised at her silence, asked her another question, *"Hm! I hear you do excellent work at Ekenge?"*

Again Mary nodded in agreement, and picked up her cup of tea, wishing that the earth would consume her. The toffee was far too big to swallow, and would take fully five minutes to 'sook' to a manageable size; taking it out of her mouth was not the kind of thing that a lady, attempting to impress, would do. In frustration, he stood up and turned his back to her; he tried a third question, couched in terms to provoke a response. *"Well, what would you think if we put in a Vice-Consul to judge in the Okoyong? He would be backed with the full might of the military forces at our disposal to rule on all native disputes."*

Repelled by the idea, Mary choked, causing the toffee to shoot out of her mouth, fly across the room and, with great good fortune, hit the fender of the fireplace and fall into the grate. Mary tried to disguise the sound by coughing delicately, as if to clear her throat. She began to talk, totally ignoring the confectionary missile, *"If I may say so, that would only lead to disaster!"*

Happy to now have her input, he turned and said, *"Ah, you have an opinion. Thank goodness!"*

Once she had begun, she did have a lot to say, *"You need someone who knows the natives, their traditions and rituals, who will respect their view o' the world. You need someone who knows the difference 'tween a gunboat and a gospel!"*

Sir Claude tried to probe further, *"I'm afraid that I don't know many men who have those qualities; the old ways have been successful in the past."*

She asked, *"Do you talk of resolving conflict?"*

"*Of course!*"

Mary continued to question, "*Are you sure? Let's put the case - whit if two men from warring tribes stood afore the court in dispute? Judgement has been made and both are content, and though the decision wis no' exactly as proscribed in yer law books, would that be an end to it? Would that satisfy the Law?*"

He mumbled, "*Well..... well.....*"

She challenged him, "*You must ask yersel', does your court demand justice, or vengeance?*"

Sir Claude was offended, "*Miss Slessor that is unfair of you.....*"

She interrupted, pleading the native case, "*These are a good people and your judgements should close and heal wounds, no' open them wide and rub salt intae them! If you perpetuate bad blood, you create an endless circle of revenge and retribution that can fester and infect entire regions, like smallpox..... I'll tell you whit ye need, you need men with the Wisdom of Solomon..... and they're few an' far atween!*"

He listened to the passion in her voice, "*I'm afraid that doing nothing is not an option for me.*"

"*I don't ask you to dae nothin', I ask that you dae - the right thing!*"

Unknown to Mary, Sir Claude had a plan, but he needed her to walk into his trap, which she had unwittingly done. "*Well, you don't ask much of me do you? Fortunately the change in Government has led to a change in attitude. If truth were to be told, to have standing armies at constant war on small battlefields is far too costly and unpopular, so what used to be the first resort has, for the moment at least, become the last. I concur with your evaluation of the situation, and would like to offer you the post of Vice-Consul.*"

This outcome had never crossed her mind; she gulped hard at the proposition; she even looked over her shoulder to make sure he wasn't talking to someone behind her.

She babbled, "*What? You mean.......... me? Me?..... But I'm a woman!*"

He smiled, "*Yes, I know it is a unique appointment, but it is a unique problem, and from all I've heard, you are somewhat unique.*"

She tried to exclude herself from the job, "*But women don't become judges, they don't become Vice-Consuls!*"

Sir Claude was unperturbed by this, "*True, but more importantly, will you do it? You have rationally excluded, as unsuitable, everyone else I had on my list for the role.*"

Mary apologised, "*That was no' my intention, sir.*"

He said, in mock judicial tone, *"I'm sure it wasn't but these are the facts Miss Slessor, these are the facts. I sentence you to one week..... to decide."*

Flabbergasted, she said, *"I, I, I, I don't know, I'll need to ask the Lord. If I do it, it'll be on meh terms, I'll act as I see fit."*

If she had meant that as a threat to dissuade him, it didn't work, *"I would expect nothing else. You would have a free hand."*

Mary thought to herself, *'how well does this man know me? Does he know I won't do what I'm told, if I believe it to be wrong?'*

Sir Claude tried to put her at her ease. *"Please have another cup of tea, and a toffee or two, I had them brought in especially, I heard you were partial to them."*

Mary, embarrassed by the toffee incident earlier, said *"Oh no I cudnae, but thank you a' the same. E'm fine."*

Sir Claude smiled, *"I'll have them give you a tin of them to eat on your return journey, and those you have left you can share with the bairns."* It would seem he did know her.

It took her the entire week to come to a decision, every waking minute going over the pros and cons of his offer. She studied the Bible for guidance, but the only quotation that stuck with her was Proverbs chapter 11 v 29, *'He that troubleth his own house shall inherit the wind: and the fool shall be servant to the wise of heart.'* One minute she disowned the offer as shameless vanity and the next defended her reasons for accepting it. She had no idea what the Church would make of it; she couldn't imagine that they would celebrate at the Mission Board. Mary hated politics and politicians and was determined not be used as a tool by them, but she knew that if she didn't do the job they would appoint someone else who would; as she trusted no one else to deal fairly and wisely with the tribes, with great misgiving, she agreed.

In the year that Susie died, Mary also lost Hugh Goldie and William Anderson; it felt as if her old world was crumbling about her. Mr Goldie had taught her so much about understanding and appreciating Africa and its people, and Mr Anderson had shown great kindness to a young, frightened newcomer. In fact, not long before, during one of her many bouts of malaria, Mr Anderson had visited her in hospital, where he recalled her early days at the Mission house with humour and warmth, informing her that it was he who had been responsible for the gifts of fruit under her pillow when, as a punishment for her tardiness, she had to forfeit her evening meals. Hearing that he was seriously ill, she made the long trip from Ekenge to his hospital bed and, although fading, he found time to joke and reminisce while she sat holding his hand until his time came to leave this world. She prayed at his side, *"Dear Lord, Mr Anderson felt no sadness at his leaving. He hoped that his time on this earth had been well spent, and he thanked You, Lord, that he had been allowed so long to do Your work. I thank you God for his life, and for allowing me to be a witness to his good works, his inspiration, and his love. Please take him to Your heart, as he will always remain in ours. Amen."*

Africa was changing and Ekenge was no exception. Many of the natives, like Eme, who cultivated the land, found the ground was now worked-out and, reluctantly, they decided to move to pastures new, to Akpap where the ground was still fertile and a market had opened. Mary informed the Presbytery, and the Consul-General, of her intention to move there and set up court, school and church. Her increasing workload, in what some believed to be an inappropriate role as Vice-Consul, was exacerbating the tension between herself and the Church and, though she had never felt she had been totally accepted as part of their world, her new responsibilities were bringing her into further conflict. But she was reconciled in her belief that she could only do what was right in her heart. If their opinion of Mary was of someone who courted favour, they could not have been more wrong; if they examined her low Christian conversion rate and used it as an indicator of her lack of success, she had no legitimate argument to the contrary. What they failed to take into account was that schools and churches were springing up throughout the region, but as very few officials would venture to the Okoyong from downriver, there was no proof.

As she had warned Sir Claude, Mary did things her own way as regards the court. The oath taken by the participants was unconventional by British standards, but, for those she was serving, it was unbreakable. The two in dispute would stand in front of her and have the backs of their right hands cut. As they clasped hands, a mixture of corn and pepper was applied to the cuts, and when soaked with blood, to complete the oath, each man sucked from the other's hand. It was based on an ancient ceremony which she believed had a greater chance of being obeyed than any British oath.

The court over which Mary presided was unusual to say the least; grand it wasn't, but she had always believed that the environment was important and should be appropriate to those she served. Similar to her churches and schools, they were neither austere nor elaborate, but fitting for the people who would recognise and respect their surroundings and feel that they were part of it, and that it was part of them. Her courts were exactly that, the buildings were rudely built and similar to their own houses. There was little ceremony in her courtly domain, though certain elements were still recognisable as legal procedure. In the main hut, on important cases, the headmen of the district would sit behind her acting as jury, while Mary sat at a table on which she placed her papers, a bowl of toffees and a cup of tea. The court in front of her was filled with those interested in the outcome of the trial. A man stood behind a bamboo rail - this signified that he was in the dock - and behind another bamboo rail sat the witnesses. As the case continued, there would be much gesticulating and pontificating, play-acting and weeping; and once all the evidence had been heard, Mary would advise the jury on how they should interpret that evidence, often being given more than a hint at the preferred verdict. The jury would leave the court and, in a smaller room attached, come to their decision. The judgement delivered by Mary was more a sermon than simply a sentence; the outcome, though not always legal, was, in her opinion, always just.

After years of living in the bush, Mary had lost almost any sense of, or indeed any need for, propriety or pomp. During lengthy court proceedings, she would often listen to the arguments and counter-arguments while knitting, not something judges would do, but it helped her concentration during a long session. Sometimes she would make her judgement with a newly-abandoned babe in arms; the natives accepted her peculiarities without question, but it raised eyebrows elsewhere. Mary had been openly criticised for her 'shoddy methods' and one missionary had called her 'that coarse woman'; it was said that 'her schools were taught by the semi-literate', and her churches were described as no more than 'mud Kirks'. It was true that when unable to find enough teachers classes were often taught by a student who was one page ahead of the class; however some items on the curriculum were to say the least unusual, such as kite-flying, football and of course, tree climbing. When Sir Claude heard these comments he was intrigued, so asked, "This is not meant as a criticism, but can I ask why, when there is money available for building, you don't use it to create a more impressive court?"

Mary answered, "What do you mean? A fine building is nae guarantee of an honest verdict!"

Knowing he had touched a nerve, he replied, "I agree, but surely more comfortable and imposing surroundings, both for your church and court, would impress those who come?"

"Are you talking of fear or respect?" she snapped.

He stuttered, *"Well....."*

She continued, *"There are grand churches in Scotland that each Sunday sit virtually empty; fine surroundings do not make good Christians, it's the people who make magnificent churches. It is the enthusiasm o' the congregation that maks the rafters ring, whether they are ornate or made fae palms. Dinnae mistake pomp for piety; and the better the jail you threaten them with does not mean the better the justice! It is important that what they come to, be it to church or court, they recognise as theirs, so they will understand and respect the words that are said. The glory of God is in the fowk, no' the building."*

As far as Sir Claude was concerned, he was content that Mary's unorthodox administration had brought peace and order to a region famous for generations for its bloody wars.

Months later - it was on the night of the eve of Christmas – Mary, still full of doubts about her decision, sat in her yard alone to study her bible. This she tried to do every night for an hour, once all other work was done and bairns had been fed, washed and safely put to bed; it was not always achieved but, come hostilities, hurricane or hippo, she always tried. As she read she became aware of the sound of footsteps trampling through the surrounding bush. Two white men and four native carriers broke into the clearing; she immediately recognised one as Sir Claude, who greeted her, *"Ah, Vice-Consul, I come bearing gifts. I hope you don't mind. Do you have room for two guests for the night?"*

Mary, always delighted to have company, led the two men into the house, and although she was intrigued by the contents of the parcels they had brought, she knew that she must be hostess first.

She was introduced to Sir Claude's dashing young companion, Captain Alan Boisragon who, two years before, had retired from the army and was now enrolled into the Consular Staff as Commandant of the Niger Coast Protectorate Force. The three sat down to a late supper during which the young man thrilled Mary with his tales of derring-do, specifically his seven years in India and those as a member of the Nile Expedition. In return he asked many questions of his hostess, who was as usual reluctant to talk of herself; that was until he mentioned that Sir Claude had told him many stories of her own conquests and adventures, adding that he had found them hard to believe, and as she would not speak of them, his suspicions were confirmed. Of course he did believe them, but the inference that Sir Claude was telling fibs concerning her, was all the encouragement Mary needed; she began her defence of Sir Claude and spoke freely, frankly and at great length.

On Christmas morning, the children woke one by one and the two men, having breakfasted earlier, were happy to sit and watch Mary greet and be greeted by each child in turn. It had been many years since Captain Boisragon had observed a family in action and was delighted and touched by what he saw. The children, so excited to have guests, smiled big smiles and lined up to be plunged into the makeshift bath in the yard, each one lifted out and left to run and play, to dry naturally in the hot morning sun. It was joyously chaotic. Nowadays Mary seldom had a chance to speak her native tongue and was now making the most of it. Politics, both local and international, the price of yams, fish and cement were all discussed in detail and rather distracted Mary from the usual early morning ritual. It was only when Boisragon counted the number of children that Mary had did he realise that one child was now standing excitedly in line for her third bath of the morning. The child's cheeky smile, and obvious delight, convinced him to keep her secret.

This was a Christmas that none of them would forget; not only had the two men brought a veritable banquet for them to eat but had somehow acquired all kinds of toys, books and dolls for the children, a Christmas that Dickens himself would have been proud of.

On the second night, Sir Claude told Mary that regrettably they must leave very early the next morning and, without an alarm clock, wondered how that could be achieved. Mary thought for a moment, then, *"I have the very thing."* She walked out into the yard and returned carrying a rooster and a long piece of string. She explained, *"This is the cockerel from the yard, he struts around and crows at day-break every morning, maks an awfie racket. If I tie this string to his leg and tie him on tae that bit o' corrugated roof, ye'll no' sleep in!"*

And this is how it happened. The two men left very early the next morning, happy and empty-handed, but they felt that they now possessed much more than they had arrived with.

1896
Death and disease

After the refusal by the Mission Board to allow her marriage, Mary had written to Charles' mother in Kirkintilloch to express both her disappointment and her determination to continue her work in the Okoyong but that, should the situation change, she hoped that they could still be married. It was obvious from his mother's sad reply that she wished them well, whilst imparting her full support for their decision to remain in their positions. The two women had continued to correspond after Charles' return to Scotland, and she informed Mary that his recuperation had been painfully slow. When unable to transfer his missionary teaching work to any other country, she had decided to send him to North Carolina to join his brother, who was working on the building of a railway. From further letters it was learned that, while based in a small wooden cabin he shared with his brother, he had continued to keep up his literary work. Mary was happy to know that, though they were farther apart than she could fathom, her thoughts and prayers flew towards him each night and she felt at one with him. Mary could not have prepared her mind, or her heart, for the next letter which she received. His mother told her the shocking news, related by John, that her beloved Charles had died. The circumstances were almost too tragic to contemplate; his health had been improving and it being a fine day Charles had left the cabin to take the air. For reasons still unknown, the empty cabin became engulfed in flames. Charles, now some distance away, turned to see a pall of smoke blackening the mountain sky, which he knew could only be from their remote home. Immediately he dashed back as fast as he could to see what he could save, only to be greeted by an inferno, in which nothing could survive. The sight before him was of complete devastation, not a stick of furniture, a book, essay or letter, could be saved; in despair he collapsed at the scene, never to recover. John added that losing his writings and his books was tragic, but losing his letters from Miss Slessor may have been too much. Though Charles had known every letter off by heart, it was all he had left of his beloved; in his frailty it may have been too much to lose. Mary's heart almost broke at the news of this gentle man's death; all that comforted her was her belief that he was now safe in the hands of the Lord. Sure that he had taken her love with him when he died, she was never without him in her mind or in her heart, and she would pray for him until her last days on earth.

She threw herself back into work, but no matter how hard she toiled, it never seemed to be done; what with the church, the school, and the court, she scurried between roles, grateful that there was little time for herself to think of her loss. Gradually the trials of the recent past grew less oppressive, her periods of deep despair became fewer and she became resigned to working and serving in this glorious and unpredictable land.

Its unpredictable nature was about to hit her full in the face. In her medical

The Court House, Ikotobong.

capacity, she was asked to accompany a man to his house on the outskirts of Akpap to attend to his family. Mary could get little information out of the over-excited man who, in his haste, pulled her out of her house and pushed her all the way to his. It was dark when they arrived; the man pointed to his house. Mary turned to ask him if he could at least tell her what was the problem, only to find that he was nowhere to be seen. She shook her head in disbelief. On entering the room, she found that there was no one to welcome her, or to describe the symptoms of the illness. The room was dark and smelled of death. She lit a match, regretting it almost immediately, for around her, lying on the floor were three children and a woman. She now understood why the man had run; it was obvious, without closer examination, to be the worst of things - they had all died of smallpox.

Mary prayed that this was an isolated incident, but knew in her heart that it was more than likely the start of an epidemic. For the next week, Mary and Jeanie, now fourteen, went house to house vaccinating everyone they could. Jeanie was a godsend, a responsible and able daughter, who would happily go in her mother's footsteps wherever they led, no matter how dangerous the destination. They worked all the hours that God gave them, foregoing sleep, trying to prevent the plague spreading any further, but despite their hard work and prayers, many died and, if not brought to their attention, many more lay dying in the surrounding bush. Soon they had little vaccine left, and what remained, they tried to use sparingly; and when Eme came running and told them that the disease had reached Ekenge and that Chief Edem was close to death, although at her wit's end, Mary immediately set off, leaving Jeanie and Chairlie in charge.

Ekenge, once vibrant and full of life, was now the scene of such awful death. The ones she could save, she did, but with so little vaccine left, she soon had to scrape the pus with a knife from those already vaccinated, to treat the survivors. When she found Edem, she knew immediately there was nothing she could do to save him, or relieve his suffering, so she prayed for his soul and wept for his wives and children. Surrounded by the dead and dying, she managed to find enough wood to fashion a rough coffin, to dig a hole and bury him as quickly as she could, with as much respect and ceremony as circumstance would allow. He had been an honourable man and a true friend. There was no need for any further sacrifice at his funeral, as most of those who had remained in Ekenge had already been sacrificed to smallpox. After days of hectic and distressing work, Mary reluctantly abandoned Ekenge and left it as a ghost town. Ekenge, considered by the natives to be merely on loan from the surrounding bush, was rapidly reclaimed by the vegetation and would soon vanish as if it had never existed.

Mary led those able to walk, and the many that had to be carried, back to Akpap. It was a tragic trail of grief, and as she had not had any food or sleep for many days she was on her last legs. Chairlie Ovens and Jeanie had held the fort in her absence and on her return both were shocked at her dishevelled and drawn appearance. Chairlie had become her guardian angel and over the next few weeks he watched her try to carry on. He saw that she found it difficult to stand for any length of time and he feared that she herself was close to death. It was this private fear that forced him to make the journey to Duke Town and insist that Mary be given some assistance. The first she knew of his handiwork was when a letter arrived from Duke Town, ordering her to leave on furlough on the next available ship. When she found out what Chairlie had done behind her back, she was furious. How could she leave at this time? As Chairlie stood before her, smiling at the results of his devious work, if she could have stood up she would have given him a clip round the ear, but as she couldn't, she asked him to take a step or two closer and bow his head, so she could chastise him without having to strain too much. He stepped forward, removed his soft flat hat and took his punishment like the good soul he was.

Mary was determined not to leave Jeanie, Mary, Alice and Maggie while the threat of contagion still existed. She would never have one restful night away if she believed they were in any danger. She told Chairlie of her very reasonable terms, *"I will not take a step without them. It's all four bairns, or I die here!"*

Chairlie raised a good point, *"But the Mission will never stand for that, forby they widnae pay for it."*

"I'll pay for them myself, I have the money."

He tried to reason with her, *"But Mary, you are hardly able to take care o' yersel', never mind the bairns. They'll be safe wi' me. You're so ill, it's no' possible."*

She was adamant, *"Not one a step from here! God can do impossible things. All my life He has made the impossible, possible; there is nothing He and I cannae do."*

Chairlie shook his head in desperation, *"What are you all gonna' wear? No-one bats an eye here in the bush, but....."*

Mary reminded him, *"We have other clothes in the case, fine clothes."*

Chairlie walked over to the battered wooden trunk, opened it, and picked up shreds of multi-coloured material that fell like snowflakes through his fingers, *"I'm afraid the white ants hae the same taste in fine clothes as you."*

"*God will provide!*" she shouted in exasperation.

1898
Bad news travels fast

As she had prophesied, a new box of clothes had recently arrived at Duke Town, sent from Scotland by supporters of their work. Soon they were dressed and looking as fine as any family for the journey. There was no time to prepare those in Scotland for their arrival, as the ship on which they were to sail would also carry any letters. The six-week journey did little to improve her health, and the accumulation of years of fevers meant that with each new bout it was taking longer and longer for her to regain her strength. At Liverpool, after dispatching a short telegram to Mrs McCrindle, Mary's disability and distress was obvious. A porter offered to help and Mary, unable to do much more than sit while being transported, handed him her purse and asked him to buy their tickets to Edinburgh, which he kindly did. When the train pulled into Waverley station, the bairns helped her to stand and extricate her weary bones from the carriage. Mrs McCrindle was waiting on the platform; she may have been expecting Jeanie, but when Alice, Mary and sixteen-month old Maggie followed, it was quite a surprise. Although the good lady was used to Mary's eccentricity, this time she was almost speechless, but warmly hugged each child in turn. The other travellers at the station stood fascinated and amazed at the sight of Mary's happy brood, helping them with their luggage into a cab. When they reached Joppa, Mary was sent straight to bed, happy and content to fall asleep to the sounds echoing through the house of happy children playing long into the night, entertained by Mrs McCrindle, her friends and neighbours.

While still unable to walk sufficiently well, it was Mary's chance to catch up on her correspondence with the friends she'd made through her many letters to the Missionary Record. The Record not only printed letters from missionaries, but kept those who were interested up-to-date with their latest news and travel arrangements. While it was ideal for friends and family to know the details of those who were on furlough and their departure and arrival times, for Mary it meant continual pressure, as news of her arrival in Britain had prompted a deluge of demands for interviews. As soon as she was able, Mary began her round of fund-raising engagements to enthusiastic audiences who, to her surprise, often quoted from her own writings and gave generously to ensure her plans could continue.

One evening in September, after dinner and the bairns were in bed, Mrs McCrindle knocked and entered Mary's room and gave her a newspaper. *"Someone handed this to me, I think you might find it illuminating; I'll leave it with you."*

It was unlike Mrs McCrindle to be so mysterious, or apprehensive. The newspaper was the Manchester Times and as Mary read the title of the article, 'A WHITE QUEEN IN WEST AFRICA', she feared the worst. She scanned the article and immediately recognised two names, Captain Boisragon and Mary Kingsley, as friends who had come to visit. She began to read:

A WHITE QUEEN IN WEST AFRICA

An extraordinary story of influence of a white lady living alone in West Africa is told by Captain Alan Boisragon in his story of the Benin massacre. After describing some of the horrible cruelties of the Niger Coast Protectorate, amongst others the custom of killing all children born twins, and driving the mother out into the wilds to die from exposure and starvation, Captain Boisragon tells the wonderful story of heroism and courage of Miss Slessor, one of the lady missionaries from the Scotch mission at Old Calabar. She has settled herself in a district called Okoyong, some way inland from the Calabar river. And of that district

SHE IS VIRTUALLY QUEEN,

as in it her word is law, and the natives, who adore her, do nothing without consulting her. She has taught herself to speak the language of the country as well as any native, and knows far more about the history and relationship of all the different chiefs of that part of the world than any one of the natives themselves. She has got such a hold over the people that all killing of twins and such like evil customs have been absolutely stopped. When twins are born, Ma, as Miss Slessor is called by her people, is at once sent for. By washing the house and all its contents herself she is considered to have purified it, and is allowed to save the woman and take her babies back to her own house – a house by the way, that she has more or less built with her own hands. All this she has done entirely by herself in a very large district where not many years ago there was nothing but disorder and trouble.

Mary slapped her forehead in despair. She thought '*what will the Mission Board think of this? All done entirely by myself ?? Oh, dearie me!*'

She read on:

Another tribute to this remarkable woman is from Miss Mary Kingsley in her "Travels in West Africa." She says:- "I made a point in this visit to Calabar of going up river to see Miss Slessor at Okoyong. This very wonderful lady has been eighteen years in Calabar, for the last six or seven living entirely alone, as far as white folks go, in a clearing in the forest, near to one of the villages in the Okoyong district, and ruling as a veritable white chief over the entire Okoyong district. Her great abilities, both physical and intellectual, have given her among the savage tribe a unique position, and won her a profound esteem. Her knowledge of the native, his language, his ways and thoughts, his difficulties, and all that is his, is extraordinary, and the amount of good she has done NO MAN CAN FULLY ESTIMATE. Okoyong, when she went there alone – living in the native houses while she built with native assistance her present house – was a district regarded with fear by other natives and unknown to Europeans. This instance of what one white can do would give many important lessons in West Coast administration, only the sort of man Miss Slessor represents is rare. There are but few who have the same power of resisting the malarial climate, and of acquiring the language and an insight into the negro mind, so perhaps after all it is no great wonder that Miss Slessor stands alone, as she certainly does."

Mary was stunned as she finished the article, she felt betrayed by her own honesty. These two people knew her but how could they have written these words? There was not one lie in the article, yet it was a dishonest summation of all that had been done and all that she held sacred. It portrayed one woman's sacrifice and bravery in the wilds of Africa amongst savages. '*How cruel and deceptive the world can be,*' she thought. Mary would maintain that as she had arrived with nothing on that continent, she had sacrificed nothing in her endeavours. The people of West Africa were the heroes and heroines, those who had bravely accepted her and allowed her to share their lives. She couldn't imagine that either of these people had sought to hurt her, but to build a myth around 'the White Queen' did all a disservice. Its only saving grace was that, when the newspapers were full of African war atrocities and the 'evil heathen', as the war press dubbed the enemy, at least these West Africans were portrayed as responding well to kindness and understanding. Perhaps all was not lost, although she seriously doubted that the Foreign Mission Board would view the article in such a light. As she read and re-read the article, she was ashamed of how self-serving it sounded; *'it was all me, me, me!'*

She had only been in Britain for a matter of months, but now it seemed imperative that she return to Africa as soon as she could. She desperately needed to escape the cold weather, the story and the public gaze, and return to her own people. Mrs McCrindle would never talk of the article again, but when Mary announced her intention to return to Africa forthwith, Mrs McCrindle tried her best to dissuade her, *"We have been friends for longer than I care to remember, I admire your dedication and bravery, but I believe this time you are being foolish."*

But Mary had made up her mind, *"We have all had such fun with you, and your kindness and generosity humbles us all, but my duty is elsewhere. The weather here is now so dreich, my bones ache for the sun to shine on them. Nowadays Scotland gives me fresh air and good, good friends but little else. But this piece of paper drives me home. I trust you'll forgive me."*

Mrs McCrindle replied with uncharacteristic frankness, *"I cannot let you leave without disputing the sense of it! I know you dislike praise, but I can hold my tongue no longer. I have opened my house to many a missionary worker, but of all those I have had the honour to meet in this world, I believe that you would be missed most of all."* She searched for the words, *"Of course your heart and mind may be fit for the greatest battles, but your body is still weak and frail. In another year, I would gladly wave you goodbye with a tear in my eye and a prayer in my heart, but please, not yet. The bairns take the air, play on the beach and paddle in the sea; can you not do the same?"*

Mary smiled, *"I'm afraid my paddlin' days are over, and now that I have my strength back, I can watch the bairns paddle in the creek at home. If you will not help me return, I'll swim back!"*

Her friend knew that any further discussion on the matter was futile, though she added, *"You are impossible and stubborn! I should have known better than to attempt to offer you advice, it's like trying to persuade a waterfall to flow uphill......... totally pointless.*" She took Mary's hand in hers and, with great emotion in her voice, added, "*But we will pray for you and your children,*" and she said her farewells.

Mary and the children made their way to Liverpool to catch the boat, the Oron 1, as was mentioned in the Missionary Record. A traveller had left his newspaper on the train and, while the bairns enjoyed the ever-changing passing scenery, she took the time to absorb the current news. As it had been in the recent past, war and the threat of war was always with them; there were reports of the Ashanti Expedition, the terrible Benin massacre and the court case of poor Mr Dreyfus, which appeared to run and run. At Liverpool, as in Edinburgh, even in this hustle and bustle, dressed as they were like fine young ladies, the bairns attracted great attention and praise from all who saw them, little knowing how differently they dressed at home.

Once on board, Mary looked forward to the peace and tranquillity of the long voyage. As was her habit, when the ship pulled into the first port, they all stood on deck to watch the hectic activity on the docks. Mary's eye was distracted by a crowd of excited people who had begun to gather around the dockside gangway. A very insistent man succeeded in convincing one of the shipping employees to allow him to climb on board. They all watched his progress with interest; she was surprised, and then shaken, when he came directly towards her. In case he was a madman, she stood in front of the bairns. "*Are you Miss Slessor?*" he asked, "*the missionary with the black children?*"

Taken aback, she replied hesitantly, "*Yes, I believe I might be.*"

"*Are these some of the twins you have saved?*"

"*What do you mean? How do you know?*" she asked.

He pulled a newspaper from his pocket and handed it to her; it was the Manchester Times. "*You're headline news!*" he announced.

Mary turned away immediately and herded the bairns below decks; the article was now following her, transforming her into the most reluctant celebrity ever known. The news that she was on this ship, including her route and destination, had undoubtedly spread. At each port, the clamour for interviews from the dockside increased. She instructed the purser that for the rest of the journey she wished to speak to no one and was not to be disturbed. From that point onwards, whenever the ship docked, Mary and the bairns kept to themselves.

The journey seemed to last an eternity and with the thought of the frosty reception she would receive at home, she had mixed feelings as they approached Duke Town. Mary was sure that the Foreign Mission Board would be livid that the Church appeared a mere bit player; the story had given Mary a starring role, a role she neither wanted nor felt she deserved. She doubted they would believe that. And would it do any good for the Mission or missionaries? She thought not; and she was fully aware that her failure to fulfil all her public speaking commitments at home would not be the only talking point.

As she expected, no one met them at Duke Town. To be honest she was glad that she did not have to meet the recriminations head on - those could wait. She employed two Krumen to take them and their luggage by canoe to the landing place. On arrival at the beach, as they gathered their belongings, she was startled by a noise coming from the bush and, ever watchful, and as the sound increased in volume, she told the bairns to stand behind her for protection. Firstly she saw Eme, then that she was leading a crowd of people, all shouting, '*Ma is back, Ma is back.*' Mary couldn't believe it, it was a welcoming committee! The journey to Akpap was such a joyous return; the bairns were carried high on shoulders and her sister Eme supported her as she wept, happy to be back with her family.

The two young women who had reluctantly, though bravely, come to relieve her at Akpap had left, having done their best under difficult circumstances. They had only agreed to go there on Mary's personal guarantee that the tribe would behave; it would appear they had let her down. She asked Eme for an explanation and Eme told her, "*They did not understand us,*" she put her hand over her ears and rocked backwards and forwards, "*and oh, the God noise!*"

Mary was impatient to hear the story, "*Yes, yes, the God noise, but tell me, what happened?*"

Eme explained simply, "*They not be you. We did nothing that we would not do with you watching. We did not do nothin' you would not have seen off with one smack of your slipper.*"

Mary raised her eyebrow in question; Eme thought, then said coyly, "*Maybe..... two smacks, but no more!*"

Mary took a deep breath, knowing that Eme's admission covered a multitude of sins. She reminded her, "*Dear sister Eme, I told you to behave.*"

Eme, feeling falsely accused, tried to justify the tribe's conduct, "*But we behave like you tell us, but they are fine, fine ladies, with fine clothes and fine manners, not like you Ma.*"

Mary was sure that Eme meant that as a compliment, but it made her wonder if she hadn't spent too long in the bush and had 'gone native'. It transpired that the complaints made by the two young women now featured in a report by the Mission Board relating to Mary's current work, attitudes and recent behaviour; allegedly it made grim reading. The course of action the Mission Board took was a surprise to Mary, but for others it was long overdue - they sent a doctor to examine her.

When he arrived at the village, the doctor seemed much affected by the strain of the journey and the oppressive heat, but despite that he appeared friendly, courteous and amiable. He introduced himself, *"Miss Slessor, I am Dr Cowan, how are you, are you well?"* While acclimatising to the intense heat from a comfortable chair on the verandah, he took time to take in the surroundings; Mary had to forget he was ostensibly an enemy agent. No matter, she was glad to have a visitor to talk to at long last. When he had revived sufficiently, they both entered the house where she was subjected to a full physical examination; afterwards, they sat and began to talk while they waited for the water to boil for tea. His conversation seemed normal, but at times it deviated and ran off in odd directions, always ending with a question, and though peculiar, she thought little more about it. They talked of many things - politics and war, Africa and Britain - she found it fascinating and felt free to enter candidly into the debate. Mary excused herself to make the tea and when she returned she happened to look over his shoulder. She could see he was completing a page of notes, then he referred to a list of typed questions; in a flash it came to her, that this was part of the examination! He was also checking her sanity! She retraced her steps, coughed to give him time to hide the papers and sat down beside him. His next question almost caused her to drop her tea cup. *"Miss Slessor, do you mind if I ask you, what colour is the Lord, black or white?"*

Up to this moment their conversation had been equitable, but now she felt as if her life as a missionary hung in the balance. She thought for a moment then replied, *"The Lord is the colour of the sun and the moon."*

The doctor thought for a moment, took a handkerchief out of his pocket, wiped his brow, and bellowed with laughter, *"There are many missionaries, teachers and doctors who have lost their sanity in this vast country, but in my opinion, you are not one of them. Given your life and your circumstances, you are one of the most sane people I have ever met. How you have lived here so long dumbfounds and amazes me. There have been so many who have died within weeks, months or years. You do very little correctly, you wear no hat, no shoes, you dress almost as the natives do, you don't boil the water, you eat all the local food, you should have been dead and buried years ago!"*

Mary shrugged her shoulders in reluctant agreement.

He added, *"I, for one, wish you many, many more years of a unique and tranquil life."* Again he wiped the sweat from his brow, *"Now if you will forgive me, I must get back to civilisation, the heat and humidity here is more than I can stand."*

The sad postscript to this story was that, six months later, Mary heard that the kind Dr Cowan had himself succumbed to fever and, while being invalided home, had died at sea.

January 1899
Moving towards war

With the threat of dismissal gone for the time being, she returned to her old routine; the months passed quickly and she began to think that another move was in order. She had been in the Okoyong for fifteen years, and as she sat watching the bairns, she imagined what a new challenge might bring. The region was working well, the school, church, and trade now had a momentum of their own. The Okoyong was now a place of relative peace, order and hard work, whereas before there had only been mistrust, abuse and constant war.

The Court had encouraged Mary to spread her work further afield; many now came by canoe, crossed rivers and creeks, walked through miles and miles of bush from regions far away, to have their disputes settled by her. During this time she began to make the acquaintance of many chiefs from the Aro, Ibos and Ibibios tribes and, though initially they seldom saw eye to eye, she gained a great deal of knowledge of their rituals and beliefs, and earned from them a grudging respect for hers. She was interested in their stories and their history; the world that they were describing was Iboland, inhabited by many tribes including the Aro and the Ibo. She remembered her brief but strangely memorable meeting with Eze Kanu Okoro, King of the Aro, and as she found out more and more, she was beginning to understand the relevance and significance of his words.

These two tribes could hardly have been more different; the Ibo were poor, industrious and good, and the Aro were rich, powerful and manipulative; they were also sly, cunning and clever and had come to dominate the region.

Their brutal dealings in cannibalism and the slave trade had made them rich and feared; they preyed on the weak and helpless tribes who lived under their shadow. Their cruelty and savagery gave them an almost mystical power, helping to create a mystique around the region of Arochuku where, in a deep, densely wooded ravine stood two grotesque and bloody sacrificial alters; behind these was a cave which was believed to be the home of one of the Ibo gods, Chuku. This place was jealously guarded by priests, and people would come from many miles away to consult this Oracle for advice and guidance. This practise had the name of Long JuJu. The Oracle's advice was believed by many outsiders to be self-serving and that the Aro preyed upon the fears and superstitions of all the other tribes. For the advice and prophesy, the attendant priests operated a convenient barter system which included payment in money, food and human sacrifice. Those who were to be sacrificed were blindfolded and led away. The only evidence that the sacrifice had taken place was when the stream ran red with blood. But things were not as they seemed. Stories told by those who had been lucky enough to escape revealed that, if the person chosen for sacrifice was also suitable for slavery, once bound and led away, instead of facing the knife, they would be sold into a lifetime of servitude. Of course the stream would run red all the same but it wasn't human blood, it was red camwood dye. Many pilgrims never reappeared from the juju hut, and if the priests were asked, attributed their disappearance to being seized by the spirits; in reality they were more than likely in the hands of slave traders. Mary liked to think that it was this outrage that drew the military's attention, but could not help believing that the practise would have continued for much longer had the Aro power and influence not blocked the main British trade route from the north.

It was a time of growing unrest throughout the region, the mounting British military presence, now armed and prepared for war, put both the guilty and the innocent on edge. Mary was glad to be called to a normal dispute to arbitrate between the Okoyong and Umon tribes further up Cross River. The fact that she was respected and well-known to both tribes made her work much easier. They were content to put their dispute into her hands and, provided the ruling was just and fair, and involved as little loss of face as possible, the matter would be settled. On her return journey, she decided to take a look at Itu, sited at the junction of the Enyong Creek, which led to Ibo territory. The rumour had been spreading that the military, in their attempt to break the Aro's stranglehold, were to establish a military base at Itu; this did not auger well for a peaceful future.

The gentle and proud chiefs here were pleased to see her and, as they palavered, she told them of her intention to move to the district and set up church, school and court. They were only too happy to offer her land for the purpose. It may have been that after so many years in the shadow of the Aro, they saw this act as the lesser of two evils, to allow this influential but meddling woman into their midst. Mary believed that they thought her presence afforded them some protection from the vicious nature of the Aro rule and might at least postpone any troop movements into the region. They may have been less confident had they known that she could only do her work with His guidance and blessing, and if the Aro tribe was to remain lawless and the military took over, there was little she could do but pray and trust in the Lord. Candidly, one of the chiefs added, *"While we will be glad to welcome you, we are not sure of our priests; they may kill you."*

As was her practise with each new region, she made several journeys into the area to test the tribe's honour and to see for herself what problems lay ahead. For one of her first expeditions, a chief sent his canoe to take Mary to Iboland. It was the furthest that she had ever been to the north and the beauty of the land took her breath away; compared to the swamps and mangroves downriver, this was a paradise of tall trees and waterfalls. On another excursion, as the river widened, there was suddenly a cry of alarm – a paddler had spotted a hippopotamus, one of the most feared creatures in Africa. These huge water monsters always seemed in a bad temper and the sight of a boat was always a territorial challenge. Firstly, the hippo used his head to try and overturn the boat. Soaken and shaken, all Mary could do was hold on to the side of the canoe and pray that they stayed afloat, but when the crew, in their panic, dropped their paddles into the water and cowered together, she knew it was time to act. Mary could see the hippo was returning with increased determination to turn them over; without further ado - although afraid of water - she leant over the side, picked up one of the abandoned paddles and, as the hippo came to the surface just by her, gave him an almighty crack on his snout. The great beast roared and turned away and vanished under the water never to reappear. The paddlers, by their leaping and cheering, *"Wonderful Ma! Wonderful Ma!"* almost achieved what the hippo had failed to do, capsize them. From that night on the story was told, with much exaggeration, around many a bairn's bed and men's camp fire, and increased her legendary reputation amongst the fighting community.

Mary's Bible

Before her plans to move had even begun, she again collapsed with overwork and fever and was hospitalised for three weeks. At Akpap, Jeanie took over her duties at home, church and school as best she could and was proving to be the young woman Mary had always prayed she would be. While bedridden, she could at least keep abreast of the latest news and there was much to take in. The representative of the British Protectorates of North and South Africa, Sir Ralph Moor, had turned his attention to the problems caused by Long JuJu at Arochuku. He believed its evil control affected the actions and lives of the people for many hundreds of miles of unexplored and untamed land to the north and east, and the bottle-neck on the river, controlled by the Aro, was making expansion of trade with the Oil River States impossible. She knew this would end in tears but was so ill that, no matter how angry she became, she could not rise from her bed. By the time she was well enough to return to Akpap, the battle lines had already been drawn. She called together the tribal chiefs at Akpap and informed them of the situation as far as she understood it, advising them that if they did nothing wrong, they would be safe from the army. Thankfully they had trust in her and her word, so agreed.

Soon afterwards an official letter came from the military, informing everyone that, due to the imminent action, all missionaries were ordered to return immediately to Duke Town, otherwise they could not be responsible for their safety. Mary knew that she was safe and immediately replied informing them of her position, adding that the tribes of the Okoyong were good friends and would not rise. Her reply came a week later, in the shape of a dozen armed soldiers. As they strutted into her yard, the soldier in charge, a sergeant, stood with a puzzled look on his face and scratched his head; he relaxed, brought out a handkerchief and wiped his brow. At the time they arrived, Mary was busily working on the roof repairing a leak, dressed in her working attire, which meant that she had tucked her dress into her bloomers, as she always found it an easier way to climb. As there were few other adults about, the soldier shouted in her direction, *"Hey you! I'm looking for the Vice-Consul."*

She supposed she could forgive him for not knowing who she was, as she never thought she looked like a Vice-Consul and replied, *"Yes?"*

The soldier huffed at her apparent stupidity and laughed with his men; as if she was half-witted, he decided to shout the same again, only slower this time, *"I - am - a – soldier,"* He pointed to his rifle and took a few theatrical marching steps; the other soldiers laughed at his performance. The sergeant continued, *"I - am - looking - for – 'big – chief' - Vice-Consul!"* To indicate 'big chief' he made an arch with his hand over his stomach, signifying a rotund appearance, alias a fat belly.

Mary stopped her work and glared at him, he took a step backwards. Her reply was accompanied with the same hand movement. *"Well – you – have – found – her – I - am – 'big - chief' -Vice-Consul."*

The laughter ceased immediately, the sergeant completely stunned stood smartly to attention and screamed, *"Tenshun!"*

Mary rearranged her attire and, as the soldiers smartened their appearance and stood to attention, came down from the roof. She sat down before them on a wooden bench.

The soldier apologised, *"I am sorry Vice-Consul, I didn't expect..... I mean, I didn't think that you was...... Miss Slessor. I've been sent to escort you, safely, to Duke Town."*

Mary in frustration said, *"Oh for heaven's sake!..... Sorry Lord..... I told them I am safe here."* She sat resolute and immoveable with her arms crossed and said, in her best Dundonian, *"E'm no' goin'!"*

The sergeant looked confused and turned to his troops for help in translation; when none was forthcoming, he apologised, *"I'm from London ma'am, I don't speak African, Vice-Consul."*

"Bah, you idiot, I - will - not - go!"

The soldier took out a piece of paper from his pocket and read from it, *"Vice-Consul, I have been told that 'if I want to keep my stripes, not to return without you!' That has a big line and dot at the bottom, writ' real big."* He drew it in the air.

She informed him, *"An exclamation mark."*

He nodded, *"That very explanation mark, ma'am."* He raised his eyebrows to emphasise how important that was.

She was not to be moved, *"I will not go, God will protect me."*

The sergeant was adamant, *"My C.O. thought you might say that....."* again he quoted from the letter, *" 'unless the Lord himself turns up, and has proof of identification with him', I am to take you back wif me, or else!"* Again he indicated the exclamation mark.

She was unhappy with his language, *"You take the Lord's name in vain, my lad!"*

The soldier explained, *"With respect ma'am, as the C.O. drums into us – 'in the army the C.O. **is** Lord God Almighty, and I better not forget it!' "* He smiled, made the sign again, and added quietly and respectfully, *"But at night, I'm a* *good boy, and say my prayers to bo'f of 'em."*

Mary was still not to be persuaded, *"I will not leave, I will not leave!!"* She made the sign twice in the air.

The sergeant shouted to his men, *"Corporal! by 4!"* Four soldiers approached her and stood to attention, two at each end of the bench. The sergeant commanded, *"On the command lift..... Lift!"* As one they bent down, lifted the bench and Mary into the air. The sergeant paused, looked at Mary, and gave the order, *"Quick march!"*

Aware that it was now a lost cause, she stopped the charade and the sergeant allowed her a few moments to pack a bag and settle the bairns, taking time to see that Dan, her newest child, was in good hands. Mary felt they would be safer here with Jeanie than in the hedonism she fully expected to be rife in Duke Town. She did wonder whether the decision by the army to protect her was in her role as a Vice-Consul or as a missionary, at the same time doubting that the Church would have taken as much care and expense over her safety.

It was her first visit to Duke Town in three years and after so long in the bush, her eyes squinted at the dazzlingly bright sun, causing her much pain. It may have been a good thing, as there would have been many *'soor'* faces to witness her entry to the town as if she was attended by a guard of honour; little did they know that she was actually under escort. Slowly her eyes adjusted and the pain diminished a little to allow her to see that Duke Town was full of soldiers. For many years she had managed to forget the back-biting and petty squabbles of town life, but was now well aware that this was not the real Africa. As she wandered the streets, she came across an event that seemed to embody all that was wrong with the 'master plan' for this great continent. It was a wedding, a native wedding; with one exception, all the participants were black, it looked more British than African. In front of her, the bride, groom and guests posed for a photograph. Mary believed it was as sad a scene as she had ever witnessed. She recognised the white woman to be a missionary, who looked as proud as Punch at her creation. They were obviously a wealthy black Christian family and their friends, all of whom were dressed like fashionable mannequins in an Edinburgh shop window. They were fitted out, head-to-toe, in European clothing, the men in brightly patterned suits and waistcoats, white shirts and ties, topped off with various styles of hat; the women, dressed all in white with veils and bouquets, looked like an illustration from a wedding advertisement. To be clothed as they were in the blinding midday heat - Mary could only imagine how stifled they would be. This seemed to epitomise all that was wrong with the colonial disease, a dream wedding for those who believed that their work here was not only to make all those they met into Christians, but also to turn them into European gentry. While she wished the pair well, she could not help but feel a great sadness for the future of Africa. Mary felt ashamed that she was so uncharitable in her thoughts and she turned away in disgust as a group of drunken soldiers joined the small crowd and shouted foul abuse at the wedding party. On another day she would have challenged these drunken ruffians, but this time her frailty militated against further action.

To Mary, this place was indeed the image of Hades. How long would they keep her here? And how long could she stand it? Weeks passed and the torture continued. Discrimination and abuse went on unchecked and she wondered, was this the price they had to pay for law and order? None here were free and there was no law, and no order, to speak of. In an attempt to regain some of her sanity, she took the opportunity to visit the Hope Waddell Training Institute. The Institute had at last been set up in 1894, after years of hard work and arm-twisting, to give young native men and women a chance to be educated and to learn a trade. Mary had been part of the main driving force behind it, and she was proud to be shown around the pre-fabricated, corrugated-iron schoolroom by Mr Thomson, the Principal. There she met some of the young people who were busily learning gardening, tailoring, baking, carpentry and engineering. The Mission Board had been reluctant to fund the project, but after years of badgering by Mary and her supporters, they eventually invested in it and it was now a great success. One of the other high points of her incarceration was meeting a young lady missionary from Falkirk, named Janet Wright. They met in the Mission House and had a great blether; she quickly found that they had much in common and shared a dry sense of humour. Janet had heard how desperately Mary needed someone to share her workload at Akpap and wondered if she might be of assistance. She seemed such a nice young lass, so to avoid any future misunderstanding, Mary decided to be as honest as she could be, *"It is a hard life, the people are good, some have become good Christians, and would grace any church in Scotland. Yet there are many, who are not Christians, but they are mostly a credit to their tribe, like Ma Eme, as good a friend and ally as anyone could wish for."*

"Well, that sounds perfect," Janet replied.

Mary, worried that she had painted too rosy a picture, decided to redress the balance, *"Wait, wait, that's no' all, no. There are others who are bad and who drink. Oh, do they drink! They drink, abuse and defile, and have no sense of honour to any God, be it Christian or non-Christian. They respect nothing but the bottle, and the traders here and elsewhere are as guilty as sin. The insidious trade in alcohol is a blight on all society.*" She realised, by the surprised look on Janet's face, she may now have said too much, "*Though I find a few whacks with my slipper often deters the offenders, and is more often than not an adequate weapon to discourage drunkenness.*"

Mary looked down at Janet's smart shoes with a solid heel, "*You might want to remove the heel.*"

"*I haven't got any slippers.*"

"*You could aye borrow mine.*"

Mary wrote and asked the Mission Board for permission for Janet to join her, but the Presbytery was heavily involved in public discussions on the unification of the United Presbyterian Church and the Free Church to become the United Free Church of Scotland, and no decision on Mary's proposal could be made. She would just have to be patient.

The start of the impending war was signified by the massing of troops and the sound of soldiers marching. A relatively small group of British officers led the, mainly African, soldiers into battle. These soldiers worked not only for a wage, but also fought keenly; due to the tribal nature of society, for many it was not seen as betrayal. To her disbelief, Mary discovered that the missionaries were one of the main instigators of military action against the Aro, so she decided it was her duty to speak up for the innocents who would die, and to register a protest with the commander-in-chief. She marched to the headquarters of Lieutenant Colonel Montonaro and demanded an interview. The sentry on guard looked at her with a sceptical eye and asked, "*And who might you be?*"

She introduced herself, "*My name is Slessor, Miss Mary Mitchell Slessor.*"

The sentry replied condescendingly, "*Well miss, we are busy at the moment. If you can pop back in a couple of year's time, I'm sure they'll love to see you.*"

Mary was not amused, "*Less o' yer cheek!*"

The sentry lifted his rifle and pointed it towards her, slowly and deliberately, "*I said..... no!*"

She tried again, "*Do you know who you are speaking to?*"

The soldier was unimpressed, "*A troublemaker, by the looks of it.*"

Mary, losing patience, announced, "*I..... am a Vice-Consul.*"

The sentry sniggered, "*Of course you are, and I'm Oliver Cromwell.*" He shouted to a comrade, *"Hey Sarg, we've got a right one 'ere!"*

A soldier came out of the sentry hut, full of bluster and ready for action. It was the sergeant who had escorted her from Akpap and when he saw Mary his shoulders dropped. Nevertheless, he stood to attention and asked with great civility, *"Ah, Vice-Consul, how may we help you?"*

*"I'm here to see **your** Lord God Almighty!"* she told him.

The sergeant knew that any interruption would not be appreciated by his commanding officer and tried to dissuade her, *"He's a very busy man, I doubt he'll 'ave the time,"* she stared sternly at him, *"but I shall make enquiries, ma'am."*

In the sergeant's absence she made small talk with the sentry, *"And how are you enjoying Africa, Mr Cromwell?"*

The sentry, knowing it wiser not to reply, simply rolled his eyes and smiled.

The sergeant returned, *"He **is** busy, but he will give you ten minutes, Vice-Consul."*

"That'll be plenty time. Thank you!"

Montonaro's office was littered with maps, his desk piled high with papers, a room being prepared for war. As she entered, he stood to attention, *"Ah, Vice-Consul, please take a seat."*

Knowing that his time was valuable, she said, *"I know you are a busy man, so I winnae waste time by sitting. I want you to stop the war!"*

He was more than a little surprised by her opening statement. *"Just like that?"* he asked.

Mary continued, *"You are in control, you could do that."*

Montonaro smiled at the simplicity of her request, *"I may have control, but the power, I do not have. Do you disagree with the other missionaries who demand that we should destroy Long JuJu?"*

She nodded, *"Undoubtedly they are correct to want an end to the barbarity; all I disagree with is the method chosen to reach such a solution. The point of this war seems to **miss** the point. From what I have heard, your orders are to 'blow the Chuku aff the face of the earth', but surely the Government and its allies give no credence to the power of Long JuJu at Arochuku? You either believe in its power or you don't. It cannae be both. If you believe it to be simply superstition and hokum, why give it mythical powers by its destruction? Does that not reinforce their belief that it is something tae be feared? It mak's nae sense. To mak' a martyr of a place gives it life, long after the last body dies and the last shot is fired."*

Montonaro clapped in appreciation, *"I can see why they chose you as a Vice-*

Consul. You should have been a politician, Miss Slessor."

There was a long pause; he sighed and added with regret, *"But **I** am not a politician, and do not wish to be; I am a soldier. If one questions orders, one will not be able to do one's job."*

She scowled, *"I despise politics and politicians."*

"Then like me, you are at the mercy of their decisions. We can only wonder from where their wisdom springs, and continue to do our duty."

She argued, *"But surely, dealing with the problem at source would save many lives, not only now, but in the future."*

He shook his head, *"I fear your wise words are wasted on me; I couldn't stop the war now, even if I wanted to do so. Write to Parliament, to the Prime Minister, but I fear the war will be over before your letter arrives. Once a bullet has been fired by Parliament, I cannot order it back into the gun."*

Mary knew the battle was already lost, *"Do you pray, Colonel Montonaro?"*

"Of course," he replied.

"Then pray for your soul, and all those souls on both sides, who will die for a piece of worthless ground." She continued with great sadness in her voice, *"We have taken years to gain their trust and respect, and this is how we repay them. What will they think o' us now?"*

Montonaro stood and shook her hand, then said, *"I shall never forget your words, and I pray that we shall meet again, in better times."*

Mary left the building with pain in her heart. Only time would tell if there was any wisdom in the carnage that was sure to follow; she very much doubted it.

Mary Kingsley, whom we met at the beginning of the story, had stayed with Mary for two weeks and during that short time the two had formed an immediate bond. Though the two Marys were very different, they were as one as far as their respect and understanding for the people of Africa was concerned. However they vehemently disagreed on one subject in particular - the sale of alcohol. Mary saw the demon drink as the cause of so much suffering all over the world, while Mary Kingsley was a strong advocate of the work done in the name of trade by the merchants of Great Britain, especially Mr John Holt, merchant trader of Liverpool. It was from his desk, at this time, that Mary received a letter telling her the tragic news of the death of thirty-eight year old Mary Kingsley. He related that the always kind and thoughtful young woman had died, not in some far-off jungle, but of typhoid fever while nursing prisoners of the Boer War. A sentence from Miss

Kingsley's observation of Mary was honest and forthright, '... *if anyone who unearths the obsolete 'Sunday school' life of Mary Slessor think that she was a pious freak, they err!'*

Christmas Eve 1901
The illusion of peace

After three months, Mary was released from the confines of Duke Town and allowed to return to Akpap. Through Eme and her confederates, she had received regular updates on the war and its affect on the people of the Okoyong and, so far, all seemed well. The treaty offered at the end of the war had still not been signed by all the chiefs who had survived the fighting. Tales of death and destruction abounded and though the Aro had brought it upon themselves, there were still many being hunted ruthlessly throughout the region, living as outlaws and scavenging in the bush. Mary was glad to be back with Eme and the bairns and to return to her duties though, for the time being, she was keeping one eye on every stranger who passed through. One Sunday, after a gruelling round of school and church visits, she reached the compound and found that all was quiet, very quiet - no birds, no bairns and no beasties. Always on the alert for an attack from renegade soldiers and warriors, she stopped in the middle of the yard and shouted, *"Bairns, it's Ma."* Within seconds she was surrounded by terrified children, swarming all around and holding on to her skirt.

Jeanie whispered, *"Ma, there are three chiefs to see you."*

Mary whispered back, *"Take the bairns and yourself to Eme, say nothing of what's happened. Me and the Lord can deal with it. Stay till I send word it's safe. Go quickly now child!"*

As soon as they were safely out of sight, she started for her house. It was dark inside; with difficulty she could see three men sitting in a row on the floor. She could just make out the lightness of their skin and knew that they were from the Aro tribe. Once she had lit the fire, she recognised one chief whom she had seen stand sentinel for King Okoro. The three men stood and bowed their heads in salutation.

The sentinel spoke, *"We wish you no harm; we are being hunted and can trust no one."*

Mary reassured them, *"You know you can trust me."*

"It is what King Okoro told us. We have come to palaver."

Mary with mission helper & children.

"Where is the King? Is he safe?"

The sentinel whispered a reply, *"Since the war, he is being hunted like a dog and now hides in the cracks of rocks, under stones, in the shadows of shadows. He will not be found. Will you help us?"*

Mary could not refuse, *"I gave King Okoro my word that I would, and I will."* She tried to put them at their ease, *"You are safe here. Please sit."*

The sentinel began, *"We have walked many miles to see you, the river is full of gunboats and the bush is our only friend, other than you, Ma."*

She nodded in thanks, *"No one will touch you while you are with me, but you know that you have done much evil to those you serve?"*

The three chiefs bowed their heads and said, in unison, *"We have Ma, we have."*

From beneath his beaded breast-plate, the sentinel produced a pile of papers, *"We have been given these pieces of paper to sign, and know nothing of their meaning. These words are like small crawling insects and snakes. We are wise Aro, but what is this?"* He held the papers in his hand and waved them towards her, *"If I make my mark, are we slaves?"*

Mary scolded them, *"It would serve ye right! Did the soldiers not explain what the paper said? Did you not ask?"*

"To ask the soldiers would be to lose face. We said we would palaver and make our answer. In defeat all we have left is who we are."

Mary realised there was much work to be done. *"First we shall eat, then we shall read and palaver."*

Over the next few days, they did indeed palaver, they argued and agreed, agreed and then argued and when things arose in the treaty that she thought unjust, she explained it to them and how to make their case. On the evening of the fourth night, the palaver over, she wished them well; they thanked her for her kindness and disappeared back into the bush. A month later, news reached her that after further palaver the treaty had eventually been signed. Mary felt an overwhelming sadness and thought, with deep regret, that if this had been done before the war, the bloodshed of countless men, women and children could have been avoided. She prayed for all those who had died and was glad that she was not a government, or an army.

It was another year before Janet Wright was given permission to join her at Akpap - *'better late than never'* she thought. From the very first they worked well together and in a very short time Janet had gained the full trust of Mary and the tribes.

Now that the situation seemed under control, Mary began to believe that a move to Itu was now possible. She gathered her belongings, said her goodbyes and began the trek to catch the weekly upriver boat. The time of the boat's arrival depended on many things, including the torrential rain and the hippos; the only certainty was that it would probably be sometime during that day. While Mary had a well-earned forty winks, she asked the two bearers who had accompanied her to waken her as soon as the boat came into sight, little thinking that while she slept, so would they. When she awoke it was dark, and the boat had come and gone. She slapped the bearers awake with her slipper, but on reflection realised it was probably as much her fault as theirs. It may have been that the Lord wanted her to miss it, perhaps He had other plans for her and after all, there was always next week.

The following week she went through the same routine, but with one exception - she stayed awake. It was still daylight as she watched the launch come round the bend of the river and pull up to the landing area. Only when her bags had been loaded and she was on board did she look to see who her fellow travellers were. It was normal for soldiers to accompany the boats, but on this launch they were exceedingly smart and alert and, unlike the regular troops, though similarly dismissive of her, they were more polite. That was until she heard a voice she recognised calling to her, *"Vice-Consul?"* She turned to see Lt. Col. Montonaro, *"Please, will you join us?"*

The soldiers, who had previously ignored her, scanned the faces of the boat's passengers in an attempt to identify a Vice-Consul. They looked blankly at each other; the attending soldiers could hardly believe their eyes as she stepped forward into their company. Seeing all these men in their smart uniforms, she said, *"I wish I had known, I would have dressed for the occasion!"*

Montonaro laughed and said, *"Gentlemen, this is the Vice-Consul, the honourable Miss Mary Mitchell Slessor."*

As she took her place beside Lt. Col. Montonaro, she began to wonder whether this was why the Lord had allowed her to miss last week's boat. As straightforward as always, she asked, *"Went the war well?"*

Montonaro smiled, *"That is unworthy of you, Vice-Consul."*

"I apologise. How goes the peace?"

He laughed and shrugged his shoulders, *"As I said to you, I am in the army not in the political service. They make war, and I execute it to the best of my ability on their behalf; the terms of peace are in their words not mine. If truth were to be told, it is an uneasy peace. They seem to want us to prosecute the war* against the Aro still further, but as they are now on their knees, it would seem there is little distance left for them to fall."

She had some words of advice, "We all have pride, and in order to move forward, if you wish those who remain to obey you, they must respect your word, not simply fear the dreaded Maxim gun."

He thanked her and said, "I agree with you, but my hands are tied. If only I had your eloquence, and the freedom to use it. What brings you out on the water - pleasure?"

"It is never a pleasure for me on the water. I am going to Itu to see if they would still welcome me. And you?"

"We have to visit Arochuku to placate the chiefs. I can't imagine you would like to join us, would you?"

He was well aware that given the invitation she would not refuse. Accordingly they sailed past Itu and on to the Enyong Creek to stop at Amasu, the landing place for Arochuku, which lay some miles further on. As they disembarked she took in the vista and was once again stunned by the incredible beauty that surrounded her - deep pools with fabulous plants, strange blossoms and tall trees. Though Itu had greatly impressed her, this was easily the most beautiful place she had ever seen.

Montonaro could see by her expression that she was mesmerised and asked, "What do you think, Vice-Consul?"

As usual, when at her most emotional, her language became broad Scots, "Oh it's bonnie, it's awfie bonnie!"

Before she could take in any more of the magnificent scenery, one of the soldiers approached Montonaro to report, "Sir, we may have a situation!" He pointed to three tall, imposing-looking, native men, armed with spears and shields walking towards them.

Montonaro cautioned Mary, "Vice-Consul, please step to the side, out of the firing line, just in case."

To the shock of the soldiers, she dismissed the warning and walked towards the three men, "Dinnae be daft! I ken them fine." They were the three chiefs who had visited Mary at Akpap.

The chiefs stood before her and bowed their heads in greeting. Their spokesman said, "Ma, you do us great honour by your visit. Have you come to stay?"

She was delighted to see them, "In time, chief, in time."

They stood talking for a while and, during their conversation, Mary took

175

great delight in laughing with them and watching the reactions on the soldiers' faces, '*it wis priceless*'. When they had finished and they said their goodbyes, with great satisfaction she returned to questioning looks from Montonaro and his men. "*Well, Miss Slessor, you are full of surprises. Here we are with guns at the ready to protect you and it would appear that you can manage well enough on your own. Of course, I shouldn't be surprised that you know these men, as it solves a mystery of my own.*"

"*And what was that?*"

He explained, "*How, during the peace negotiations, they always seemed to be one step ahead of us.*"

Mary avoided answering directly, "*Like yourself, they are wise men.*"

He had his answer, "*Yes, Vice-Consul.*"

While she made plans for her move, her work carried on as usual, and to mark fifteen years in the Okoyong she felt that, although the Church had not acknowledged her work, they should at least honour the large congregation at Akpap. She fully expected her plea to once again fall on deaf ears, but to her surprise and delight, they agreed to send an ordained minister. On the day of the service and celebration, when the natives were invited to step forward and, by the taking of bread and drinking the wine, take the sacrament, not one would step forward; the ritual seemed to strike fear into the large crowd. Thankfully, seeing the lack of movement, Jeanie led the bairns forward en masse and Mary was filled with pride. Eventually only eleven of the congregation came forward. It slowly occurred to her that the ritual had many similarities to that of the Esre bean, that ceremony consisting of the drinking of a poisonous liquid and the taking of an oath which, if falsely foresworn, would mean death to that person. The irony of the situation made her smile.

Throughout the years, she had done all she could to raise the profile of the Mission in Africa through her writing; yet she felt that her work, as far as the Mission was concerned, could have been taking place on the moon, as they seemed not to understand the region, its people, or the complexity of her work, or appear to want to. There was no glory where she worked, other than His; she wished no recognition or thanks, but there were many times she missed their support. Yet she remained committed to work for both the Church and these people, as long as He would give her the strength to continue. Without the support of the Church, all her plans to move upriver were pointless, for without additional missionary workers to take her place, moving from Akpap to Itu or Amasu was an impossible dream. She had to find another way. It didn't help that she was once again feeling physically weak, even while her resolve to find a way to spread the word was stronger than ever. She had the germ of an idea which she played with in her mind. What if she could leave Janet and Jeanie to carry on her work at Akpap? Would it be possible to travel regularly up the river, build and attend to schools and churches all the way to Amasu? Laying out her plan in a letter and, attempting to second guess the Mission Board's response, she added a sweetener, *'As you know, I am overdue a furlough; if I forego my time away will you allow me six months to try out this scheme? I will do so at my own expense.'* And to pre-empt any lengthy correspondence she pointed out that, *'this will save the Board the cost of travelling expenses and accommodation, usually incurred with a furlough in Britain, and providing my health will allow me, I believe it is possible.'*

Late into the night, and during a hurricane, with great excitement she completed the long and hurried letter by candlelight. Writing at night in such conditions was difficult; eventually she needed an umbrella to deflect the rain, which fell freely through the holes in her roof. The use of candlelight also brought its share of problems, attracting all kinds of creepy crawlies and flying beasties that crawled up and down her pen and across the paper. She sent the letter off and awaited their reply.

The letter arrived at the fine offices of the Foreign Mission Board, where a smartly-dressed man named Buchanan sat behind his desk, in an elegant, leather, high-backed chair, and shuffled his papers around. There was a knock at the door; he called, *"Come!"*

The door was opened by a tall, thin junior official, named Smout, who held Mary's letter well in front of him. He looked at his superior man and raised his eyebrows. Mr Buchanan said derisively, *"I see we have yet another missive from The White Queen! Yet another demand, I suppose? She is well aware we have no money for any of her harebrained schemes."*

Smout squinted at the storm-damaged letter which he was holding gingerly by his fingertips and replied, *"Oddly, no."* He read in silence for a few seconds, *"She is asking that instead of going on furlough, she wants to spend the next six months setting up schools and churches, by travelling up and down a river."*

The two men grinned at each other and Buchanan dismissed her appeal out of hand, *"She seems to think we are made of money, we have stopped any expansion, as it costs too much. How much will it cost? If it's a farthing, it's too much!"*

His junior, still trying to decipher the letter, added with enthusiasm, *"No, no, she asks for no money, only time."*

Buchanan replied with scorn, *"I doubt we can afford the time!"*

Smout tactfully reminded him, *"It is worth remembering, she has made many friends and allies as Vice-Consul. Her letters home, and her countless articles are read by many, many church-going people; she seems to have gained quite a following. You remember the fuss she caused on her last furlough?"*

Buchanan pondered, *"You're right, it might be as well to keep her out of harm's way. If we have to do nothing....."* he paused, *"and if it **is** to cost us nothing....."* he paused again, then smiled, *"we will back her all the way! But you must put in the reply a note of censure. Tell 'Her Majesty' that her letter is a disgrace, it is filthy and almost illegible. Even she must observe social etiquette. We will simply not countenance another in this condition; tell her we will put it in the fire unopened. Has she no pride in how this looks?"*

"And that is not all there is!" Smout turned over the envelope and a number of dead, many-legged insects fell out. Mr Buchanan stood up in a panic, immediately flicking them off the fine leather of his desk and on to the floor, before hurriedly standing on them.

Unfortunately, when the good news reached Mary, she was very ill and incapable of carrying out any plan. She was given the sternest advice by the doctors in the hospital that she should leave Africa immediately for a long rest or they wouldn't be responsible for the consequences. Although she took their advice seriously, she was well aware that, if she weakened, her plans would be put back years, or might never happen at all. Her normal workload was testing, but what she was now proposing would require every ounce of strength she possessed; something would have to change. That change came reluctantly, after hours of soul-searching and prayer; she would have to resign as Vice-Consul. Mary felt satisfied that she had served her country well for twelve years in that role, and though she had refused personal payment, they continued to pay her £1 per year; the balance was given to the Mission, and she knew that **that** was something the Mission would miss. Her duty was, as it had always been, to serve the people and the Lord, and she knew in her heart He wouldn't miss the money. Mary expected no argument, or reaction to her letter of resignation, so when a reply arrived, it came as a surprise and in the strangest of guises; it arrived in the form of an invitation. It was a printed invitation from the High Commissioner, asking her to attend a formal reception in **her** honour at Duke Town; she was speechless. Mary checked the envelope many times, just to make sure it was actually addressed to her; her eyes moistened with excitement and pride, *'imagine a wee Scot's lass with such an honour'*. She thought, *'Lord I can't believe it, Lord I can't imagine it, Lord I can't go!'*

As her vanity was replaced by reality, it was obvious that she was in no fit state to travel, and even if they carried her all the way, the white ants had eaten her last respectable dress. The Lord had made up His mind for her, that it was not to be and she was more than happy to remain at home. Yet, when she wrote to decline the invitation, she did so with a little sadness, and a great deal of relief. Now free from the strain of attending, she returned to making plans for her greatest adventure. It was a few weeks later, while hard at work in the schoolroom, that Eme interrupted, excited and breathless. *"Soldiers march to you Ma, you best run!"* she screamed.

Mary, used to Eme's flights of fancies, told her, *"Dinnae be silly, I don't run, in fact, I'm no' sure if I can."*

Eme insisted, *"I see them with my peepers!"*

Mary, in front of a class of students, corrected her, *"How many times do I have to tell you, they are not peepers, they are your eyes."*

Her 'sister' pointed out, *"Ma, you say peepers."*

Mary could only giggle, as did the class of students. *"That's not the point, silly woman!"* she scolded.

When Mary reached the doorway and looked out she could hardly believe her peepers. She still had vivid memories of their meeting and the toffee incident. There was no doubt who he was; tall, thin with a long waxed moustache - there could be no doubt it was Sir Claude Macdonald, the High Commissioner, and he had come to visit. He greeted her, *"Good afternoon, Miss Slessor, if you couldn't come to me, I hoped that you would not think it inappropriate for me to come to you."*

Mary found it hard to keep her emotions under control and only managed to hold back the tears with the greatest of difficulty; she welcomed him as she did all her visitors, *"Would you care to come in for a cup of tea?"*

He smiled and asked, *"If you have the time?"*

"Oh, I always have time for a cup of tea."

Mary dismissed the class and put on the pot of water to boil while they talked. She excused her poor dress, *"You find me dressed for work, not entertaining."*

He insisted, *"I would have you no other way. You seem to have an engine for work that those who know you admire greatly. The social niceties are for those who crave the admiration of society; I believe you to be the antithesis of society. My uniform is a convention, to inspire confidence in those who lack it; your actions and success speak louder than any fancy dress."*

As Mary poured the tea, Sir Claude explained, *"I come as a Government official to ask you to reconsider your decision to resign....."* Mary tried to interrupt but he raised his hand to stop her, *"but I am sure that you have your reasons. We keep a close eye on your movements, in a paternal way of course, and think your plan to service many stations on the river to be one of great merit. All I would ask of you, is that once you have this under way, and have regained a surfeit of time and energy, you will keep the door open to take up a judicial role in the future?"*

She replied with her usual humility, *"The Lord guides my hand."*

He knew that only too well, but asked, *"But does he tell you what to say? I hear your court is the most respected in the entire region. Not only do they come from far and wide to consult you, but even the most fearless of fighters abide by your decisions! Other courts, much less successful than yours, are manned by soldiers with guns, great powers and fearful punishments. These courts are not the courts talked about by the natives, they are not feared. No, they fear the little woman with the fiery hair and her slipper! From the tales I have heard, and the accounts I have read of your work as Vice-Consul, if I had another two or three Miss Slessors, I could let the rest of the staff go."*

She gave him some advice, *"If you respect and understand these people, they will honour you, and give you their trust. They are good and loyal friends; treat them ill at your peril; they mak' poor enemies."*

Like moths to a flame

The work of establishing outposts on the river had, so far, gone well. Within a short space of time, which is African time, the first school and church were up and running and it was time to announce to the people of Akpap that she was to leave. Mary knew that this would be sad news to them, but she had confidence in the two women who would take her place. Well before the day of her leaving, people began to arrive from villages far and near to say their farewells, or so she thought - their tears were not at her leaving, they had gathered to plead for her to stay. They came with gifts for her and the bairns, all kinds of fruits, chickens and goats as tribute. She felt their sadness through their love, but assured them as best she could that they would be safe without her, and so, amidst tears, they began to load the boats.

The weeping and wailing was heartfelt and humbling, and to the ringing of their mournful song, she set off on her journey. Their deep affection and sorrow had touched Mary deeply, and once out of sight she fell prostrate on the floor of the canoe and wept.

In time, she gathered the strength which she would need for the work ahead. Once again there was much to be done to make it resemble anything like home and to make it safe and secure so that the bairns could join her as soon as possible. Immediately on arrival she set about doing just that. One of her first jobs was to make the long trip down to Duke Town to 'procure' some tools and wood. After much bargaining, dealing and cajoling, when she returned to Itu, laden down with building materials, including bags of cement, she was surprised to be greeted by Lt. Col. Montonaro.

He said fondly, *"Well Miss Slessor, I came to offer my assistance, but by the looks of it you have the situation well in hand."*

They worked together; he and his three soldiers helped her unload the wood and tools. He looked on in amazement at her ability to tackle any job without fear. Confidently she began to empty out the cement and add water. *"Where on earth did you learn to mix cement?"* he asked.

Mary confessed, *"I never did."*

"How do you know what to do?"

"All I do is add the water and stir it like porridge, level it wi' a stick and wi' the Lord's help it dries flat and hard."

He admitted, *"I am impressed, and somewhat surprised, by your faith in cement, but as usual I am unsurprised by your faith in the Lord."*

Cement was essential to Mary's house building, as it was the only way to interrupt the march of the driver ants and curb their voracious appetite; the crowd of interested children were put in charge of keeping all the beasties away while it was drying. To Montonaro she related a recent incident with the ants, *"Mind you, cement is no guarantee of immunity fae the driver ant. Late one night, while in bed, I began to feel that I was no' alone. I started to feel itchy, and when I staggered to my feet and lit a candle, I could make out that it seemed the floor and wa's were alive. Then I saw that I was being invaded by thousands and thousands o' the wee beasties; they were pouring in from every door, window and gap in the wa's. They covered me from head to toe, and while I brushed them off my body, and tried to shake them out of my hair, I could feel more drop on tae me. When I looked up I could see the ants were dripping aff the roof. I abandoned the building for the night and it took me, and others, hours and hours*

181

the following day to retrieve what remained o' my belongings."

Mary had come to believe that, although she disliked the creepy crawlies, in moderation there was enough room for them all to live in harmony.

The opening up of the river was now drawing missionaries of every religion in an unseemly rush to convert the new market for souls. This may have been the reason behind the Mission Board's decision to actively support her strategic staging post at Itu. The house needed to be as good as she could make it and, as was well known, she would never turn away a child from her door; the house was soon overflowing with new bairns. When a government doctor arrived one evening to review the building's progress, he found her with her hands full. He was struck dumb by the sight that greeted him - Mary was holding two bairns and there were a dozen more infants lying around her on the floor, wrapped in brown paper.

Once he had recovered his composure, the doctor introduced himself. Relieved to see him, and not standing on any ceremony, she said, *"A doctor, good, tak' ane of these."*

She handed him one of the infants, while she dealt with the other. He looked totally confused at the scene that surrounded him. He found it hard to find the words, *"I can't criticise what I can't comprehend."*

Not sure what he meant, she replied curtly, *"Good!"*

He continued, *"I know you work wonders with few resources but?"* he paused, *"but why are these children wrapped in brown paper?"*

Now she understood. *"Oh I see. That's easy to explain."*

He felt relieved, *"That's good, I was sure there would be a reasonable explanation. Have you run out of cots?"*

She laughed, *"Dinnae be daft, it's 'cause I ran out o' milk crates."*

He repeated her answer, *"Milk..... crates?"*

"These wee souls need love and care, no' the bed o' a princess. If I turned them awa' fir the lack o' a bed, or milk crate, or brown paper, the Lord would no' forgive me."

Mary knew that her house looked like the inside of an Overgate slum, yet how things appeared did not concern her; love had nothing to do with money, poverty was not the father of cruelty. She knew well that the house of the pauper was often the home of love and miracles.

The visits of the Aro chiefs had become more frequent and their requests for her to go and live amongst them had intensified. They had learned during their treaty negotiations that, if she taught them reading and writing, they could take their place with those in power and fight for themselves. They also announced that they wished to be taught about God, which was fortunate; they knew of her reputation, when they asked for one they got both, whether they liked it or not. They promised her land for a school, but as there was still much work to be done at Itu before any move could be considered, that would have to wait. She was much in demand for advice and instruction on all native matters by a multitude of agencies and individuals, and when asked to report on her progress at her first Mission Council meeting in six years, she leapt at the opportunity. In her address, she told of her steady, if limited, success so far. She proposed that the use of native workers, at all levels, could lead to a self-supporting native workforce, proudly naming the Hope Waddell Institute as a shining example to make her point. What they made of her speech she had no way of telling, but with the grace of God they would not only see the thrift in her plan but also the wisdom. The result was gratifying, for soon afterwards they allowed her another six months to continue her roving commission. This appeared to be a change of heart by those in power, but the letter concluded with the proviso that this could only happen '*if they would incur no expense*'; as always, she had to accept that a little change was better than none. From this point on, until her death, with the Church's less than enthusiastic backing and with money more scarce than ever, she felt an exasperation, which she described in a letter as '*dragging a great Church behind her*'.

It was not all penny-pinching as the Foreign Mission Board decided to put some money towards the medical base at Itu. This was great news which they all celebrated. When a benefactor came forward with an offer to finance the hospital, they were even happier, though the Board was not so delighted by his insistence it be called the Mary Slessor Mission Hospital.

Amidst so much work, plus the distance she had to travel, Mary again began to feel isolated and abandoned; so much work and so few people to do it. Mary desperately needed workers who would follow in her footsteps and take over from her, so that she could go to new places so desperately in need of education, with a settled mind. She did at least have a core of invaluable native workers, but it was still not large enough to make her plans succeed; she prayed that some Scottish lassies would come and join her, '*what a difference it would make*'. Her frustration spilled over from day to night, torturing her mind; it would not let her body rest. Though exhausted, she wandered the house throughout the night, watching the bairns sleep, not knowing how much longer she could keep going before she collapsed. She prayed, *"Surely, surely, God, who takes care of little ones, will take care of me."*

The Church Officer, Mr Stevenson, had sent her a letter congratulating her that the new hospital at Itu was to be named after her and asking if he could write her history. His kindness, though well intentioned, Mary felt was misplaced, as she politely told him in her reply:

Dear Mr Stevenson,

You're a fine flatterer I can gather from your letter, and the present occasion gives you a good chance I must say, to set it off, but O if you only kent how small and ashamed I feel at the very thought of such a piece of Christian philanthropy being associated with my poor name you would never speak of writing about myself or my wanderings, for I feel as if I can never come out of the bush and go among people with this distinguishing mark on me. Why should I be lifted up above the others who are working better, and perhaps far more successfully in God's sight than I am? And what have I ever been able to do except what God has done Himself, and could have done easily without me...

While she had his good wishes, and while she had his good ear, she thought she might as well tell him a few home truths, so continued:

... Also the weak part in our Calabar Mission is the want of any industry or shelter for women. Where are Mrs Goldie's Girls? And many more brought up in the Mission when the Missionaries do not need them in their service. Either living with coast men, or sitting anyhow, rather than go into a harem. For there is nothing but market and sewing machines for women, and every woman has a machine and all women can't earn a living in the market. We must have something at which a decent Christian woman who wishes to earn a living, can do so, apart from native marriage. We must really try at once to get something done, and that something must not be in the evil overcrowded environment of a shipping port like Calabar. Every woman born here can work land, raise stock, and etc., and we could get land up country for this purpose...

Then there should be Elementary schools both for boys and girls, with farm works, mat making, and etc., attached, and these scattered about will supply the Sabbath services just as well as the formulae of the Church and the Minister would. This is an absolute necessity at once. The value of land will soon rise to a fictitious value, and it is true economy to invest in something that will be the basis for work in the future. Had our Church kept on her brickfield, and got a sawmill 5 years ago, we would have had practically all the workmen in the country under our influence. It has been lost to us, and we have not only lost our moral influence, but the Government employ hundreds of men at these two branches alone at immense profits in £. s. d. The same salaries as we are paying. If scattered over new places with inexpensive houses, and with a girls' school, a Minster with a boys' industrial school station, would cover the country with a network of simple agencies, and let the old stations be manned at Calabar by one man, one man at a station...'

Whether Mr Stevenson, or the Church, would pay any heed to her words, she had no way of telling, but she lived in hope, she always lived in hope.

When at her lowest ebb she learned that one of her best workers was to leave - it was her daughter Jeanie, who wished to marry. Her husband-to-be, Akibo Eyo, was one of Mary's brightest pupils at school, and Mary was delighted. Crucially, he was well aware that Jeanie had been born a twin. They had been offered work on Eme's farm and were to leave to start a life together. At this moment in time, Mary was mother to nine babes and would greatly miss Jeanie's help and her work on behalf of the mission but she could see that they were in love. As she had experienced the loss of a loved one to duty, as if it were yesterday, she readily gave her blessing and performed the wedding ceremony. Jeanie wrote regularly to Mary of their lives and progress and when she told her the joyous news that she was with child, Mary could not have been happier.

Late one night, many months later, when Jeanie turned up at her door, she was surprised and delighted to see her but was aware that something was seriously wrong. Jeanie, always smiling and confident, stood before her a shadow of her former self; she was dreadfully thin and seemed to carry the cares of the world on her shoulders. For a few seconds, the young woman stood and looked intently at her mother, then flung herself into her arms, and wept for what seemed like a lifetime. Mary knew better than to interrupt, knowing that when she felt able to tell her what was wrong, her lassie would. Once Jeanie had regained some control of her emotions, she began to talk, *"Oh Ma! My baby is dead and Akibo has gone and my heart is broken into pieces."*

Mary whispered, *"Oh you poor, poor lass."*

The young woman mourned, *"I have asked the Lord to take the hurt away; I have prayed and prayed, but the hurt, it does not go."*

Mary could only hold her tightly with every fibre of her being; she had no words of comfort, the pain was too deep. Mary still had pain in her own heart for Charles and knew that this kind of love was outwith rational thought; it was all heart and no head.

185

Jeanie needed to tell her sad story, *"We were happy, so happy the night our child was born, and it died without ever seeing the sun. My man, who had loved me, and stood in the field with me, shared the pain of our loss, I know. He wept as much as me, he built a small coffin for our bairn, but as we prayed over the grave, I watched him change. I could see that he had lost his faith. From then on he had no more smiles for me; he was no longer part of me. No matter his love for me or the Lord, he now believed that the shame of a wife being a twin had cast too great a shadow. He left the farm without a word and did not return."*

Mary tried as best she could to be supportive, *"The Lord will give you peace when you accept him back into your heart; he has already begun if you had eyes to see. You have come home, and have a family here, and a Ma's embrace to give you love and comfort. For the time being, it's all we can ask."*

They knelt down together and prayed for the Lord's guidance. Mary put her to work with the bairns, and once Jeanie had washed them, heard their prayers and put them to bed, Mary went to find her, taking a cup of tea for sustenance. She found Jeanie lying fast asleep on the bed, surrounded by her many brothers and sisters. The Lord had begun his work.

1904
That man Partridge!

The new military administrative centre was based at Ikot Ekpene, twenty five miles west of Itu. With each new administration, the rules of governance were re-drawn, as was the internal map of the country. The country had been dissected into new regions by a distant hand in some far-off place. This latest version had split West Africa into blocks, the boundries drawn with an unfeeling, blunt pen, annexing communities, irrespective of which tribe had occupied these ancient kingdoms for centuries; they simply appointed and anointed new kings to rule. These kings were, more often than not, those preferred by the ruling elite and in no way reflected the wishes, or customs, of the population. Often these men proved to be weak and divisive choices, with little or no right to their thrones; contentious appointments to satisfy political objectives. This was how external control worked, or rather, didn't work. It led to territorial, language and cultural confusion and conflict, creating dissent and intense inter-tribal rivalry. In a short space of time, those administrators on the ground soon found that by this arbitrary partition they had created more problems than they had hoped to solve. In desperation, some sought methods of slowing down, if not halting, the downward spiral of local disputes into anarchy. Some believed Mary could help bridge the chasm between high expectation and poor deliverance.

She had been informed that the new District Commissioner was thirty-three year old Charles Partridge; while she wished he would be successful, she was suspicious of any change not fully considered and wondered if he would be up to the task.

By now, she was not surprised by the arrival of any visitor, be they Chief, King, High Commissioner, Lieutenant Colonel or foundling - they all made their way to her door to find a pot of tea bubbling on the fire. One such visitor, unheralded, came to call. He introduced himself, *"Miss Slessor, I am the new District Commissioner. I am acquainting myself with the region, and thought I would seek out the fount of all knowledge."*

She wasn't sure how to interpret his introduction, so decided to test him out, *"I am happy to meet anyone who has the good of the country at heart."*

Charles Partridge was up for the game, *"Which country are you referring to?"*

"Africa, of course!" she said defiantly.

Mary eyed him suspiciously; her first thoughts were that, yes, he was smart, self-assured, tall, with dark hair and moustache, handsome, but far too young for the job.

He changed his tone and topic, *"I spent some time at Duke Town, I found it very pleasant."*

*'Is **he** now sparring with me?'* Mary thought to herself. She shrugged her shoulders, *"It has many good points, I am told..... though I can't remember what they were."*

He looked questioningly at her. Had she gone too far?

She corrected herself, *"E've a poor memory."*

He seemed to ignore her and asked, *"Your plan to use native workers to man the stations on the river is ambitious. Do you really believe they possess the skills?"*

With great annoyance, she replied, *"Of course they do!"* Believing she may have seemed a little too severe, she tried again, *"I'm sure with the correct guidance, they can do our work as well..... if not better."*

"Our work? We would be out of a job." he noted, rather flippantly.

Mary advised him, *"We are only here for a blink of an eye. We are here to teach them what we know, to share our knowledge and skills, so that they can have a future when we leave."*

*"That is not why **many** are here, they come for conquest, and what they can*

take out of the country......"

She interrupted him, *"I, am not many!"*

He stood corrected, *"No, I don't believe you are."* He looked at his watch and stopped playing the game, *"To be perfectly blunt, I have little time for missionaries."*

"I am one..... have you little time for me?"

He smiled, *"I believe you to be atypical."*

Playfully she asked, *"A typical what?"*

They both laughed and he clarified, *"Unlike the others."*

She giggled, *"Yer right there laddie!..... But there are many, many good missionaries here..... finding them is more of a problem, but they are here and serve well."*

He seemed confused, *"Do you serve God, or the people?"*

"Do you not mean the Church, or the people?" she enquired. *"It's quite different."*

"How so?"

"The Church is man's interpretation of the glory of God's word; His words are far too often used, and misused, for earthly advantage, and not purely for the glorification of His name, or the love of humanity." She picked up her Bible, every page filled with notes of her own, and handed it to him, *"I read the Bible every day. You see my own scribbles alongside man's interpretation, sometimes disputing and doubting, sometimes praising the words of the Scriptures others would hold sacred. Is it sacrilegious? To many, if they could see my Bible, it would be. Yet all I question is **man's** word, never the meaning of the Lord."*

He gazed at the scribbled pages and read aloud from her Bible, *"The Pharisees also with the Sadducees came and tempted Him that He would show them a sign from Heaven."* Then he read her handwritten comment, *"Man's cry for the moon! What does a sign prove? Is God known by magic?"* He smiled at her temerity in challenging the Gospel and admitted, *"I wish I had your faith..... and conviction!"*

Mary assured him, *"You have, you just hivnae found it."*

Mr Partridge walked across to look at her other books, commenting, *"I see from your choice of reading material you have catholic tastes."*

Mary almost dropped her teacup for she took great exception to the term and exclaimed, *"What!?"*

He corrected himself, *"Sorry, that's catholic with a small 'c'."*

"Oh..... that's fine then."

He reached for another book, *"Ah, Dickens - he is a favourite of mine, too."* He picked up her copy of 'Sketches by Boz' and, before she could stop him, he had opened it and glanced at the private inscription from Charles Morrison. He realised its personal nature, gently closed the book and handed it back to her. She took it and cradled it warmly in her arms.

Mr Partridge, aware that he had touched a raw nerve, said, *"I have taken too much of your time, Miss Slessor. I hope you will not take it as too much of an imposition if I call on you again for your unique and insightful views. I'm off to talk with the Ibibios chiefs, and am not sure of my ground; with your help I may avoid mutually costly mistakes. I respect your candour, I find it better to have my mistakes pointed out before I make them, rather than after."*

"What you need to remember, is that we are different people from them."

He was surprised, *"Not words I would have expected from you."*

"It's no' as it sounds. While they are being constantly punished and kept down, they will never aspire to be better. If they continue to believe themselves inferior to us, why should they look up to the skies and bless the Lord? Give them respect and honour, and they will rise to be the best of people. Educate them, employ them, pay them for honest labour, and they will work hard and wish to prosper. It's their country, train them to be proud, and no' ashamed of it."

He nodded, *"Now I understand your meaning. I thank you most sincerely. May there be many more times you will correct me, and put me in my place with such grace."* He stood up, *"Oh, as it is nearly Christmas, in the spirit of the season, I have a gift for you and yours; I hope you will save it for the day, and enjoy it as much as I have our conversation."*

He smiled, and with two hands presented her with the large gift wrapped up in brown paper. She was taken by surprise, so surprised in fact that she couldn't think of any words to thank him properly; she felt somehow offended, deeply offended by this man. What a cheek for a young man to presume that a grand old lass of fifty-six would appreciate any gift he could give. Mary made up her mind that the next time they met, she would give him a piece of her mind, a big piece. As Christmas Day approached, she found it harder and harder not to peek inside the parcel; every day she cursed *'that man Partridge!'* for putting such great temptation in her way. When her resolve eventually ran out, and she opened the gift, she saw it was a magnificent plum pudding; she was beside herself with delight. As soon as she could, she put pen to paper to thank him:

6th Jan 1905

Dear Mr Partridge,

*I can't help it! I **must** write a "Thank You" for such a Lovely Huge Pudding! I'm only afraid I shan't get a chance to send part of it to the dear Sister at Okoyong & the bairns. We had nothing at all to differentiate last Xmas from other days, except that 5 days seat amongst the flies & dirt at Ikoneto Beach and this will be such a treat. It is simply lovely! Surely it is a Home made one Eh? & what about the basin? Am I to keep that too? For such a basin is in itself a big thing here.*

*I had a good shake of fever the night you left me. I had scrubbed all morning, having the rain water, & that was the price! So I refused to let the Children boil the Pudding till yesterday morning, & we had it for breakfast, tea and dinner, & again to breakfast this morning. A Plum Pudding is my weakness, & it was always on the table on my birthdays (when I had a home and birthdays) which is in the far past now. All I want to make perfect, is someone to share it with, who **understands**.*

This is not leap year is it? & I am over 50 years old!! & probably you have a wife, so there's no manner of shadow of my being immodest. Eh? Well, I can keep a pudding for a week at least in good condition, so I don't despair of getting a bit down to Okoyong before that.

Many, many thanks! & for your visit as well, & and I trust you will use the freedom of saying, or sending at any time, if you are out of anything, or are in need of anything I can get. I would do the same to you as my neighbour, & I keep most stores here, so though you would not think of it, I have almost anything for ordinary use beside me.

I am Yours very sincerely
MM Slessor

It was only after she had written and sent the letter did she consider its schoolgirl impetuosity. Though he was a young man, he had a position and power that should be respected; her letter, as far as she could remember, was naive and far too familiar for a woman of her age. For some reason, Charles Partridge seemed to bring out the worst in her. In the future, would he ever trust the judgement of such a childish woman? She was ashamed of herself and her emotions and resolved that, should he deign to reply, she would never let it happen again. But it was such a very thoughtful gift.

Mary's affect on men, young and old, had been noticed and commented on. One such observer noted, *"She had the power of attracting young men, and she had great influence with them. Whether they were in Mission work, or traders, or government men, they were sure to be attracted by her vigorous character and by the large-hearted, understanding way she would talk to them or listen to their talk of their work or other interests. She loved to stir them to do great things."*

The Aro war had been the precursor to the inevitable opening up of West Africa and, with the authority of the army established, expansion began to tear down the bush, and road and bridge building began. Like General Wade's roads in Scotland, they had always been the government's best and quickest way to control an unruly population. Though her future destinations would be literally off the beaten track, the new road at least made some of the journeys easier on her auld tired bones.

As a consequence of her previous experience as peace-broker, and her recent meetings with Mr Partridge, she was approached by the High Commissioner to become Vice President of the native court. Had it not been for the strange affinity that was beginning to blossom between the two, she may have refused the position. With her acceptance, she now had the honour of becoming the first woman Magistrate in the British Empire. On one of Mr Partridge's too infrequent visits to her, he did, in her opinion quite indelicately, remark on her inability to walk as easily as once she did. She believed that this young man's presumption had to be curtailed, so she replied in a high-handed manner, *"Young man, when you have the experience and knowledge that I possess, and you have come here to plunder, I imagine that someday, a long way off, you too will be weighed down by this great responsibility."*

She stuck her tongue out at him and he laughed, *"I bow to your superior intellect. Ma, if I can think of any way to aid you on your lengthy and arduous journeys, I will do so."*

A month later, a present arrived from Mr Partridge, with a note attached:
Dear Miss Slessor,
I hope this may aid you, and your great weight of responsibilities,
Yours, Charles Partridge

The parcel, whatever it contained, was very large and again wrapped in brown paper. When unwrapped, she found to her amazement and amusement that it was a bicycle! As with the plum pudding, this seemed at the same time bare-faced cheek and a wondrous gift. Soon she was to be seen on the bush paths, or on the new road, doing her rounds of church and court, peddling through puddles with her skirt tucked in her bloomers, freewheeling down hills with her bare feet raised high in the air. She had tried cycling in Scotland in her younger days and had been so *'faird'* of dogs that, if she saw one, she would immediately dismount and push the bike until the animal was out of sight. Here in Africa, unless she was being chased by a leopard, she cycled through all that the Lord put in front of her - *'she wis fearless!'* The bicycle took years off her and she soon began to miss cycling when called to places it couldn't go. She would cycle as far as was possible, leave it at a village or station and pick it up on her return. The natives would wave and cheer as she sped past, shouting, *"Here's Ma, on Enan Ukwak!"* the iron cow.

As the area's administrators, Charles Partridge and Mary worked well together and, though from completely different backgrounds, he a Cambridge graduate, she a graduate of Baxter's mill, and taking into account her dislike of politicians and administrators, and his of missionaries, their mutual respect and love for the people meant that, for most of the time, they read from the same page. He would seek her advice on various troublesome events and, even if he didn't ask for it, she would give it to him anyway. Mary liked to think that their relationship was similar to that of an elderly aunt and her favourite nephew, she being kind and guiding, and he eager to learn from her wealth of experience; though whether he saw himself in the role of nephew is quite another matter. Between them, they kept peace in the district as best they could, with as little fuss or confusion as possible. Mr Partridge was also a powerful buffer between herself and the influx of administrators, both black and white, who came in on the new roads, and brought new ideas and new problems.

Her ventures to spread the Gospel further afield were yet again seriously curtailed by the lack of new recruits so desperately needed to take over the work she had begun. It had never been her intention to have an empire of stations run solely by her; she would create a working station and the Church would supply a replacement to take it over. Only when that was satisfactorily achieved, would she feel free to move on. She had come here to serve and not to rule; once stability, trust and trade were established, she could leave well alone and return the authority and the land to the tribes. It was never easy to find suitable replacements to work in these areas; they needed to be hardy, enthusiastic and fit for the tough challenges ahead. Many were good God-fearing Christians, but in most cases that was not enough: God had to be in the hearts of the workers, not only on their lips.

Mary was beginning to believe that cutting her financial ties with the Church and funding the work herself with money from her court work, and the generous donations she now received from numerous sources, might be the way forward, but that would be for another day.

As she worked between the new stations and busied herself with court work, Charles' thoughtful gifts continued to arrive – books, including the poetry of Burns, and the annual Christmas pudding. On returning from furlough in England, Mr Partridge arrived with yet another unexpected gift; to protect her reputation for awkwardness, she was her usual scathing self. Charles entered the room carrying a very large object covered by a blanket. In a humorous attempt to pre-empt the surprise, she began to try and guess what it was, *"Well, I know it's not a bicycle..... and it's definitely no' a plum pudding!"*

"As perceptive as ever, Miss Slessor, this..... will make you talk."

She assured him, *"I will certainly tell everyone that you brought this very large contraption into my house. Will that dae?"* Impatiently she asked, *"What is it?"*

He removed the blanket but even unveiled she still had no idea what it was, so he told her, *"Its a phonograph,"* and added enthusiastically, *"they are very fashionable."* He could see that she was not impressed, *"They are in the very best of houses."*

"How can I be without one? It goes fine wi' the mud sideboard."

To give him time, he suggested, *"While you make us some tea, I will set up the machine."*

Mary left the room and, though still decidedly unimpressed, she was desperate to know the gadget's use. When the gentle sound of singing filtered through to her, she was intrigued; the hymn 'Abide with Me' filled the air, not sung by one voice but by a choir. The music took her over, so she ran into the room to find its source. All she could see was Mr Partridge, with a smile as broad as the Tay, standing beside the phonograph.

Tongue-tied she babbled, *"Who?..... What?....."*

With great satisfaction, he pointed to the machine and said, *"All the voices, all the people, are on the wax cylinder!"*

She looked at the size of the cylinders and commented, *"They're awfie wee."* She lost herself in the music, *"It's like being back at the Wishart Church!"* and stood enthralled by the magic of the moment; tears welled in her eyes.

He picked up two cylinders and explained, *"There are other songs on these, this one is 'Holy, Holy, Holy', and you can play them over and over and over again."*

This was totally beyond her comprehension, *"No, surely not!"*

"It's a gift for you," he said, then added, "but only if you do something for me."
"I won't stop trying to turn you into a good Christian!"
He knew that she would not do that, "No, that's too much to ask..... I want to copy your voice."
She was mystified, "Why would anybody want to do that?"
He was still not accustomed to her modesty. "Miss Slessor, even though you wish to be everywhere, it's simply not possible; I want to put your words on this wax cylinder so that at least people can hear you in two places at once."
His reason was still unclear, "Why on earth would people want to hear me?"
"Simply put, you are the voice of Africa," he announced.
The expression made her blush, "Awa' ye go and dinnae be daft!"
He no longer attempted to convince her by flattery, but when he reminded her of her duty, she knew she could not refuse; this man knew her far too well. Mary spoke into the contraption's trumpet and recorded the Parable of the Prodigal, Luke XV. Not only was it like her voice, but it repeated the mistakes she made from that moment on, and would forevermore! On the following Sunday, Mary and Mr Partridge gave the people of the village a treat, by playing the phonograph recordings to a mesmerized congregation in the Court House. While they listened to Mary's reading, Scriptural slides were projected on to a white sheet as an accompaniment. It was an inspirational event.

Things seemed to be going well. In the spring when Janet Wright went on furlough, Mary was joined at Ikot Obong by Mina Amess. Mina arrived well prepared for anything that the bush might inflict, including water filters and mosquito nets. Mary was impressed by her preparedness, though slightly dismissive of the young woman's lack of faith that the Lord would protect her. However, Mary soon learned to rely on Mina's hard work and ability to handle difficult situations, so much so that she would soon be able to leave Akpap in her very capable hands.

Dan the man

Mary had tried to keep work going, but illness was her constant companion and a visit from the doctor only confirmed her fears. After examining her, the doctor looked sternly at her, not that he had ever looked at her in any other way. He stood above her bed and talked at her, not to her, "Well Ma, you always ignore my advice, so I will not waste my breath giving you my expert *analysis of your health. Based on many years of practise and expertise, I'm telling you to go on furlough, or die!"*

Mary's reply took him by surprise, *"I agree. I'll take Dan with me."*

The doctor, with a bemused look on his face, smiled and exhaled. She continued, *"Doctor, you look disappointed that I have taken your advice."*

He shook his head and said with some reticence and a quiver in his voice, *"Ma, I am not disappointed, but I was ready for such a fight, it's as if..... as if, for the first time, I've said something that you have heard and you have agreed to!"*

She shook her head and smiled, *"No doctor, I always hear you, but it's the first time you've been correct."* There was a short, awkward silence, and then they both laughed, possibly for different reasons.

Before leaving for Scotland with Dan, Mary received another gift from Charles Partridge which, even by his standards, was exceptional. It was an elegant cloak with a fur hood. Her thank-you letter to him was similarly extravagant:

"Oh Mr Partridge!!!
I'm just speechless!! I simply don't know what to say! And I have just been fairly crying because you went past and did not call. I threw myself on the bed... And now comes the cloak which says, "Here your needs are all met."... Oh my cloak! O you dear!! It is so good of you and your family circle to care for me like this... Thanks beyond speech, and a good night's rest to you, Mary..."

The journey back to Scotland refreshed her failing body, and six-year-old Dan, whom she had adopted as a baby, was such a bright and attentive boy, each smile made her spirits rise. As always, from the time they left their village on Mission work, they were at the scrutiny of all who saw them. He was a perfect companion. Dressed in fresh, clean, smart clothes donated by friends of the mission, Dan seemed to glow. Seeing his Ma in a poor way, he took on the mantle of the man of the house. Even for such a young lad, he had always been adaptable and a quick learner and now, out of their normal world, as only young people can, he took the new manners, habits and language in his stride. He quickly picked up the social graces in Scotland and led his Ma on to public transport at every opportunity, insisting that she gave him the money to pay the fare, *'as the Gentleman always pays for the Lady'*. Dan, whose 'Sunday name' was Daniel Henryson McArthur Slessor, had been named after Mrs McCrindle's son and it was such a proud moment for them all to have the boys photographed together.

She had shipped her bicycle with her which she believed would give Dan a continued purpose while in Scotland. Once again, Mrs McCrindle's house was their home and, as always, they were made to feel most welcome. The house at Joppa was set high on a steep hill which ran down to the promenade at Portobello. This was the ideal early morning exercise before the traffic became too heavy: Ma freewheeling downhill, as out of control as she ever was, and Dan running as fast as he could beside her to keep her safe. They would set off from the grand house, over the bump in the road as it lifted over the railway track leading to the nearby local railway station, down and past the large church and through the narrow criss-cross of roads and lanes that led to the beach. Once at the bottom, if required, the soft sand of the beach became a natural and gradual brake to her momentum. Too exhausted and infirm to cycle back, the young boy was only too happy to push Ma's 'iron cow' on the return journey.

This was to be Mary's last trip to Scotland. Although she was unaware of the fact, she felt by a curious instinct that it was the right time to honour a promise she had made many years before to two good friends. Mary and Dan set off on the morning train in the direction of Dundee on a beautiful, sunny, cloudless day. It was a journey she knew well and as the train rattled and trundled its way up the east coast towards the River Tay, many memories of her past life flew by; but this time Dundee was not to be her destination. They left the train in Fife, at the East Newport station from where she pointed out to Dan the interesting aspects of the Dundee skyline across the estuary - 'the Law', the name given to the extinct volcano on whose shoulders the city nestled, the forest of factory chimneys belching smoke appeared as if vents, releasing the pent-up anger of the ancient eruptor. They walked through the affluent precincts of Newport to reach Kilnburn Villa, where, as she took the last few steps, she felt that she had almost come full circle. She took a moment to gather her thoughts and then knocked on the impressive front door, that of her mentor, James Logie. The door opened and Mr Logie stood before her, not the young man she had once known, but now seventy-three, white haired with matching beard. Mary, her face lined and tanned with age and the sun, hair cut short, looked little like the girl of her youth. Had they passed in the street, would they have known each other? The question would not arise. They looked fondly at one another, instantly there was a gleam in their eyes, which they both recognised. The awkward decision as to whether to shake his hand or not, was immediately taken out of Mary's control, as Mr Logie stepped forward, gently took her by the shoulders and hugged her warmly.

He and Dan were friends instantly. Mr Logie, now a widower, and father to three grown-up boys and three girls, who had long since left home to pursue marriage and careers, brought out some of their old toys from the spare room and spread them on the floor for Dan to play with. The large reception room was elegant, light and airy with fine furniture and filled with framed photographs, each one described in detail with pride and delight by Mr Logie. Once they had had tea and biscuits, Mr Logie suggested that the three walk down the steep hill to 'the Braes' on the banks of the Tay to take the air.

Dan was given leave to clamber down the rocks which led to the water's edge, with a typical mother's proviso, *"only if you are careful, and don't get wet".* Unlike Africa, there was no sandy beach, but under the clear, cool water there were large stones covered in slippery seaweed to negotiate. Mary and Mr Logie sat on a bench on the grassy embankment overlooking the beach to converse and enjoy the afternoon sun. Until then there had been no mention of Africa, both hesitant to bring up the subject, but now the time seemed right. Mr Logie began, as if their last meeting had only been yesterday, *"Well Mary, did you take on the world?"*

"No, no..... But there were times when I thought the world had taken me on."

He admitted, *"I have read many reports of your adventures in Africa. I, like many others, am a great admirer of your work. But I have to ask you, did you ever learn to curb that sharp tongue of yours? Or did it get you into trouble?"*

"Tae be honest..... on balance, it probably got me out o' trouble, more often than in."

Mr Logie chuckled. *"And was Africa all that you thought it would be?"*

She answered enthusiastically, *"Oh yes, and mair besides!"*

Mary was keeping one eye on Dan's antics and watched him remove his shoes and socks and begin to paddle. *"You be careful!"* she shouted.

In admiration, the old gentleman commented, *"You seem to be a natural mother, Mary. How many children do you have?"*

"Oh hundreds, Mr Logie, hundreds.......... I heard of your loss."

"I do miss my wife and mother of our children. Since her passing I have come to realise how much I depended upon her. Mrs Logie was an exceptional woman; she understood without complaint or explanation but, in this age, there is neither respect nor place for a clever woman: subservience to men is the order of the day. She greatly admired your frank views on the subject of women's rights, though not

always on your method of delivery. She was content to sit in my shadow while I appeared to be the centre of the universe, but it was she who was the centre of mine. Yet I believe in life, we were equal partners, in an unequal partnership." Mr Logie faltered; he began again, *"I have no right to ask....."*

"Mr Logie, there is nothing you cannae ask me. And you hiv mair right than any."

"Do you have a man to take care of you?"

Mary had not expected **that** particular question, so had to pause before she could reply with confidence and conviction, *"I am in love with a man called Charles Morrison. One day we will be together, of that I am certain."*

"Good, I am glad to hear that," and he returned to the subject of her work, *"How did you find the heathen?"*

"I went in search of the heathen and discovered that heathen was but a vague and derogatory term for any non-Christian. It was an easy word to describe what was not understood and never explained. I did not find any heathens."

Mr Logie was slightly surprised, *"What do you mean?"*

"I never found any. I found many natives who didn't believe in my God, but gey few who believed in no god at all. If I have learnt anything, I have learnt tolerance of other's beliefs. Just cos' they are no' mine, it doesn't mean that they've no place, and whilst I will encourage them to listen to what I teach, if they chose no' to accept, I don't close them from my heart, or turn them from my door. We're a' His children."

Mary watched Dan climb with some difficulty back up the rocky outcrop to where they sat. She asked if there was something wrong, only to be told that he simply wanted to check with his Ma that it was all right to play on the beach a little longer. Mary examined his clothes to satisfy herself that they were still comparatively dry; affectionately she ran her fingers through his hair and let him climb back down to the shore.

Only once she had observed that he had safely reached the water's edge did she continue, *"Oh, at first it was far from the experience I had expected. It was hard work; in the baking heat even the simplest job became a mighty labour. It was perplexing and frustrating until I learnt the language and I began to comprehend those I was there to serve. I have to admit, I stopped listening to the advice of others, and began to listen and understand for myself. I found the natives' needs to be real, not imagined, not outrageous or fanciful. Their aspirations I could understand and once we began to work with a common purpose, and in harmony, which at times wis mair difficult than it sounds, I saw that their goals were not* only achievable, but with a bit of common sense, patience, much palaver, and some arm-twisting, I found that between us they were attainable."

Mr Logie was impressed by his former pupil, *"You sound so self-assured and the reports of your countless successes have caused many to believe you should be rewarded for your sterling work."*

Mary was shocked by his suggestion, *"God forbid! You should know better than anyone whit I think o' rewards."*

"Mary, your words are full of passion and humility, a rare combination. You seem content, but are you happy?"

Mary turned to Mr Logie and smiled, *"I, like you, have a family, though mine continue to take up all of my time. I love them, I depend on them, I need them. Can there be any greater gift or more profound happiness?"*

They sat and talked until it was late afternoon. The time had passed quickly, as it does in good company. It was the dinner hour, the two rose from their seat and Mary called to Dan to come and join them.

Mary had been delighted to spend a few days with Mr Logie in the peace and quiet of Newport, but the return to Edinburgh's hectic hustle and bustle was unsettling. Mary felt that since her last furlough the pace of life had increased to an unimaginable level, so much speeding traffic, so much noise, such crowded streets. She reported in correspondence to Charles Partridge details of the visits she and Dan made to the centre of Edinburgh. Writing before one expedition, *'I'm not feeling very patriotic at all but we expect a visit from the Prince and Princess of Wales in a few days time.....'* In her next letter, in typical Slessor fashion, she described what she had witnessed of their visit, *'The Prince and Princess of Wales were passing..... but they might have been in Africa for all that I could see.'*

In one of her rare moments of self-indulgence, while window-shopping in Edinburgh, she saw a grey silk dress-suit that so enamoured her that, when she tried it on, she felt compelled to buy it. She looked, and felt, like a bride. Such an extravagance for this modest woman; was this purchase the ideal and irresistible accessory to the elegant cloak? As she returned to Joppa with the dress, she was filled with guilt and remorse at her impulsive buy. Was she losing her focus? Was she becoming too comfortable in these plush surroundings? While her old bones sank deeply into the soft chair, the thought came to her that many native missionaries, who had been sent to Edinburgh to study missionary practices and scripture, often returned as pale shadows of their former selves, becoming more anglicised and less African;

a sad loss to themselves and their home nation. As they sat relaxing that evening, she asked Mrs McCrindle, if it were not an inconvenience, if Dan could sit on the floor. Mary did not want him to get used to a life he would soon have to leave. She was well aware that it would be hard for such a wee laddie to walk away from the treats, the mechanical toys and fine books, but this was not his life, or now, Mary's. She saw this as a sign that Africa was urgently calling them back, and though her body was not repaired, for her age, it was as good as it was going to get.

They said goodbye to their friends, fairly sure in the knowledge that they would never meet again, but Dan's presence made the leave-taking manageable and formal. On the train journey to Liverpool, Dan, confused and crestfallen at the thought of all he was leaving behind, cried himself to sleep. Mary held him closely; each teardrop that fell became etched on her lap as a censure, but it was something that they both had to deal with. To experience another's culture was valuable, but Dan's own culture was as rich, if not richer, than any. If he were to carry this knowledge with him into the future, he might have the wisdom to help his country adopt, from others, elements worthy of adopting; or not, as the case may be.

On her return, they settled at Use where Mary began to work on a home for women and children. She bought the land in her girls' names and set about building a house suitable to take in waifs and strays and train women and girls. Here they would be taught how to make shoes, clothes and bamboo furniture, basket weaving and basic husbandry, the agricultural kind. This was a long term project and, while it continued, so did Mary.

Her Sundays, especially, were full of frantic activity. She walked many hours to hold services at, at least, ten villages. Her court work was taking up more and more of her precious time, often presiding for over ten hours at a sitting, and settling other disputes, informally, after lengthy palavers. Treating the sick, looking after her growing brood of bairns was only a small part of her duties, which regularly included roof repairing, laying cement, hammering, sawing, chopping, digging, planting, constantly battling to cut back the ever-advancing bush, which left her hands and feet bruised and bleeding, her body tired, almost beyond exhaustion.

Owing to illness, Charles Partridge had been sent home to Britain on furlough and, in his absence, her court work had taken on a more onerous significance. Word had reached her of other courts making illegal arrests without warrants and, due to official and officious intimidation, natives had become too frightened to leave their homes, causing essential markets to close. Mary waited patiently and prayed that on Charles' return things would go back to normal, but that was to prove a forlorn hope.

1908
Lagos for Charles Partridge, courting disaster

She was sad and upset to read in a letter from Mr Partridge that, on his return from furlough, he was to be posted to Lagos. She could not hide her feelings and, in a fit of pique, she wrote to him:

July 14th 1908
Dear Mr Partridge,
Your letter has quite upset me! What a sell! What a dead down dump!! Of course it means promotion to be called to the Lagos side, but woe's me for those left at home! And when we were resting on the assurance that we were just out of the wood and that all was to be well once more. Things have been so unsatisfactory somehow, and no one seems to see... I've not begun to wonder yet whom we shall have for a Boss! It will be all the same who comes now it is not you.

Mary knew that her words had been written in haste and frustration, yet they needed to be said; she had tried to keep to her side of the bargain, to serve the community in his absence. And furthermore, with the invasion of the district by officious men, both black and white, who had the law in their hearts but not justice, life had become almost unbearable.

The incident which brought the matter to a head concerned the death of a native woman who, by the accounts of the natives, had fallen on to a broken bottle and bled to death. Mary, unaware that an official murder investigation was already underway, was severely censured for her meddling in the affair, bringing her into direct conflict with the new District Commissioner, R.B. Brooks. Mary's patience with officialdom had been sorely tested since Charles Partridge's departure and, in an act of desperation and to show her displeasure at their high-handed treatment of those they were purportedly here to serve, she offered her resignation. If she had thought that this would bring them to their senses she was sadly mistaken, as Brooks moved quickly to accept it. At first, she was hurt that these *'utter strangers'* should choose to treat her so badly, yet on reflection, she viewed the current situation as ridiculous, verging on the ludicrous, making her decision easier to live with; she could now happily disassociate herself from these courts. It had become a choice between trying to fight a vain battle against colonial injustice and losing the respect of hundreds, perhaps thousands, of those who trusted her word. She could not, and would not, remain a government tool in what she believed had become an unfair and unjust system.

No doubt the Presbytery was happy at her decision, as they had never approved of her court work, commenting, as they had, "*...that acting in an official or semi-official capacity in court is calculated to compromise her position and interfere with her usefulness.*"

'*Her usefulness?*' she railed, '*whit a cheek! Surely it was useful to try and stop the murder of twins, the abuse of women, stop battles, wars and sacrifices, all this while setting up churches, schools, hospitals, training facilities. If **I** was not useful to **them**, I know that the Lord still has a use for me.*'

She returned to work with all the strength she possessed; unfortunately, at that time she had little to spare, and despite the short furlough in Scotland with Dan, her health was bad and mirrored her temper. Mary was hard at work, though now resting on a chair, repairing and white-washing a fence around her yard. Her helper, a young man, drew her attention to the arrival of an official car in her yard. Mary looked over her shoulder at the impressive motor. Out stepped the smartly-dressed driver who opened the rear door. Out stepped a man she recognised, it was District Commissioner Brooks. Mary's assistant was leaning languidly against the fence with paint brush in hand. To everyone's surprise, she bellowed at the young man, "*I've telt ye afore, don't stop working till I give you leave!!*" She threw the pot of paint over him, covering him head to toe in whitewash. "*Now go to the creek and wash it aff, I'll give you such a leathering efter!*"

As the young man ran off, a grinning Mr Brooks approached Mary, "*Well done Miss Slessor, it's often all they understand.*"

Mary wiped the paint off her hands and asked Brooks if he would care for a cup of tea. Brooks smiled and said, "*No, I have only a short time, my men and I are hunting a desperate fugitive.*" He took from his pocket a photograph of the man he was looking for. "*The man I'm after is a slave, who was very well treated by his white master and with absolutely no cause, callously murdered him in cold blood. He must be brought to justice and hung for his crimes. He was last seen, still brandishing the gun, running in this general direction.*"

"*I heard he had been ill-treated for years and could take no more. His master beat and whipped him, and in a drunken fit he tried to shoot him. The slave fought back but the gun went off, accidentally. Is that not the case?*"

"*Miss Slessor, I know you believe you have a conduit to the native mind, but you cannot believe all you hear, especially from certain members of 'that' community.....*" He took her by the arm and whispered to her, "*To be honest, I actually came to have a quiet word with you, Miss Slessor.*"

They sat down on two chairs outside her house. Mary stayed silent, not wishing to pre-empt Brooks' dialogue. He began, "*It's about your court work.*"

"*But you accepted my resignation!*"

"*I know..... but you continue to..... continue to.....*"

She interjected, "*To have an opinion?*"

"*Well yes..... but my officials find your 'opinions'..... while they are greatly respected by the native population, we feel they undermine the Law.*"

It was out of Mary's mouth before she realised, "*The law is a ass – a idiot!*"

Brooks was much offended; Mary defended her words, "*It's a quotation, the words of Mr Bumble, the Beadle, in Oliver Twist! He was a man with little education and too much power..... It seems that ever since Charles Partridge left, the Law has taken over from justice, now it is all about revenge and vengeance.*"

Brooks smiled smugly, "*To counter your quotation - in the judicial profession, we say, as you do in the missionary, 'vengeance is mine!'* "

Mary bowed her head in utter frustration. She quickly considered the consequences of hasty words, but saying what she thought would now no longer endanger her position, so she gave him both barrels, "*I've held my tongue lang enough!* **Don't you dare quote scripture at me!**" and she glared at Mr Brooks. Then speaking as if to the heavens, "*Why do those, with no legitimate argument, hide behind the Bible, misquoting or editing to justify injustice.*" She rose to her feet and directed her gaze back to the District Commissioner, "*You edit, no' fir brevity but to turn a great truth into a great lie! The quotation is - for it is written, vengeance is mine; I will repay, saith the Lord'.*" She repeated, "*'Vengeance is* **mine***; I will repay, saith the Lord' It is not* **your** *place to extract retribution, it is the* **Lord's**.*"

As if an imaginary alarm clock had suddenly rung in his pocket, Mr Brooks immediately reached into his waistcoat, pulled out his watch, looked at it blankly and said, "*Oh, I must go!*" He walked quickly to his car, shouted angrily at the driver and, in a cloud of dust and wheel-spin, was driven off at great speed. Mary watched them drive away through a cloud of choking dust and when out of sight she ran, as best she could, down to the creek to find her young helper. There she found him, sitting in a pool of milky water, still trying to rid himself of the paint she had thrown. As she got nearer, she stopped and looked at him sternly, then smiled and smacked him playfully over the head. She examined the man's back and gently touched the many, still open, wounds on his back, *"I'll give you some medication for these cuts and once we get rid of this paint, you must go. You'd better leave me the gun. You know if they catch you, you will surely hang. Run quietly, run far and hide well."*

Since his move to Lagos, her letters to Charles Partridge had continued, but at a much slower pace and with less emotion than before, mainly due to the hundreds of miles which now separated them. His father continued to send the weekly newspapers to her, which would arrive in a bundle each month and which she would read avidly from cover to cover. Although she appeared to have chosen to work as far away from the European contingent as she could, she cared greatly for the world and all its people and prayed for their future.

Mary's health was now almost constantly poor. The bicycle was a godsend, the second to be gifted by Charles Partridge as she had worn out the first. Dan was delighted to be part of his Ma's mission work. He accompanied her on her travels, pushing her up steep inclines and enjoying with great relish the screams of joy as his Ma careered at speed down the other side. He would run down after her and inevitably catch up as she would soon be immobilized by thick bush or mud or sand. Over the next year, she measured her health by how far she could cycle. If she was well, she could cycle unaided, though Dan continued to stay with her; if unwell, Dan was essential; and if she did no cycling at all, she was very ill.

By 1909 her gruelling schedule again brought her to her knees. In July she suffered from a massive outbreak of painful and unsightly boils, her hair fell out in handfuls and she succumbed to malarial fever. This may have been a slight to the vanity of many, but the fire in Mary's red hair had long ago been amalgamated into her personal armoury. Despite her agonies, she was glad that two of her daughters, Mary and Annie, had found men whom they loved and who loved them in return, and they were now to be married; but she did not relish her next task. For her two boys, Asuquo and Dan, it was time to let them go, but not to work in the fields - she had found places for them to start school at the Hope Waddell Institute as boarders. Asuquo was a good but lazy boy and she prayed that the regimentation at school would be the making of him, but Dan would be a greater loss to her. He was a great comfort as her son and an invaluable help to the ageing woman in her work. She would not be selfish, she knew that it was the best thing for him, but how would he take the news? She decided to speak to them both together but, as usual, Asuquo was nowhere to be seen.

She found Dan nearby, sitting in a tree, gazing out over the bush; she smiled as she approached, recalling her younger, tree-climbing days. Dan spotted his Ma, stood up in the tree's branches and waved; a broad smile spread across his face, *"Ma! Ma! Wait, I'll come down!"* She shouted back to him, *"No, I'll come up."* Dan waited patiently, but when he saw the difficulty his Ma was having, he joined her on the ground. No matter how much he pushed and pulled his Ma, they both soon realised it was one climb too many.

Instead, Dan helped her to sit under the shade of its branches; Mary put her arm around his shoulders and hugged him, *"Dan, there are times when the Lord asks us to do difficult things, he tells us it is time to move on. In fact, He has just told me that my tree-climbing days are over. I will miss climbing, it has always been a great comfort and escape for me."*

Dan, never one to give up, said, *"But I am always here to help, Ma, let's try again."* Dan's enthusiasm was infectious, but today it only made Mary feel sad. And how could she tell him that he was being sent away? How could she make it sound an adventure, not a punishment? She said, *"Dan, I would like you to do something for me."*

Always ready to please, he proudly replied, *"Anything for Ma."*

Mary explained, *"I need you to go away from here, and learn for me."*

Dan had no idea what she meant, but agreed, *"Of course, Ma."*

"I have no learning, and need someone to go and find out what the world has to teach, so that he can come back and tell me, and our people."

"But Ma needs me near to push her up hills, then find her at the bottom, to help her climb trees."

She felt a different emphasis on the truth might make him feel better, *"You're right, but the Lord needs you to be my eyes and ears now. I am too old to learn or understand. I need you to pay attention and be smart. I will miss you but it is important work you must do. I have taught you all I know, and that was gey little, now you must go and learn, then return and teach me."*

Now, with a sense of purpose and pride, he understood, but it did not stem the tears that they both shed as they sat beneath the shade of the tree.

Hellos and goodbyes

Though Mary no longer held court in an official capacity, it did not stop her, when asked, giving judgement on native issues to those who still came from far and wide to consult her and settle their disputes. Naturally this led to her falling foul of those who were now commissioned to do that work. She had inadvertently crossed swords with Assistant District Commissioner Falk who had come to the end of his patience with her repeated intervention. He wrote to his boss, District Commissioner Brooks, asking for his advice. Part of his reply was – *"I beg to point out the extreme difficulty of giving any orders to natives who have, and have had, any dealings directly or indirectly with Miss Slessor."*

Over the past few years, Mary had shared these judicial concerns in her many rambling letters to Charles Partridge, but whether due to pressures of work or possibly due to Mary's apparent fall from grace with the new administration, he may have been advised, by his superiors, not to encourage her 'involvement' in colonial affairs. His letters were now few and far between and when he did write his replies seemed distant and somewhat detached. With a growing sense of isolation, she became almost frantic to rekindle their old relationship, leading her to write to him in somewhat desperate terms:

5th Oct 1910

Dear Old Friend

If I have grieved you in any way surely it is not beyond forgiveness, & surely you will let me know, so I can explain it, or try to. I can't afford to lose your regard in that respect, without making some effort to avoid such a sorry debock - & I can't spell the word!! Guess it. Please! Dear old comrade! Give me, if only a PC to say "All Right", & if it has been a sickness which has caused the silence...

Mary hid her loneliness well from those around her and went on with her work at Use and Ikpe which continued to progress slowly. However, the arrival of Miss Crawford made her life and work much easier. It could not have been easy for such a smart and attractive young lass to share Mary's spartan lifestyle but, with her help, Mary now felt confident enough to expand her work further from the normal pathways, visiting many villages and towns that had once been impossible to reach. Often she found tribes of natives ignorant of the Gospel, and devoid of any education or clothing, yet her visits were generally welcomed as the legend of the 'White Queen' had gone before her. Often she would spend weeks in a mud hut or in a lean-to, just to get the lie of the land and to establish if it was a suitable place for a mission. Her fragile frame would bend to whatever she lay upon, though standing up straight in the morning was becoming much more difficult. When she became so ill that she had to be moved around in a basket chair, the doctors who saw her had serious worries about her future. It seemed to Mary that whenever they had no one else to look at they turned their attention to her. One doctor in particular, Dr John William Hitchcock, seemed to take great delight in standing in her way, or so she imagined. After he visited Mary at Use to examine her, he was so concerned about her living conditions, her health and diet, that on his return to the hospital at Itu he sent her a chicken and insisted that she eat it all. She wrote back and asked why he had sent it to her. In exasperation he replied that he had sent it *'because it could not come by itself!'*

Hitchcock had been made well aware of Mary's uncompromising attitude, and after the chicken incident, and despite his repeated warnings, he received reports that she was to continue her punishing schedule. Cognisant of how that course of action would inevitably end, he decided to try and save her and not simply be a spectator to her death; so he ordered her to report to him at the hospital at Itu to have a few words. Although a comparative newcomer, he had been given charge of the facility and, after a brief examination of Mary, which confirmed his previous diagnosis, he sat down and faced her to talk, *"Well, Miss Slessor, how are you?"*

Mary shook her head in impatience and disbelief, *"Excuse me, Doctor, I believe that that is your job."*

He laughed, *"Well, I like to think so, but some of my 'awkward' patients think otherwise and disobey my orders. In fact, you do."* She began to speak, *"But I am well....."* The doctor stopped her abruptly, *"Please Miss Slessor, if you would allow me to finish!"* He leant forward and continued, *"Miss Slessor, we all have our roles; I minister to the body, and you to the soul. Can we agree that I will not attempt to teach you the bible, and you will not try to teach me medicine."*

She tried to have her say, but again he stopped her, *"Oh I know you know something of medicine"* - his tone became assertive - *"so why, if you will not listen to me, do you not follow your own advice and give your body time to heal?"*

Her reply further infuriated the doctor, *"I'm fine."*

He huffed in exasperation, *"Miss Slessor, I have heard tales of your self-medication. It is legend!"* He opened and read from the thick folder which lay in front of him. *"Before long canoe journeys, if you are feeling unwell, you take laudanum, and covered by a blanket in the bottom of the boat, you sleep through the night and wake in the morning refreshed! Well, is that true?"*

"I cannae say it isnae, but....."

"No buts!"

"But, I'm fine."

"No, Miss Slessor, you are not fine, you are not well, you are very **ill**. How can I make you see sense?"

"Sense?!" she exclaimed, *"Doctor, I've nae time tae be ill."*

"Possibly not, but it seems you have plenty time to die!" He realised he had sounded unfeeling, so attempted to regain his bedside manner. *"To every thing there is a season, and a time to every purpose under the heaven, a time to be born, and a time to die.......... Miss Slessor, it is not your time."*

Flippantly she reminded him, *"Doctor! I thought we were not going to do that."*

He stood up, raised his arm and pulled at his hair, *"You are an infuriating woman, Miss Slessor!!"*

She was impatient to leave, *"I know you have the best of intentions, Doctor, and I know you have many responsibilities running the hospital; your skills and counsel are much in demand, so if you will 'release' me, I will be one less body to trouble you."*

He remained silent; she looked at him with a little concern, not knowing what was on his mind. As the silence lengthened, she rose from her chair and said, *"Well, I will take my leave and get back to my work. Dinnae you worry, I'll tak' it easy."*

Doctor Hitchcock remained deep in thought. When Mary turned to leave, he broke his silence, *"Well Miss Slessor, I take it that you propose to return to your schedule?"*

She reached for the door handle, *"Yes Doctor, I do."* As she opened the door, she heard him say, *"Well, I cannot allow that!"*

Mary stopped in her tracks, closed the door, turned slowly towards the doctor, and said measuredly, *".........Whit?"*

The doctor quickly considered the consequences of his course of action and was as ready as he could be for her response, but just in case, he added, *"If you care nothing for your health, there are many, many people who do. I cannot trust you to 'take it easy' as you say. If you insist on careering around the country until you become too ill to be saved, then I will have to accompany you, every..... step..... of the way."*

Mary could not believe what she was hearing, *"You cannae be serious?"*

"Oh believe me, I have never been more so!"

She was silent for a moment then smiled when she believed she had found the flaw in his plan, *"But what about the hospital? You cannae leave."*

"I will close it!"

Aghast at his words, Mary returned hurriedly to the centre of the room and retook her seat, *"But whit of a' the poor fowk who rely on you?"*

*"Miss Slessor, **you** are one of those poor folk, and I have absolutely no intention of letting you die before your time."*

Realising that the doctor meant every word, she surrendered, *"Doctor, yer a bad man, you micht be a grand doctor, but oh, yer a bad man."*

*"My wife and I will welcome you to stay with us until **I** think you have improved enough to be 'released'."*

Mary was almost dumb-struck; her final words on the subject had an emphasis and tone not normally associated with the words, *"God save you!"*

To begin with, Mary was cantankerous with the Hitchcocks, but given a legitimate reason to rest and, at least for the latter weeks of her confinement, she became a pleasant, amusing and entertaining house guest.

Her general health had improved with the enforced rest, but her ageing body greatly limited her mobility; as usual, Mary found advantage in adversity. She wrote to Charles Partridge to describe her proposed new mode of transport:

Ikpe Ikot Obon

1ˢᵗ January 1912

My Dear old friend,

... I have sent home for a small carriage of some kind, (a cape cart, a large, basket-type, wheelchair) which can take me over bits of the road on which I can't cycle so that I can cover a larger area, and in a small carriage shall only want two boys and I can take my lunch, and a baby or two inside with me...

Doctor Hitchcock, in his short time in the region, had not only crossed swords with Mary but had also discovered a great respect and fondness for her; he would not have taken this extreme course of action for any of his other patients, but she was not 'any'. He was to write of Mary: *'She is quite a small woman – fair hair, clear complexion, exceedingly vivacious, an excellent conversationalist... But what a fine woman she is, with a magnificent brain...'*

Though she much improved under his care, later the next year, her health was once more in decline. This time it was decided that going on furlough was the best course of action. Miss Cook, who was now in charge of women at the Foreign Mission Board, convinced her to go to the Hotel Santa Catalina on Grand Canary and, despite Mary's protestations, insisted on paying for everything. As she was in no fit state to travel alone or to walk more than a few steps unaided, Jeanie was sent with her; as she mentioned in a letter to Miss Crawford, it was the best trip of her life:

The Hotel Santa Catalina
Grand Canary
The last Sabbath of October 1912
My Dear Friend,
... Blame, or thank – as you feel and see fit – my dear old faithful friend Miss Cook, who suggested it, and dear heart: wants to pay for it!! It is the first trip in my life, and were it not an expensive one, I should say it's perfect. The expense appals me, as they would not let me go without Jeanie. I am so lame and feeble and foolish... The sunshine and the breezes, and the blue expanse of ocean, the gardens, and the atmosphere of love, make it like a visit to Paradise...

The trip did her a great deal of good, and she was once again ready to take on the world; she would need all her strength for the extraordinary events which were to come to pass over the next year.

In early 1913, she was invited to Duke Town to meet the new Governor General of Nigeria, Sir Frederick Lugard, and, no matter how much she protested, she had to go. Being 'unwell' and having 'nothing to wear' were not accepted as excuses, as the Governor General had asked to see her in person. A car was sent for her. She tried to put on a brave face and, for the occasion, wore her best (only) dress, stockings, shoes and an odd little hat, far from fashionable but it was all she could manage under the circumstances.

Duke Town was buzzing with those and such as those. She felt out of place in a town so full of ambition and ego. Many residents, wearing elegant dresses or smart uniforms, stood in line waiting to be introduced to the man on the platform. Mary hung back, hoping they might forget the wee woman in the plain dress and the odd hat, but they found her and led her to wait in line by the platform. As she watched others being introduced to the Governor General, all she saw was a light shake of the hand and she thought to herself, '*I could do that*'. The two Duke Town merchant women had been watching closely and nudged one another as they spotted Mary in the crowd.

Mrs Crabbe was somewhat aghast, "*Look who's come for a nosey - I'm sure it's that awful Miss Slessor. Just look at what she's wearing! It's a disgrace. Look at her hat; it's like a bird's nest.*"

Mrs Smylie concurred, *"Let's hope no one sees her. She is an embarrassment to the community."*

As an official came to escort Mary and guide her on to the platform, they watched with glazed looks and open mouths.

Mrs Crabbe could not believe her eyes, *"Oh no! It cannot be!"*

Mrs Smylie agreed, *"It must be a mistake, they must have mistaken her for someone of importance."*

Mrs Crabbe put her hands over her eyes, *"I can't watch, oh, the shame of it!"*

When Mary reached Governor General Lugard in his plumed official dignity, his aide told him her name. He appeared to awaken from his automatic motion. He looked straight into Mary's eyes, took her warmly by the hand and said with great sincerity, *"Ah Miss Slessor, I'm so proud to shake your hand."*

"What's happening?" asked Mrs Crabbe.

Mrs Smylie narrated the scene, *"You'll never believe it!! It is that awful woman, she's actually being introduced to the Governor General!!!"* the pitch of her voice rose higher as she continued her report, *"she's offering her hand..... he's taking it..... he's actually.......... speaking to her!"*

Mrs Crabbe had heard enough, *"It's too much, I may faint! Oh!"*

She fanned herself quickly then collapsed out of sight. Her friend, who had not noticed, advised, *"Try not to Mrs Crabbe, the ground is so dusty at this time of year. Well, there's obviously much more to this than meets the eye, don't you think Mrs Crabbe? Mrs Crabbe?"*

Mrs Smylie turned round looking right and left to locate her friend. She looked down on the ground and saw her lying in the dirt. *"Oh dear, I warned you not to do that, and in your best dress too, it's so dusty. I must come to your aid,"* and she shouted, *"Boy! Boy?"*

When Mary was introduced to Lugard, she was blissfully unaware of what he had had in mind for her. Lugard had earlier that year noted in his diary an outline plan concerning Mary - he had been '*...drafting a dispatch to the Secretary of State asking H.M.'s bestowal of some kind of recognition of her great service (this is confidential and must not be repeated until the award appears). A great lump rises in one's throat. The long years of not quiet but fierce devotion – for they say she is a tornado – unrecognised and without hope of, or desire for, recognition, in these blatant days of self-advertisement. Her great work has been combating witchcraft and the awful custom of murder of twins, and always has some little black urchin about her. But she has not feared to go under fire to* *separate warring tribes...'* Had she known, she may have given him the slipper treatment but, for now, as the ceremony concluded, she was only too happy to be released from her obligations.

Mary's escape from the excesses of Duke Town was hurried; she left as quickly as she could as she had nothing to say and had no wish to talk of nothing to those who knew even less. Why had they asked to see her? Mary felt that those in attendance were much more deserving of tribute, and would be happier to speak of it. All she wanted to do was to run as far away as possible from this sycophantic pageant. However, soon after, she was to be invited to a much more pleasurable event, the opening of a new church in the Okoyong, which she was delighted to attend. She had left that place eight years before with such pride and sadness; would she be as proud on her return? This would be a test of the success, or failure, of her 'harebrained schemes' to develop an area and put in trusted people - in this case Mina Amess - and move on. Mary knew that God had been watching over her and, having had no secret messages from Eme, she prayed that all was well.

As Mary approached Akpap, crowds were beginning to gather. This was not unusual for, at any event, markets would always spring up and various sellers would congregate; at least it demonstrated that there was a certain amount of wealth and stability for them to sell their produce. But her first priority was to find her sister Eme, whom she had so much love for despite the fact she had never accepted the Lord into her heart. Had others been successful in converting her where Mary had failed? She had prayed every day that she would see the light; she would soon discover if her prayers had been answered.

Mary reached Eme's home; the signs were not good for native symbols were in abundance. In the centre of the yard stood a mud figure of a woman painted with whitewash and with egg shells for eyes; on the figure's lap lay offerings of eggs and fowls. Next to the statue was a sacrificial altar, on which had been placed food, gin and palm wine for the gods. The dream of Eme's conversion was only that, nothing had changed.

Eme came out to meet Mary and, though older, she was much the same; her broad grin and open arms welcomed Mary back home. They wept as they hugged each other, a hug for the times they had spent together and to make up for the years they had been apart. Mary ignored the surroundings and greeted her sister, *"I'm glad that you are well."*

Eme asked impatiently, *"Are you with man, have you bairns?"*

"Oh, I have many bairns, but no man."

Eme's eyes bulged, *"And you, a good Christian woman?"* And they both laughed.

Mary reflected, *"Eme, it has been many years we have been sisters; I cherish every one that I have known you. How is your life?"*

Eme shook her head and shrugged her shoulders, *"Many bad things have gone, and the God noise is not talked to those who do not want to hear it. We live as one, as people of the Okoyong. You have touched us all, and spread goodness. Children and women now have a voice and a place. The men, who once lived only to fight, now work for trade and not to destroy."*

"Will you be at the church opening tomorrow?" Mary asked.

"No God noise for me," Eme reminded her.

Eme's love for life and all that that entailed had always been a great lesson for Mary. Her affection for the woman had been viewed by the missionaries as her greatest failure. They asked how she could call her 'sister' if she were not a Christian. As far as the Africans were concerned, they saw the strength of their relationship through the tenderness, understanding and compassion between the two women of different race and that Mary could be trusted with their friendship, without asking anything in return. They bowed to different gods, but their aim had always been the same, to do the best for Africa.

If Eme would not attend the ceremony, Mary suggested, *"Come with me now to the Mission house, I have bairns to feed and people to meet."*

Not wishing to place Mary under a cloud with those from the Mission, Eme replied, *"I am not a Christian, they will not want me."*

But Mary held Eme in very high esteem, *"You are my sister, and one of the Lord's children, we will have time to talk of our past, and our future. They will welcome you..... or I'll hae somethin' to say!"*

The following day was a day of wonder. Mary could not believe the size of the crowd who had come to praise the Lord, over four hundred filled the nearly completed church, and almost everyone, man, woman and child was clothed! In the centre of the church were the men and boys, the women stood at the sides, and the children sat in rows on the floor at the front. They had all come to celebrate their new life. Unlike the previous ceremony, Mary was only too happy to take part, thrilling the congregation by preaching in Efik for over half an hour.

This was to be the last meeting of Mary and Ma Eme, as shortly afterwards her sister became ill and died. Mary, for the rest of her life, kept the memories of that great woman in her mind and in her heart, proud to have had a good, loyal friend, proud to have known such a fine human being.

A new cross to bear

There was hardly any time to catch her breath, for the next momentous event in her life was about to unfold. A native runner arrived with the mail, and amongst the usual correspondence she was surprised to receive an invitation and a large imposing envelope. On opening the envelope she saw that it was a certificate informing her that she had been appointed a member of the Order of St John of Jerusalem, an award given '...*to encourage the spirit of mankind, to encourage and promote humanitarian and charitable work aiding those in sickness, suffering, and/or danger*'. She noted that King George V was at its head and that he had personally sanctioned the award. The invitation also instructed her to attend a ceremony in Duke Town to be awarded the Maltese Cross medal. Her first thought was '*how kind it was of the King to spare a thought for the people of Africa and me*'. She was delighted that he even knew of their existence and cared enough to send a certificate to her. Her next thoughts were, '*Why am I to receive it? What have I done to deserve such an honour? All I have ever done was my duty, no more; it is the people of Africa who deserve the acclaim*'. She wrote back and asked them, politely, if they would be good enough to send the medal to her. Such a celebrated and unique decoration was obviously not to be sent by post and she quickly received a reply informing her of the date and time that a car would arrive to convey her to Duke Town. They knew in Calabar how she would react; her prevarication could go on for days if not weeks. So in anticipation they had also sent her a telegraph form, ready for despatch, with the reply '*Coming*' written in large letters. They knew that while it sat in her house, unsent, it would bother the life out of her, so to avoid any further stress, and strain, she ordered it to be returned forthwith.

When the day arrived for the ceremony, Mary was so self-effacing that she could hardly walk to the chauffeur-driven car. The natives sang and cheered for their Ma and the great honour she had brought to them, but she could barely raise a smile as she was driven off. Mary's friend and admirer, Lord Lewis Harcourt, Secretary of State for the Colonies, who was in charge of the arrangements for the ceremony, had attempted to make it as painless as he could, so had indicated to her that it would be held in the intimate setting of the Mission House with only a small number of invited guests. On Mary's arrival in Duke Town, she was less than delighted to be taken to the much larger venue of Goldie Hall, where a far greater number of guests eagerly awaited her arrival. All the Europeans for miles around were gathered to see her accept the medal. Merchants and their wives, the military and their wives, African nurses and teachers were there to honour one of their own. Throughout the speeches of praise and congratulations by Lord Harcourt and Mr Horace Bedwell, Provincial Commissioner, she sat on the platform with her face in her hands, unable to look at the audience. The mill lass had never understood fame or adulation and was repelled at the very thought that any of it should be wasted on her. It was not until she was asked to give an address in Efik did she become herself again and proceed to entertain her audience.

Pre-empting her reaction to the whole affair, Lord Harcourt had guaranteed that, for her next few days in Duke Town, she could spend them as she pleased, visiting old friends. She was reunited with Ma Fuller for the walk through the town; they shared many memories and recalled times past. It was a suitable time for reflection so she asked Ma Fuller if they could visit the graveyard and pay homage to their many mutual friends who were buried there. She sought out their lasting resting places and took time for silent prayer for those who had touched her life. During their sad meander, she noticed two, modest, recently-erected stones. The two gravestones stood side by side, the deaths were but a month apart. Reading further, she noted that they were both merchant women, and then she recognised their names - Mrs Smylie and Mrs Crabbe. Although the two women had never welcomed Mary, they had caused her no harm. She felt no animosity, but acknowledged that they had played a valuable part in her life, helping to mould the woman she had become; she stopped and said a respectful goodbye before moving on.

Their next visit was to the Hope Waddell Institute where she had tea with her two sons and talked to the new Principal and old friend, Dr Macgregor, and the teacher, Thomas Hart. In her constant quest for news, she asked Mr Hart if had read anything of interest in the special Reuters reports. He mentioned that there was one story that had caught his eye, that of the assassination of the Archduke and Duchess of Austria, little knowing at the time what that event would soon precipitate. She remembered writing to him after the outbreak of the war, *Little did we think when we sat there that the spilling of a drop of blue blood – with the Jesuitical microbe in it too, would send Europe into bloodshed*.

She had received a beautiful bouquet of flowers from Mrs Bedwell at the ceremony which she treasured and handled with extreme care all the way back to her bush home. They were her favourite flowers, roses. As soon as she could, she removed a few of the stems with unopened buds and planted them next to the steps in the yard. There she could tend to them with only a little exertion and, with much loving care, they took root. The roses became a constant reminder to her, not that she really needed one, of what was possible with a little patience, love, care and attention, of what one could plant that would grow and flourish in this wonderful country.

Governor General Lugard and his brother Edward, both devoutly religious, may have recommended the Maltese Cross award partly as a consequence of their reading reports and articles on Mary's life. One especially, which had appeared in the Missionary Record, romantically related her life and times. After the ceremony, she was asked by the editor to write her life story in her own words. She refused as courteously as she could, '... for one thing, I haven't the time; and for another, I haven't the strength, either physical or mental. When one gets into the sixth decade one is the wrong side of the line, and the pace doesn't slacken on the mission field... If I were sitting down in Edinburgh and the kindred spirit asked me questions, I might recall the dear fellow-labourers and the days in Calabar when it wasn't a picnic. White and black, there were giants in those days, and were I to record some of the manifestations of God's power and guidance and loving patience to myself through times of loneliness and stress, it would doubtless strengthen the faith of His people; but to sit down and conjure it all up then write it out, makes me feel faint. One cannot do much amidst schoolboys and visitors, and sick folk and a household, and through the long sleepless nights which are now my portion. It would be too strenuous, and as the shadows lengthen and no sound of a fellow-traveller's voice comes up behind, and so much lies to be sorted out before the sun goes down, one's energies are watched like a miser's hoard...'

They wrote of her in British Weekly – '... Mary Slessor, to those who personally know her, stands a genius among women because she has "consecrated" a good Scots head and a vigorous Scots will to the redemption of a people with an absolute contempt for convention and the un-needful...'

1913-1914
The beginning of the end

It had been a hard year, with both sunlight and shadow. Mary had begun to worry that there was something amiss with her, confused as she was by a world that gave awards to honour such small success. She felt unworthy; she had done nothing, the Lord had done it all, and she was ashamed of the celebrity it had brought. There was so much work still to do. Once back in her distant isolation, she wore the medal with pride as it had been given by the King, on behalf of a higher King, to the people of Africa. All she was sure of was that she must move on further, as far away as she could from all the 'stooshie' that the medal had created, to go to areas that were desperately in need of the teachings of her Lord. She continued to make good friends and allies wherever she went; one man in particular, whom she befriended, was viewed by many to be an inappropriate confidant. While passing regularly through Use, she would often visit an old Hausa trader, not in itself a serious caution, but when he was observed to run to greet her, kiss her hand and take her arm, then, on parting, respectfully bestow a Muslim blessing upon her, this was considered to be beyond the pale by her detractors.

While on her travels, she had spotted an abandoned Government Rest House at Odoro Ikpe and late one Saturday evening, with Jeanie's help, she struggled desperately to climb the steep hill to see what she could see. It was a hard walk, the highest she had ever been in Africa. The sun began to set as they reached the top and Mary shuffled around the abandoned house to see what still remained; as usual, she did not notice its obvious faults, only its potential. She didn't care that the four-apartment building was empty of any furnishings and had only holes for windows, doorways but no doors. She stood on the verandah and gazed at the black velvet night, with millions of diamond stars above and out to the darkened landscape beneath her. Her physical pain, gone for the moment, was replaced by the hurt she felt in her heart for those living nearby, who had so far refused to accept learning or to allow the Lord into their lives. Suddenly, she fell to her knees in agony. Jeanie, who had been watching her closely, came running to her aid. She sat beside her and held her closely.

Her mother rallied a little and told her, *"It'll be hard to mak this work, but I'm determined to try."*

Jeanie stroked her forehead and pleaded, *"Ma, it is time for you to rest."*

Mary had never learned when to stop, *"But I'm well enough to carry on, the Lord needs me to."*

Her lassie tried to make her see sense, *"But He will be sad if you can do no more. If you rest for a time, go home to Scotland and become new again, He* would rejoice, we all would.*"*

In the coolness of the night, they sat in silence and looked out into the darkness. The young lass cradled her mother's head and held her small, wrinkled, bony hand; Mary could hear Jeanie gently weep.

As if in a dream, Mary continued, *"**This** is whar we'll set up our new home, it's perfect."*

Jeanie still tried to reason with her, *"But there is nothing here, Ma! There are many stations that have much to comfort you! They have beds and chairs and plates..... and windows and doors!"*

Calmly Mary responded, *"Jeanie, I had nowt tae start wi', and hae nowt noo, but I have a full hert, and the Lord will provide."*

Soon Mary had managed to procure a pail, cooking pot and plate, her wheelchair to sit in, and the loan of Miss Peacock's camp bed to lie on, not much but it was a beginning. It was the perfect base, mid-way between her past and her future endeavours; she could work at Odoro Ikpe, Ikpe and Use from this vantage, it felt right. At least the bairns were settled; Mary and Annie were married and had homes of their own; Alice and Maggie were in Duke Town learning to wash, iron, cut and make clothes; and the boys were doing well at the Hope Waddell Institute. In time, with patience and a great deal of persuasion, one by one the chiefs allowed her to enter their lands and trusted her to teach there unhindered. As the months passed, she became increasingly deaf and blind, and even more immobile if that were possible, but the work had to continue, so she kept going. Mary was now struggling to walk even short distances, yet even at her worst she insisted on being pushed in her wheelchair, and when the wheels lost purchase she was carried. When visited by a churchman, a Mr Bowes, she was so happy to meet someone who could tell her of the world outside and to show him around her domain. Proud of her new home, she struggled unsteadily to her feet. Though not going far, the gentleman was surprised when she picked up a cumbersome shoulder-bag and wore it for her walk. When they reached the verandah, she pointed to places of interest in the landscape and described her future plans. Mr Bowes could clearly see that she was finding it difficult to stand, and said, *"Miss Slessor, you should sit and rest, at least let me take that bag."*

He was more than surprised when she took the bag from her shoulder and disclosed its contents, saying, *"Na, na, laddie, I have my cat in here, it helps me balance."*

Reluctantly, Mary had to admit, at least to herself, that she was becoming seriously ill and she had to consider the consequences of her death in such a remote place. What if she were to die here alone, her body found, and her skull taken by natives? That would be juju to rival any and be an instrument for such disorder that it might ultimately challenge both the Mission and the Government. And as she didn't want to leave any personal correspondence lying about to be read after she was gone, late one night she destroyed all her letters, although she need not have bothered, she could have left them lying on the floor. As she wrote in her diary, *"Dirt reigns supreme. Rats dirt everywhere, clothes eaten by them, and bottle of milk eaten through by white ants..."* If that were not enough, by July the signs of trouble abroad were beginning to have an effect in the region. Canoes travelled the rivers empty of produce, no building materials were available and the price of food had doubled, confirming the extent of the insidious spread of the dreadful War. In the latest bundle of newspapers to arrive, with horror she read for herself the brutal details and she feared for all mankind:

Saturday, September 5th 1914

Reported loss of 10,353 men of the British Expeditionary Force.

The Kaiser... reined his finest troops in its lines at Cambrai and Le Cateau to which they had retired fighting fiercely all the way for three days.

... The British were to continue their retirement at daybreak, to take up position in line with the French at La Fere. To prevent that retirement, and to cut off the British from their allies, five German corps were hurled against them, and the result was one of the fiercest that was, perhaps, ever fought.

Stubborn and superb was the stand made by the British against tremendous odds.

In dense formation the Germans advanced right across the open, and artillery, machine guns, rifles mowed them down in hundreds.

They staggered under the terrible hail of lead, went back, and then came on again. Five times and with splendid courage the German hurled their masses against the British troops but all was in vain...

Tremendous German Losses: 1,000 upon 1,000's fell, and with thinned and shattered ranks the soldier of the Kaiser reeled back and came not again; they had had enough. The slaughter was terrific.

Saturday, September 12th

British Forces Almost Annihilated At Mons

Saturday, September 19th

Germans Shock Humanity
Appalling Atrocities Committed by the Kaiser's Hordes
Men, Women, and Children Burned and Bayoneted
... But why wreak vengeance on woman and children... But how about
the woman I saw with the hands and feet cut off, how about the white-
haired man and his son whom I helped bury outside of Sempst, and
who had been killed merely because the retreating Belgians had shot a
German soldier outside their house? There were 22 bayonet wounds in
the old man's face. I counted them...

This was the conflagration she had feared, only worse, much worse than her blackest nightmares. She prayed and wept at so many deaths. All she could hope for was that it would soon be over, but she knew that the madness of war often takes its own time to die. *'If they would only palaver!'* she thought, yet was well aware that the bullet had left the gun. That was not the only catastrophe; King Okoro, who had been hunted after the Aro war, had been captured and imprisoned in Calabar. News had reached her, unofficially, that he had died while incarcerated but not of natural causes; it would appear he had been poisoned.

Her feelings of hopelessness and isolation were not lessened by lengthening periods of chronic illness and self-imposed exile in the worst of conditions. Was it that her lifelong dislike of what others called 'civilisation' was now beginning to encroach and cast its dark shadow over the entire continent? There was no hiding place in a world that had no respect, or value, for human life; would the war soon destroy cultures and heritage that had taken millennia to build and, once destroyed, would their very existence be forgotten? What would be left when the guns of war ceased? Once again, it would be the women and children who survived who would be left to mourn fathers, husbands and brothers. The winners would count the acres of land they had won; she doubted that they would count the dead bodies with the same relish.

On the 24th September, Mary collapsed. After two weeks of raging fever, help was sent for; on medical advice she was immediately transported to Ikpe, carried on her camp bed. During the journey her long-term companion, her yellow cat, vanished into the bush, never to be seen again. On her arrival, the doctor examined Mary and, in his opinion, she would not live till morning.

By the time Dr Wood arrived from Itu, Miss Peacock, who had seen Mary recover from the brink before, did not think she had the strength left within her. Yet Mary, as she had done so many times, would not give up and, though in a poor condition, by the turn of the year, somehow she was back at work. She now had to be carried to her many church services and teaching. For those who watched, it was a sad sight, yet her determination and belief drove her on beyond all expectations.

Her diary of 1914 tells of her pain and devotion:

Thursday 1st January... Strong fever ague all night crawled to church.

Tuesday 16th June... This deserves red ink. A sheet of iron fell from the roof and cut my chair in two, the wind made my hair fly, but it did not touch me. A miracle, life rededicated.

Wednesday 17th June... Crazed with pain, but none the worse.

Sunday 19th July... Marvellously helped! A fine Sabbath, but bodily strength at lowest ebb.

21st September... Unable for duty, Weariness intense, Dan keeping school.

Her correspondence with Charles Partridge, her good friend and confidante, was of the utmost importance to her, and when his letters slowed almost to a stop, she felt more alone than ever. But when two plum puddings, and a letter, arrived from him, and surrounded on Christmas Eve as she was by most of her adopted family, she could not have been happier, as her letter in reply confirms:

Use Ikot Oku

24/12/14

My dear old friend,

The plum puddings have just come in, and as this is Christmas Eve, I have ordered one to be opened and the whole lot of us are to have it tonight, which has caused great excitement and all are jumping about like Crazy things... Please to forgive me for my want of Faith, but I thought you had let me drop out of your regard and memory, and it pained me exceedingly. Specially since this terrible trouble of German Hatred and jealousy has come to involve our Empire, and threaten our Home life with unspeakable gloom. So my joy and comfort is profoundly deep and is better than the medicine I am forced to take nowadays in order to help the old machine to run till the warm weather, and rest comes to the Homeland. O I have missed you, and I have had to tear up and burn so many of your letters since I was able to get about a little, that it ached more, only I had to clear out my desk, as one never knows how soon an attack may pick me off, and I don't want to leave anything of personalities lying about for prying eyes.

Now here is a sheet of paper filled with my precious self! What about you? Where are you? What are you doing? How do things go with you? O you old dear. I am overjoyed to know you have thought of Me...

She had begun the letter on Christmas Eve and had described the almost Dickensian joy which surrounded her; nearly all her adopted children were gathered, including Annie and her new baby. In Mary's frail state, their youthful exuberance began to take its toll on her and she excused herself to find some peace and quiet to finish her correspondence. The sad fact was that this would be the last letter she would write to her 'Old Boss'. Ever the eternal optimist, her letter continued in that vein, but soon returned to more serious matters as if she had the weight of the world upon her shoulders:

... But this is Christmas morning, and I must wish you – out loud with my voice – a very Happy Christmas and a very Good New Year. God can carry it to you, and give you all I wish, without interval in telegraph or post, and He will. May 1915 be the best year you have yet known... When the first serious 'reverses' in Flanders and France came it shook me so. I thought it was a shock, and for so long was so ill, that when they carried me to Ikpe, and then brought me here, I was almost unconscious, and three months have made little way towards recovery. But I can hold out till March, and if things are not worse at home I shall probably then take a trip to Scotland, or at least to Canary... I find this is a half sheet of paper. I'm sorry it is so untidy, but it carries much loving grateful regard all the same, and the household joins me in it. Hoping you will soon write if only a scrap to say how you are, and where & etc. I am dear Old Boss

Yours ever Affectionately
MM Slessor.

Dan had returned home from school for the festivities to find his mother painfully thin, drawn and unable to walk more than a few steps; at the sight of her he burst into tears. All during the short vacation, he begged his Ma that he be allowed to stay to tend to her. She would have none of it and reminded him that his duties were to his studies, adding that she would soon be well and would see him again soon. The morning Dan returned to school followed its usual pattern. Mary said her goodbyes, waved and waited on the verandah until he was out of sight, but this morning he thanked God that she could not see the floods of tears that cascaded down his face.

Although she rallied slightly in the second week of January, she had a relapse and lay in a semi-conscious state for several days. Her five girls, her two Scottish aides and Dr Robertson did what they could but could now only stand around her bedside, helpless in silent vigil. Mary fell in and out of consciousness and, each time she woke, she found Jeanie and Alice at her side. Often she simply smiled at her daughters and managed a few words, but in the dark of her last night, Jeanie woke with a start; she heard her name being whispered. *"Jeanie! Jeanie!..... Are you there?"*

Jeanie was glad to be awoken. She retained the hope and desire that her Ma would revive, but with one look she knew that it was not to be, *"Ma, I'm here."*

"Good girl, I knew you would be. Are you feedin' the yellow cat?"

Jeanie laughed at the urgency in her mother's voice, knowing that the cat had gone, *"Of course, Ma."*

Mary was satisfied and reflected, *"Good. It's been a long journey for us a', bonnie Jean, and you have still so far to go, but I think God is telling me to rest. When I'm no longer at your side, I will only be a prayer away, so you can aye speak to me. We have been through so much thegither and you have never let me down. I'm sorry that **I** have so often. All I can hope is that you will find it in yer heart to forgive me. But our roles seem to hae been tae serve and no' enjoy the sunshine when we saw it. Not tae paddle in the stream and play wi' the fishes, no' to stand on the hilltop and fa' asleep in the evening sun, but tae let others, by our work, a chance. I leave you nothin' but my name and the responsibility that it brings. There will be a big stooshie when I'm no longer here, pay nae heed, that's fir others. I will not have gone, my weary body will be resting. Take care o' your brothers and sisters and work hard; it is a' I have ever done."*

The other members of the household had heard Mary's voice and now gathered round her bedside as they heard her last prayer, *"I ask you Lord tae keep our people safe, tae protect those unable to do so fir themselves, and to give them a chance to make a place o' their own in the world. As I'll be safe wi' You, You may have mair time to look after others, as I know I have been a trial to You. Amen..... But now Jeanie, I am weary and need to sleep, forgive me lass."* Appropriately, her last words were in Efik, *"O Abasi, sana mi yok."* Oh God, release me.

Before dawn on the morning of January 13th 1915, Mary Slessor went to join her Lord.

The news of her passing was immediately conveyed to the District Commissioner and the Mission at Duke Town, notifying them that unless they heard to the contrary Mary's funeral would take place at Use at four o'clock that afternoon. On receiving the news the District Commissioner put plans into action, informing everyone of the tragic event and sending the Mission launch to transport Mary's body downriver for the last time.

At school, Dan was called by Principal Macgregor to his office; being a typical schoolboy, he wondered what indiscretion he had committed to be called to the steps of No.1 Bungalow. He knocked and entered, but to his surprise it was not Mr Macgregor who met him but his wife. Her eyes filled with tears as she took the young boy's hand, *'poor Dan'*. At that moment he knew he was not there for punishment for an offence, but for a much heavier punishment. Mr Macgregor entered the room and told Dan to sit by him; then he said the words Dan already knew, but dreaded hearing, *"Your Ma has died."* This brought such an uncontrollable torrent of tears from the young boy. The two sat with their own memories and grieved without words at the passing of this remarkable woman. No words were needed as the tears spoke for themselves. Dan was excused classes to compose himself for his Ma's funeral, which was to take place at 7.30 the following morning.

Lord Harcourt reminded all government employees that Mary had been a great friend of the Government and the Mission and a treasured personal friend, so decreed that all should attend the funeral. The following morning, before dawn, the crowds began to gather. Countless hundreds of natives flooded in from every corner of the district and from far beyond, to say a last farewell to their 'Ma'. Chiefs and Kings, slaves and freemen, Christian and non-Christian, men, women and children, came and lined the route to pay their last respects to *"Eka Kpukpro Owo"* Everybody's Mother.

As the steamer *Snipe* set off on the journey from Queen Beach to Marine Beach, Dan was escorted down to meet it. In attendance were the High Commissioner, senior British Officials and the commanding officer of the 3rd Battalion of the Nigerian regiment, all proudly wearing medals on their dress uniforms. Leading members of the mercantile community and heads of ruling houses in Calabar and surrounding areas gathered, while the band of the regiment played the 'Dead March in Saul'. As the *Snipe* moored, all flags were lowered to half-mast. The mahogany coffin, draped with the Union Jack and adorned with a beautiful cross of frangipani blossoms, was lifted by Kru boat boys and in turn, the launch boys, all dressed in black singlets and navy blue loin cloths, and passed on to four non-commissioned officers. Marine ratings in starch white were brought to attention as the coffin began the mile and a half journey towards the cemetery. While Dan watched in admiration at the spectacle he was now witness to, it was only when the procession began to move did he feel a weakness in his legs, a reluctance to move on to see his Ma's body placed in the earth. Each step forward was one step closer to his Ma being no longer with him to talk to, no longer by him to scold or comfort, and no longer near him to tell him that all would be well. It mattered little that her farewell was worthy of a monarch, this was his Ma. He was hardly aware of the huge crowds that thronged the streets and hilltops, many only managing to get a glimpse of the precious coffin by climbing trees; through his sadness he did manage a wee smile, knowing how much his Ma would have appreciated **their** efforts. The police force manned the route, and as the coffin passed, fell in behind the procession. Despite the vast number who had come to mourn, the town was hushed. The boys and teachers from the Hope Waddell Institute formed part of the honour guard, but as the procession came in sight over the hill from the beach, the native 'death wail' began. A voice from the crowd ordered it to stop; it was Ma Fuller, who cried out in Efik, *"Don't wail! Praise God! Praise God!"* With respect to the old woman and, in Mary's honour, the death wail subsided, never to be heard again that day.

The site of her last resting place was an area of the cemetery close to the graves of her friends, Mrs Sutherland and the Andersons. Missionary teachers lowered her body into the earth, Mr Wilkie and Mr Rankine led a brief memorial service and African Christians led the mourners in singing the hymns 'When the Day of Toil is Done' and 'Asleep in Jesus'. Birds sang, the sun shone as if it were any other day, but it was not; this was the day when Mary Mitchell Slessor was laid to rest and, though the world had only lost one simple soul, it was such a great loss.

A few weeks later at a separate ceremony, on a hillside above Duke Town, a large Aberdeen granite monument was erected in her memory. Chairlie Ovens, who knew her so well was there and, with honesty and affection, remarked, *"She was nae jist a' that holy!"* As the large stone was manoeuvred into place, he was heard to whisper, *"It'll tak mair than that tae hold doon oor Mary."* Though some may have thought it irreverent, this was a fitting and heartfelt tribute to the feisty and indomitable spirit of his great friend.

In 1956, Queen Elizabeth II, visited Mary's grave and placed a wreath in her honour.

Mary had come to Africa to serve her Lord; she felt that, with His guidance, she had done her best, no more. She had left in her footsteps, wisdom, tolerance, learning and love, plus countless schools, hospitals, workshops, farms, churches, and refuges for women and children. She had given, and received, love and respect from all those who knew her in Africa and wherever her words were read. This very mortal woman is remembered with affection in Africa and by anyone who believes in and respects goodness and kindness.

The End

Postscript

Mary's unique magnetism is personified in the reaction to the last letter she sent to Charles Partridge. While we often ignore the power of personal charisma, it may give pause for thought to consider her quite extraordinary personality and influence. In 1950, at the age of eighty, thirty-five years after her death, her old friend presented his collection of letters, books, voice recordings and photographs to the Dundee Museums. He wrote this moving tribute as part of his accompanying letter:

Dear Sir,
... During my long life, I have had intercourse with many distinguished people, chiefly men. Of the women, I place first Mary Slessor whom you call "The White Queen of Okoyong"! She was a very remarkable woman. I look back on her friendship with reverence – one of the greatest honours that have befallen me – and I had and still have a superstitious feeling that she has been and still is one of my Guardian Angels. (I have been twice seized by cannibals, thrice shipwrecked, etc, etc!) This belief exists in spite of my being agnostic (non-knower) and non-religious, though as we all are, thoroughly inbred of the ethics of Christianity. Excepting Miss Slessor, I thoroughly disapprove of all Missionaries!...

Just now I have read Miss Slessor's last letter to me, dated 24th December, 1914, written three weeks before her death. I dare not read any other letter – it hurts!
Yours sincerely
Charles Partridge

Scots Dictionary, for use with this specific text.

A' – All
Abodie – Everybody
Aff it – Off it
Aiberdeen – Aberdeen
Ain o' they – One of those
Ain or twa – One or two
Alow – Underneath
Anither – Another
A'right – All right
Atween - Between
Awa' – Away
Awfie – Awful
Aye - Always
Bairns – Children
Bobbies - Police
Bonnie – Beautiful
Brak – Break
Braw – Fine
Ca Cannie – Go warily
Cannae – Cannot
Claes – Clothes
Come in by – Enter
Cudnae – Could not
Daein' – Doing
Deid - Dead
Didnae - Did not
Dinnae – Do not
Disnae – Does not
Drearie – Dull
Dreich – Miserable (usually when discussing the weather)
E'm – I am
E'll – I will
E've – I have
Fae – From
Fair get my goat – You annoy me
Faird – Afraid
Faimlie – Family
Fiddle – Cheat
Fir – For
Fit? – What?
Flit – Move (as in - move house)

Forby – Besides, in addition
Fowk – People
Gey – Very
Gie – Give
Greetin-face - Person with a miserable expression
Guid – Good
Hadnae – Had not
Hae – Have
Hame – Home
Haud – Hold
Hert – Heart
Hisnae – Has not
Hivnae – Have not
Intae - Into
Keaker – Black Eye
Ken – Know
Kent – Known
Leathering – Beating
Losin' – Losing
Mair – More
Maks – Makes
Meenester – Minister
Meh – My
Micht – Might
Mind – Attend to
No' – Not
Nowt – Nothing
Naebodie – Nobody
Neibour – Neighbour
Nicht - Night
Onie – Any
Peepers – Eyes
Peeked – Took a look
Polis – Police
Pooches – Pockets
Raggie man – Man who collects rags
Sark – A man's shirt, a woman's long loose vest
Scunner – Nuisance
Seterday – Saturday
Skinnymalink – A thin, skinny person
Sodger – Soldier
Sook – Suck
Souter – Shoemaker

Stour – Dust
Tak' – Take
Telt – Told
Thegither – Together
The Morn – Tomorrow
The Night - Tonight
Thocht – Thought
Wa's – Walls
Wee – Small
Whar – Where
Wha – Who
Wi' – With
Wifie – Woman
Wid – Would
Widnae – Would not
Winnae – Will not
Wis – Was
Ye'll – You will
Yersels - Yourselves

Bibliography

Atbush, Peregrine (Charles Partridge) – King Edward's Ring

Zweineiger-Bargielowska, Ina– Women in twentieth-century Britain

Buchan, James – The Expendable Mary Slessor

Christian & Plummer – God and One Redhead

Dickens, Charles – Sketches by Boz

Enock, Edith E – White Queen, The Missionary Heroine of Calabar

Fage, J D – A History of West Africa

Hardage, Jeanette – Mary Slessor, Everybody's Mother

Huxley, Elspeth – The Kingsleys

Livingstone, W P – Mary Slessor of Calabar

Livingstone, W P – Mary Slessor, The White Queen

Luke, James – Pioneering in Mary Slessor's Country

Macdonald, Lesley A Orr – A Unique and Glorious Mission

Livingstone , Mrs W P – The Mary Slessor Calendar

O'Brien, Brian – She Had a Magic

Pakenham, Thomas – The Scramble for Africa

Perham, Margery –Lugard, The Years of Authority

Macnair, James I –Livingstone the Liberator

Jeal, Tim – Livingstone

Kingsley, Mary H – The Story of West Africa

Kingsley, Mary H –Travels in West Africa

Robertson, Elizabeth – Mary Slessor

Wallace, Kathleen – This is Your Home, Story of Miss Mary Henrietta Kingsley

McLennan, Bruce– Mary Slessor, A Life On The Altar For God

Compiled by a Committee appointed by the Synod of the Free Presbyterian Church –
History of the Free Presbyterian Church of Scotland

Dundee Museums –Mary Slessor's Diary

Wellgate Local History Library – Hugh Goldie's Efik Dictionary

Wellgate Local History Library –Letters of Daniel Slessor

Wellgate Local History Library –Letters to Charles Partridge

Wellgate Local History Library – Mary Slessor letters, various

Liverpool Museum –Mary Kingsley's letters to John Holt

various –The Missionary Record

various –The Children's Magazine

various -D C Thomson publications

various – Quarterly Magazine